PRIME MINISTER

AINSLEY BOOTH

SADIE HALLER

BOOTH HALLER BOOKS

CANADA

PRIME MINISTER — PREMIER MINISTRE

Happy Reading

Your friend,

Gavin Strong

DEDICATION

The sexiest part of a man is his brain
And his forearms
Bare feet are hot too
Hands...
A sense of humour
Kindness (this list is in no particular order)

For every man who is smart enough to put his partner first
and for every woman who knows that one day she'll find that
man (or woman...group of people...whatever works for you)

He's the most off-limits man in the entire country, but Gavin Strong looks at me like I'm everything he's ever wanted.

He thinks I'm smart.

So even though I'm only an intern, I get pulled into meetings where he wants my opinion, and we work late into the night.

And when I call him Sir, he gets hard and I get flustered, and then he calls me his good girl and it doesn't matter that he's the Prime Minister of Canada.

In those moments, all that matters is that he's mine.

FOOTNOTES:

1. This is a fictional erotic romance. No prime ministers or interns were harmed in the making of this book.
2. Except it's a BDSM romance, so they were hurt a little.

GLOSSARY OF CANADIANISMS AND ACRONYMS

Toque - wool winter hat
Donair - like a doner kebab, but with a unique Canadian sweet sauce
Chesterfield - couch

PM - Prime Minister
MP - Member of Parliament
DND - Department of National Defence
CANCON - Canadian Content (specifically referring to television and radio requirements to play a % of CANCON)
RA - Research Assistant
TA - Teaching Assistant
ABD - All But Dissertation

FOREWORD

This book is a work of fiction. Hot, erotic fiction, set against a political backdrop that may seem familiar. We promise you that Gavin Strong and Ellie Montague are figments of our imagination and any similarities to real people are entirely coincidental.

For purposes of keeping this story focused on their romance, we've simplified some of the complex realities of political life. We've reduced the number of principal staff that the prime minister relies on. We assumed you wouldn't want to read about the dozens of awesome, smart people who support a nation's leader. That's what watching re-runs of West Wing is for.

ELLIE

THE ONLY THING worse than being late for your first day of work is when your first day of work is at the Parliament Buildings and your new boss is the prime minister.

Who you have a secret crush on, except it doesn't need to be a secret, because he's single and hot and every other woman in the country also has a crush on him.

You could wear a placard that says **I want to bang the PM** and nobody would even notice, because they would all be wearing variations on the same theme.

Of course, it should be a secret because I'm going to be working for him.

With him.

Under him.

Stop it, Ellie.

It's only a three month internship, and technically there's a deputy director of communications and a chief of staff between us in the chain of command. But my nipples don't understand that and they're super excited about working so closely with Gavin.

Mr. Strong.

Like every other straight woman, gay man, or anyone in the middle of the Kinsey scale, I've got a crush on the man. Which is why I should have been early for work, and is also why I'm running late.

I should have been focused on making a good impression.

Instead, I'd changed my outfit three times and chose heels that made it impossible to hustle when I realized just how late I was.

I squeak in the front doors at 7:59 by the clock on my cell phone. But of course there's a security line to get through and—

"Ms. Montague?"

I'd recognize that voice anywhere. Thick with humour, warm and rough enough at the edges to appeal to steel workers and farmers—that was the panty-melting voice of our nation's brand new prime minister.

I know that voice.

Until this moment, I had no clue he might know me.

So I stare at him dumbly.

This is not my finest hour.

"Sir," I finally stammer out.

The women behind me in line giggle.

That's the effect this man has on people. I'm now officially blocking the security line into the building and nobody cares because Gavin Strong, The Honourable Prime Minister of Canada, is flashing his baby blue eyes at everyone in a thirty foot radius. He's done this before—stop and talk to his staff on the way in, but I'm still flustered. I don't think I ever expected to talk to him, and definitely not before my first day has even begun.

"Shall we head inside?"

"Yes, of course." I yank out my wallet. "I'll see you in there."

He holds my gaze for a moment, probably a second or two, but it's the kind of second that stretches. Long enough to be meaningful for me but nothing for him.

And then he's turning, shaking hands with the people in front of me. Welcoming them all to work today.

Who does that?

Gavin Strong. Union lawyer, community activist, Habitat for Humanity volunteer. The most personable man in the entire country, possibly the smartest, too, although he likes to play that bit down.

Surround himself with experts, he says.

That's where I come in.

I'm hardly an expert, but I'm getting there. Bachelor's degree in Women's Studies and Sociology. Master's in Women's Studies. One year into my doctorate, which is loosely a business degree but specifically a communications specialty.

And I've scored one of ten brand-new internships with the federal government. Cultural Change Officers, we're called. I've taken a three-month leave of absence from my studies to do this job.

To work under the prime minister.

And I didn't make it three minutes into the role without my panties getting wet.

Fan-fucking-tastic.

IT TAKES five hours for my crush to die a miserable death.

Gavin might be hot, and smart, but he's also a perfectionist, and he expects that of his staff. Which is fine for me, because I haven't pissed him off yet, but by lunch I've witnessed enough to know that if I don't lock down my libido and bring my A-game, I'm going to get called on the carpet.

The showdown he had midmorning with his Chief of Staff—Stew Rochard, my boss—over fundraising and lobbyists has the entire office in a panic, because we've got a private event in five weeks that might need to be cancelled if the PM decides to take a hard line on influencers.

That's how I've decided I need to think about Gavin. The PM. The Prime Minister.

I'm not going to notice how good he looks in a suit or how his powerful thighs are outlined every time he sits down. The suit represents the position. It demands my respect, nothing else.

Instead of taking me out to lunch for my first day, Stew gives me half of the ham and Swiss on rye that his wife made him, digs two cans of Diet Coke out of a box he keeps under his desk, and tasks me with figuring out how we can spin the $5,000 a plate dinner into something that won't offend our boss quite so much.

Because I'm a freak for these kinds of problems, this makes me happy. A nice lunch would probably be nothing but small talk, and I'm kind of awkward when it comes to that. Like I should have asked Stew about his wife and kids when he gave me the sandwich, but I was already poring over the file on the fundraiser—the history of it, the host, the criticism on the other events that led to the PM's edict two hours earlier that we would *not* be in the pockets of the wealthy.

"One problem with him saying that over and over again is that he's rich, too," I point out as I lick mustard off my fingers. "And everyone knows it. Don't get me wrong—most people like that about him. But he's hardly one of us with the sandwiches from home."

Stew snorts. "Don't let him hear you say that."

"He's a man of the people in many other ways. He knows how much a loaf of bread costs, that's all that matters. But he's also comfortable with these donors, right? What if it wasn't a fundraiser for the party? What if it was…like a kick-off for a community challenge?"

"Keep talking." He roots around in his lunch bag. "Chocolate chip cookie?"

I shake my head. "But I'll take another pop if you've got one."

"He shouldn't shut himself off from business leaders. He needs to stay connected to them, and show them who's boss. Canadians just want to know that he's not in their pockets. They'll be thrilled if he can turn it around, make them bend to his will."

"Shit." He rocks back in his chair and shoves the rest of his cookie in his mouth. "That's good."

The truth is, it's not a new idea. It was a critique I wrote six months earlier for a class, as a response to a hypothetical case study that was eerily similar. I got lucky on my first day, but I'm smart enough to pretend that my luck is actually talent. "Thanks."

"It'll need some work. You'll need to present it with the repercussions forecasted out in all directions."

"Of course." I've done that at school before, too. If I've got time, I'll tap a couple of my profs and get their—

"I want you to pitch it tomorrow in the morning briefing."

Oh, crap. So no time, then. "Tomorrow. Right."

"That a problem?"

"No."

Stew opens his mouth, maybe to warn me about what the PM expects, or maybe to question how sure I am, I don't know, because before he can say anything, in whirls a six-foot-three-inch hurricane wearing a suit and righteous indignation.

"This report from the Ministry of the Environment is fucking bullshit, Stewart," the PM growls as he storms in from the hallway.

Stew doesn't miss a beat. "I'm in a meeting, Gavin."

The PM's gaze swings around to where I'm sitting. "Ms. Montague. Would you step outside?"

My immediate reaction is yes, of course. But that's the wrong answer.

That's the woman inside me doing what a man has asked of her, because he doesn't want to make her feel uncomfortable.

Seriously? Fuck that noise. "I'd rather stay."

He gives me a hard, unreadable look.

"Sir," I add, swallowing hard. "I'd rather stay, sir."

His eyes flash in surprise and anger, and my palms go all sweaty.

"Because…I'm the barometer, right? Without me, you're talking in an echo chamber. That's what you said in your announcement about these internships." I turn to my boss. "I don't think your office is an echo chamber, of course, Stew."

Gavin chuckles, an unexpected sound after a day that's felt beyond tense. "No, Stew has no problem telling me when I'm wrong."

I take a deep breath. "Neither will I. Sir."

He gives me another long look, this one more complicated, but just as hard to read.

Finally he nods. "But stop calling me sir. That's my father's name."

His father's name is Vince, but I get the point. "Okay. So what part of the report is fucking bullshit?"

He laughs and turns back to Stew. "This one can stay."

2

GAVIN

By ten o'clock this morning, my day had completely derailed — not an unusual situation. Twice my assistant Beth quietly suggested that we change our estimated arrival time at the City Farm Camp. There's a press conference at five thirty, after the kids have left for the day. I only need to be there for an hour beforehand to get a tour and have a photo op with some of the children.

But I'm only three months into my first term as PM. I'm not interested in doing the bare minimum. I've heard amazing things about this program, and we've got a plan to greatly expand the tax credits and subsidies for ones just like it across the country.

I'm not going to talk about that without actually spending some real time with the kids and the counsellors.

Plus, horses and sheep and chickens. What's not to love about that? It's certainly more fun than a bullshit environmental report that completely misses the mark —

I cut myself off. I'm not going to get worked up about it. The delightful Ellie Montague is going to tear into that report and tell me all the ways we can render it null and void, and justify spending the money on a new one.

I need to have Substantive Fucking Policy tattooed on all deputy ministers' foreheads, clearly.

I've just finished the most intellectually stimulating conversation I've had in weeks in Stew's office, with Ellie… Ellie, who I can't get off my mind.

Dangerous territory, I tell myself. I don't listen. There's something about her that fires me up in a long-dormant way.

"It's two o'clock," Beth says as she strides into my office. She's going to try again to rearrange my day.

"You haven't had a chance to return these four calls yet," she says smoothly, sliding a call sheet on top of the report I was just about to open. *Reading time is over*—her message is clear.

I give her a side-eye and she just smiles sweetly at me.

Beth. She's like the sister I already have. Between her and Pia, my actual sister, I don't get cut any slack. So Beth is like the baby sister I never had, and when she's not riding my ass about the damn itinerary, I like her a lot. Even the bossy parts.

She's adjusted amazingly well to the new role. I hired her on my first day in the city as an MP two years ago, and everyone said she was too young and inexperienced to be the executive assistant to a national leader. Everyone was wrong. She's my secret weapon for keeping a tight schedule —every day except today.

Today, I'm going to camp whether she likes it or not.

She doesn't.

Oh well.

I grab the call sheet and wave it at her. "You sure you don't want to come with me?"

She gives me a look of great alarm. "To muck out barns?"

"Yeah."

"No. Make those calls or I'm coming to find you later! Remember I can see who you call on your cell phone."

Yeah. That's why I have two phones. The official phone of the Prime Minister of Canada, and the burner phone I use to call my best friend, Max, when this all gets to be a little too surreal.

As I hop in the back of my armoured town car, I think this should be one of the times I call him. But I've got four phone calls to make in a thirty minute drive to the Agriculture Museum, and I have a certain doctoral candidate to do a little more research on, too.

Ellie Montague.

I try to tell myself that my interest is purely professional. She's smart and capable and she's only on loan to us for three months from the University of Ottawa. If she's impressing Stew on her first day of the job, we need to be amping up her responsibilities while she's here.

But first, phone calls.

***

CAMP IS in fact more fun than reading reports or even fighting with Stew.

I find myself wondering if Ellie likes animals, and shove that thought away as fast as it pops into my head.

The most amazing discovery about the camp I make this afternoon is what a difference the experience makes for kids who are struggling in school. So, after I spend nearly three hours being taught by children how to care for the animals and manage the other farm chores, I get a little pissed off when the first question I get from the press is about how much my shirt cost—because it's now smeared with mud.

"I'm going to be lucky if that's mud. Pretty sure I got that when we were mucking out the horse stalls," I tell Rick Stupes, a reporter with CAN News who is always out to make me look like Richie Rich. I don't respond to the rest of his question because it's stupid.

He tries again. "When your staff set up this photo op up, did they advise you to wear anything different?"

Seriously, what is this guy's problem? I'm only slightly more GQ than the last guy.

Okay, no, I'm a thousand times more GQ than the last guy.

I kick my foot out from behind the podium. "I've been wearing these boots since I left the house at half past five this morning, because I'm not a toddler, and I know how to dress myself appropriately. As a side note, they're the boots I hiked Golden Ears in after we won the most recent election." Take that, Rick. "Nobody had to remind me to put them on. Coming to City Farm Camp has been the highlight of a difficult week, something I've really been looking forward to, and if I didn't have a full day of work tomorrow, I'd be back in a heartbeat."

The next question is similarly off-topic. Inside my head, I'm calling the press corps all sorts of names, but we've practised this over and over again. My natural propensity to snap at stupid people is well and truly beaten out of me now. Or at least well internalized.

I smile and give a short answer. Rinse and repeat, until the fifth question gets to the heart of the announcement I've just made, about funding for such activities needing to be a two-fisted approach, because not all parents can wait for a tax credit to justify the upfront expense.

And sometimes, those are the kids who need the alternative learning experience the most.

I smoothly reiterate what the camp director has already said, about how the hands-on care of animals instills empathy and compassion that translates well back to human interaction.

I know as soon as I finish the spiel, with an extra charming smile for the reporter who asked the right question, that's the clip that'll run on the news.

We don't always nail it this well, but when we do, it makes the rest of it worthwhile.

3

ELLIE

I DON'T LEAVE the office until after eight. I only stumble as far as a sushi restaurant three blocks away, where my room-mate, Sasha, is waiting for me.

"That bad?" she asks, flagging down the waitress. "We're going to need sake."

"No sake. Green tea. And then I'm hitting the last yoga class of the night."

"Ew."

"I'm not making you come with me."

Sasha's a runner. Uptight, controlled…she's practically allergic to finding her resting place and just breathing.

Me? I'm spastic, anxious, and a chronic worrier. I hold it all at bay by doing yoga five days a week.

Not usually this late at night, but hello real world. I've been spoiled by being a grad student—it's hard work, but I can mostly do it on my own schedule.

Not anymore.

I have to be back at work at six thirty tomorrow morning. Tell the PM he's wrong at seven. Then probably fight with people all day as I convince them I'm right. If I don't centre myself and get a good night's sleep, that's not going to go well.

4

GAVIN

THE FIRST THING I notice when my senior team files into my office for our daily briefing at seven is Ellie Montague. This doesn't surprise me, because I haven't been able to stop thinking about her since yesterday. She looks tired and my imagination takes off in search of a likely explanation. Most of them involve her being kept up all night by a man. Narrowing down her type was proving problematic. She didn't seem like she'd go for the muscle-bound studly type with more balls than brains, but I've been surprised more than a few times by what can get a woman wet and needy.

I watch her from the corner of my eye as Stew talks to my staff—his staff—about what's come up overnight, what our priorities are for the day, and a number of other things that he doesn't need me to listen to. Which is good, because I'm too busy cataloguing all the ways she fascinates me. What I notice most is Ellie's fidgeting. She keeps catching herself, and I find it hard not to smirk.

She smooths the front of her skirt with her hand and leaves behind a long streak slightly darker than the khaki fabric. Her palms are sweaty. She's nervous. I barely have time to wonder why when Stew invites her to speak.

Her head comes up at the sound of her name and our gazes lock for a moment, then she drops her clear grey eyes to the binder she's holding in her shaking hands. I'm glad I'm sitting down because I'm pretty sure waving my raging hard-on around the room is not on the briefing agenda.

I watch her lips as they form the words I'm not really hearing because I'm busy imaging what they would feel like on my cock.

I should be paying more attention to what she's saying, but I already know I'm going to agree with whatever plan she's laying out.

She wouldn't be speaking right now if Stew wasn't already going to back her recommendations on how to keep these outrageously expensive rubber chicken dinners that are supposed to be party fundraisers from becoming opportunities for big business to buy some private time with the prime minister. Pay to play, they call it.

Confident this embarrassing little hiccup is already handled, I drift back into my fantasy. Something I shouldn't be doing for so many reasons, not the least of which is she's young enough to be my niece.

But I can't help myself.

She's on her back, draped over my desk with her head tipped back over one edge, her legs dangling over the other.

I unzip my trousers and free my long-suffering erection.

"Open," I demand.

Her lips part and I trace them with the tip of my cock until they're glossy with pre-come. I want to be rough, make her take me all the way down, but for some unknown reason, I hold myself back. Her tongue swirls around the head as I slide in.

The sight of my fluid smeared all over her lips makes me want to mark her other places. Her tits, her back, her ass.

As I slip farther into her hot, eager mouth, I take her hands, weaving our fingers together. I hold them against the surface of the desk and lean forward, stopping just above her mound of soft red curls. In my fantasy they're a bit darker than the strawberry blonde waves I've seen her twist her fingers into more than once.

She's ethereal and bright. Impish and totally captivating. "Spread your legs, Sprite."

I slide out and in with shallow strokes as I move my head lower so I can tickle at her clit with my tongue. She squirms and I stop.

"Don't move."

Curious to see how much she can take, I push my cock in until it barely touches the back of her throat. Her belly lurches a little, but she swallows against it. Her mouth is hot and wet and tight around me, and I want her to take even more but I won't push her. Not the first time.

"Good girl," I say. Because she is. I resume my shallow thrusts into her mouth and lower myself back down to feast on her pussy.

This time she stays perfectly still while I suck and lick at her clit. I catch that firm nub between my lips and tug gently. She struggles to keep still and I get a thrill from her obedience.

While I'm consumed with her delightful pussy, she's working away on my cock. Even with the position of her head restricting her movement, she does an excellent job of giving me all the suction and friction I need to get me where I want to go. She's gotta come first, but her mouth is unbelievable. Distracting.

Fuck, I want to rut against her and let myself go, but I can't.

I concentrate harder on my goal. She starts to moan and—

Ellie's lips stop moving and I'm yanked back to reality. Not that I was all that far away. I may have been having wildly inappropriate fantasies about my Chief of Staff's far-too-young-for-me intern, but I was present enough to keep from making a complete fool of myself.

"Thank you for your presentation, Ellie. I'll take it under advisement." Stew gives me the look. The one that says I am going to have some explaining to do. And I am going to have to do some fast thinking, because I sure as shit won't tell him the real reason my mind wasn't where it should be.

"Okay everybody, I think that's everything for today." Stew gestures towards the door, but doesn't exit with the rest of the group.

I watch as Ellie leaves. Damn that skirt looks good on her from the front, but it hugs her ass tight, and the rear view is spectacular.

The last person is barely out of the room before Stew shuts the door.

There are only two men in the entire world who know me for who I really am. Who would watch me in that briefing and see where my mind really went. One of them is safely on the other side of the country living his own life.

The other is standing in front of me, trying his damnedest to keep *my* life on track.

Stew shakes his head. "What the fuck got into you?"

I haven't thought fast enough and I'm saved from having to give an excuse by his ire, because he's already worked up and intent on pointing out how much of an ass I just was.

"That girl was working all night because yesterday at lunch I told her to have that presentation ready for this morning's briefing. The least you could have fucking done, you inconsiderate piece of shit, was listen to her proposal. Instead, you had your head up your ass thinking about God only knows what, and I don't want to know."

I wince. "Was I that obvious?"

"Only to me. You've got to come up with a new phrase when you mentally return to meetings because it won't be long before others will figure out *I'll take it under advisement* means my brain had more important matters than whatever twaddle you're peddling."

"Twaddle?"

"Gavin, it was her first briefing. She was nervous and you were unbelievably rude. And that's not like you."

"You're right. I should apologise."

"Nah, she was too nervous to notice you were being an asshat. I think you'll do more damage than good by drawing attention to it."

"Are you sure?"

"You're willing to blindly accept my recommendations when it comes to how we deal with this fundraiser business, but on something as trivial as this, you question my wisdom?"

"Fuck, Stew. How did I even get here? Two years ago I was happily spanking shitty employers for mistreating their workers and now I'm running the fucking country."

"Not for much longer if you don't keep your head in the game. What if that had been Question Period instead of your morning briefing?"

He's right and I know it. "Point taken. Now, don't you have work to do?"

Stew shoots me his middle finger and walks out the door.

I lean back in my chair and prop my feet on my desk, crossing them at the ankles. The same desk I'd just been —

Fuck. I need to get laid. This dry spell is completely fucking with my judgement.

And I need to stop thinking about Ellie Montague's ass. Her mouth. How pink her pussy will be when she's wet and swollen for me.

Most of all, I need to stop finding her fidgeting so damn endearing.

5

ELLIE

By Saturday, I'm totally ready for the weekend.

Except Stew emails me at six in the morning and I end up working until noon. There are a few people in the office, but everyone is heads down on their own stuff. I'm in and out in five hours, and I've still got two days of down time to enjoy.

Okay, so I'll get a day and a half. Maybe a day and a quarter, because there's some serious reading I need to do tomorrow night to be ready for Monday morning.

But a day off still sounds heavenly. Yoga, brunch, lying on the couch like a vegetable and watching something on Netflix. I can squeeze all of that into a day and a quarter. Maybe brunch can be something delivered and easily consumed while lying on the couch.

I check the yoga studio's schedule. My favourite teacher has a class at three today and another at seven tomorrow morning. That is not happening, so this afternoon it is.

I change out of my work clothes and pull on red yoga pants, a bralette with fancy braided straps, and a floaty black scoop-neck t-shirt that falls off one shoulder and

20

shows off the twisted black and red fabric. I'll pull it off when I get to yoga, but I'm not so one-with-my-body that I'll walk to the studio in a top that anyone outside of the studio would see as a bra.

I'm halfway there when my phone pings again.

I wince as I check it.

Another email from Stew. Apparently getting lucky and proving myself helpful in the first week has consequences.

No good deed goes unpunished. Or…I'm establishing a reputation in a city where I want to have a long and productive career. I take a deep breath. The environmental report on the pipeline needs to be read from a youth jobs perspective. Can I have some thoughts for him by Monday?

I can, and I will, but I need the report, which can't be transmitted electronically yet. Crap.

So much for yoga. I glance at the clock on my phone screen. Quarter after two.

A gentle screech of bus brakes behind me makes the decision easy. It's a quick trip up the street. I can get to the office, get the report, and get back here in time for class. I spin around and wave my bus pass at the driver.

Twelve minutes later, I'm sprinting past the security guards, who laugh at me because I was already there once and it's Saturday and ha ha ha, not funny.

New girl is trying to make a good impression, okay?

Upstairs, pretty much everyone is gone. I let myself into the office I share with a couple of other junior staffers and grab the confidential report from the locked cabinet beneath my desk. The cover is stiff, though, and I need it to roll up so it will fit into my yoga mat bag.

Stew's copy has a floppy cover. I head to his office, but I can't find his copy anywhere. Frustrated, I check my phone. I'm not making that yoga class. Maybe I'll go to the one at four, even though the instructor is way too obsessed with the sound of her own voice for it to be truly Zen.

Then I call my boss. "Stew, I'm standing in your office. Where would I find your copy of the environmental report?"

"What's wrong with your copy?"

It won't fit in my yoga mat bag probably isn't the right answer. But it's the only one I've got, so I tell him the truth.

It takes him a while to stop laughing, so I lean on his desk and consider just taking a nap there like that, bent right over.

Once he stops laughing and tells me where to find it on his bookshelf, I say a muffled thanks and hang up the phone.

I don't get up right away.

It's been a really long week.

I groan and mumble to myself, "Might just stay here for a while."

"Are we working you that hard, Ms. Montague?" a voice asks from the doorway. A rich, warm voice with a now familiar-in-person rough edge to it.

The PM.

And I'm sprawled across my boss's desk in yoga pants and a bra. Kind of wearing a t-shirt, but when you're in front of the nation's leader, does *kind of* count?

No, no it does not.

"Sir," I gasp, pushing myself upright, suddenly aware that my ass was just in the air.

"I thought I told you not to call me that," he says.

I spin around and he's looking at the floor, and then the shelves, and finally his gaze settles on a point just past my shoulder.

That's weird, because he's usually such an eye-contact kind of guy. And it makes me self-conscious, like, he was also aware that my ass had been in the air, and is now behind me, but the rest of me is still clad in yoga wear.

And normally, this is not a big deal. I didn't think twice of wearing it in front of the security guards, for example.

But after a week of trying very hard to not be aware of the PM as a man, and at the same time being rather painfully aware that he is a man, with eyes, and…

All of that.

Sigh.

He's not the person I want to be standing in front of in skin-tight cropped yoga pants.

I'm not even wearing underwear under them, and I swear he's got Superman's X-ray vision right now, which is why he's *not* looking at me. Because he already did and he saw under my clothes and oh God, I need to work under him for another two months and three weeks.

With him.

I really need to stop making that slip inside my head. One of these days I'm going to say it out loud and everyone will know that I'm thinking about how big he is and how heavy he would feel on top of me.

While all this is rioting through my head and he's waiting for me to say something, *not* looking at me, I consider hiding behind Stew's chair to remove the inappropriate clothing from being a factor. But at some point he's going to expect me to leave this office, so I just stand where I am, suddenly feeling very, very naked.

Naked and slowly turning red.

"My apologies. I was just here to get…" Something I can't remember. Luckily the PM doesn't have that problem.

"The environmental report. I heard. Stew keeps his on the bookshelf." He clears his throat and points behind me. "Over there."

"Right." I turn and look at the second shelf.

"Next one up, I think."

I push up on my toes, because I'm short and Stew is not. Yeah, I can't reach.

"Here," Gavin says, and he's right behind me now. My pulse is jackhammering away in my neck. I can hear it in my ears. Can he hear it? It's loudly pronouncing my lascivious thoughts. The arm of his suit jacket brushes my bare skin as his hand reaches easily past mine and grabs the stack of nearly identical confidential reports.

How many of those does my boss get in a week? I only have the one to read. Suddenly my whining about my workload seems to lack perspective.

I turn and press my back against the bookshelf as he flips through the stack, finding the one I need.

"Here you go." He hands it over, and I press it to my chest as he leans over me to put the rest of the stack away again.

He's taller up close. I have to tip my head back to look up at him. Of course, I usually wear heels, and the canvas slip-ons I wear to yoga have zero lift.

"Thank you," I breathe, about to add *sir* when I catch myself. He laughs as he watches me form the start of the word, then press my lips together.

"Gavin. You can call me Gavin."

"I'm pretty sure I can't," I laugh, turning my head to the side in embarrassment.

"You need to, because this *sir* thing is killing us both and it's only been a week." He steps back and taps his index finger to his bottom lip. "Let's practise."

"Really?"

"Yes, really. Try… 'Hey, Gavin, how's your weekend going?'"

"Hey…Gavin." That feels weird. And nice, kind of, but

mostly weird and possibly dangerous because his eyes are extra blue right now.

He laughs, his shoulders shaking silently at what I can only assume is the dorkiest look on my face, but it breaks the ice. I square my shoulders and give him a stern look. He cocks one eyebrow and sobers his mouth. "Keep going."

"How's your weekend going?"

"Ah, you know. Had to work on Saturday."

"Me too." This is actually working. It's fun to talk to him like he's a regular person and not someone who over-whelms me at every turn. "Well, part of it, anyway. I tried to go to yoga."

His eyes twinkle as he follows my lead. "What happened?"

"Got stuck at the office."

"Bummer."

"It was okay. I almost got a mini nap on my boss's desk. But then I got busted by his boss, which was awkward."

"Sounds awful."

I grin. "Not so bad, actually."

"Phew."

I wiggle the report in the air between us. "Thank you, again. And I'm going to get out of your hair now, so you can get on with that mythical weekend thing."

He gestures his hand gallantly toward the door. "After you."

He's standing in front of my yoga mat. I point to it. "I just need…"

Instead of moving, he reaches down and grabs it. When he hands it over, his fingers brush mine, and I'm reminded again why everyone and their brother falls in love with this man.

There's definitely something about him, a heat that's

impossible to resist, but safe at the same time. It's super sexy, and my breath stutters on the inhale.

His gaze drops to my mouth, and when he looks back up at my eyes, the heat's gone, like he's purposefully made himself cold inside toward me, and after the stupid teasing conversation about names, I've gotta say it's unexpected.

It reminds me that I'm underdressed and overexposed, especially when it comes to my reactions to him.

He doesn't want me perving on him.

Nobody would. It's not professional. But before I can apologize, he's muttering a goodbye and on his way down the hall.

I follow slowly, pausing at the door, my hand on the light switch. I thunk my head against the wood paneling.

New girl made an impression all right.

I'm just not sure it was the right one.

6

GAVIN

My gut twists as I make my way back to my office. The sight of her bent over Stew's desk in those yoga pants made me hard, and then our conversation made me even harder. Who am I kidding? Her being in the same fucking building makes me hard.

I don't have a masochistic bone in my body, but there was something twisted about leaning over her and helping her get that report.

I know fucking better. I'm completely aware it was inappropriate and self-punishing, since I couldn't do anything else once I had her pressed against the bookshelf.

But her hair smells like lavender and her breathy little exhale is too addictive not to tease out of her.

I'm out of control and there's only one person I can turn to.

I check my watch and subtract three hours. Lunchtime on the west coast, so Max should be free. And if he's not, who cares? I'm the effing PM and for the first time in our adult life, I pull rank on him. If I need to get one of Vancouver's most renowned physicians out of bed or off the hospital ward to deal with a personal crisis, I damn well will.

I pull out the burner phone I keep just for occasions such as this and scroll to the entry labeled only, **Hawkeye**. I close my eyes and picture Max looking at his call display on the other side of the country. I'm BJ. The M*A*S*H references for our secret handles sums up our relationship pretty succinctly. I'm sure he's rolling his eyes as he picks up on the third ring, knowing that if I'm calling under the radar, this isn't just a social call.

"It's about time you called me," he says lazily. "I was beginning to think you'd found a newer, shinier best friend."

I wince. "You know what it's like when you start a new job. It takes a while to get up to speed."

"What can I do?" That's my best friend right there in a single question. He's a self-absorbed, narcissistic, egotistical bastard, but he's always got my back, no questions asked.

The vision of Ellie's perfectly spankable ass bent over Stew's desk slides back to the front of my mind and I rethink my decision to discuss my problem with Max on the phone. I need space. The better part of five provinces kind of space.

"Listen, I'm heading home in a couple of hours." And now I have to make that true. "I was hoping we could get together tonight."

I hate myself a little for being impulsively frivolous with the jet, but I justify my actions. It's not like I'm taking a taxpayer-funded holiday to the Bahamas. I'm flying to my riding where I have obligations outside those of PM. And if I can score some action to get my mind off Ellie and her all-too-tempting ass, even better.

"You bet. Anything special I should arrange?" Typical Max. He knows me even better than Stew does. I want to say yes, so badly, but even though I'm on a burner phone, and we're both very careful to avoid saying anything overtly recognisable, I'm still taking a risk.

"I'll give you a call once I get home so you can swing by."

"Sounds good."

I slip the burner phone into my briefcase and use my office phone to call Lachlan Ross, the RCMP officer in charge of my security.

If he's surprised by my sudden decision to go home, he doesn't let on, and he doesn't question it. Ever the professional.

Seven hours later, I hear a car pull up and park in the driveway of my Vancouver home. The band of stress squeezing my chest loosens a little.

It doesn't take long for Max to clear through my security detail. He's one of the few people in the city who can get to me with nothing more than photo ID.

He's got a big grin on his face as I open the door, and I suspect he's arranged something special anyway.

I close the door and turn to him. "What have you done?"

"Relax. You tell me what's eating at you and then we'll talk about what I may or may not have done."

My heart speeds up and I feel a little sick. It's hard enough acknowledging to myself all the inappropriate feelings and urges I have towards Ellie. But confessing them to another human being, even if that person is my best friend in the world, makes it way too real. But I need help, and coming clean to Max is my only option.

I lead the way into the kitchen and grab us both a beer from the fridge.

"There's this girl," I begin.

"Well, duh." I open one and turn to hand it to him. His expression softens. "Sorry. There's this girl…"

I open the other beer and take a long swig. "Yeah. She's an intern."

Max's eyes go wide. "Good God, man. Did Bill Clinton not teach you anything?"

"I haven't touched her. Not outside of my very vivid fantasies, anyway."

Max nods. "But you're finding it harder and harder to keep your hands to yourself." Not a question. As a doctor and long-time Dom, Max is a master at reading people. Add best friend to the mix and yeah, he's got my number. And my back.

"Yeah," I confess. "It's not just her looks, although she does have an ass that is just begging to be spanked. She's got brains and spunk. Seriously smart and deliciously sassy, and I love that." I take another swallow of beer. "But over and above the inappropriate workplace boss-subordinate romance thing, she's too young. I should not be perving over a woman that young who exists in my real life."

"So, you ran away."

"Yes, I fucking ran away. It's been too long since I've been laid, and I'm so wound up, I'm worried I might make a mistake I can't recover from. She's a scandal I just can't afford."

"And getting your kinky itch scratched in Vancouver is?"

"Dammit, Max, you're supposed to be helping me, not making me feel worse."

"What do you want me to do?"

"I don't know. Find me a way to let off some steam?"

"I thought you might be angling for something like that."

"I'm not angling for anything. I'm flat out telling you I need help."

"It's not like I can take you to the club and find you a willing sub for the night."

This is the bullshit that nobody tells you you'll have to put up with when you go into politics. Not if you want to stay out of blackmail range, anyway. But Max has a glint in his eye. And he seems to manage to find himself plenty of discreet, willing company.

"What are you suggesting?" Honestly, I'm game for anything. I trust him with my life. And my kink is nearly as precious. He knows that better than I do. He was the one who introduced me to it in the first place, when I stumbled into BDSM in college and freaked myself the fuck out.

His gaze darkens, like he's trying to warn me off. "I've got options, of course. I'll have to pay handsomely for them. Are you…"

"Anything, Max."

"Then yes. I've got an idea. But it'll take a few days."

We spend the rest of the evening drinking too much beer and catching up. Max takes me up on my offer of the spare room instead of taking a cab home.

I SPEND the next four days keeping my mind off my needs by throwing myself full-throttle into work at my constituency office, but issues are piling up in Ottawa and I'm running out of time and patience.

Stew has been on my ass at least twice a day wanting to know when, exactly, I plan to return. And every day it gets harder to put him off.

I'm just about to eat supper when the phone rings. I check the caller ID. Finally.

"Max. What's up?" I try to hide my excitement. *This is why I can't have nice things. I'm like a kid in a candy store, except*

I'm a grown man and my best friend is hooking me up... Definitely not the public man that everyone is looking to for a fresh new direction for our country.

Doesn't stop me from having the conversation I'm about to have. Just means I co-opt my best friend into playing spy talk as we do it. Lesson number one the RCMP taught me after I was elected: you never know who's listening.

Max has no guilt about subterfuge. He sounds totally relaxed, like this is the kind of bromance conversation we'd ordinarily have. "Just wondering if you're free to come over to my place tomorrow night?"

"Sure. What time?"

"Seven."

"Great. I'll see you then."

Thank fuck the wait is over. Now I can get Stew off my back and, after tomorrow, I'll be able to get Ellie's delectable body out of my fantasies. I pull out my laptop and start preparations for my return to Ottawa.

In the morning, I'm exhausted. I had a hard time getting to sleep. Too excited about what tonight has in store. Too busy wondering what she'll look like. How she'll react. How rosy her ass will get after my hand has warmed it up. Will she gag, or swallow me down like a porn star?

I spend the rest of the day in meetings and clearing up loose ends at the office, thoughts of the evening ahead never far from my mind.

Months without sex, and even longer without any kind of power exchange has been rough on my mental and physical well-being. If I have any chance of remaining sane, I'm going to have to find myself a regular sub in Ottawa — soon. Not exactly sure how I'm going to swing that miracle.

I used to have a regular thing with my friend Andrea here in Vancouver. Neither of us were romantically involved, so we were always each other's plus one with vanilla sex on the side. It worked well for us. Then things started looking shaky for the government and for a bunch of reasons, I pulled away from her.

She was fun to go to functions with and really good in the sack, but she wasn't wife material. Not my wife material, anyway.

I couldn't afford for the public and the media to get too attached to her. Better to be single and lose the election than run the risk of people thinking I'm using her for political gain.

If or when I get involved in another relationship, it'll be the real deal. Like what Stew has with his wife. A partnership that works on every level. And since I've never come close to that in thirty-nine years, I'm not holding my breath. Better that the country accept me as the bachelor leader I'll probably be for the entirety of my term.

It's nearly six by the time I get home, barely enough time to choke down some food, shower, and dress before I need to leave for Max's place.

There's leftover pizza in the fridge, and I grab a slice to eat while I grab clean clothes. I open my dresser and pull out my favourite jeans.

I wear a suit every day. When I'm going to do a scene, I prefer fabric I can move in, but that still carries a certain image. These are soft and faded from years of wear and washing. I doubt I'll be in them all that long, but I need to be comfortable. I open the next drawer down and root around until I find the right t-shirt. Black cotton, and just tight enough that my chest and biceps push at the fabric but not so tight I look like a juicer.

I pop the last of the pizza into my mouth and check the time on my way to the shower. Fuck, I have just over half an hour to be at Max's and the drive will take at least fifteen. I could do it in less, but it's probably better the PM doesn't get pulled over for a traffic violation on his way to a bit of spanky-panky with an escort sourced by his Dom best friend.

I'm out of the shower and dressed with five minutes to spare. I throw on a jacket and grab the keys to my Tesla on my way out the door. I considered taking my toy bag with me, but decided that was also an unnecessary risk. Max would have a few extra goodies at his place I could use if I wanted.

I close the door behind me and turn to the officer who's been assigned to me for this shift. "Come on, Tim, I'll drive."

7

ELLIE

THE SECOND WEEK of my job proves both easier and harder than the first.

Easier, because the PM is gone for the first part of the week.

Harder, because he's on the west coast and all of our work days just got longer.

Easier, because I don't have to deal with the fact that I can still feel the brush of his hand against mine as he reached past me to grab the report.

Harder, because I find myself looking for him constantly.

I go to yoga every single night, the extra-long class.

I ignore the dreams that wake me up in the middle of night. Gavin holding me against the bookshelf and kissing me. Touching me.

By Friday, I've made zero progress on not fantasizing about him, but fantastic progress on laying the groundwork for Gavin to make a significant statement about corporate giving at the fundraiser planned for the middle of July.

It's a little awkward, because Stew doesn't want me to

loop in the event organizers, who are political party activists. But I did get the green light to work with the PM's speechwriter, Dave, who comes over from the office block across the street bearing gifts of coffee when we meet, and Stew pops in and out over the course of the week.

We map out a communications strategy that softens the landscape in a subtle way. I'm so stoked about it, and when Stew tells me on Friday that Gavin likes the plan, I grin like an idiot all the way home.

Sasha is on the couch when I walk in. She does a double take. "Did you get fired?"

I laugh. "No."

"But it's only six."

"It's the end of the week, and the PM is currently flying back from Vancouver. I got an unexpected night off."

She snorted. "How long is this internship?"

Three painfully short months. "Until the end of the summer."

"Phew. Because you seriously can't work at a job forever and ever where Friday evenings aren't de facto nights off." She leaps up and claps her hands. "Come on. You look happy. And awake. Let's celebrate that with a drink."

I quickly get changed, then we walk down the street to the gastropub that serves warm pretzels and a to-die-for ham and salami tray with pickles.

We're nearly to the end of our first round of drinks and the food has just arrived when my phone vibrates. It's an email from Gavin's assistant, to the entire PMO group, advising us that they've arrived back in the city on time, but he's cleared his schedule for the weekend and would be taking work up to Harrington Lake, the summer residence north of the city.

I can feel my face falling before I remember that Sasha is watching me.

"Bad news?"

"No." I reach for my drink. It's completely stupid that I'm disappointed I won't see him tomorrow.

It's completely stupid that I was already planning on going to work tomorrow.

I need more beer.

"What is it?"

"Nothing that drinks tonight and yoga tomorrow won't fix."

"You've been on a real kick all week."

"Since when do you pay such close attention to how often I go to yoga?" My phone vibrates again.

This time the email is from Gavin, again to the entire PMO group.

Thanks for your hard work this week. See you all on Monday.

Seeing his name at the bottom of the message makes me tremble from the inside out. And just like that, my grin is back.

"You want another drink?"

I do and I don't. "One more. Something light."

"Because of yoga?"

"Don't mock me. I never make fun of you for going on a long run when you're thinking about stuff."

She's giving me this look. A clever one, a thinking one. Something that says she sees right through me.

"So you think you've been going to yoga all week because it's stress-relief?"

It is. I look at her, confused. "Yes."

"Well that's your first mistake."

"What is?"

Sasha gives me a bland look over the top of her beer. "Shavasana doesn't help with horny."

"I'm not —" I blush. "Horny."

"Who was the email from?"

Oh my God, I'm so busted. "Nobody."

"You work for the hottest bachelor in the country, Ellie. I don't believe you. Who. Was. The. Email. From?"

"The PM," I squeak, sinking low in the booth.

"Not horny, my ass. You're thinking of him right now."

Well, that wasn't fair. I think about him constantly. "Only because I got an email from him three minutes ago."

"Was it dirty?"

"Of course not."

"Wanna bet it was dirty between the lines?"

"I'd take that bet in a second. There's zero chance that the PM would ever do anything inappropriate like that."

She narrows her eyes at me. "Interesting."

"No. Nothing is interesting."

"You didn't say that he wasn't attracted to you, that there was nothing there, that he's in a relationship or gay, or any other excuse you could give for why there'd never be anything dirty between you."

"Are you out of your mind? I'm…" I lower my voice. "I'm an intern. He's the leader of the government. If for no other reason than the optics of that are *awful*, I'm sure I'm not his type."

"Because beautiful, bendy redheads are never anyone's type."

"I'm really more of a blonde."

"Those are also known to never, ever get any action."

"I'm awkward."

"It really trips over the line into adorably nervous most of the time."

"I'm…" I flail my hands in the air. "Sasha! Listen to me. I'm just a regular woman. I'm *nobody* that Gavin would ever be interested in."

"So why do you turn pink every time you read your email?"

Because I have the most insane visceral reaction to him. To even just see his name on the screen. "I'm like everyone else in this country. I think he's incredible."

Her face softens and she tips her head to the side. "Awww, El. I'm sorry. I shouldn't tease."

"It's fine. I brought it on myself."

"And is he incredible?"

"Absolutely. He's one of the good guys. He's also brutal to work for." I laugh ruefully. "I think he only sleeps like four hours a night."

"So it's just a crush?"

I nod. "Yes. And now we're going to pretend it doesn't exist, okay? Because he's exactly what this country needs. And I want to help him in any way possible. Drooling over him isn't conducive to that plan."

"Cool." She lifts her hand and waves down the waitress. "Let's toast him with another round."

MONDAY MORNING I wake up at four. Might have something to do with the fact that I went to sleep at nine the night before.

Probably has a lot to do with the fact that I'm giddy at the thought of seeing Gavin today.

It's Sasha's fault. Well, Sasha and beer equally carry the blame. Friday night I tumbled into bed and my dreams went from naughty to something way more dangerous: romantic. I can't even remember all the details when I wake up, but each morning I'm a little more gone for him.

And all weekend, that warm, tingly crush feeling carried me through a few hours of work and a trip to the market, dinner with friends and two more delicious nights of being stripped bare and consumed by the prime minister.

I get up quietly and shower, grateful that Sasha and I have separate bathrooms on opposite sides of the apartment.

I dress carefully. A black pencil skirt, my beloved pair of black Louboutin pumps, and the short-sleeved sage-green silk blouse I got at Holt Renfrew on clearance last year.

It's by far my most sophisticated outfit. Sexy, professional, and not to be ignored.

What are you doing, Ellie?

It's a fair question. I don't have a plan, because my heart is beating so fast my mind can't get a word in edgewise.

I let my hair dry on its own while I check my email. Twelve messages for the PMO, and while I'm in beast work mode, I fire off a quick stay-in-touch email to my PhD advisor, filling him in on my first two weeks. I finish off the note with a question, because otherwise he'd recognize the email as the noise it really was.

Starbucks won't be open for another hour, so I make a travel coffee for myself, pack my lunch bag, and head out the door. There's one bus running up Bank Street this early, and I'm not waiting another hour to get to the office.

And I'm not so twisted up in my feelings that I'll grab a cab or walk.

I'm not crazy.

I'm also not alone. There are a few others heading downtown at this hour. Most get off one block before me, heading into the offices across the street from the Parliament Buildings.

I stand on the wide walk up to Centre Block for a minute, wondering how much my emotions are being manipulated by this place. Probably a fair bit. I get a little thrill every time I walk past security, and today is no different.

"You're here early, Ms. Montague," the guard says. He knows my name from my badge, but I feel badly for not returning the acknowledgement.

"Lots of work to do." I give him a quick smile, but my lips shake from the effort.

I take the elevator, grateful for both the wait and the slow, creaky ascent. A few more moments of fantasy time.

I know that when I see Gavin, it'll be the same as it was the first week. *Terrifying.* Okay, not quite the same as that. Or yes, but in a different way.

But he's not going to see me. Not like I see him.

The office is empty. I let myself in and turn on my computer. Dave has sent me a draft of a speech, and it's good. I flag a couple of points of language that I know will drive Gavin mad, and email it back, suggesting I come over to his office later to discuss it. I'll need a latte anyway, my coffee from home is awful.

Maybe I should steal a Diet Coke from Stew. I stand up and grab my keycard lanyard, slipping it around my neck as I step into the hallway. I'm just tugging my hair free when the elevator dings and off steps Lachlan Ross, Gavin's chief of security. He's an RCMP officer, I've learned, but everyone on the PM's security detail dresses in plain clothes.

Next off is the man himself, and I eat up the sight of him. Today's suit is dark blue, and the tie is red and navy stripes. The shirt is white, as always. I add it to the mental catalogue of his outfits in my head, with a tagline note that he doesn't look rested in the least after his weekend in the country.

Our gazes tangle as he slows his long strides.

"Gavin," I breathe. "Good morning. Welcome back."

Something hard snaps in his eyes, and his lips tighten. "Ms. Montague."

His response couldn't be more chilly, and I step back in shock, bumping into the door frame of my office.

Of all the fantasy possibilities of how this moment might go, I forgot to consider something like this.

Lachlan is well past us now, but there's another security team member trailing behind Gavin. I'm painfully aware that we're not alone.

That doesn't stop me from still searching for something more as I look at him — an explanation, maybe.

There's something hard about his face, and it takes me a moment to realize he hasn't shaved today.

Or yesterday, and maybe a few days before that.

You stopped shaving is a stupid thing to say to someone who's just put you in your place for being overly familiar.

"Gavin. You can call me Gavin." Where the hell has that teasing look in his eyes gone?

I cross my arms and force myself to be professional. "I'll see you at the briefing."

He nods curtly and moves past me, finding his speed effortlessly again. But when he gets to his office door, which Lachlan has opened for him, he stops and looks back at me. "Actually, if you have a minute now."

I nod, dread sliding into my gut. There's only one answer when you work for the prime minister. "Yes, of course."

8

GAVIN

I'M A COMPLETE ASSHOLE.

That's the second thought that pounds through my brain after I get off the elevator.

The first was, she's beautiful. Like, steal my breath and smack me in the face with it gorgeous. Her hair is loose today, long golden waves with touches of burnished copper here and there, and I just want to wrap my fists in it and crush my mouth against hers.

But I flew across the country to drum my want for her out of my system, so even if I could want her, now I don't deserve her.

"I owe you an apology," I say brusquely as she stands in front of my desk. Her fingers are wrapped tightly around her lanyard.

I want to take her hands in mine and stroke away that worry.

Which I've caused.

I told her to call me Gavin.

Everyone does.

And then I threw it back in her face.

She stiffens. "I'm sure you don't, sir."

Fuck me. There it is. Did I do that to myself? Did I push her away just to hear her say it again?

"That's for me to decide, Ellie." I tap my fingers on the back of my chair as I stand behind it. I need to get us back on track. "Stew tells me that you're working closely with Dave in our communications team."

She nods, her lower lip caught between her teeth. "I'm heading over there as soon as he gets in. We'll have a draft speech for you by the end of the day."

"Perhaps you should work over there for the next few weeks."

She blanches, and I kick myself because now I've made it seem like she's being moved out of the office—right after I told her I had something to apologize for.

Which I never exactly got to, because how do I find the words to say, I'm sorry I can't stop thinking about fucking you on this desk? You don't.

That's the kind of secret you bury deep.

"Look, you're spending most of your time working with Dave, and it'll save a lot of time if you're not traipsing back and forth between here and the PMO."

"True."

Fuck, she still looks so damned dejected. I second guess my decision to get her out of the way for a while, even though I've convinced myself my reasoning is sound.

I give her what I hope is a reassuring smile. "Don't worry, your desk will be waiting right where you left it once you and Dave have this communications strategy nailed down."

She nods. "Anything else?" Her eyes shine bright with unshed tears. I can see she needs to escape, and as much as I want to pull her into my arms and soothe her, I do the kinder thing. "No. We're done."

She turns to leave and I'm faced with her beautiful ass, all wrapped up in that tight black skirt. I look for panty lines. Nothing but smooth fabric that leaves very little to my imagination.

The knowledge that she's naked under that skirt makes my mouth water and my cock throb.

I cross the room and close my door. I need a few minutes alone. I pretend it's to calm my raging hard-on, but in truth, I want to indulge in a little fantasy. Max's arrangement did nothing to curb my all-consuming hunger for Ellie.

I walk back to my desk and glide my fingers along the smooth surface, imagining her bent over it. Because she's so short, she's up on her toes. Her skirt is stretched even tighter over her ass, and I decide to leave it where it is.

Somehow I find the idea of spanking her fully clothed in my office hotter than the thought of her naked.

I stop directly behind her and grip her hips as I grind my erection against—

There's a knock on my door and reality catches up with me too soon.

Nearly two hours have passed by the time Stew finally fucks off to his own office.

The way I left things with Ellie has been eating at me all morning and I need to do *something* to try and smooth things over without giving her the wrong impression.

After several minutes of replaying every encounter we've had, I come up with the answer and leave it in my assistant's very capable hands.

Now that I've got a few spare minutes, I pull out my burner phone and dial Max's number.

"Do you have any fucking idea what time it is?"

I look at my watch and wince. "Time you got your lazy ass out of bed."

Max just laughs. "Glad your flight went well, sorry it took you three days to let me know you arrived safely."

"That's what the national news is for." The words fall out of my mouth before I remember why I'm talking on a burner phone.

"Fair enough. I noticed you left my gift unopened." Max doesn't have any problems speaking in code.

I feel a twinge of guilt over bailing on the escort Max arranged for me. It's not like I can reimburse him for the expense. "Yeah, turns out it was more your style than mine, but I appreciate the thought."

"Well, you're going to need something to keep you active."

"If you were here, we could find ourselves a pick-up hockey game somewhere."

Max chuckles. "Really? Take a look outside your window. Do you think that's going to be an option for you?"

"Won't know until I try, will I?"

"More power to you. I'll see you in just over three weeks."

"I didn't know you were coming to town."

"I gave that cute assistant of yours the heads up that I'd appreciate any opportunity to visit."

"Don't hit on my staff. And why on earth would you want to visit?"

"Maybe I've grown tired of never experiencing minus thirty degree winters."

"It's summer. More like plus thirty."

"It is, and an excellent time to go house hunting."

"You wouldn't move here."

"I just might."

I've missed having my best friend nearby, and a little bubble of hope starts to grow in my chest, but I can't acknowledge his statement without taking this conversation to a really emotional place—I can't wrap my head around the fact that he would actually move across the country, but I'm also the only family he has. "Listen, I've got to run. Back to back meetings. I look forward to seeing you."

Max hesitates, then says, "Catch ya later."

I disconnect and call Lachlan into my office.

"You've been in Ottawa awhile, yes?"

"You could say that, yes."

"And if I needed something a little…*un-Priministerial*, you could probably arrange it, yes?"

Lachlan stiffens slightly, but his expression remains neutral. "What exactly are you looking for?"

9

ELLIE

I won't lie — at first it felt like Gavin rejected me.

But since everything that transpired between us can be summed up as the understandable delusional fantasies of a girl with a crush on a man that everyone is crushing on, and in the days and weeks that followed, life carried on and I got over it.

Mostly.

It helped that two days after I moved over to the block of offices across the road — where in fact I *was* more productive — I got a thank you gift from the PM.

Part of me wanted to see it as an apology, as well, although a travel mug branded with the Government of Canada's wordmark wouldn't defrost many hearts. The note inside, though…that did funny things to my chest. Handwritten in his own sharp, spiky block writing that I'd already come to recognize, it was short and to the point.

You're a valuable part of my team, Ellie. It's my loss that you're only on loan from the university. Thank you for keeping me on my toes. ~ G

I tucked the note away in my purse and now use the mug every day.

It also helps that there's a ton of work to do, and a lot of it happens away from him, although his presence is felt in every project. He's running this country with ease, it seems, even though that's a daunting, overwhelming task — and he's doing it at an exhausting pace.

I've settled into a routine that starts with checking my email while it's still dark out because it's easier if I get a head start on anything that's come up overnight.

My job seems to morph on a daily basis. The biggest project to date was moving the goalposts on the fundraiser, which is just a week away now. I spent most of that time in the PMO offices across the street, and after the sting of feeling like I was exiled, I realized that much was happening there that I was missing out on.

Since this internship will further my own career goals as much as it is a public service, I want to get as much out of it as I can.

However, most of the time I'm asked for informal position papers, a page or two of tight, sound-bite fodder on any number of issues. Some of them I can anticipate from the election and the PM's first three months in office. Others come out of nowhere — storm clouds gathering in the dark and bursting at the start of the day, derailing the news cycle.

I'm mainlining coffee and packing brown bag lunches because invariably the thirty minutes it takes me to step out to grab something is the same window where all hell breaks loose and I have to play catch-up when I get back.

I'm already working at the disadvantage of not being able to read anyone's mind. Stew and Gavin only seem to speak out loud when they're barking at each other. The rest of the time they communicate in grunts and nods that I can barely follow—and they expect me to keep up.

When I wake up on my fifth Tuesday on the job and reach for my phone, eyes still blurry with sleep, I'm almost convinced I've got a handle on what today will look like.

I am, of course, completely full of shit.

We're well into the summer break for the House of Commons, but the PM plans for us to hit the ground running when the House reconvenes after Labour Day. That's part of what these internships are about, I've realized —not just making sure that young people from all sectors have voices in the various departments of the government, but so the government quietly has in-house sounding boards.

He's scary smart, Gavin is. I'd never want to cross him. I'm not sure who he's more intent on besting come the fall —the Opposition, or the doubters within his own party.

And Stew has his back. Today, that means that Gavin sent a terse email to his Chief of Staff at…

I blink. Jesus. Ten after four in the morning. My sleep-deprived heart whimpers.

Since then, there's been a chain of emails, mostly between Stew and someone in the party I don't know, and I've been copied on the entire exchange.

I look at the clock.

Quarter to six.

That's a lot of emailing in an hour and a half.

Another email lands in my inbox, this one from the PM, replying to the chain.

Call Ellie and wake her up. I need her thoughts on this by breakfast.

Seriously? For one thing, I *am* awake, like I have been

at this hour every day since I started this job. I've responded to emails at this time of day at least a dozen times.

It's the height of arrogance to assume I'm still asleep.

Sure, I'm lying in bed, because it's still dark outside. But in forty minutes I'll be walking into his office, my brain at his disposal for what will surely turn into a ten or twelve hour day, so he can suck it.

I need coffee. Honestly, I can understand why some people in politics do cocaine. Coffee barely touches the level of fatigue I'm working at right now.

And Gavin Strong was up at four in the morning, stewing about…

I scroll back to the top of the email chain. I'm not awake enough for this yet, but I read it twice.

It's dense. I think Stew and I were looped into the conversation after the first few exchanges, but they're talking about—

I jerk upright in bed.

They're talking about radically changing the tax code.

Fuck.

It's too early in the morning for a conversation that's way out of my depth.

And Gavin wants my thoughts on *what?*

My phone rings. Stew. I sigh and hit answer. "Morning."

"Are you on your email?"

"Yes. Reading it now. I'll be there in forty minutes."

"Make it thirty."

"Stew…"

He sighs. "It's fine, Ellie. He just wants your opinion."

"I don't know what I'm supposed to say."

"Tell him what you really think."

Easier said than done.

But as I hang up and flop back on the bed, a stupid grin spreads across my face for the first time in days, maybe weeks. Gavin wants my opinion.

That shouldn't make me nearly as happy as it does. But it's all I get of him, so I'll grab on to it with both fists, earnestly and eagerly.

I WALK in to the main reception area of the PMO and Gavin's assistant is waiting for me.

"Stew wants you to join them in the PM's office."

I give her a quick nod and say thanks before dumping my messenger bag at my desk. I sling my lanyard around my neck. It's become a bit of a security item for me. I've discovered that if I hang on to it during meetings, my fingers looped around the cord, I don't futz with my skirt and my hair nearly as much.

I was mortified when someone asked me if I was nervous.

I mean, of course I am. By all rights, I shouldn't be anywhere near the leader of the country. Definitely not being pulled into his office to talk about tax law.

Of course, when I knock and enter, it turns out that's not why they've asked me to join them.

The real reason is even worse.

"Thank God you're here, Ellie," Stew says from the corner, where he's leaning against a glassed-in bookcase. "We have a tampon problem."

First issue with this statement: Stew has never been grateful for my sudden appearance before.

Secondly, I'm not a tampon expert. Yes, I use them. No, I don't want to talk about that with either of these men.

My cheeks grow warm, and I'm sure they're fast on

their way to burning red, and I hate myself for that reaction. Because there is a small chance that this is a reasonable request for my expertise.

Probably not, but it could be.

"Jesus, Stew, you have a way with words." Gavin turns from where he's been standing in front of the window and gestures for me to sit. He's looking extra tall and broad this morning. He doesn't look tired in the least.

He looks fantastic. Black suit today. I can't help myself from noticing, even when grumpy. Mental image recorded…white shirt, red tie. Classic. Into the memory bank it goes.

He leans on his desk. "You saw the emails."

"I did."

"What do you think?"

This is the moment of truth, because I'm smart, but I'm not that smart. Not universally smart like Gavin or bone-deep smart like Stew. Sometimes, the bravest thing to do is be honest. "I have no clue."

He laughs, and it takes me by surprise because it's been a month since I've heard that sound.

I miss it. A happy warmth fills my chest as his blue eyes look straight at me. Something else I've missed way too much.

"I don't expect you to intuitively understand the technical side of it," he says roughly. "I just need to know if I'm barking up the wrong tree."

I flick my gaze over to Stew. "What's the tampon problem? We don't tax feminine hygiene products anymore."

The previous government had been embarrassed into action by a series of online petitions campaigning to remove sales tax on what is obviously a necessity. Gavin presented them in the House of Commons.

"Exactly. So we've set that precedent—and it's one

we're committed to. Taxation shouldn't discriminate or take advantage of different needs based on any—"

"Let's cut to the point," Gavin interrupts. "The real question is, what's the next tampon problem that we're not seeing here?"

"I don't know." I shrug. "I won't know until I see the list of products that will and won't be taxed. That's what you're talking about, right? You want to change what consumption products people are taxed on. Move more of the daily consumables into the necessity column, like tampons and diapers and groceries."

Gavin snapped his fingers and pointed at Stew. "See? She gets it."

She really doesn't. I wrack my brain trying to see the complete picture. "But that's not all you were talking about in the email. That's just the thin edge of the wedge."

"Yes…" He's staring at me intently now, waiting for me to see it.

See what?

"Wait." I swivel my head back and forth between Stew and Gavin, moving closer and closer to his desk as I fit the puzzle pieces together. "You don't want to add individual items to that necessity column. You want to somehow work it so that nothing at the grocery store is taxed. You want to remove sales tax completely at that level."

It's huge. Stupid and expensive, but huge.

Gavin holds my gaze, his eyes glittering with intensity as he nods. "It was an idea put forward by one of my economics advisors."

"That's a big hit to the budget."

"Massive."

"So it's gotta be worth it."

"And that's my question for you. Is it worth it?"

I want to say yes. And a part of me wants to say no, too,

because I can see arguments on either side. But something I've learned over the last month is that my role isn't to say yes or no, but to voice the perspective that doesn't yet have a seat at the table. I take a deep breath. "Not right now. This isn't what will make the biggest difference in people's lives."

"Sales tax is regressive." He's not lecturing. It's debate-bait.

I nod. "Definitely. And a year or two into your mandate, it'll be a strong re-affirmation that you're committed to easing the cost of living for lower and middle class Canadians. But if I don't understand it immediately, neither will the average voter. Don't give them a headache in your first full session of government."

"And you thought you didn't know what to tell me," he says softly.

"Is that what you wanted to hear?"

"No." But his eyes are smiling. Not his mouth. That's set in a firm, thinking line that's ridiculously hot. "But it's what I needed to hear." He turns and nods at Stew. "Thanks. We're done."

This time those two words don't turn me inside out.

I go back to my desk, and when I get called across the road to a meeting about the fundraiser, I'm practically skipping.

I can see how people get sucked into the pulse of this world. Sliding back into academia at the end of the summer is going to be a challenge.

10

GAVIN

ONE OF THE first lessons drilled into me by the protocol officer assigned to my transition into the role of prime minister was on the role of official gifts. They can't exceed a certain dollar amount, for example. Any gifts I receive in my role really become national property.

Max mailed me a gorgeous leather flogger as soon as he heard that, the fucker. I pointed out to him that, one, I don't open my own mail any more, and two, my assistant has almost certainly read Fifty Shades of Grey, so there's no pretending it's some kind of Western paraphernalia. Having a harassment charge levelled against me in the first week on the job would have been awkward.

He sent her the largest, most ridiculous bouquet of flowers by way of apology. Now she thinks he's the funniest man in the country, and she bends over backwards to accommodate any request he sends her way—like an invitation to the party fundraiser next Friday night.

I'm ninety percent thrilled that my best friend is considering a move to the capital. Ten percent of me is seriously worried about the impact his lifestyle will have on me—the me that is now the PM, which I've fragmented from the rest of me. But that makes me a shitty friend, so I shove that worry to the back of my mind.

Anyway, at the moment I have the much more pleasurable task of figuring out how to present the gift I had commissioned for Ellie.

Because she's an intern and we don't officially have a personal relationship, there are rules of protocol around what is an acceptable gift. I may have bent them a little. I felt the need to make up a little for the weak coffee cup apology.

If only circumstances were different. In my perfect world, I'd be giving her a strand of pearls. I'd have her strip, stand before me so I can inspect every last inch of her, then drape the pearls around her delicate neck.

Instead, she's getting an eighteen karat gold Canadian flag lapel pin. Because nothing says I want you body, mind, and soul like a fucking symbol of patriotism.

And as much as I hate to admit it. I do want her mind and soul every bit as much as I want to dominate her body. Maybe even more.

I cut myself off from another fantasy. It took a few weeks, but Lachlan's found a Sunday morning hockey game for me that he assures me will be private. It's a summer thing, but then so is Ellie's internship.

Come September, we'll need a new plan.

Maybe one that involves pearls.

For now, I have to behave.

I leap out of my chair and lean out my office door. "Beth, does Ellie know she should attend the fundraiser?"

"I don't think so—do you want me to send her an invitation?" She holds up a creamy envelope. "I've got an extra right here."

I reach for the envelope. "No, I'll walk it over. If I've got fifteen minutes?" The pin has been burning a hole in my jacket pocket for days and I'm grateful for an innocent opportunity to pass it along.

Other than Stew, Beth has known me longer than anyone else on my staff. Unlike Stew, she doesn't know how much of a bastard I am. And she's a diehard romantic. Her eyes light up and I groan inside.

"Actually, I probably don't have time." I step away from her desk, back toward my office.

"Not at all." Her fingers fly fast across her keyboard then she beams at me. "You have thirty minutes."

Lachlan appears as if conjured from thin air—probably by Beth—and before I can think better about this plan, we're heading out.

My security detail is actually pretty light. An officer heads across the street before us, then I've got two men behind me. It takes a solid fifteen minutes because I need to stop and take pictures with two groups of tourists on the lawn, but these kinds of impromptu walks aren't that big a deal. I've got it easy compared to some international leaders.

The Langevin Block is where most of my staff work. Some of my predecessors have spent more time over here than I do, and I'm sure once the House is in session, I'll do the same. But there's something about working in my Centre Block offices, something that appeals to my domi-nant nature.

I want my staff to come to me. For them to understand the weight of the authority I carry every day. That when I make decisions, sometimes against their counsel, I do it from the seat of power.

That took some of my newer staff by surprise.

Stew and Beth? They weren't shocked at all. They

know I'm ruthless when I want something. Everyone else sees a dragon slayer fighting the good fight.

The truth about that knight in shining armour? He doesn't think twice about cutting the heart out of his enemies.

I finally make it to Ellie's office. Lachlan and the rest of my security detail don't follow me around inside the PMO, so after I make sure to make everyone else feels like they've gotten a slice of my attention, nobody pays any notice to the fact that I've really just come to see her.

Her door is open and I stand there for a moment, just watching her. She's so fucking sexy when she's thinking.

I knock on the door frame and she looks up. "Got a minute?"

"Absolutely." She leans back in her chair.

I close the door behind me and walk to her desk, but remain standing.

"The fundraiser is just over a week away, and it's only just come to my attention that you might not be aware that your presence is required." I pull the invitation from my jacket pocket and hold it out to her. "You'll need this."

Her eyes dart to the creamy envelope. "Oh. It never occurred to me that I'd be invited. I'm just an intern."

"Actually, you've been the driving force behind keeping this fundraiser from being a public relations disaster. You're definitely more than *just* an intern."

Her face turns the most adorable pink and suddenly all I can think of is what kind of pink I can turn her ass with my palm.

That is an incredibly distracting image, and my body instantly reacts to it, but I force myself to stay on point. "And on the subject of your stellar performance, I wanted to present you with a small token of my appreciation."

I dig into my pants pocket and retrieve the little gold pin. It had come beautifully boxed, but I didn't want to make it appear a bigger deal than it was, so I thought I best present it naked.

I can't risk touching her skin. My groin is at her eye level and I'm already fighting off an erection, so I lay it gently on the desk in front of her.

She picks it up and studies it for a moment, a small smile turning up the corners of her mouth. "It's lovely. Thank you."

"You're welcome." I pause a beat. There's so much more I want to say. None of it appropriate, and the door to her office has been closed long enough. "I look forward to seeing you at the fundraiser."

I turn to leave, but stop when she makes an indecisive noise, almost a little whimper. It's official—everything between us turns my mind to sex now. "About that. Um… I'll let Beth know…I mean, of course I'll try to be there—"

I spin back towards her and lean over her desk, my face inches from hers. Fuck, she's got such pretty eyes. "The invitation is a formality. Your presence is not optional. And the correct answer is *yes, Sir.*"

Her breathing becomes shallow as her lips make a silent O that would look perfect around my cock. I squelch that thought, reminding myself where I am and who I'm with, before I do or say something neither of us can recover from. I try like hell not to notice how her pupils dilate and her lips darken as her system drives blood to the body parts she's suddenly aware of.

I fail spectacularly.

I straighten up and take a step back and repeat myself. "I look forward to seeing you at the fundraiser, Ellie."

She nods slowly and gives me the most perfect response. "Yes, Sir."

IT'S BACK-TO-BACK meetings all day and I don't get home until well after ten. I'm starving and after the nearly disastrous visit to Ellie's office this afternoon, I need to talk to Max.

I toe off my shoes as soon as I walk in the door. Like at the PMO's office, my security detail stays on the other side. Even when I'm not here, 24 Sussex is always secure, and while there's a complicated security system inside, I've been assured I have relative privacy.

I toss my suit jacket and briefcase onto a sofa on my way to the kitchen. I've been looking forward to last night's leftover pizza and a beer all day.

I grab the pizza box along with a bottle of my favourite beer from the fridge and return to the living room.

Max picks up on the first ring. My mouth is full of pizza, but it doesn't matter. He just starts talking.

"That assistant of yours, man. She's all the fucking awesome. She's already got me set up with a real estate agent and has agreed to come with me while I look at houses because I'll need a woman's perspective."

I nearly choke trying to swallow my half-chewed pizza and I wash it down with a quick swig from my beer. "I told you not to hit on my staff."

"Oh, I wasn't hitting. She offered. I accepted."

I make it a policy not to meddle, but knowing Beth and her boyfriend have recently split, Max's careless enthusiasm concerns me on many levels.

He's way more than just a player. He makes me look positively vanilla.

And it's not some fling Beth is on the rebound from. She and her boyfriend had already been living together when she came to work for me more than two years ago.

I don't know what went wrong. The only reason I even know about the split is because it's the sort of thing my security team keeps me abreast of, and Lachlan thought I ought to know she was in some emotional turmoil.

"I've never, ever interfered in your social life, so you need to understand just how serious I am. Don't lead her on. Don't give her any mixed signals. I'm not saying don't flirt. Just make sure she doesn't misunderstand. Okay?"

"Wow, you're a bucket of cold water."

"I need you to trust that there are reasons and leave it at that."

"Understood. So, what were you calling about that couldn't wait until Friday?"

And now I'm not so sure this is the time to discuss the insanity of this afternoon. "Nothing. Just had a long day and didn't feel like eating my pizza alone."

"And this is why I'm moving there."

I close my eyes and thud my head back against the couch cushions. But I'm grinning as I do it.

11

ELLIE

I FLING the door to our apartment open and point at my roommate. "I need a dress."

Sasha nods like this is a completely normal way to start a conversation. "Start with my closet, or go straight to maxing out the credit card?"

And the correct answer is yes, Sir.

I can't wear one of Sasha's dresses. If the fundraiser goes anything like I hope it might, I'm going to want to put that dress in a sex museum. Also, I think it violates a number of articles in the Roommate Accord to have sex in someone else's clothes.

Not that we're going to have sex. Necessarily.

But...

I lick my lips nervously as I look at my roommate. She knows about the crush. She knows he sent me away from his inner circle and how devastated I was, and she knows about the coffee mug.

Can I tell her about this?

At what point can I start to trust that what we're doing

—this slow, seductive dance of looks and words and arcing chemistry—is actually going to lead somewhere? After his visit to my office in Langevin Block...

Well, if it is going to lead somewhere, then it can stay our secret.

But if my heart's going to get broken, I'd really like my roommate to be on guard with ice cream and Doritos and a Heath Ledger movie marathon.

Luckily after two years, I don't need to tell her anything. Also, I have the world's shittiest poker face.

She squeals. "You have a date."

My face crumples. "No."

"Oh."

"I have a fundraiser."

"Oh, Ellie." She groans and waves me to her room. "Okay, you can pick a dress from my closet. And then we need to have a long, hard talk about unrealistic expectations."

I follow her, but my heart is already set on a dress of my own. And I'm irrationally annoyed that she thinks I'm delusional about Gavin. No way am I telling her about the pin and what he said.

I perch on her bed and she pulls out her three go-to cocktail dresses. Two black, one dark green. They'd all look good on me, although her boobs are bigger than mine, but none of them are strapless, so that's probably not an issue.

"Hmm," I say, and she rolls her eyes.

"You really want to go shopping?"

"I..." I blush. "Yes."

She blinks twice, clearly processing my stupidity, then nods. "Okay. Let's go."

And that's why we're not just roommates, but friends. Because even though she thinks I'm a loon, she's going to make sure I'm the hottest, sexiest redheaded loon at that fundraiser.

We don't bother with the mall. My credit card screams as we head straight for Holt Renfrew, the fanciest department store in Canada, but I trust Sasha.

An hour later, we're home again with the perfect dress —a strapless sheath that hugs me like a glove. An open black lace pattern reveals a lot of the champagne satin underneath, and paired with my second most prized shoes, the nude Jimmy Choos, it'll scream sex to Gavin and look perfectly professional to everyone else.

I hope.

I try on the dress with the shoes while Sasha plates up the Pad Thai we picked up for our dinner.

She whistles at me as I skip out of my room, showing her the two earring options I've got on.

"Left or right?"

She gives me a carefully appraising look. "Hmm. The dangling ones are hot, but the pearl drops are classier. And I take back any doubting noises I made earlier. He's going to lose his mind when he sees you in the dress."

"It's classy enough?"

"Shut. Up. Go take off the fancy clothes, put on your sweatpants like a normal person, and eat this take-out food."

I do just that, on the couch, watching a re-run of a fashion reality show that Sasha pretends to hate, but I've already mostly lost her to whatever book she's reading anyway.

I wonder what Gavin's having for dinner. He must eat, but then again, I assumed the man slept, and that proved untrue. What would he think of takeout on the couch?

Is he one of those "food is fuel" workout freaks? I've seen the videos of him at the gym. The entire country has.

It's such a refreshing change of pace having a leader who can bench that much weight—and look that good in shorts. And the photos of him kickboxing…they may be saved to my phone.

I try to think of the last time I saw the inside of a gym. Yoga doesn't count, and I also haven't done that in almost a week. Undergrad, probably. Seven years ago?

"What are you thinking about?"

"Working out."

"Oh!" Her eyes get all big and hopeful. I'm so mean. "Wanna go with me to the gym in the morning?"

"Nope." I laugh as I twirl up another forkful of noodles. "I was just thinking about…" *Gavin*. "The PM. I think he works out a lot."

"I read somewhere that he plays hockey. I think any gymming he does is in support of that."

"Oh!" I like hockey. I file that tidbit away to research further. "Cool."

"So that's a no to the gym?"

"I have to be at work first thing in the morning." Gavin's giving a tech sector speech tomorrow afternoon that lays another bit of the groundwork for his big speech at the fundraiser. It's his fourth event like this, and the media is starting to pick up on the hints. Stew expects a lot of calls in the afternoon, which means we need to have everything done in before lunch.

For some reason, I'm anxious about this. About tomorrow, and the fundraiser. Not because of Gavin. Something else that I can't quite put my finger on.

Sasha takes our empty plates away and I stretch out on the couch, trying to figure out what's bugging me. Something's not right.

But I'm tired and pleasantly full and still on a shopping

high about scoring that dress, so I tell myself I'll give the worry more thought in the morning.

Before I can convince myself to crawl off to bed, I've zonked out on the couch. When I wake up in the middle of the night, I'm covered in a blanket, and Sasha's tucked my phone beside me.

12

ELLIE

IN HINDSIGHT, I probably should have seen it earlier in the week. Maybe I'm too innocent about the ways of politicos.

Maybe I was unforgivably distracted after Gavin hand-delivered the invitation—if you can still call it that when your presence is *required*.

Either way, I had no clue that Dave the speechwriter was going to turn out to be such a total dingus.

I use other more colourful language the next morning when, with plenty of time to prime the news channels before the end of day politics wrap up, Gavin's speech for the fundraiser next week is leaked.

Such a stupid, pointless move.

Yes, it derails the day. That storm cloud you don't see rolling in. But once it bursts, it's done. Everyone gets wet but they dry out, and the cloud has spent itself.

Dave's just killed his career for a touch of notoriety.

Stupid.

And as I have that thought, I realize that in the five weeks I've worked in politics, I've used *stupid* like a thousand times more than in the preceding seven years of academic work.

Of course everyone is furious. It doesn't take long for someone from IT to identify that Dave was the person who'd sent the speech out—and used a throwaway Gmail account, but didn't think twice about the fact that he was using a government computer to do it.

Total dingus.

Stew fires him, behind closed doors but loud enough for everyone to hear every last expletive-enhanced word. Then after the writer is escorted out of the building by security, the Chief of Staff stops by my office.

Fury twists his words and his short instruction to me is so sharp I nearly jump out of my skin. "Write a new speech. He's going in front of a hostile room now. I want to see it by end of day tomorrow."

Okay. I'll just pretend that I know how to write a political speech. No biggie. I wince as I turn back to my computer.

Sasha brings me dinner on her way home from the university. I stay until eleven, then Uber home and I'm back again at six, freshly showered—but that's about it. No makeup, hair twisted in a damp bun on my head.

I try to imagine what he needs to say about corporate giving that will break through their stony assumptions.

Midmorning, someone from the communications staff brings me coffee. I make them sit down and listen to what I've written. It's not awful, and they give me some good feedback which I incorporate into the next draft.

It's like writing an essay, except I've got twenty-four hours instead of four weeks. But the process is the same. Write, write, write, nearly to the end, and *then* discover what the real point is. Go back and revise.

I'm flying by midafternoon, grateful that I had stuff to

throw in my lunch bag that required zero assembling. Apples, a bagel, a chocolate bar and half a package of cheese strings.

My diet resembles that of an eight-year-old these days, and I don't care.

If I can pull this off, it's going to be amazing.

I finally finish it at six. I hit send on the email to Stew before I can second guess myself.

New speech is attached. Let me know what the PM thinks.

Thirty seconds later, Stew forwards it to Gavin and copies me.

You wanted to see this as soon as she was done.

Well, crap. My heart pounds in my chest. I stare at my inbox, but he doesn't reply right away.

When my stomach rumbles, reminding me that the eight-year-old school lunch I brought is long gone, and by the way, it's dinner time, I grab my bag and dash out for some food.

And then I come right back to my desk because I'm not going anywhere until he reads it.

An hour ticks by. I read an academic journal article my advisor sent me. I email the grad studies coordinator about a tuition bill I received earlier in the week—it should have had a small rebate on it because of the leave of absence I took for this internship.

I watch the clock.

Another half hour.

Tick. Tick.

When his reply pops up, I'm in the middle of watching

baby animal videos on YouTube, and the bolded unread email registers in my brain before my eyes catch up.

There is no better feeling than the warm thrill of attention from a man you have a crush on. Even if he's unattainable.

Even if he's the prime minister.

I'm hot and cold and aching all over, and it's just a damn email.

Hopeless.

Hands shaking, I click on the message. I'm already smiling like a goofball when I read it.

Fantastic work. Thank you. If you have a few minutes, I'd like to discuss a few points.

I look at the email header. Stew isn't copied on it. My breath stops in my throat.

Of course. I'm over at Langevin.

Can he hear how eager I am? If he does, it doesn't bother him. His reply is instant.

Good. I have a phone call in five minutes. Come over at nine.

Here's the thing. I'm not one of those women that carries a makeup bag. I own makeup, I like it, but it's at home on my dresser. In my bag, I've got a round Blistex pot of lip balm.

Not sexy.

I still put some on. Better than nothing. I'm tempted to run to the drugstore, because I've got thirty minutes, but no

—I'm saving all my foolish dress-up plans for the fundraiser next week.

I'm wearing a basic black pencil skirt and a boring ivory dress shirt. There is nothing that can be done about that.

I stop in the washroom and look at myself in the mirror. I pull the clips out of my hair, letting my bun tumble free. Marginally better.

You're an idiot. He wants to talk to you about a speech.

Well, I'd rather be an idiot full of hope and desire than a cynical shrew any day of the week.

Hair down it is.

I get over there a few minutes early. His door is closed and Beth is at her desk, packing up for the night.

"Late night," I say quietly, not wanting to startle her.

She glances over at me smoothly. Maybe nothing rattles her. She shrugs. "Some weeks are like that. Yesterday was a bit rough, so we played catch-up all day today."

"My roommate thinks the hours are insane."

She groans. "So did my boyfriend. Ex-boyfriend, now."

"I'm sorry."

She straightens up. "I'm not. This is a once-in-a-lifetime opportunity. I don't want to be with anyone who doesn't understand that."

"Fair enough."

She grabs her keys off her desk and slides them into the outer pocket on her bag, giving her desk a last once-over look. "Anyway, I'm off to Byward for a drink. Hope he doesn't keep you too late tonight. If you want to join us, we'll be at the Clocktower until eleven, at least."

"We?" I've been shit at socializing, clearly.

She lists a few names I recognize.

"Okay. I might, thanks."

She gives me a friendly smile and disappears as an RCMP officer I don't recognize takes her place at the desk.

Finally Gavin opens his door. I swear the temperature in the building goes up ten degrees but the security detail doesn't seem to notice. Exceptionally good at pretending nothing weird is going on here at all.

Maybe nothing is.

The first thing I notice is that his tie is missing. And his top button is undone.

Then I catch his gaze again and my steps falter. It's been a long week, but I'm not imagining the way he's looking at me.

Be a professional, I tell myself. "The speech works for you?"

He steps out of my way as I slide past him, then closes his office door behind me. "It's extraordinary, Ellie."

"Thank you." His praise slides through me like a knife through warm butter and I give him a smile that must make me look like a fangirl. "You have some notes?"

"A few." He strides across the room and grabs a sheaf of papers. The speech, I realize. "I prefer to scribble my notes on a hard copy, if you don't mind."

"I don't, of course."

"You're a deft, clever writer." He pauses as he hands over his notes. "A few points I want more repetition on. Sometimes you're too clever for the audience. Don't be subtle. We're making a grand statement about how money flows through our political system."

"Noted." I flip through the speech. Quick, dashed-off notes decorate the margins. "I can fix this tonight."

He gives me an amused smile. "Sure you're not one of them?"

"The politicos?" I laugh and shake my head. "Only for the summer."

"And then back to school."

"Yes."

"Are you looking forward to that?"

Was that a loaded question on purpose? "I'll miss this."

His lips twist in amusement. "That's not an answer."

"Sorry," I whisper.

"Well? Are you looking forward to returning to the quieter pace of academia?"

Slowly, shyly, I nod.

"That wasn't so hard, was it?" He gestures to the speech. "Can you make those changes tomorrow?"

"Yes, sir."

If I wasn't watching his face, I would have missed his reaction completely, but the slight shift of his jaw, the parting of his lips as he controls his exhale…and mostly the momentary glitter in his eyes. Definitely the right answer.

He watches me tuck the speech away in my bag, then he undoes the remaining two buttons on his jacket and gestures to what I assume is a liquor cabinet against the wall. "Would you like a drink?"

Yes. But I feel obligated to decline, even if it comes out weak and unconvincing. "I should get back."

I hold my breath after I say it because I know it's not the right answer.

His lips tighten, but he nods. "Is anyone else still over there?"

I lift one eyebrow. "Are you kidding me? There's a skeleton crew of them who won't leave until they get the notice that you've left the building."

He ducks his head. "I swore I wouldn't be that kind of boss."

"Don't feel bad about it. It's what they want. Every single one of them lives for the moment they're thrown into battle."

"How about you?"

"I'm an academic. I live for studying people like them."

He huffs a quiet, rueful laugh as he opens the cabinet. "You sure I can't offer you something?"

"What are you having?"

He lifts a bottle of Crown Royal in the air. "On the rocks."

I should say no. But for the first time since I've met him, he looks tired. And if I let my imagination run wild, as it wants to, he looks lonely, too.

"Sure. A small glass."

I look at the pictures he has lining the mantel while he pours our drinks. A family portrait. Gavin and a dark haired man who looks vaguely familiar. Gavin and Stew on election night. I catch the corner of my lip between my teeth as I lean in and look at their beaming faces.

"You really didn't expect the election win to happen, did you?" I ask as he joins me.

He makes a noncommittal noise.

"I'm sorry, is that rude?" I shoot him a quick look over my shoulder. "I guess you've never answered that question."

"It's tricky. I don't want anyone to think that I don't want to be here."

"I'd never think that."

He gives me a long look, and his normally icy stare is darker. Murkier, like a thawing spring lake. Finally he tips his glass up to his lips. After taking a slow sip, he licks away the whiskey and looks back at the picture of himself and his Chief of Staff. "No," he says quietly. "We didn't expect it to happen."

"I'm glad you won."

"Me too. The other guys were ruining this place." A faint smile plays at his lips as he glances toward the arm chairs. "Let's sit. Tell me how it's going."

I settle in the chair furthest from his desk, smoothing out my skirt after I cross my legs. I keep my eyes down, because I don't want to know either way if Gavin's looking at my legs.

If he is, that's complicated.

If he isn't…

"Ellie."

I still don't look up. "It's going just fine."

"Is the pace too much for you?"

"No, sir." I look up. "It's not the life I'd choose for myself for the rest of time. But like you said, I'm glad it happened."

"Was it your idea to apply for the position?"

I shake my head. "My faculty advisor thought it would be a good opportunity. My research will take place in elementary schools and daycares, and the summer isn't a great time to start that. So my options for these three months were…apply for this, or work as an RA doing data review."

"Research Assistant?"

I nod. "I promise you're a more interesting taskmaster."

Another slight reaction, well-controlled, but not completely hidden.

"This is a once-in-a-lifetime opportunity," I whisper, echoing Beth's words. But I don't own them the same way she does.

His gaze darkens. "I'd never want to interfere with that for you."

I frown. Maybe he didn't hear the doubt in my voice. And I genuinely have no clue what he's talking about. "I'm really…my time to date has been fascinating. I've learned so much, seen so much…If I were done tomorrow, I'd call it a successful experience. Definitely."

"But you aren't done tomorrow."

"Of course not." I give him a nervous smile. "I've been ordered to attend the fundraiser next week."

He takes a long, slow sip. The whiskey leaves his upper lip wet, and the slick welcome to his mouth makes hot, hungry heat unfurl low in my belly. "You're a big part of making sure the event is in line with my principles, Ellie."

"I'm happy to be there. I…" You know when you say something and you can hear yourself saying it, and you know it's extraneous information that you should have kept to yourself? Yeah. That. "I got a dress for it. Wednesday night. Before… you know. Last night I worked until eleven. I didn't go shopping yesterday."

"Ellie."

"Yes?"

"Stop."

"Okay."

He grins, unexpectedly, and it lights me up inside. "A dress?"

I blush. "Yes, sir."

His eyes flash dark again. "Good."

Ha. That was dirty. Even I know that was dirty. I knew something was going on. And there's no way the PM is ever going to act on it.

I'm his intern.

So if someone's going to do something… it has to be me, right?

What's the worst that could happen?

I touch my fingertips to the hollow at the base of my neck. His gaze follows.

My cheek. Still with me.

My lips, a glancing swipe with just one finger as I slide my hand in front of my face and sweep my loose waves behind my ear.

They tumble free a second later.

He's still looking at my mouth.

I've never played the seductress before. With enough

chemistry, it seems it's not so difficult after all. I give him a slight smile and lean back in my chair, crossing my legs the other way as I reach for my drink again. "I've never been one for whiskey, but this is excellent."

"I'm more of a beer guy," he says, his eyes twinkling as he leans back in his chair. "But I haven't worked up the courage to ask them to install a beer fridge in here yet."

"Yet?"

"It's not in my nature to deprive myself forever."

When I find my voice again, it's breathless. "You usually take what you want."

"Usually."

"What stops you the rest of the time?"

"The greater good."

"Ah." I tip back my glass and finish my drink. It burns going down and fills me with warmth. Liquid courage indeed. I uncross my legs and push myself out of the chair. My glass swings loose in my hand as I carry it across the room and set it on the tray next to the bottle.

When I turn around, Gavin's standing as well.

I press my hands to my skirt, which is suddenly too tight across my hips. I wish I wasn't nervous again, but when I stood, the seductress act fell away, and now I'm standing here, just me again.

Young, awkward, unworldly in many ways.

He's not just a guy I like. I can't invite him out for beers and let my arm brush against his. Tip my head sideways and ask if he wants to come back to my place for one last drink.

We only get this. I glance around. There are probably security cameras, anyway.

"Not in here," he says, his voice low and strained.

"Did I say that out loud?"

He nods roughly.

I take a step closer.

He doesn't move.

"Gavin…"

A muscle clenches in his jaw and two more steps get me close enough to touch him. I press my fingers to his cheek and feel him shudder. His hand comes up and his fingers circle my wrist.

I hold myself still, bracing for his rejection.

It doesn't come.

His grip tightens on my wrist and he tugs me closer, his other hand settling at the small of my back as we stare at each other. I'm breathless, and inside I'm screaming at myself to kiss him already, but then he takes control.

Both of his hands rake over my body and drive into my hair, fisting together at the back of my head as his mouth slides hard against mine. I gasp and twist my fingers into the front of his shirt, holding tight as he parts my lips with his and wipes all fantasy kisses from my mind.

This is way better than my imagination.

He tastes warm and sexy, a whiskey-laced man, and I press onto my toes, hungry for more. His hands tighten in my hair and he eases away.

"Ellie," he says, his lips brushing mine, and I don't know if it's a warning or a plea.

I slide my hands inside his jacket, over the smooth, fine cotton of his shirt. It does nothing to disguise the solid bulk of him beneath the clothes. Firm, fighting muscles I want to feel on top of me, moving against me.

I scrape my teeth against his jaw as I press my body tighter against his. He hisses and shifts his hold on me, moving me backward until my bottom bumps into his desk.

Effortlessly, he lifts me at the hips and settles me on the mostly clear surface.

"Is this thing an antique?" I ask, my voice shaking as he shrugs out of his jacket.

"I really don't give a fuck," he growls, caging me in as he leans over me. "No biting."

"Or what?" I snap my teeth at the air in front of him and his entire face darkens in the most delicious way.

"Jesus, Ellie, you're playing with fire."

"So maybe I want to get burned."

13

GAVIN

She leans forward and nips at my lower lip. My reaction is swift and instinctual. One of my hands is pinning both her wrists behind her while the other is fisted in her hair, pulling her head back. Her lips are rosy and swollen from our last kiss and I crush my mouth to hers, forcing it open while my tongue delves deep inside.

I half expect her to struggle. Instead she leans in and lets out a small moan.

I'm done for.

I release her wrists and hair, then work my hands down her back until I'm cupping her ass. I slide her off the desk to her feet and pull her in tight, trapping my erection against her soft belly.

I can't get enough of her. I squeeze her hips, her ass, her waist. She's pliant and sweet, like a willow, but with enough snap to draw out the part of me that wants a challenge.

I twist her body away from me, one hand dangerously low on her belly, the other cupped around her throat as I continue kissing her. She rocks her bottom against my cock as I swallow her gasping pleas.

I'm so lost in her taste, I don't come to my senses until I've got her bent over my desk with one hand on the small of her back and the other mid-swing.

What the fuck am I doing? Heart pounding, I freeze for a second, then let go of her and help her up.

I apologize in a rush, needing to smooth this over. "Ellie, I'm so sorry. That shouldn't have happened. Actually none of what I did here tonight should have happened. My behaviour was inappropriate and inexcusable."

I can't believe I lost control and nearly spanked her.

My gut is all twisted up and my knees feel like rubber as all the consequences of my actions race through my head.

For probably the first time in my life, I'm at a complete loss on how to handle a woman. It's the first time since I've taken public office that I've wanted a woman as much as I want Ellie. No, scratch that. I've never wanted anyone as much as this.

And I can't have her.

She touches her fingers to her lips, then drops her gaze to the floor. "No, it's fine. No harm, no foul. Really. I shouldn't have...I...I should go."

"Ellie, look at me." I pause a moment, then use my thumb and finger to gently lift her chin. She still won't make eye contact, so I adjust my posture until she has no choice. "You didn't do anything wrong. I think I made it clear I'm genuinely flattered by your interest and that it's mutual. But, we're not... compatible, and I let blind lust get in the way of good judgement."

She shakes her head and pulls away from me. "But I—"

I drag my fingers through my hair and pace the room. "Just stop. You did nothing wrong. Nothing at all." How the fuck am I supposed to make her believe it?

"I need to just go."

I look at the clock. It's late. And fuck, Max is due to

arrive soon. "At least let me arrange a safe ride home for you."

She nods and I open my door. "Tim, I'm just about ready to leave now. We'll be dropping Ellie at her place on our way home."

MAX IS WAITING for me with pizza and beer when I arrive. Yet another reason why he's my best friend. It doesn't matter where I hang my hat, he has no problem making himself right at home.

"I thought you'd forgotten I was coming."

"Long, hard day."

"You look more like it's been a long, hard night. Where were you?"

"At the office."

"Your hair looks more like you've spent the last few hours rolling around in bed."

"Fuck."

"Oh hell. Sit down, eat some pizza and guzzle some beer. We've got all night."

"I messed up royally tonight."

"I got that much from the *fuck* and your expression. Care to elaborate?"

I do and I don't. I'm still processing, but the only person who could possibly understand and help is sitting right here on my couch. I've missed being able to have candid conversations where I don't have to worry about anyone listening in.

I take a deep breath. "It's Ellie."

Max rolls his eyes. "Can we move on to the stuff I don't already know?"

I can feel my face burn as I recall the details. "What you

don't know is I kissed her silly and came within a heartbeat of spanking her ass scarlet."

"What made you stop?"

"The one functioning brain cell that deactivated my lizard brain. Fuck, Max, she made the sweetest pass, and instead of being responsible and letting it go, I acted on it. And to make matters worse, she somehow feels like she's the one who fucked up. I need to fix this, and I have no idea how."

"Well. That is a bit of a pickle." Max grins at me, then takes a massive bite of his pizza.

Outwardly he's being an ass, but I know that big brain of his is churning and I can afford to be a little patient.

I take a long swig of my beer, grab another slice of pizza, and wait.

Finally, three beers and an empty pizza box later, Max speaks.

"Well, my friend, you've got some serious thinking to do."

"That's all you've got? Really?"

"No, that was me prefacing what I've got. Do you want to hear this or not?"

"Carry on."

Max bowed his head in mock salute. "As I said, you've got some serious thinking to do because all your options have a downside."

I nod and wait.

"And before you can even evaluate them, there are factors you need to consider. You're kinky. Is she on board with that, or are you going to turf the toybox? Your thing with Andrea was totally vanilla—how'd that work out for you?"

Not satisfying in the least. And not because of Andrea or the sex—I'm not the kind of guy who needs to be all kink, all the time. But because that door was kept firmly closed when it's in my nature for it to swing open. Sometimes…a lot.

"You need to figure out exactly what your feelings are on that point, first. Then you've got some options." Max holds up a finger. "Option one is do nothing. Pretend like it never happened and hope she doesn't hit you with sexual harassment." Another finger. "Two, you have a clandestine affair with a subordinate and hope like fuck nobody finds out." A third finger. "Last, you fire her, and get it all out in the open."

Truth is, he's not telling me anything I don't already know. But after spending the last few weeks acting irrationally, it helps to have an objective party weigh in. I desperately search my brain for a fourth option with no downside. Of course, all I come up with is the one problem he didn't—her age.

She's fourteen years younger than me.

On the other hand, I've memorized her birthday. She's turning twenty six in August. That's not too young for a man my age. But is it too young for a man in my position?

I've made a lot of deals to get this chance to lead my country. Tucked away my desires and set aside my wants.

Even with all the downsides racking up in the cons column, I'm bitter at myself for giving up Ellie, too.

THE NEXT MORNING I'm feeling a little fragile. It's a rare Saturday off for me, orchestrated by Beth, who deserves a raise. Too bad her salary is dictated by the federal government and I'm not allowed to give her lavish gifts.

We'll have to find a workaround there.

I'm infamous among my staff for being an early riser,

but the truth is, on a day off I like to sleep in—add in a few too many beers last night, and I'm up earlier than I want to be today.

Max has arranged to spend the day house-hunting with Beth, and that isn't going to happen without me along to supervise. I never did manage to extract a promise from him not to mess around with her. Besides, I'm feeling pretty fucked up from the way things went with Ellie and the distraction will do me good.

Max is already in the kitchen preparing breakfast when I show up. He looks too fucking cheerful. Must be all that doctor training shit that makes him never need a full-night's sleep.

"Morning. You're looking a little rough, there, Gav."

"Fuck off. I need coffee."

"You don't have to come with us today, you know."

"Oh, you know I do. Now stop talking until I've at least had a cup of coffee. As your prime minister, that's an order. I'm sure there's a piece of paper somewhere stating something like that."

Max just laughs. "Suck it up, princess. To the outside world you're the prime minister. To me you'll always be nothing more than the sad-sack I got stuck with for a roommate that first year at UBC."

I want to stay grumpy, but I can't. I'm too happy to have him close.

"You don't have to buy a house. You could just live here. It's way too big for just me."

"And how would setting up a dungeon in the prime minister's official residence go over?"

Because for Max, kink isn't optional.

He's got me there. No dungeons allowed. I slide the pile of house listings across the table and start leafing through. There aren't as many as I would have thought.

"No row houses or condos, I see."

"Back to that whole dungeon thing. Single family dwellings make for good neighbours—and better play parties."

Jesus. I know he'll be discreet, and he's a private citizen, so it's nobody's business but his—and a play party is a fun fucking time—but I'm nervous about the potential exposure. Which makes me a terrible friend. I shove that thought away.

"Any front-runners?"

"Yeah, there's one near Civic Hospital that looks like it might do."

I shuffle through until I find it. "Four bedrooms? What on earth are you going to do with four fucking bedrooms?"

"Have sleepovers?"

I shake my head and smile. He can live in whatever house he wants if it's going to be within an easy drive of mine.

"What time are we picking Beth up?"

"Ten. You really could stay here and go back to bed."

"Nah. I'm up." I take a long sip of the coffee Max had placed in front of me. I'd almost forgotten how good his coffee was. I pay closer attention to what he's doing and spot the waffle iron on the counter. My morning is definitely looking up.

"Waffles will be ready in a few." He places the bottle of maple syrup on the table.

"Where did that come from?"

"Beth had your housekeeper do a more thorough grocery shop this week in anticipation of my arrival." He flashes me a wicked grin intended to get my back up. "I told her I'm a gourmet cook."

"Hands off."

He just winks.

I study the label. Product of Quebec. It reminds me that he's going to be here for winter and I make a mental note to get him a toque for his house-warming.

By six that evening, we've seen every house on Max's list and the only positive thing I can say about the entire experience is Beth made it through unsullied.

I had hoped it would help keep my mind off Ellie. It didn't. Every house we entered, I saw the counters I'd bend her over, the walls and doors I'd fuck her against. The showers we'd share.

If she wasn't my intern and if I had a clue how to broach a real, honest conversation…if that didn't expose me politically in a dozen different ways…but I've pushed her away twice.

I'm not going to get a third chance.

14

ELLIE

Fool me once, shame on you. Fool me twice…

Nope, I still think Gavin needs to wear the shame on this one. And the first time was a pseudo rejection. Didn't really count.

This was a definite, shut-it-down rejection, but everything that happened before that?

I was just going to kiss him.

Now I'm not even sure I know what kissing is. Because what we did? Or what he did to me, because beyond the first touch, I was hardly in control…that was unlike anything I've ever experienced before.

Friday night I went home and crawled into bed.

Saturday I went to yoga, then let Sasha drag me out for drinks.

Today?

Today I started thinking.

We're not… compatible, and I let blind lust get in the way of good judgement.

I pulled a notebook from the box of unused notebooks

in my closet. This one has Japanese cherry blossoms on the cover. Super pretty. Gavin doesn't really deserve it, but it's got a spiral binding and after I make this list, I can tear it out and the pretty notebook will be pristine again.

Not Compatible, I write at the top of the page.

Then I draw a mad face beside it.

Age difference, I write beneath that.

West coast/east coast?

Experience…

I draw a lazy line beneath that one. I'm twenty-five.

There's no way he thinks I'm a virgin, right?

But even if that were the case…

I draw a circle around compatible.

Something's missing.

Sasha knocks on my door and I shove the notebook under my pillow. "Yes?"

She pokes her head in. "Brunch? My treat?"

I shouldn't take advantage, but Sasha's loaded. And I maxed out my credit card buying the dress that likely won't have any effect on the PM.

No, that's not true.

I glance toward the dress, hanging in a place of honour on my closet door.

"Yes…brunch." I hop off the bed. "And maybe we can go to Sephora and find me a new makeup look for the fundraiser, too."

"So that's still happening."

I have no idea. "Yes, of course."

"You were out late Friday night."

"Working."

"Mmm."

"Are we going for brunch or having an inquisition?"

"Who says the two things are mutually exclusive?"

"I want fancy brunch."

"I want fancy gossip."

We go to the diner and neither of us gets what we want.

"I can't believe you're seriously not going to tell me anything," she grouses as we head back to our apartment.

"There's nothing to tell," I say more smoothly than I expect. But it's true. What happened—what happens—between Gavin and me is private.

I wasn't sure before, but I am now.

"In fact," I add, stretching out my words. "I think my crush on the PM is over."

Sasha snorts.

"Really. We're…not compatible."

"Unless you're into something really kinky, I can't imagine how you aren't compatible with Prime Minister Hottie."

I wince. "Don't call him that."

"Whatever your complicated feelings about our nation's leader are, they don't do anything about the objective fact that he's smokin' hot."

"Now you're just trying to bother me."

"Okay, I'll stop." I can feel her gaze burning into me as we climb the stairs to our apartment. But when we get inside, she stays true to her word and disappears into her room.

I do the same, because I suddenly have some research to do.

How do you go about asking the prime minister if he's kinky? Is that even the right word? *What exactly are you into, sir?*

If I even got a chance.

And what if I'm wrong? It would be easy to let my imagination run away from me here.

I open my computer.

I've done two Women's Studies degrees. If he thinks I'm some innocent flower, unaware of the wide spectrum of sexual desire—

Oh. Warm, embarrassed heat sprints through my body.

So "incompatible kinks" brings up some interesting search results. And I'm getting way ahead of myself.

I can't ask Sasha where I should look…but one of my classmates in Toronto was openly kinky. I go to her Face-book page and scroll back. She'd posted something a few months ago—a munch meet and greet—and thankfully she's one of those people who only posts a few times a week so it doesn't take me that long to find the link.

I hit the motherload.

An entire website with kink organized by subject.

But I need a profile to go any further. I tap my finger against my chin. Is this a dumb idea?

Fingers flying, I type in a made up username and pass-word that doesn't match anything in my real life, and use a throwaway email address. *Don't be like Dave*, I tell myself, and make a silent promise never to check that email at work.

Location…well, I'm definitely not saying Ottawa.

I click back to my friend's page. Is she open about her username? No such luck. But a couple of the people attending the meet and greet apparently live in Antarctica.

I snicker and type that in for myself.

Then I click on the location, and gasp. Apparently thirty-seven thousand other people had the same idea.

Kinky sneakers.

But now I'm at a loss for what to look up. A few groups are suggested for me, based on the short questionnaire I completed.

Gender…female.

Sexual orientation…straight. Straight? I want to put heteroflexible because I'm a Women's Studies major and fuck the patriarchy, but it would have to be a pretty specific set-up for me to want to have any kind of sex with a woman. Maybe if Gavin…Nope. Straight. And suddenly quite selfish, apparently. No sharing Gavin.

Role…

Role. This drop down menu has twenty, thirty…too many to count very specific sounding roles. Some I know. Others I can imagine. A few make my fingers itchy to Google, but I shut the computer instead.

I can't get ahead of myself. I need to figure out what *role* Gavin is. And only that will properly frame the million dollar question.

Are we really incompatible?

Or does the prime minister have a secret kink that just maybe could work for me too?

That question gets under my skin. I clean the fridge and make a grocery list. Sasha's doing marking for the summer class she's a TA for, so I head out by myself and stock up on everything we need for the week.

And I'm still thinking about it, because until this week-end, kink has always been an "other" in my life. I know of it, of course. Paddles. Discipline. Release. Submission. Bondage. Control. Power Exchange. And then on the edges of my awareness, the other things that drop down list of roles alluded to. Role playing. Humiliation. Pain.

After re-stocking our kitchen, I go to yoga and push myself hard—to the point where my muscles are shaking and sweat is dripping down my face and making my hands slick.

This is discipline. This is pain. Control, too. But I've

never wanted anything like this in my sex life—of course, I've never thought about it like that, and if you asked me to score my sex life on a scale of one to ten, I'd probably give it a five.

When I have one, which I currently do not.

Sex is nice. I've never had awful sex, but I've never had sex so good I've wanted to post about it on a message board, either.

Really, my favourite part of sex is kissing and touching. Ben in Toronto was pretty good at going down on me. That would have notched it up to a seven, although I never came like that, so maybe he wasn't *pretty* good.

Kissing Gavin, though, that was a ten. When he spun me around and ground his erection into me—although that might have been me doing the grinding—that had been a ten, too.

Everything except the bucket of ice water had been super hot.

So if his desires create that level of heat, I'm game to at least try something different.

Is kink-curious a role? Maybe that's what I am.

I shower at the yoga studio, taking my time to strip out of my clothes so by the time I step under the steamy spray, I'm alone with my thoughts.

Making a mental list of questions I have, I decide to dig a little deeper into the website I found.

When I get home, Sasha's gone out for the evening.

Somehow I feel better about being alone for my research, anyway.

I log back in and join a couple of groups.

One of the newbie threads is about books and movies. I flag a couple of books to read as soon as possible, but I need more immediate intel. After reading the film reviews, I hop over to YouTube and check out a few trailers and clips.

An older James Spader and Maggie Gyllenhaal movie, *Secretary,* makes me gasp out loud.

I watch the clip three times over. A man in a suit telling his secretary to read a letter she's typed—as she's bent over his desk. And as she reads, he spanks her.

Replay.

Replay.

By the time it stops, my eyes are already closed. My fingers are pressed to my mouth as I remember our kiss. Gavin's hands in my hair, the way he moved against me.

The way he moved *me.*

How he bent me over the desk.

Is that what his face looked like, that twisted battle on James Spader's face, not sure if it was right or wrong, but hellbent on doing it anyway?

I roll onto my side, sinking into the fantasy. Gavin holding me down. Telling me to keep my hands flat on the desk. Standing behind me...

We're incompatible.

Hmm.

If he just wants to spank me, I'm not sure that we are. But nothing is that simple, surely. I peel my eyes open and watch another clip from the movie.

I need to watch the whole thing. Thank goodness for iTunes.

My stomach growls, so I go to make some popcorn before I hit play.

Three minutes into the movie, silent tears are rolling down my cheeks. This is not a popcorn movie. I set the bowl aside and curl my arms around my legs, transfixed by the story unfolding on the screen, but worried inside my head because *this* is a movie beloved by many in the BDSM community?

It's so sad.

Except…the heroine has a spark to her. You can see it even as she drifts and I want her to find her way. I want that desperately for her.

The lawyer she goes to work for is no Gavin, that's for sure. But if I squint I can see some similar traits. I file that away. Would he like this movie? I find myself thinking about that question more than searching for commonalities, because this is a specific story about two damaged people, and that's not us.

Well, that's not me.

And everything I know about Gavin's life, that's not him, either. Except you never really know someone from their public biography, do you? And it's human nature to have hidden desires. Secret pasts and transformational moments that twist us in weird ways.

The more I watch the movie, the less I'm looking for what Gavin might like and the more I'm seeing myself in the heroine. Not the darkest bits, but she's endearing in her awkwardness, and I don't know if I'm endearing, but I'm certainly awkward.

And the way she lights up at praise. Jesus, I can feel my cheeks pinking up. I know I do that, seeking out approval and leaning into it when I get it.

It sounds crazy for a grad student to say that, because doctoral studies are notoriously brutal and advisors mostly tell you how much you suck. But not my advisors. I chose Ottawa, and Toronto before it, for my studies because of the faculty members and a certain kindness I sensed in them.

Another point in my personality where I'm open to pain and pressure, as long as someone tells me at the end of it that I've done a good job.

Maybe all grad students are submissives. We're definitely masochists to one degree or another.

And isn't that really what it is for everyone? A spectrum? I just always assumed I fell on the...

Don't say normal.

But I'm watching a movie where the heroine wears a saddle.

I always assumed I fell on the more *conventional* end of the spectrum.

I don't want to wear a saddle.

That's a hard limit.

But maybe everything that I've done before isn't the sum total of all that I might like to do, with the right person.

Before Gavin, I had a completely unremarkable dating life.

Don't put the cart before the horse. You and Gavin don't have a dating life yet. Yet. We will. I'm eighty-three percent sure of that fact.

I had two boyfriends in high school. One in college, until he cheated on me toward the end of second year. I dated casually until grad school, then dated one guy, Ben, more seriously for about six months, but it was mostly itch-scratching on both our parts and we ended things amicably.

None of them ever turned me around and bent me over a table—to spank me or anything else.

The closest I've ever come to this feeling of something kinky is a pretty innocent flirtation I had in my fourth year of undergrad with one of my sociology professors. I was the best student in his seminar, would always stay late afterwards to keep talking, and a few times he walked me back to my apartment.

We never crossed the student teacher line, but I wanted to, desperately, and it felt like this attraction I have toward Gavin. Hot and secret. More significant, emotionally, than the more conventional relationships I've had.

Except now I'm five years older and hopefully wiser, at least when it comes to who I am and what I want.

Who I want. The real measure of wanting someone is not having them: losing them or missing out on having them at all.

That prof? I can't even remember his first name. I left Montreal that summer and went backpacking in Germany without another thought.

In six weeks I'm moving back to an office ten blocks away from Gavin and I'm already aching at the distance.

I curl up in a tight ball and watch the rest of the movie. It gets dark in places and I give a grumpy side-eye to my laptop. Surely this isn't the best how-to on BDSM.

That's not exactly how it was praised on the website.

No, but it's what I wanted.

Oh well. If life wasn't a little challenging it wouldn't be interesting.

I do a search for *Secretary* on the fetish site. Tons of comments and threads. Some critique, lots of love, especially for a couple of the scenes, including the one I watched the clip of earlier—the one that hooked me into the movie.

Hmm.

Gavin's always reacted well to pencil skirts. I'll wear one tomorrow.

But when I sort through my closet, the only blouses are ones he's seen before, and none of them are even remotely like what Maggie Gyllenhaal wears in the movie. I'm just as likely to wear a blazer over a tank top, and that doesn't scream submissive in the least.

I carefully hang my skirt over the back of my chair and put my Louboutins beneath it.

"Hey, Ellie?" Sasha calls out.

I meet her just outside my room. "You're back."

"I am."

"Good."

"Everything okay?"

"Yep."

"You're being weird."

"I'm just trying to find something to wear tomorrow."

"Want to raid my closet?" She tries to peek around me.

Did I close my laptop screen? Better if we go into her room just in case. "Yes I do."

"What kind of outfit are you looking for?" She throws open her closet door and steps back. Our apartment is nice enough in general, but Sasha's room is awesome, and the best part of it is the walk-in closet.

That's because it's supposed to be a study. It has a window and everything. But who has a study off a master bedroom? That's weird. And since Sasha's clothes take up a lot of space and her computer is a laptop that fits in her purse...

No brainer.

"Just a blouse," I murmur, looking for something white, maybe. Classic. "I only have like four of them, and I've worn them all a fair number of times already."

"Well, take whatever you want. I'm making tea." She disappears and I start to move hangers down the rod. No, no, no...

Oh my God.

In front of me is a pretty close facsimile of the black and white polka dot blouse from *Secretary*. I can't *not* wear it, right?

It's silk. It looks expensive. I look at the label. Moschino. I don't even want to think about how much this blouse cost.

I'll be so, so careful with it, I tell myself.

And hands shaking, I lift the hanger off the rack.

This is the perfect thing to wear tomorrow. I just need to wait for an opportunity. And if one strikes—when one strikes, because power of positive thinking and all that—I'll do my best to see if maybe I can inspire some spanky-panky with the PM.

15

GAVIN

WE ARRIVE at the rink twenty minutes before our game and Tim leads us through the building to one of the two locker rooms designated for our rink rental. On the digital board it says, **Private**. All other slots for the day have a team name or last name attached, but it's still pretty low-key. I'm getting pumped.

Lachlan is already there, and given all the guys we're playing with have been carefully vetted beforehand, we walk right in.

Lachlan raises his hand and motions for us to join him. "Max, Gavin, glad you could join us."

Activity stops, but not for long. Apparently these guys are more interested in getting on the ice than taking selfies with the PM. I'm actually relieved. I really needed this to be a place where I'm just Gavin. Then I realize, Lachlan has already figured this out.

While Max and I are getting ready, Lachlan starts putting names to faces. "Tate's our centre and Derek plays right wing. You'll meet our goalie, Corinne on the ice. I play left wing and you two newbies are on defence. Don't fuck up."

I grin. Yup. Just Gavin.

Despite the fact that *Tate* turns out to be Tate Nilsson, captain of the Ottawa Senators, the game is played at exactly my speed—a little rough, a little fast, and rules are really just suggestions.

Like a lot of adult pick-up games across the country, we don't have refs. No such thing as a penalty, but everyone wants to go to work tomorrow with all their teeth.

I've got the easy end of the ice for the first half of the game. This isn't a bad thing. It's been months since I've been on skates, a couple years since I played consistently. Max plays once a week back home, and even he's sweating by the break at half-time.

Then Tate switches himself out for one of the substitute players waiting on our bench, a friend of his who obviously likes his beer more than his ice time, and my game gets a hell of a lot harder.

Suddenly the other team is constantly in our defensive zone and I barely catch my breath before I'm hustling to block another attack on our net. With each burst of activity, each burn of my muscles engaging to just fucking do it, stop him, get the puck, my worries over Ellie and our kiss get pushed further and further from my mind.

An hour later, I'm tired, sweaty, and ready for a nap.

The concern about Ellie slams back with a vengeance, but that's to be expected. I can't hide on the ice forever.

Back in our change room, I thank the players for coming out.

"Anytime," Tate says, shaking my hand. "I'd have done it anyway for you, of course, but Lachlan's been a good friend to me since I joined the Senators."

My security chief waves him off with an easy grin. "I pride myself on making sure that people are taken care of."

"Ha. Right. You're the go-to guy for a lot of things that are hard to find."

Lachlan gives him a weird look. "And I get to play with some half-way decent talent over the summer, so it works out nicely." He turns his attention to me. "Tim's outside. I'm going to get the cars pulled up at the back, as there are more people in the building now than when we arrived."

I thank him and start packing up my bag. When I'm done, I glance over at Max, who's still just wearing a towel. Fucking exhibitionist.

"So what else can Lachlan hook people up with?" Max waggles his eyebrows as he leans his arm against the wall next to Tate. "I like resourceful people. And I've got a lot of…hard-to-accommodate interests."

I groan. "Max. Boundaries."

He throws his foul-smelling socks at me. "You're no fun."

"Yeah, I know. It's like playing hockey with your dad."

Max turns back to Tate. "Maybe one week I'll come and play with you guys without this one, and you can give me all the dirt on Lachlan."

"Out," I order, and we wave goodbye as Tate leans back against the painted brick wall of the locker room, still chuckling.

We can't talk about whatever Max picked up on in the car, and by the time we make it back across the city to 24 Sussex, Stew is waiting for me—we have a scheduled phone call with the Premier of Saskatchewan.

MONDAY MORNING I arrive in the office to find Stew has moved Ellie back to her desk in Centre Block.

"She's figured out what makes you tick," he says to me when I ask him about the change. "She's the best fit since we're down a speechwriter and she seems to read you better than anyone else."

I am not happy about this at all. I've spent the better part of the weekend obsessing over the events of Friday night and what I need to do about it. I'm leaning heavily on the do nothing option. I think my feelings for her go beyond lust and are well on their way to…something else. I need to rein that in because the way things are going, I'm on the road to political suicide.

I pick up the latest version of my fundraiser speech from my desk and start reading. Damn, Ellie's really good at this. If only I didn't have a relentless hard-on for her, I'd seriously consider hiring her on as my speechwriter. I briefly toy with the idea of doing it anyway, but dismiss it for the ridiculous notion it is.

Not that she'd want it. She made it pretty clear on Friday night that she's looking forward to returning to her research at the university in September.

I'll miss her, but it's for the best. Six more weeks, and then it'll just be me lusting after a former intern.

I wince. The optics of that aren't any better.

I'm nearly done reading when there's a knock at my door. I look up and see Ellie. She's wearing a slim black skirt with a slit off-set in the front and white blouse with little black polkadots. It's got a high neck and long sleeves. A lump forms in my throat and my cock grows thick and heavy. It's been a few years, but I'll never forget Maggie Gyllenhaal in *Secretary*.

Ellie wears it even better, and I'm quite certain it's a

deliberate thing she's doing, because it's unlike anything she's ever worn before.

It's the last thing I expected to see today—or ever—and it turns me on in a dozen inappropriate ways.

The little minx is cosplaying a BDSM movie. In my office.

And I have this urge to recreate a scene or two.

She saunters in and closes the door behind her. Fuck.

"I was just wondering if you've had a chance to go over the speech so I can get to work on the changes," she says, wide-eyed and innocent.

Yeah. She's figured out what makes me tick all right.

I return my gaze to the papers in my hands. "I'm nearly finished. Just a couple more pages to go."

"Shall I wait, Sir?"

I make a point of not reacting even though I can practically hear the capital 'S'. "Yes, yes. Have a seat, I just need another minute or two."

I don't look up. I can't. I need to focus on the way forward. Pretend like Friday never happened and remind myself that we are not compatible.

I watch her from the corner of my eye as she sinks gracefully onto the chair in front of me and places her hands, palms up, on her knees. Then she bows her head.

Fuck. Me. It's like she's spent the entire weekend studying *One Twue Way: Rules for Submissives*.

I struggle to read through the last of the speech because I'm a combination of amused, flattered, and horrified by her behaviour. It's all I can do to ignore it. Because not being able to clarify to her what Dominance and submission mean to me is like being forced to sit and watch my house burn down.

The *Secretary* thing is really hot, though.

I slog through the final paragraphs as fast as I can

because if someone comes into my office, I'm not sure she would adjust her pose to something more appropriate.

"There's not a lot that needs changing." I don't look up as I slide the papers across the desk. "You've done a great job, and I appreciate all your hard work. Once you've finished the revisions, you can send it on to Stew for approval."

I immediately pick up some random piece of correspondence from my desk and pretend to read it, hoping she recognises she's been dismissed.

"Oh…yeah…okay. I mean, yes, sir." She's flustered and that 's' is no longer capitalised. She picks up the speech and slips silently from my office, closing the door behind her.

I feel guilty for making her doubt herself, but I need to focus on the greater good. Now, I'm no longer sure what that is.

I bury myself in work, but that capital *Sir* keeps bouncing around inside my head like a pinball and big red letters keep flashing TILT. She's thrown me off balance.

I don't see her again until the afternoon when I meet with her and Stew to finalise my speech for Friday night.

She's back to calling me Gavin and I hate it. I also hate that she no longer has that little glint in her pretty grey eyes. It's like she's gone dark.

My chest hurts and guilt gnaws at my gut.

Regardless of whether she's actually interested in exploring the darker side of my desires or just tire-kicking, she'd taken a huge chance this morning.

I totally shut her down. And not gently, and not just once.

Ellie is damn brave, and I have to do something to make this right.

Act in haste, repent at leisure. Yeah, sounds about right.

I'm so twisted up in knots when it comes to Ellie, I can't seem to act rationally.

When I get home, Max is sitting in the living room with papers spread all over the coffee table.

"Looks like you've had a rough day. Sit down, I'll get you a beer."

I throw my things on the nearest chair and park myself on the sofa. I pick up one of the sheets and read the notes he's added.

He returns and hands me a beer. I hold up the paper in my hand. "This one?"

He glances at it and nods. "Yeah. That one screamed *buy me* the minute we got there, but I didn't want to be hasty. It's a pretty big spend."

"When are you putting in the offer?"

"Already done."

"Then why are you still comparing houses?"

"Because if this doesn't go through, I need a backup plan."

"You really are going through with this move, then?"

"I really am. Now, what's going on? You look like someone just set fire to your favourite flogger."

I can't tell Max what Ellie did this morning. Even though he's my best friend in the world, this is private. But I need advice. I tap my finger on the bottle I'm holding while I think about what I want to say.

"It's Ellie."

He gives me a rueful smile, but says nothing. I'm grateful. I'm not up for cheeky comments right now.

"Something happened today and I didn't handle it well."

Max shifts to the edge of his seat and leans forward a little. "What did you do?"

"No details. All I can really say is when it comes to Ellie, I'm not in control of myself. I keep making mistakes and handling them badly. I act before I think. And it's hurting us both." I take a long sip of my beer. The cold liquid soothes my aching throat. "I made a decision and then a thing happened and made me question it. But my reaction was immediate and based entirely on my original decision without taking more recent…developments into consideration."

"Sounds to me like you've got a lot more thinking to do. There's no shame in changing your position when something isn't working out for you."

Nodding, I toe off my shoes, then lean back in my seat. "What's for supper?"

"I don't know. What are you making?"

THAT NIGHT, I lie in bed replaying the morning's events. Searching each detail for clues as I try to find the real explanation for her actions.

Was she honestly trying to tell me she's interested in more than one flavour? How am I supposed to be able to tell?

I delve further back—to Friday when I had her bent over my desk…

And I'm an idiot.

I was so caught up in my own bullshit this morning, it didn't occur to me that by telling her we weren't compatible, coupled with my behaviour, I'd unwittingly sent her to parts of the internet where no amount of eye-bleach could scrub out what she'd seen behind those doors—if it horrified her.

And if it didn't?

I realise the choice I'd made was the coward's way out of the situation I'd found myself in with Ellie. It was time I put on my man pants.

The next morning, I summon Ellie to my office. I see she's back to her regular wardrobe. I realise her choice of clothes is not all that different from what she'd worn the day before, except somehow, it is, in a vague way I can't name. I'm such a man when it comes to women's fashion.

"You wanted to see me?"

"Come in and shut the door, please." I use my Dom voice. Slightly lower, and far more commanding.

I watch her throat bob up and down as she swallows. The latch clicks and she starts across the room.

"Did I do something wrong, Gavin?"

"Sir. Did I do something wrong, Sir?"

She swallows again.

"Did I do something wrong…Sir?"

"Actually yes, Ms. Montague."

Her eyes go wide, and she fiddles with her hair. Yeah, I'm so fucking gone.

I pull out a page from her speech. "There is a typo." I point to the spot I'd circled in red. Fuck, it had taken me forever to find one. There was a point where I thought I might have to make one up. But she went to all that effort yesterday. I owe her at least double in return, and this is the safest option for the middle of the work day. "It should be than. You've put then. Do it again."

"Yes, Sir." She keeps a straight face, but the glint is back in her eyes and there's no missing that capital 'S'.

A weight lifts off my chest. I want to reach over my desk and pull her in for a long, hungry kiss. She touches her lips, like she knows what just bulldozed through my head.

"I want the corrected copy on my desk first thing in the morning. Now, off you go."

"Yes, Sir."

There's a bounce in her step as she leaves that has me

grinning like a fool. I only have a few minutes to tame my erection before my first meeting, so I slide my joy aside and focus on the doom and gloom report my finance minister wants to discuss.

The next morning, I meet with Ellie first thing. She's tried to second guess me and added a new typo. She seems to be under the misguided impression I intend to follow someone else's kinky road map.

The only reason I'd gone with a little *Secretary* roleplay yesterday was so she'd understand we're in the same library. We're just not in the same book. Yet.

I pull the yellow highlighter from my drawer, draw a line through her newly developed typo, and slide it across the desk to her.

"When we meet tomorrow, I expect a three page essay on why it is unacceptable to purposely add typos to my speech. That is all, Ms. Montague."

She wants to argue. I can see it. But she holds back and gives me the response I crave. "Yes, Sir."

I pick up the finance report from yesterday. Nothing like mind-numbing negative forecasting to kill a perfectly good hard-on.

Thursday morning, she smiles wide as she hands me her essay. I skim it first and am thrilled to see she has a basic handle on where she went wrong yesterday. I flip back to the first page to read it more thoroughly and she starts to sink into a chair. "No, I'd prefer you stand, today. At that window, looking out."

I may have made a tactical error. It's hard to concentrate on giving her essay a thorough reading when her perfectly delectable ass is taunting me at eye level. I make a valiant effort. If there's a mistake, I can't find it. Time for her reward.

I get up from my chair and move in close behind her,

not quite touching, but my body still knows how soft she is and aches to press against her. I don't give in to that. Instead, I bring my lips close to her ear. "Excellent job, Sprite. Take tomorrow off and have a nice relaxing day so you're well-rested for the fundraiser—and all it entails."

16

ELLIE

WHEN SASHA WAKES up and I'm still in the apartment on Friday morning, she asks if I've been fired.

"No! I'll be working late tonight and…I got the day off."

"Spa day!" For an uptight academic, Sasha really likes going to the spa. She's already on the phone. She has two of her favourite places on speed dial. "What do you want done?"

"Uhm…manicure?"

She wiggles her index finger at my face. "And your eyebrows, right?"

"Sure."

Then she points at my crotch. "Wax?"

"What? No." I cover myself for good measure. One perk of being a redhead—I don't have a ton of hair between my legs, and what I do have is kind of cute. It's staying put.

I shower and shave my legs before we go, and when we get there, Sasha surprises me by having my hair done as well.

"You're the world's greatest roommate," I tell her as we sip mint tea in the waiting room.

"Care to reward me with any Parliament Hill gossip?"

"I can't really tell you about political stuff..."

"I mean PM gossip."

"Then...no."

"Did he like the blouse you borrowed?"

Somehow I manage not to blush. "I can't remember if I saw him that day."

"Liar."

Yep. "Are you all done with your marking?"

She accepts the change of subject. "Indeed I am. I'm heading to the cottage tonight, actually."

"Did I know that?"

"I mentioned it. You've been distracted."

"And now I'm the worst roommate ever."

"Only if I wanted you to come with me, but I do not, because my brother's brother-in-law is coming, and I'm going to angle for a double date."

Sasha's brother is two years older than us and is already on his second marriage. "Might as well while you still can?"

She snickers. "This is why I love you, Ellie. You're sweet as can be, but deep down you've got an edge to you."

"Do I?"

"You couldn't be my bestie if you didn't."

Our conversation is cut off by the arrival of the aestheticians, and off we go to get beautified. Me for the PM, Sasha for a dirty weekend away at the cottage.

EIGHT HOURS LATER, my face hurts from smiling. The room isn't as hostile as we expected—if anything, the leaked speech lowered expectations, so when he leans against the podium and tells the wealthy attendees that they can do better...well, who could argue with that?

I mouth along as he delivers the speech I'd written. He ad-libs in a few places—making it better, of course, on the fly like he does—but the key message is one I've now permanently engraved on my soul. One of respect and acknowledgement in the same breath as he pushes them to do more.

"The very fact you're here," he says, spreading his arms wide, his voice ringing strong as he smiles at the crowd. "That says so much to me. It says you understand there's a need for change. A need to do better. It's time for a new model of public-private partnerships in Canada, and I trust that the leaders of industry in this room will champion innovation—"

God, I love how he pauses here, mid-sentence, making eye-contact with more people than you'd think possible, those icy blue eyes silently gaining their promise that yes, of course they'll champion anything he wants.

"And sponsor community projects that make a difference at the same level you back political parties. I don't just believe that you can do that—I'm going to hold you to an *expectation* that you will do that. Some of you may be used to an older model of doing things. Buying a ticket to a dinner to shake my hand and whisper something in my ear."

He shakes his head and I swear, I might just have a small orgasm if he bites his lip.

He grins, softening the room for what comes next. Then his face sobers and he rolls his bottom lip between his teeth.

I die.

"You want to impress me? More to the point, do you want to impress the collective strength of the House of Commons? Do something incredible for your community. Lead innovation and give back to the people who work for you, who live around you, and who support your company. Do that, and you'll have the ear of the entire nation."

And now my hands hurt just as much as my cheeks do, because everyone is on their feet and I'm applauding like mad along with them. It took a minute, but a few tables rose, and then everyone else joined them.

Peer pressure is a powerful motivator. Stew taught me that. I glance across the back of the room, looking for my boss. He gestures me over and I make my way through the boisterous crowd. Half of them are heading for the bar. The other half are crowding around the PM, and he'll give them each a warm smile and a quick handshake, but nothing else. Not tonight.

"Fantastic speech, Ellie. Well done." Stew lifts his glass as I beam at him.

Beth sees him toasting me and excuses herself from her conversation, joining us just as Lachlan materializes at Stew's side and whispers in his ear.

My boss nods, then crooks his finger at Beth and me. "Come on. The PM wants a private word."

My heart flails like a muppet in my chest as we follow the Mountie back through the hotel, weaving down one hallway, then another. We stop in front of a private room, guarded by another member of the security detail.

Lachlan pulls out a room key and lets us in.

Gavin is standing at the window, his back to us. He turns.

He's got a drink in one hand and the other is tucked in his pocket, sweeping his open jacket back on that side.

Do not eye-fuck your boss's boss.

Do not eye-fuck the prime minister.

Too late.

It's his own fault, I whimper silently. He looks good

enough to eat. Black suit, white shirt, black tie. Fitted and sleek like a panther.

And we've been priming for this all week.

So why are Stew and Beth here? Maybe I've read all the clues wrong.

We need a kinky affair bat signal. Like, handcuffs spotlighted on the Peace Tower or something. But subtle.

Clearly this is why he pushed me away last week. I don't have the faintest clue how to be sly about this.

Luckily Beth pushes a champagne flute into my hand. I hadn't allowed myself to drink before now, being too nervous, but now I take a sip and it's lovely.

I take another and feel myself relax.

Then I hold the flute in front of my face because there's a limit to how chill I can be, and any second Stew or Beth or Lachlan will notice how I keep staring at Gavin in that suit.

But it's not my fault.

That suit is…

"Did you say something, Ellie?" Stew turns my way.

I shake my head like mad. "Nope."

Gavin lifts one eyebrow at me, but the rest of his face doesn't move. He's either really good at sly or we're not on the same page. My chest flutters with nerves, but I won't let myself doubt that this means something more for the two of us.

Picking up the last flute, he raises it in the air. "To my staff," he says quietly, taking the time to make eye contact with everyone in the room. "Thank you for helping me blueprint our policy in a clear and compelling way. We're laying a strong foundation for a fall session of Parliament."

"You're the one who wowed them tonight." Stew laughs and glances at me. "With Ellie's words."

Gavin was already looking at me, but his eyes darken. "Definitely."

Beth says a few nice things about what she observed from the back of the room, then we're interrupted by a knock at the door.

The guard pokes his head in. "Max Donovan wants to know if Beth would like to have one last dance before he turns in for the night."

Gavin groans and lifts his free hand in a wave. "Send him in."

Beth shakes her head. "No, I'm leaving. Because yes, I would like a dance." She winks at me and heads for the door.

Max Donovan. The dark haired man in the picture on Gavin's mantel. The name clicks with the face, and I realize who Gavin's best friend is—a former child television star who retired from Hollywood at eighteen to move back to Canada. I vaguely recall that he went to medical school and is a doctor in Vancouver now.

He was here tonight?

"I'm heading back in. Need to do some glad-handing," Stew says, looking at Gavin. "Are you done for the night?"

"I think it's for the best that I am. Can't make a grand statement about separation of industry and the executive branch of government and then rub shoulders the same night." He looks past me to his ever-present chief of security. "Lachlan, will you give Ms. Montague a ride home?"

My breath catches in my throat as Lachlan nods. "Of course. I'll just arrange for another member of the security detail to cover for me. Give me five minutes."

Stew taps my forearm on his way out, giving me one last nod of approval for tonight's event. I want to revel in the success, but even more than that, I want to be alone with Gavin for a minute.

The door clicks shut softly behind us and I glance over my shoulder, making sure Stew and Lachlan are both gone.

When I turn back to face Gavin, he's closer.

Much closer.

My fingers itch to reach out and grab the lapels of his jacket.

Instead, I flex my fingers and wiggle them at my sides. "Home?"

"My home."

I let out a nervous laugh. "You're good at the sly thing."

He gives me a knowing look that melts my insides. "Yes."

"Good. I'm not."

"I'll keep that in mind."

"What are we doing?"

"Whatever you want."

"I want what you want."

"Do you know what you're asking?"

I shake my head. "Not really. But I'm not completely innocent. Do we need a contract, or anything?"

"A contract?"

"I've been doing some research."

He smiles, a slow, amused curl of his lips. "Have you?"

"I know about safewords and hard limits."

"Mmm." He leans in, his lips brushing my cheek before he whispers in my ear. "Do you want a safeword, Ellie?"

My nipples do. Not that they'd ever use it. "I don't know that we need one."

"No. I react instantly to *stop*. Unless you ask me not to."

"Stop is good. But I won't be saying it."

"We'll see about that." He brushes my hair out of the way as he gets closer to the curve of my ear. His breath is tantalizingly hot. Slow. Controlled.

By comparison, my chest is rising and falling like a roller coaster car halfway off the rails.

I suck in a shallow breath. "Do we need to talk about limits?"

He grazes the edge of my ear with his teeth. "I won't be doing anything that approaches a limit tonight. You need to get in the car and go to my house. When you get there, you need to take off this dress. Take off your panties. I want you waiting for me, naked. That would please me immensely, Ellie."

Oh.

"Do you want to please me?"

"Yes, Sir."

"Good. Now go with Lachlan, Sprite."

———

LACHLAN APPARENTLY KNOWS that home doesn't mean my apartment.

He also doesn't seem to think this is a big deal, when in fact it's the biggest deal ever.

It's a short drive from the Chateau Laurier to 24 Sussex. We slide quietly through the gates and he parks right at the main entrance, then comes around to open my door.

"This way, Ms. Montague." He guides me to the front door, where he punches in a code on a keypad. There's a light on in the hall, and he turns on a few others as he leads me into a private sitting room. There's one window, heavily curtained. It's nicely decorated with antiques, but everything screams *don't touch*. It's like a museum.

"I'll wait here?" I ask, my voice shaking.

The Mountie gives me a gentle smile that softens his usually stern expression. He's probably about the same age as Gavin, maybe a little older. "You can wait wherever you'd like. The PM would like you to make yourself comfortable." He hesitates, then adds, "There's nobody else in the house. There are a few RCMP officers on guard outside, and the alarm system is armed. The only other person who will be entering the home tonight is the PM."

Oh. "Thank you."

He steps back, then stops. "Your privacy will be respected as much as the PM's. You have my word on that."

I give him a tremulous smile. "Thank you, Lachlan."

"No thanks required. Good night, Ms. Montague."

"Good night."

I stand stock-still as I listen to him walk away. I have to strain to hear the quiet beep of him letting himself out of the house. Another beep tells me he's re-armed the security system.

Naked.

Gavin wants me waiting for him naked.

I reach behind my back and tug on my zipper. My fingers slip the first time, but I take a deep breath and roll my shoulders. I shudder as the zipper slides open, freeing me from the snug satin and lace dress. I'm not wearing a bra, and my slight breasts feel impossibly sensitive at the brush of air.

I carefully drape the dress over an armchair in the corner. My underwear needs to come off, too. Leave my shoes on? He didn't specify. But I feel like a fake porno character trying to tug my panties off over my heels, so I kick them off.

And once they're off, once I'm fully naked, I realize I'm not putting them back on.

He wanted me naked. This is me. Small and slight, nervous and unsure. Ready and completely turned on, too.

Desire slicks between my thighs. No way can I sit on an antique. I look around the room. I could stand beside the chair, one hand casually draped over it. Or against the mirror. Just in the middle of the room, covering myself like Botticelli's Venus?

"Do you want to please me?"

"Yes, Sir."

Heat pounds through my body as I glance to the floor. Maybe I should…

I halfway sink to my knees, then right myself again. Oh, God. I'm shaking now. I should have asked him for more specific instruction, clearly.

Worst sub ever.

So much for my research.

But kneeling does seem to be standard. At least on Tumblr.

I swallow and sink all the way to my knees, spreading my legs a bit as I get comfortable.

I twist my hair loosely so it curls together down my back and lift my chin. Yes, I'm nervous. I've never done anything like this before.

But as a faint beep tells me Gavin's arrived, all my fears are driven away by the sheer rush of anticipation that swirls through me.

I'm his.

17

GAVIN

SHE'S EXACTLY as Lachlan said he'd left her. Except naked.

The sight of her is like kerosene being dumped on the fire we've been stoking all week.

I undo the buttons on my jacket and shrug out of it, leaving it on the chair near the door. I flex my biceps and roll my shoulders as I look at her, while I try to figure the right way to do this.

She's kneeling in some kind of pose I can only imagine came straight from the internet. Her legs are spread and her hands are clasped at the small of her back, forcing her perky breasts to stand out. My mouth waters in anticipation.

I loosen my tie and undo my top button as I approach her. She doesn't move a muscle.

"You're a good girl, Sprite." I reach down and gently stroke her hair. "But that's not where you belong. Give me your hand."

She wobbles a little as I help her up from the floor, so I wrap my arms around her until she's steady, then tuck my knuckle under her chin and lift her face to look at me.

"We haven't had a chance to talk yet," I say as I rub my thumb against her lower lip. She holds still, and her natural obedience thrills me. "So we're going to do that now."

She blinks slowly, a delicate frown tugging her eyebrows together. "Talk?"

I press my thumb a little harder, keeping her lips parted after her question. My first instinct is to slide in further and make her suck on it. Show her what her being on her knees makes me lust for. Her mouth. My cock.

But there's time for that later, and I owe my sprite a kiss.

Curving my hand around to the back of her neck, I hold her in place as I force myself to stay in control. Just a kiss.

"It's been too long," I mutter as I curl over her, brushing our faces together. My nose against her nose, my forehead against hers. My lips just ghosting hers, savouring the feel of her breath against my mouth.

"A week."

"Too. Long."

"Gavin…"

And that's what does it. That's what breaks me. My name on her lips. The rest turns me on, but maybe I needed to know that she really wants me. Just Gavin. With all my limitations and dirty kinks.

I crush my mouth against hers. She reaches for my face and I catch her wrists.

One thing at a time.

I tug her hands behind her back and circle both of her wrists in a fist.

My other fingers itch to explore her body and discover where the edge of her pleasure is, but for now I satisfy myself by gathering her hair in a loose ponytail and holding her still as I love her mouth.

Slowly. Sweetly.

Sometimes that's my favourite kind of cruel.

But we *must* talk. With a tortured grunt, I release her and lead her to a big comfy armchair, where I sit before pulling her into my lap. She burrows her head in the crook of my neck and I wrap one arm around her while I stroke her hair with my other hand.

"Ellie, I should have been more open about who I am with you. I appreciate all the research you've put into figuring out what makes me tick. And I have to tell you, the whole *Secretary* thing? Blew. My. Fucking. Mind. But I'll let you in on a secret. When it comes to BDSM, I'm really not all that complicated."

She whimpers and tries to bury her face in my chest.

"None of that," I say roughly. "It worked to get my attention."

"I feel ridiculous. Embarrassed."

"You've done nothing ridiculous. You tried to please me. You *did* please me in an unexpected way. It's my fault for not anticipating your pro-active enthusiasm and giving you some direction. My only excuse, and it's a shitty one, is denial. I was in denial about how I feel, I was in denial about what you could handle. Truth is, I was a coward. I was too scared to open myself up for rejection."

"And now?"

Now I know she wants me for me. "Now, I'm still scared. But optimistic."

"Me too."

Part of me just wants to just sit there and cuddle her warm, naked body. The rest of me wants to play. But there's more to discuss. And after her admission about feeling ridiculous and embarrassed, I need to tread very carefully.

"So, *Secretary*? What did you think of it?"

Hands down, my favourite thing about Ellie is her honesty. When asked a direct question, she always answers, and fully. She's the least political person I've ever met in that regard. I can feel her tense up, but she doesn't hesitate to tell me the truth. "A lot of mixed up feelings. It was different than I expected. But there were parts that were pretty hot."

Promising. "Like what?"

"When she's reading the letter bent over the desk while he spanks her."

Promising, indeed. "And the second typo you added to my speech? Was that you asking for a spanking?"

She smirks and lifts an eyebrow, an unusual expression for her, but I think she's a little smug about this. "Maybe."

It's adorable, of course, but I can't let her get away with that. "Communication is key, here, Ellie. *Maybe* doesn't cut it."

"I don't know. But I want to find out."

Now we're getting somewhere. "That works. What else did you find hot?"

"When she got praise for doing things right."

"Did you like it when I called you a good girl?"

She nods her head up and down.

"I need words, Sprite."

"Yes, Sir."

My cock twitches eagerly. I ignore it and kiss her on the head. "Very nice. What didn't you find hot?"

"I didn't like that she didn't fully understand what it was they were doing at first. But it's not like it was a healthy relationship at the start, was it?"

"No." I rub my lips against her temple. "And that's a key difference between BDSM in film and literature and real life. Although everyone is different, of course."

"What about you? Because the saddle thing. Total hard limit for me."

I laugh. "Fair enough. No pony play." I tease her a little. "I can live without it."

"Pony play? That's what it's called? I'm sure I saw that somewhere during my research. Maybe—"

"I'm teasing," I cut her off. Jesus, she's so earnest it hurts. I bet she thought about it from every angle so she'd make sure not to sound judgemental. "Pony play is not my kink. Back on topic, Ms. Montague, or we won't find out if you like being spanked, and that would be a disappointment for us both."

"What is your kink?"

"I have plenty. Dominance and submission. Power Exchange, to a degree, but I'm only into kneeling if there's a blowjob involved and I don't answer to Master. Oddly, Sir never did it for me until I met you. I like it, Sprite. A lot. It's a gift you give me, one that I treasure."

She smiles into my neck. I feel her lips curl and I make a mental note that she likes acknowledgement.

My cock is throbbing now, but I need to get through this. List everything I can think of so I can feel her response inside the circle of my arms. "Some light bondage. Impact play. Mostly I like to spank with my bare hand, but I do like to play with floggers and paddles on occasion. I'm not into punishment, though. So, if you're looking for a spanking, you won't get it by adding typos to my speeches."

"I'm sorry, Sir."

"Nothing to be sorry for, Sprite. You were testing things out, and on the whole, you did a pretty good job of pushing my buttons. I think it's time to see what pushes your buttons." I loosen my hold on her. "Up you get."

She climbs off my lap and for a moment I consider having her turn over my knee so I can spank her right here. But once I get started, I'm not going to want to relocate. Besides, my newly acquired stash of condoms is in my bedroom. Boy, do I owe Max big for taking care of the sensitive purchases for me.

"Bring your clothes with you."

She follows me upstairs to my bedroom. I decorated it out of my own pocket, and by decorated, I mean I bought an awesome four-poster bed and some comfortable chairs. The bed is the perfect height for so many things, none of which have been tested before tonight.

The chairs will come in handy for us at some point in the future, too.

I had no idea I designed my bedroom to fuck Ellie Montague, but now that she's standing in the middle of it, I never want her to leave.

"Put your clothes on the chair, then bend over the end of the bed."

"Yes, Sir." She saunters across the room like she owns the place. No self-consciousness about that beautiful body of hers.

She drapes her dress over the back of the chair and carefully sets her shoes under the seat. I watch her position herself on the bed as I remove my shirt and tie. I choose to leave my pants on for now. I want to keep her at a slight disadvantage.

"Your safeword is stop, or don't, or anything that sounds or even looks to me like you're not having a good time. Understand?"

"Yes, Sir."

Don't let me fuck this up.

I stand behind her. Close, but not touching. Like I'd done yesterday when she was looking out the window. My heart is racing as I reach down and stroke the creamy skin of her ass. First one cheek, then the other.

I take a step back and slightly to the side so I have more room to work. I pull my hand back and lay a firm slap on one cheek. Hard enough for her to feel a little sting. She lets out a small squeak, then a moan as I rub circles over the spot. I do the same to the other cheek. No squeak this time, just a low moan while her hips grind against the mattress.

She's got the most beautiful ass. And now it's marked with my hand prints.

I rub her right cheek and down her thigh, then slide back up between her legs, my fingers sweeping along her seam. Just a whisper of a touch, but she spreads her legs. Eager again. Fuck me, she's perfect.

"Hold still," I admonish, touching the outside of her thighs firmly. "Hold your position and I'll reward you."

A rough jerk of her head accompanies a mumbled apology and I lean over her, kissing her shoulder as I gather her hair again, twisting the silky smooth strands together.

I want her to braid her hair one night so I can tug on the heavy plait as I train her throat. I add it to the growing list of specific scenes I imagine us enjoying together.

"You're beautiful," I murmur as I lay another series of lazy swats on her backside. "Your ass is turning the prettiest shade of pink."

A whimper. Her fists squeeze against the bedspread, not in reaction to the spanking, but my words.

"Do you like that?" I rub my erection through my suit pants as I wait for her answer. "Sprite?"

She whispers something.

I tap a new spot on her bottom, harder this time. "I can't hear you."

"Yes," she gasps. "Please…"

Another dip of my fingers into her folds covers my hand in pussy juice.

"You're soaked," I say, and my voice is rough. My muscles strain as I cup my hand and deliver a new round of stinging, warm spanks against her ass. Each one makes her arch her hips into the heat. "You're bent over my bed, dripping wet because I'm spanking you. And you like it."

Another whisper.

My cock throbs as I lean over her. "What was that?"

"I love it," she says more clearly. There's wonder in her voice. I've given her this. She pushed me so hard to show her what I like. Why did I doubt that she might be a natural?

My dirty girl.

"Good." My voice is rough, raw. The primal part of me that craves this is taking over, fuelled by her scent and her sounds.

I've waited long enough for a taste.

I turn her onto her back and sink to my knees as I lose myself in her perfection. I had no doubt she was a cute red-head from head to toe, but it pleases me enormously that she's done nothing to hide it.

I want to spread her wide open and tie her legs to the posts of my bed. I settle for covering as much of the creamy pale skin of her inner thighs as I can with my hands and pressing her legs up and out.

She's perfect.

I can feel her eyes on me as I dip my head low and snake my tongue through her folds for the first time.

She's swollen and pink, slippery and delicious. I lap up the proof of how much she enjoyed my brand on her ass, then set about showing her that this, too, can be about submission.

Her orgasm still belongs to me, although I'm not telling her that tonight. She can come whenever she wants, as many times as she wants. I'll ease her into the fact that I want that control.

When I'm done showing her how good it can be, and

what the pay-off is for her, it'll be something she gives me freely.

Or not. I shove that thought away. She's a natural. She's mine. We'll find the places where our kinks intersect and play there.

I suck harder on her flesh, making her gasp. She floods my fingers, too. I stroke inside her, one finger first, then two. I want to give her three and stretch her to the point of aching, but there's time for that tomorrow.

And there's still so much of her body for me to explore. I give her clit one last lingering kiss, promising to return, then I lick my way up her body.

"Play with yourself, Sprite." I settle on my side next to her so I can watch.

Her breath is shallow and weak as she skims her hand down her quivering belly.

"Wait."

She stops immediately. Fuck, I love that response. How it's instantaneous and without question. Makes me hard. Makes me want to climb on top of her and take her without another moment passing.

"Slowly."

"Yes, Sir."

I kiss her because I can't help myself. Because she tastes like sun-warm raspberries fresh out of the garden. Because of the sounds she makes when I thrust my tongue against her. Because I need to be inside her and I need to wait and the tension there is killing me.

I push away from her just long enough to stand at the foot of the bed and strip out of my pants. Watching her leisurely stroke her fingers around her clit is a sweet bonus. "Is that what you like?"

She pinks up as she nods. "Yes."

"Do you ever put your fingers inside yourself?"

She shakes her head. "No, Sir."

"Why not?" I'm naked now and I prowl closer, leaning against the posts of the bed. The sight is hypnotic.

"It doesn't feel the same."

"As?"

"As I imagined your fingers would."

That little admission—she'd thought about me fingering her—has me vaulting onto the bed. My fingers are inside her before my mouth crashes against hers. She's still rubbing her clit as I fuck into her with two fingers. I need to slow down and learn her body, but she drives me insane. Maybe once I claim every last inch of her I'll have more control over this raging need to possess her.

"Like this?"

"Yes."

"You've thought about this?"

"Yes."

"And is it as good as you imagined?"

She gasps and rolls her hips into my touch. "So much better."

She's going to come. I want that. I want to feel her spasm around my fingers. I want to feel her spill all over my hand.

But I had a plan.

What the hell happened to my plan?

Ellie happened.

Gorgeous, responsive, eager as hell Ellie.

"Slow down," I rasp, finding my senses. I ease my fingers out of her snug channel and she protests. "Shhh. Trust me."

She presses her lips together and nods.

I suck my fingers into my mouth, enjoying another taste of her. Never enough. New plan. I'm going to find out how much nipple play she likes, then I'm eating her out until she comes on my face.

My fingers are still wet and sticky, so I paint her nipples with them, then lean over her and suck, back and forth, until she's panting and her peaks are puffy and swollen. She's the perfect picture of a debauched woman, warmed up and restless for more.

I pinch and pull one nipple while sucking on the other one. Switch. Repeat. I hold myself back from testing her limits, and I tell myself it's because I want to go easy on her.

Don't want to scare her.

But there's nothing about this woman that says she's scared.

She's writhing and stilling herself when she remembers. She's trying so, so hard to be good.

I reward her by working my way back to between her thighs and sucking her clit hard into my mouth.

Her thighs shake and she cries out my name. I give her my fingers, and two strokes in, I feel her climax begin, a tightening inside her that makes my dick pound against the mattress. He knows he's missing out, but we're going to make her do that all over again soon enough.

And again.

Over and over again.

Because when Ellie comes, it's a gorgeous fucking thing.

She's trembling as I grab a condom and fit myself between her legs.

No secrets. No made-up rules or artificial boundaries.

I want to say no limits, but fuck, I'm still worried I'll scare her off.

But as I sink into her, as she wraps her legs around me and welcomes me into her body, none of that matters. I'm drowning in her pretty eyes and being saved by the clarion call of my name on her lips, breathless and pleading.

Lost and found, rolling in an ocean of sex and desire.

Our hands twist together as I surge into her. Her legs pull up on either side of me and she whispers, "Deeper."

Harder.

Faster.

A million emotions roll across her face as I do all that and more. Slower. Cruel, short little pumps, giving her just the tip of my cock. She's so wet, but it's a damn tease, because I think I'm going to slide right in, but every time, she's tight. Every time, I stretch her and she cries out.

And still she wants it deeper.

I hitch one of her legs a little higher, reaching down her body to give her a swat where I pinked up her ass before.

"Gavin..."

Yes. My name, over and over again. I want to hear her scream it as I come deep inside her. "This is just the start," I whisper as I press into her, holding her down. "I never want to stop fucking you."

"Yes," she breathes, her eyes bright and her lips wet.

I spank her again and her breath hitches. "Like that?"

"Love it."

"Gonna come for me?"

"Yes."

"Yes what?"

"Yes, Sir."

"Come for me, Ellie." Swat. "Give it to me."

She wraps her arms around my neck as I fuck her faster, roughly now, deep and grinding, and on the next slap of my palm against her skin, she clenches all around me. This time her climax is the shockwave of an explosion, and I'm caught up in it.

I shout her name as I jerk inside her, burying my cock deep in her pussy. Mine. I come hard and fast, and blackness darkens the corners of my vision.

Drowning.

Broken into a million pieces.

There isn't a metaphor in the world for what Ellie's done to me.

After I get rid of the condom, I roll her onto her side, spooning her from behind as she sighs and snuggles close. She's blissed out and I'm...messed up. But in the best way. I cup her breast possessively and bury my face in her hair.

That was so much more than I expected. And we've hardly scratched the surface of what I want from her. What I want to give her.

My Sprite.

I close my eyes, hating the flood of competing thoughts that are trying to crowd into this moment. They can't have me yet. I'm still hers right now. I'm going to hold her until she falls asleep. She hardly needs aftercare after what we did, but while we didn't do a scene and push her into subspace, we did something.

Intense in a different way.

If I'm reeling, maybe she is, too. But she's wiped out and it's our first date, so I can hardly roll her over and say, "So hey, that was crazy emotional and maybe I more than like you...cool?"

Not cool.

I grin. No, when it comes to Ellie I have zero game. I'm the classic lovesick idiot. And that's probably going to be my undoing, but I don't care. I've waited nearly forty years to meet her, and now that she's in my bed I'm never letting go.

18

ELLIE

I WAKE up in Gavin's bed. It's early-ish, although I don't see a clock anywhere and God only knows where my phone is. I didn't bring my purse upstairs with me last night.

Rolling over, I look at the prime minister.

My lover.

Holy crap.

Last night wasn't at all what I expected it would be. It was just…real and natural. And hot. Very, very hot.

I press my thighs together. For all I know he has a full day of official duties today. But *God*, I want to do it again.

He's fast asleep. He doesn't even move when I touch his face. His stubble catches on my finger pads, sending shivers down my spine, and even as the deliciously wicked licks of feeling curl under my bottom and between my legs, I'm pulling my hand back.

The urge to molest him is strong, but I need to wash up first. I slide out from under the incredibly nice bedding and reach for my clothes.

Oh, God.

No. I cannot wear my dress. I can't wear it downstairs

to discover if he's got a coffee maker I can figure out, let alone home.

And how the heck am I getting home, anyway?

Intern Does Walk of Shame Out of 24 Sussex. More at 11.

Last night, we were the only people in the house. Is that still true? I could go to the bathroom naked but **Intern Discovered Streaking Past 24 Sussex Staff** is another headline I'd like to avoid.

Gavin's shirt is on the chair next to my dress. I pull that on, smiling as the faint whiff of his scent wraps around me. Then I tiptoe into the hallway, listening for any hint that I'm about to encounter someone who isn't expecting me.

I find a washroom first, then take a few tentative steps down the curving staircase.

"Good morning. Can I assist you in any way?" Lachlan steps into view at the base of the stairs and I press Gavin's shirt tight to my body.

"Hi."

He gives me a friendly nod and gestures down the hall. "I put coffee on for the prime minister."

"Is that a normal part of your duties?"

He laughs. "No. I'm not usually here on his day off. I wanted some. I was just being polite in saying it was for him."

I shift my foot to move further down the stairs, but I'm not wearing nearly enough for this conversation. "Would it be a terrible imposition if I asked you to bring coffee upstairs?"

"Not at all." He pauses and glances at my legs, but not in a creepy way. He keeps his gaze on my ankles. "Could I perhaps assist in retrieving some of your clothes for you?"

Surreal conversations I never thought I'd have. "Umm…How…private is the entrance in the daytime?"

"Reasonably private."

"I…"

From behind me, Gavin clears his throat. "Good morning."

I turn as much as I can without flashing Lachlan a view of my butt. As much as I wanted Gavin when I woke up, my heart still melts further when I see him standing on the landing in nothing but a pair of dark grey cotton shorts, his hands on his hips.

And an amused smile twisting his lips in a way that ratchets up my internal temperature.

"Where is your purse?" he asks me quietly.

"I think it's downstairs."

He nods, then raises his voice and directs his next words at Lachlan. "Find Ms. Montague's purse. Her keys are inside it. Go to her apartment and get her some clothes." He looks back at me. "Any specific directions for him? Closet? Dresser?"

My cheeks burn up.

Gavin smirks. "Any drawers he should avoid?"

The top one. "I have yoga stuff in the bottom drawer. Pants and a top would be great. And flip flops—they're in the bottom of the closet."

He looks past me again. "Got it?" Lachlan must have nodded. "Thanks. And we'll get our own coffee. Stay out of my kitchen today."

A chuckle below tells me Lachlan doesn't take offense.

As his footsteps below fade away, Gavin holds out his hand and I hurry back to him.

"I didn't like waking up alone, Sprite."

"I had to pee."

"And talk to my chief of security?"

"That was an accident."

"You're naked."

"I'm covered up."

"Barely. Are you arguing with me?" My eyes must light up because he laughs. "I told you, I'm not interested in punishment. If you want to be a brat you'll need to tell me so I know we're playing."

Brat. I roll that around for a second. No, I don't want to goad him…much.

"You don't like to wake up alone?"

"That's not what I said," he whispers, brushing his mouth against mine. Minty fresh. Someone brushed his teeth before coming to find me and order me back to bed. "I wake up alone every single day. Today I wanted to slide into you while I was still half asleep. Make you come before my eyes were even open. I wanted to feel your nipples get hard against my hands and sink my teeth into the nape of your neck as you got close to orgasm number two."

"Wow." I slide my hands over the hard planes of his chest as he undoes the buttons on his shirt. My pulse picks up as his fingertips not-so-accidentally brush the curve of my breast. "I really missed out."

"We have all day for you to make it up to me."

"We do?"

"Do you have other plans?"

"No."

"Then we have all day." Tension tightens at the corner of his eyes. "I'm not going to be able to give you a lot of days like today, but I want to start this right."

This? What is this, exactly? But I'm not asking that right now because he's finished with the row of buttons and his fingers have found me slick and ready for him.

"Back to bed, Ms. Montague." God, I love that shift in his voice.

"Yes, Sir."

He picks me up and carries me to his bed, where he lays me down and stretches out on top of me, heavy and hard.

Very hard.

I push at his waistband. I want him inside me, now.

He grabs my hands and pins them above my head. "Patience."

"I have none."

He grins and knees his way between my thighs. He trails a finger down my torso, then back up again, circling first one nipple, then the other. "What did you think about last night?"

He doesn't stop touching me. How am I supposed to answer that question when I want him to pinch me already? That's what he's going to do, right?

I loved that last night.

But since I'm not answering, he frowns and lifts his hand.

Seriously?

I lick my lips and force my thoughts together. "It was wonderful." I hesitate, and he doesn't miss that.

"But?"

"No. No buts. It was perfect." For our first time.

"Sprite, this works best if you don't cut yourself off like that." He touches me again, his thumb and forefinger on either side of my already hard nipple. "What else did you think?"

"Pinch me," I whisper.

"Please?"

"Pinch me, please. Sir."

His eyes flash as he presses his fingers together firmly, pouring heat straight into my belly. I moan and he ducks his head, sucking the peak into his mouth.

"Teeth, please," I breathe.

He bites me gently and tugs, pulling my breast as he

rises above me. "So polite," he mutters roughly. His mouth is wet and I want to touch it, but he's still pinning me down. "So polite, and still such a bad girl."

"What?" I struggle against his hold. "I'm not!"

"You didn't answer my question."

"You're distracting me."

"Focus, Sprite. Wait until I ask you not to come while working you over with a vibrator. You need to learn to control your desire."

That sounds awful. And amazing. "Why would you do that?"

"Because I'll enjoy it." He grins, feral now, and I squirm at the idea of him liking that control so much. And still he pushes me further. "What else did you think about last night?"

"It was…"

"Wonderful." Now he's just mocking me.

I struggle again and his grip tightens on my wrists. And my pussy swells. Like, I can literally feel myself fucking bloom for him. What the hell? "Yes. It was amazing. But I thought it would be more like this."

He's breathing hard now. We both are. He pulls a condom packet out from beneath his pillow and holds it in front of my face. "Hold this."

My hands are pinned to the bed. How…? Oh. Swallowing hard, I open my mouth, and he lowers it just enough that I can bite it gently.

He rises above me onto all fours, then flips me onto my stomach.

"Unnnh," I whine around the condom, but I'm lifting my hips in the air at the same time.

I have no shame when it comes to asking for what I want.

He's not going to give it to me. Instead of spanking me

again, he presses his entire body on top of mine. "Stay still, and we'll put that condom to good use. Move, and I'm taking you downstairs and feeding you breakfast."

That doesn't sound so bad, but I can't say anything, so I just nod.

"And not letting you come until very, very late tonight."

My nod gets more intense. I'm not going anywhere.

He chuckles in my ear and it's such a dirty sound. I shiver as he leaves the bed. It doesn't take long for him to return, the bed shifting slightly beneath his weight as he climbs on top of me again.

Straddling me this time. He carefully gathers my hair and moves it off my back, then he takes my arms, one at a time, and moves them from above my head to behind my back.

Then he ties them together. Something silky slides against my forearms as he binds my wrists. "My tie from last night looks better on you than me," he says gruffly.

Oh God. I lay there, arms bound, face down, and for a split-second, I wonder what the heck I'm doing. Then he's guiding me up onto my knees, lifting me upright. He moves in front of me and any doubt flies away fast as his gaze finds mine and locks on.

He settles me back on my heels, my pose not that different from how he found me in the living room last night. But this time I'm kneeling between his legs on the bed, not at his feet. And I can see his plan—he wants me to ride him.

He takes the condom from my mouth, then leans back against the headboard and opens it, slowly sheathing himself as he looks at me. His cock is thick and hard, the dusky red head darkening as he squeezes with each stroke.

He's put the condom on, so it's not like he's just going to jerk off as he looks at me, right?

But the question…ahhh. It pokes at me. I want him more because I wonder if maybe I won't get him. I want him with an intensity, a craving that is sweeter for the doubt.

I let out a shaky breath when he reaches for me. He sets one hand on my hip, the other curls around my rib cage, keeping me steady because I can't do that myself.

"This more like what you were expecting?"

"Yes," I breathe.

He wraps his arms around me, holding my bound wrists in his hands as he pulls me tight against his body. I'm so wet, his cock slides easily between us. "Can you take more?"

My pulse jumps. "Yes."

"Do you want more?"

"Yes." Oh, yes.

"You know how I told you last night what I like? I want you to make a similar list. Things you'd like to try."

"I want to try everything you like." Do I sound too eager? Is that possible?

"That's good," he says, squeezing my ass hard enough to make me squeak as he lifts me up onto my knees.

I roll my hips, hungry for the stretch of him inside me again.

"But…" He stills my body as I sink onto him.

I cry out and he grabs my hair, wrapping it around his fist. One hand on my ass, the other tangled in my hair, and my hands are tied behind my back. Surely this is perfection. How can he possibly have anything he wants to correct about this? I just want to pause the world and have him take me, over and over again.

"But what?" I pant.

"But sometimes I want to know what you want. Sometimes I want to make your fantasies a reality, too."

I didn't know that I had any fantasies before I met him. "I want this. I want you, and I want it hard."

He pulls me down onto him, his entire length filling me in one breath-stealing surge. "Hard?"

"Harder."

"Oh, you wicked woman." He flexes his hips, dragging his cock out of me, then pushing inside again. This has always been my favourite position, but Gavin's taken it to a whole new level, keeping me slightly off-balance as he fucks into me slowly. His eyes flash. *Take it. Take it hard.* And I do, letting my body go soft as he holds me on his lap. I'm utterly helpless—his plaything.

Once he finds a rhythm that works—rolling his hips up, dragging them back—his mouth gets busy again. He licks and sucks down my neck and across my collarbone, pulling harder when he reaches a spot that will be hidden when I'm dressed.

Mark me. I sigh as he lets go of my flesh with a wet pop.

"Gorgeous." He inhales roughly as he shifts us so my breasts are in his face. "So gorgeous."

They're small. I like that I don't need a bra most of the time, and can easily find one when I want it for fashion purposes. I don't love that in the past they've felt…not enough.

I've hated that I've let myself think that for even a second. Bad feminist.

But with Gavin, I trust that he wants *me*, however I'm packaged, and he proves that to be true, over and over again. Like now, as he starts to whisper all the things he loves about my chest.

"This freckle here…" he licks a circle just above my right nipple. Inside me, his cock flexes and I pant at the new stretch deep inside. "Feel what your *freckle* does to me, Sprite?"

"Yes."

"One of these days I'm going to cover this freckle with my come. Paint it with the evidence of just how hard it makes me."

"Ahhh…" The image of him jerking off on my chest makes me crazy. I try to shift my legs so I can get better purchase on the bed, ride him harder—make myself come.

Gavin's one step ahead of me. "Don't do that, Sprite."

I stop immediately, my thighs shaking with the need to come. "Please."

He waits.

"Please, Sir. I want to ride you harder."

"No. You want to come. You want to force it. You want this to be over."

"No…." I close my eyes and sag against his arms.

He rewards me with a hard thrust that makes me scream his name. His cock pounds into my cervix and rubs against my G-spot on the way back out again. How does he have this much leverage? "I want you to come, too. I want your tight, beautifully pussy to cream all over me—once we've both had our fill of pleasure and pain. Unless you want to start coming now, and not stop until I'm done?"

I shiver and moan, because comprehensible speech is beyond me now.

"Yes," he says gently. Clearly a sign he's about to do something maniacal. He tugs at my hands and the binding comes loose. "Ride me, Ellie."

He rubs my wrists as he eases my hands in between us. The tone has shifted, and I worry for a second that I've broken a spell. But Gavin is just as intent on fucking me as Sir was. I settle my hands on his shoulders and press up on my knees, rubbing my nipple against his mouth on the way up. He captures it on the way down.

I slide my fingers through his hair, grabbing a handful

as I bottom out. Grinding myself tight against him, my clit never loses contact with his body. His cock is angled just right to hit my G-spot and I make a few long, slow passes, forward and back. He bites my nipple and I'm almost there. I pump my hips hard and fast while he sucks and bites at my nipples.

I yank his head back by the hair I'm holding and take his mouth in a greedy kiss. I'm so close.

He snaps his hips up hard, meeting me thrust for thrust and when he pinches my nipple hard, my universe shatters. He plunges deep one more time and I can feel him pulse inside me as he comes.

I'm a boneless rag doll as he gently lifts me off him and lays me down.

"Was that okay?"

He grins down at me. "That was wonderful."

I blush at his teasing echo of my earlier words. "Shut up."

He kisses my nose. "It was perfect."

"I'm still learning."

His face goes serious. "Ellie, I don't need you to learn anything. I'm sorry I ever told you we wouldn't be compatible. Obviously that's not true. You're perfect exactly as you are. And that you're interested in letting me play, giving me the control…that's a cherry on top. I don't want you to worry about that again."

WE FINALLY MAKE it down to the kitchen after a leisurely shower where Gavin washes my hair and holds me close. Never before has a lover cared this much for me, physically. Of course, never before would I have described any of my boyfriends as a lover.

The kitchen is eye-poppingly dated. "Oh, wow," I say as I take in the vintage cabinets and utilitarian, first-generation stainless steel appliances. The rest of the house has an antique appeal. This is just…fugly.

He grins as he opens the fridge and pulls out eggs, sausages, tomatoes, and mushrooms. "There should be bread in the bread box behind you."

I turn and investigate. There is—really nice bread. Fugly kitchen, fancy food. Decent trade off. "Who does your shopping?"

"I have a housekeeper who comes in a few times a week. She's part of the Governor General's staff. It doesn't make sense for me to have an entire household staff when my household is…me…and I primarily eat pizza and drink beer."

I give his magnificent body a disbelieving look. "Pizza?"

"Lots of veggies." He gives me a boyish grin that turns into a dirty-as-sin, not-boyish-at-all up and down. "And I make sure to work it off."

An unexpected pang of jealousy shoots through me. "How often do you do that?"

He freezes. "No." He shakes his head. "That was just dirty talk. I don't do this, Ellie. Not with anyone else. There's just you."

Butterflies take flight in my belly at the reassurance. I smile. "Okay."

"Come here." He sets aside the food and pats the counter. I slowly slide in front of him and he lifts me up so I'm sitting on the edge. This puts us at eye level, and I lean in to kiss him.

He lets me, parting his lips and slowly tasting mine. I slide my tongue against his, inviting him to play.

He takes the invite. He explores every inch of my mouth, learning what makes me groan and tighten my legs around him. His kiss scrambles my brain cells and makes me weak in the knees, and when he lets me up for air, I can't remember what prompted it in the first place.

He does, of course. Mr. Always-In-Control.

"I think technically this is still our first date," he says roughly, running his knuckles along my jaw before settling his palm against the side of my neck. The warmth from his touch slides under my skin and settles nerves I wasn't even aware were jangling. "But we've been circling around each other for weeks, and my position makes for some interesting challenges when it comes to dating."

Ah. The earlier mentioned *this*. "Are we dating?"

He smiles gently, but his eyes are a bit tense. "If you're willing."

"Oh, Gavin." I reach for him, touching his chest, his shoulders, and it's not enough until my hands are cupping his face. "Yes, I'm willing. I just didn't know if that was… possible. Or desired. Or…anything. I'm stumbling a bit blind here."

"Me, too." His lips tighten. "We can't date publicly for a while. And I hate to say that, because that sounds sordid but—"

"No, the optics are horrible."

"But when you return to your research…?"

I lean in and kiss him softly. "I don't mind keeping you all to myself for as long as I can. I'll be careful. I haven't told anyone. Not even my roommate, although she knows I have a crush on you."

He turns pink. The PM. I can't even with how adorable that is. "Really?"

"Yeah."

He clears his throat. "The crush is mutual."

"Oh, good. I was worried there for a minute." I wink, because one thing that I'm not worried about at all is how much he wants me. Gavin makes me feel like the most desired, precious person in the entire world.

He strokes my cheek so softly it makes me want to cry, his eyes two mountain lakes of the clearest blue as he searches my face for something. I think he finds it because he smiles and steps back. "Now…breakfast?"

19

ELLIE

GAVIN'S DEFINITION of taking a day off work means only spending two hours in the late morning reading briefing papers. I don't mind, because I spend most of that time curled up in his lap, reading his favourite book from the last year—a pulpy thriller about black ops agents and a pharmacological weapon that's turning people into zombies.

It's now my favourite book, too, although it could have used a kick-ass heroine. Before I can point that out, he says the same thing in a distracted way that tells me he really means it, and I kiss his neck.

It's going to be super hard not to fall head over heels for this guy. I'm not sure I'm going to even try to stop myself.

Lunch is a delicious Cobb salad—apparently Gavin makes crisp bacon better than any other prime minister in the history of the country, or so he claims. I agree with him, it's pretty good. I chop ham, cheese, cherry tomatoes and hard-boiled eggs. The eggs were already cooked and peeled, too, which is kind of unfair.

"How many people are lucky enough to have perfectly hard-boiled eggs show up in their fridge?" I point at him across the kitchen. "You don't just have a part-time house-keeper. Someone is spoiling you."

"I don't ask for them!"

"But do you appreciate them?"

"Of course I do." A hint of colour dusts along the top of his cheekbones. "And I'll be sure to leave a thank you note in the tray on Monday."

"That's better."

I don't want to think too hard about anything domestic on our first date, but he gives me a funny look that makes my stomach flip-flop. This is turning into a marathon, ultra-domestic double sleepover.

We spend the afternoon swimming in the private pool. It's in a separate building, accessible through a tunnel in the basement. I feel like I'm being let in on a weird state secret. Then we end up back in the library, curled up together reading. That's when Gavin informs me that I'm staying another night, but he has to leave first thing in the morning.

"I can go home tonight," I whisper, peppering his face with kisses. I drop my book and straddle him. I love this big leather wingback chair. There's something seriously dirty about it, like it was built for sex.

Or maybe that's just us. Gavin strokes his hands up and down my bare thighs. I'm still wearing his shirt and nothing else.

"Try getting past the RCMP officers stationed outside," he rumbles.

"Think they'd handcuff me if I tried to escape?" I gasp as he pulls my hands behind my back. That's all it takes, and I'm grinding against his erection through his pants. "Take it out," I pant, suddenly hot and desperate for him again.

"Condoms are upstairs."

"I'll be good. I just want to rub against it."

"Jesus." But he does as I ask, releasing my hands so he can undo the fly of his jeans and fist his already raging cock. I watch him stroke himself for a minute, then push his jeans lower on his hips, making room for me to wiggle closer.

I bite my lip as I fit my sex against the length of him. I'm on the pill. I trust him. But it's our *first date*. And he bought all those condoms upstairs, so being safe is important to him, and I love that…

"Sprite." A warning. Like he can read my thoughts.

"I'm just playing a little."

"Okay." He flips up my shirt and palms my ass, then strokes up my back under the fine cotton. "But I'll be most pleased if you remember to control yourself."

A tremor wracks my body. "I will."

"Good girl."

I roll my hips as he touches me, gently at first, then as my belly pulls tight and my desire starts to spin faster, he slides his shirt off my shoulders and begins to work on my breasts.

Work is exactly the word for it. It's methodical and precise, and incredibly hot. He warms me up by stroking and squeezing my flesh, his eyes flicking up to my face, then back to my breasts. Watching and learning what I like. It doesn't take long until he's pinching my nipples to the point of discomfort—and then pushing a little further, making me squeak.

"You can take it," he says with confidence. And I believe him.

His erection throbs between my legs and it pleases me so much that this turns him on. I want to rub against him like a cat, except in a dirty, human way.

"Do you want to come like this?"

I nod through my lust-filled haze.

"You are the sexiest woman, Ellie. God." His voice catches and he pulls my face to his, kissing me roughly as I rock my clit harder against his cock, catching just the right angle that feels *ohmygod* so good. "I want to do so many things to you."

"Yes," I pant, keeping myself this side of the point of no return. He doesn't want me to come, I won't come. I might die, but I won't come. "Tell me."

"Later."

I whimper and he nips at my lower lip. The hot rush of his breath against my mouth makes me melt.

"Right now," he whispers, "I want you to come on my cock. And then I want you to use your juices to jack me off. I want to come all over your stomach, Sprite. And when I do, you're going to rub it into your skin and wear my mark for the rest of the night."

"That's so dirty." I try to smile but I'm close now, so close, and all I am is a bundle of nerves between my legs, rubbing bare against the man of my dreams. It's too much, and as he whispers again for me to come, I do, in a dazzling, dizzying orgasm that starts at my core and radiates out through my entire body.

Even my fingers tingle, but I remember what he wants. Even as the aftershocks ricochet through me, I'm shifting back so I can wrap my fingers around his cock.

He's so wet from me already, and he groans at my touch. "I'm close, too."

"Good," I breathe. "I want to feel your come. I want to touch it and taste it. I want you to come all over me."

"You're the dirty one," he grins, dropping his head back against the chair. I lean in and kiss his neck. His erection gets trapped between our bodies and I stroke him in the snug space, rubbing his wet crown against my belly.

He grunts, a short, harsh sound that fills me with pride,

and his hands clench and release on my hips. "Faster. You can be a little rough."

"That's your job."

"Jesus…" With a shout, he shoots come all over me, and I start snickering. I can't help myself. It's hot and sticky. "No laughing, Sprite."

"Sorry," I say sweetly. I'm not yanking my hand away or anything, so that's something. Besides…I like it. And I'm pretty sure he knows that. I like everything he's introduced me to, including messy hand jobs.

He snorts.

I wait for him to take a few deep breaths, then when he opens his eyes, I do exactly as he asked, and rub his mark into my skin. He watches, transfixed, and when I'm done, we tumble to the ground and make out for longer than I thought possible for two grown-ups who'd had sex a dozen times already in the past eighteen hours.

And I'm only slightly exaggerating.

APPARENTLY "WEAR IT ALL NIGHT" translated to thirty minutes, because we end up taking another shower together, and I actually put clothes on for the first time since Friday night.

Which is the only reason an argument about what to order for dinner doesn't turn into sex against the wall—not that I would have been complaining if it did.

"Chicken and caramelized onions is my current favourite."

He gives me a shocked look.

"What?"

"That's not pizza."

"Excuse me?" I shriek as he advances on me and

crowds me against the wall. I'm breathless by the time he cages me in, one of his arms braced beside my head, the other curled around my hips. "It's delicious."

"You're delicious. But that's not pizza."

"What would you order?"

"All pizza must have pepperoni on it, unless you're a vegetarian. Then you're allowed to substitute mushrooms or tomato slices."

"That's it? Pepperoni?"

"No, that's the start. The base. Then you can pile on mushrooms, green peppers, sausage, onions — not caramelized. That's weak. Red onions. Olives are good."

"Oh my God." I lick my lips. I shouldn't be turned on by a disagreement about what to put on pizza, but I am. "You're a reverse snob."

"I am not."

I nod, seeing it so clearly now. "Your whole every-man routine. It's not a routine. You're actually a beer and pizza guy."

"Of course I am."

I laugh. "You're so perfect it hurts."

"Hardly. I've got a beautiful woman over and I'm arguing with her over pepperoni. If that's not a tragic personality flaw, I don't know what is."

"I like arguing with you."

"Maybe after pizza and beer we can debate clean energy initiatives and whether or not we should eliminate the Senate."

"Seriously, take me now."

"Can't." He kisses me softly, then a little deeper when his first kiss sends a sizzle of energy down to my toes and I make a little sound that he correctly interpreted as a plea for more. But that's all I get. "Need to order pizza. Two pizzas."

"I can handle pepperoni. If you get the black olives, I guess."

"This way I can have leftovers tomorrow while I'm prepping for the summit."

"If only the voters could see you now."

"Stop making me blush."

I'm still giggling when he picks up the phone and dials a number that he's clearly memorized. He orders two pizzas, adding sundried tomatoes and black olives to mine. He winks at me when I raise my eyebrows. "What? I guess I can choke down the caramelized onions if there are other flavours around them."

"You're a fascinating man, Mr. Strong."

He just grins.

"And do you really order delivery like everyone else?"

"I *am* just like everyone else."

"Well…"

"No, that pizza place is vetted or something. Lachlan gave me a number I can call, and they get checked out at the gate. But I made it pretty clear that I wasn't going to have catered pizza or something weird. I need this little bit of normalcy and they make it happen."

There's something there that makes my heart pang, and I press up on my toes to give him a gentle kiss. Then I go back to my book while we wait for the pizza. He takes a phone call upstairs, then answers the door when the pizza arrives.

"Here's your pizza," I hear from my perch just out of sight. "That'll be thirty dollars."

"Thanks, man. Keep the change."

I follow him into the kitchen, where we plate up our pizza—and he takes a slice of mine, because even with his opinions, he's still game to try it—and he offers me a beer.

"Or we could open a bottle of wine," he adds when I don't answer quickly enough.

I blink in surprise. "Do you like wine?"

"Yes."

I search his face for signs that he's fibbing, also being polite.

He laughs. "I prefer red, but will drink white. Champagne is only for special occasions, toasts, and drinking off the body of a beautiful woman."

"Do that often?"

"Not recently."

I smile. "Beer's good."

"Was that some sort of test?"

Now it's my turn to laugh. "No. Sometimes you just work at a faster speed than I do. I was still thinking about if I wanted one or not."

He holds out the bottle of beer, but doesn't let go when I reach for it. "It's really not been recently."

"I…" My pulse skips a beat. "It's been a while for me, too."

"I don't want there to be anyone else, either."

I nod. "Just us."

"Is this too heavy for our first date?"

No, not too heavy at all. "You just bought me pizza. Maybe this is where the second date starts."

He gives me a crooked smile that crinkles the corners of his eyes. "When it comes to you, I'm going to be very possessive. Fair warning."

"Same." I stick my tongue out. "Fair warning right back."

He lets go over the beer and we leave that conversation in the kitchen.

After watching TV while we eat pizza, he opens the doors on a cabinet built into the bookcases, revealing a treasure trove of board games. "What's your poison? Monopoly? Clue? Scrabble? Yahtzee?"

The vintage Clue set tempts me, but I want to play Scrabble with the smartest man I've ever slept with.

It turns out he's a dirty stinking cheat.

"Stop that," I protest, pointing to yet another S he's pulled off his tray. "How many of those do you have?"

He shrugs and uses it to not only turn my HOOK into HOOKS—making a joke about how the S is called a hook in Scrabble, so it's extra-fitting—but then he also builds STAINER down from it, using all his letters.

"I hate you."

"That's not a good sign for me getting lucky at the end of our second date." He winks, and that's when I realize that teasing aside, hate is exactly the opposite of what's coursing through my body.

Scrabble cheating and all, how I feel for Gavin is rapidly shifting from a crush to something much more serious. "No," I say weakly. "You're pretty solid on that bet still."

2 0

GAVIN

IT WAS SUCH a perfect weekend and I'm stuck on a plane headed for a climate change summit in Amsterdam, instead of learning my way around my sweet Ellie.

I cross my legs and shift myself a little sideways to hide my inconvenient erection. I can't even think her name without seeing her beautiful, naked body draped over the end of my bed, her ass freshly pink from my hand.

I return my attention to the speech I'm meant to give on Wednesday. It's fine, but it's missing something. I make a note to get Stew to have Ellie do something with it.

If Ellie and I are going to keep things between us on the down-low, it's best to keep things absolutely professional at work. And that means not skipping links in the chain of command.

According to my watch, there's still another six interminable hours until we touch down. I need to prepare for this summit and I make a deal with myself. If I get through all my briefing material on the flight, I can call Ellie as soon as I settle into my suite at the hotel.

As soon as I'm alone—well, as alone as I can be when

I've got Lachlan camped out in the next room—I pull out my burner phone. Ellie's number is already programmed into my contacts. I tap the number for Lee—nope, I couldn't resist the *Secretary* reference—and wait. By the fourth ring, I'm mentally formulating the message I will leave.

"Hello?"

"Is this a bad time?"

"No, of course not. How's your day been?"

"Tedious. Yours?"

"Same."

"Maybe some yoga might help."

"Any pose recommendations?"

Hell yeah, I did a bunch of yoga research after I'd discovered how much she does. "One or two."

"Like what?"

"Oh…Cow, Locust, maybe Reclining Twist…" I grin at the thought of her in Locust Pose. Mental bondage at its finest.

"Mmm. Too bad yoga will have to wait until I get home from work." Her voice is light and teasing.

"Just remember what I said about controlling your inner light," I warn.

"Namaste."

I just want to talk to her for hours, but I know she's at the office. And we're already taking huge chances. The time difference is almost as unbearable as being away from her. Friday night can't come soon enough. "I should let you get back to whatever I interrupted. Call or text anytime you need me."

"I will."

We disconnect and I return the phone to my briefcase. Then think better of it and move it to the bedside table. I don't want to be fumbling around for it when she needs me.

I lie on the bed and replay our conversation in my head. My hand slips down the front of my pants and I rest my palm at the base of my cock while my fingers tease at my balls. I want to come, but not without her.

In this, my self-control is rock-solid. Just because she has to wait until Friday night for relief doesn't mean I have to. But I will. Even if I did let myself go, I know in my heart it'll be nothing more than release—not the mind-altering bliss I only seem to find when I'm with Ellie.

I'm hit with the realisation that Ellie seems to have a thing for roleplay. I stop fondling my balls and start thinking. Then I reach for my phone and start tapping away.

BJ
Have a good day. Make sure you get that paper submitted on time and don't forget your apple.

I'm tempted to send the text right way, while she's awake, but I want to draw this out over the coming days, so I schedule it so it'll arrive around the time she wakes up for work. Conveniently, that should work out to be around the time I'll have a break for lunch tomorrow.

I'M NOT SO CRASS as to text while I'm in meetings, but I'm not above taking every little opportunity that comes my way.

I'm in the meeting that just won't fucking end when I feel the phone vibrate in my pocket. We were originally supposed to have broken for lunch, but some asshole suggested we have food brought in and continue.

Too many participants nodded their fucking heads and now instead of reading and replying to a text from my girlfriend—I let that roll around in my mind for a minute because I love the way it feels—I'm stuck in a room full of imbeciles incapable of basic reading comprehension who require every fucking thing in the report we're discussing explained like they're fucking toddlers.

I'm probably being unreasonable, but I've never been a prime minister with a girlfriend before, and my tolerance for extended anything that doesn't involve said girlfriend—preferably naked—is completely gone.

Predictably, the meeting runs over, and I've only got five minutes to get to the next one and I over-did it on the coffee. The only thing in my favour is the washrooms and the room my next meeting in are close to each other.

Lachlan is waiting at the door to escort me. Even though the venue is supposed to be secure, nobody is taking any chances.

The next meeting mercifully runs a little shorter than scheduled and I have an extra half hour to get shit done before I need to dress for dinner.

I want to read Ellie's text the minute I'm alone in my room, but I have responsibilities, so instead I check messages on my official phone, wrangle my email into submission, and call Stew for a briefing.

My time is finally my own just before six, which leaves me an hour before I have to leave for dinner.

I pull the phone out of my pocket and tap in my code.

Lee
Paper delayed and it's a banana day.

She wants to play. A mixture of joy and relief wash over me. It takes me a minute to come up with a response I'm comfortable with.

> **BJ**
> As I recall, late papers come with penalties.

My phone vibrates seconds after I hit send.

> **Lee**
> I can take the hit.

Fuck. Me. I've hit the jackpot with this woman. Smart, witty, and loves a good spanking. I wish I could just jump on the plane and go home to her, or at the very least phone and hear her voice. But duty calls. I compose one last text.

> **BJ**
> Will discuss later.

I tap send and head for the shower. The hot water helps loosen me up. I've been tense most of the day. Beyond a quick soap and rinse, I ignore the erection that's been raging more on than off throughout the day. I have plans for my next load of come, and it's not down some Dutch shower drain.

I resist temptation and hold off on checking for a response until I'm ready to go. Of course, there's a text.

> **Lee**
> K

Perfect. I double check the phone is set to vibrate and tuck it in my jacket pocket.

It takes a while to get all my responsibilities squared away when I return from supper. I'm conscious of my need to rush, so I'm extra careful, which means everything takes longer than necessary.

Finally, my time is my own, and while I know Ellie's technically on the clock, she works way more than she's paid for and is entitled to a few minutes of personal time to talk to her prime minister boyfriend. Such a juvenile term, but really, the only one that fits—for now.

She picks up on the second ring.

"Hi."

"Hi. How was the yoga yesterday?"

"Disciplined."

With that word, my cock immediately shifts from politely reminding me of its presence to kicking and screaming for attention. "Good to hear. And how was the banana?"

"Nice and firm. Much yummier than mooshy."

I nearly choke on my spit-take. This is not a conversation I'm capable of having in code.

Ellie laughs and takes pity on me. "How's it going?"

"It's going. Lotus pose was on my mind a fair bit."

"I'm off to do some of that right now."

I don't know if she means real yoga or she's teasing me about sex again. And I can't ask, so I'm going to have to go to sleep with that torturous question bouncing around in my head.

THE NEXT DAY, I have to give my speech. Thankfully, Ellie's given it a thorough polishing and made it come off as more—me. There's enough of my personal philosophy in there to keep me from feeling like a total hypocrite without contradicting our official position on climate change.

I schedule her morning text just before I head out the door.

BJ
Have a good day. Be careful not to jay walk.

Lee
What if I'm in a hurry and there's no traffic?

BJ
You never know when a cop might
pinch you.

Lee
I guess I'd best keep my get out of jail free
card handy

Fuck. Me. I can only guess what she means by that, and sure as shit want to find out if I'm right. Now I know *exactly* what roles we'll be playing Friday night when I return to Ottawa. I just need to find the right opportunity—and words—to bring the subject up with Lachlan.

I decide to call Ellie right away because I want to hear her voice before I do anything else work-related. I've been good this whole trip and for once, I'm going to put my wants first.

"Hi there." Just one ring this time. I puff up at the knowledge she's waiting for me.

"Hey. How's it going?"

"It's been another cop-free day."

How did I get this fucking lucky? "Yeah, well, I hear Fridays can be killer when it comes to getting pinched.

"I appreciate the tip. Do you have any advice—in case I should find myself in a spot of…bother?"

"In case you're searched, don't put up any resistance. And take particular care to avoid anything that could get you nailed for obstruction."

"I'll bear all that in mind. Thank you."

"Happy to help. I need to get back to work. I'll catch you later."

"See ya."

I disconnect and start working my way through the mountains of email that have accumulated throughout the day.

THURSDAY IS another long day of meetings punctuated by a brief flurry of texts. Roleplay is definitely a thing for her, but apparently, she's not much into playing the part of a maid. I'm good with that.

> **BJ**
> Have a good day. Don't forget to dust under the desk.

> **Lee**
> I don't dust. Nor do I do windows.

> **BJ**
> I see. What do you do?

> **Lee**
> Hire someone

> **BJ**
> Makes sense. Watch out for cops.

> **Lee**
> Don't worry, I'll be fully prepared.

By the time I'm done for the night, I'm too exhausted to talk on the phone with Ellie. I wish I weren't, but I'm realistic and know this is the way it's going to be sometimes. I have one last breakfast meeting in the morning before we fly back to Ottawa. I send her a final text before sleep.

> **BJ**
> Lucky number is seven. Be prepared.

The smiley face emoticon I get in response tells me she understands loud and clear that I'm telling her I'll see her at seven when I get home.

FRIDAY AFTERNOON, after a long, tedious flight filled with too many people with functional hearing, I'm finally back on Canadian soil and still haven't had that chat with Lachlan.

Time and opportunity are running out, so in the car on the way home from the airport, I finally broach the subject.

"Lachlan, can I ask a rather delicate favour?"

"Of course."

I'm glad he's driving and not really able to look at me. "Any chance I might be able to borrow your dress uniform tonight?"

I was wrong. He gives me a long, hard stare in the rearview mirror and I try not to cringe.

"Okay. But only on the condition there will be no blue-dress type evidence when you send it out for cleaning.

I get the message loud and clear. No bodily fluids. "No problem. Thanks."

After a long silence, Lachlan clears his throat. "If you need anything else…"

"Anything else?"

"Yes."

"Did you trail off for a reason?"

"Only if you need…anything else."

"Good grief. Are we talking in code?"

"Well…" Another long pause. "Straight out telling your boss you're kinky and have resources is a little tricky. So, yeah. Code."

"Ah."

He looks at me in the mirror. "Did I misread the situation?"

"No, not at all."

"Okay. So…anything else."

"No, no. I think that's it. For now."

I ponder this revelation about my head of security for a while.

"Lachlan, the hockey team?"

"Yeah."

"All of them?"

He shoots me a grin. "The ones on our side."

And now it all makes sense. The entire team is kinky—which means Lachlan's connected.

"I assume you knew about my…uh…preferences?"

"And Dr. Donovan's. There had to be a certain amount of…poking around when you became prime minister."

"Yes, I suppose there would be. Who else knows?"

"Me and the regular members of your security detail. CSIS. I suppose those on our hockey team may have assumed. But leaking what they suspect to be true would only put the spotlight on their own activities."

"I see. So, risk of this information getting out is minimal?" I can take care of myself. So can Max. My only concern is for Ellie.

"I'd say so, yes."

I'm relieved. How did it not occur to me that I, along with those closest to me, wouldn't be thoroughly vetted for vulnerabilities?

We both remain quiet until we arrive home. Lachlan gives me a hand carrying my luggage into the house. Ellie is due to arrive at seven and I still have things to organise.

"I'll go grab that uniform for you. I'm not kidding about making sure there's nothing left on it that could bite either of us in the ass."

I nod. "Pristine or I'll burn it and pay for your new one."

"Pristine is your only option, sir."

"Understood. And thank you."

21

GAVIN

I've sent Lachlan to "bring Ellie in." Fuck, that turns me on. He's not going to actually cuff her, but I imagine it and that's good enough.

When Ellie walks through the door, she's looking at Lachlan kind of strangely. "Where'd your sense of humour go," she teases, no clue that I'm standing in the shadows of the center hallway.

"This way, miss. The inspector won't be long."

"The—" She gasps, low and sexy and steps closer to Lachlan. Fuck, no. But also, *fuck,* maybe yes.

No.

God. I'll just watch for another minute. She's so fucking beautiful.

"Can you give me any clue as to why I've been brought here? I'm so nervous," she breathes. My dick throbs, and the uniform pants don't give me the usual snug constraint of jeans or my tailored suit pants.

My cock likes the freedom. I'm not sure how I feel about it, but Ellie's one hundred percent into the roleplay already.

But it's been a week since I've held her, and Lachlan needs to leave. Now.

I step into view and she grins at me. Cheeky. Good, I'd like to play with a brat right now. "Thank you, Lachlan. That will be all."

He leaves without another word and I stalk toward her. "Up against the wall, arms and legs spread wide."

"Am I in trouble offi-Sir?"

I don't miss the change in inflection. It makes me harder than I thought possible. I want to be inside her. I want to fuck her so hard the smell of her permanently imprints on my skin. I bury that need deep and give her the roleplay I've planned. "That depends."

"On what?"

"What you're hiding under your skirt."

"I'm not hiding anything, honest." Breathless anticipation decorates every word.

"Well, I need to check for myself. Can never be too careful."

I run my hands up her thighs and over her ass, sliding the skirt up with them. I tuck the fabric into her waistband to keep it out of my way.

She's not wearing panties, just as I'd hoped. "It *looks* like you're telling the truth, but I'd best make sure." I pull a small plastic bag containing nitrile gloves and a small bottle of lube from my pocket. I'd promised Lachlan pristine and I'm a man of my word.

I pull on a glove, and give it a little snap at the wrist for emphasis, then cover three fingers and my thumb with lube. She doesn't need it, she's plenty wet. I can see her pussy glistening. But I want to keep my options open.

I slide two fingers inside and pump them a few times, then add a third. I can feel her squeezing them, and I so desperately want to replace them with my cock. She's tight. Warm and welcoming.

My voice is getting strained. *I'm* getting strained. "Nothing unauthorised in here. Still one more spot I should try, though." I slide my fingers out and through the crease of her ass before I gently press my middle finger against her tiny hole. A wordless request. We haven't talked about this limit.

She pushes back against me and the tip pushes past the ring of muscle. I don't venture very far, just to the first knuckle. Her reaction is promising and I file that away for another time. "Nothing here either. I think we may have to do a more thorough search."

I withdraw from her ass and carefully remove and discard the glove into the small garbage can in the corner.

"Turn around."

She does and I take her mouth in a deep, savage kiss, swiping my tongue all around inside her mouth. I release her and we're both breathing hard. "Nope, nothing in there that shouldn't be, either. I think I should pinch you anyway."

I'm struggling to keep up the game. All I want is to free my erection and take her hard against the wall.

I skim my hands up under her top and discover she's not wearing a bra. She's taken the no obstruction thing seriously. I cup her breasts, then pinch her nipples with ever-increasing pressure.

She watches me, her mouth open, her lips wet. An offer. A filthy invitation. She pulls it into the game as she runs her fingertips over her lips, sucking on them for a second before letting go with a wet slurp that makes my balls draw tight. "But I have a get out of jail free card, offi-Sir."

I'm totally corrupt. I'm going to let her off with an oral

warning—after she pays the price. "I'll still have to take you to the station."

I take her hand and lead her up the stairs to my bedroom. Point to a chair. "Strip and wait for me over there." She slowly lifts her top up and over her head, then drapes it on the back of the chair. She shimmies out of her skirt and adds it to the pile. And there she is, standing before me, naked save for a pair of very sexy heels. My slutty little jail bird. She shoots me a wide grin and sits on the chair, knees together, fingers back at her mouth. She watches as I carefully remove Lachlan's uniform. I make a mental note to get one of my own. I can see this becoming a popular game, and I'd like a lot more freedom to play.

"So, what about this get out of jail free card?" I ask when I'm finally naked with Lachlan's uniform out of harm's way. What was I thinking borrowing the fucking thing? It's been more bother than it's worth.

I walk towards her and she slips to her knees in front of me. "It's right here in my mouth," she says as she takes hold of my raging cock.

I'm not sure I'm going to be able to last.

Seeing her on her knees with my cock in her hand while she smiles up at me, the twinkle in her beautiful grey eyes tests my control to the limit—I haven't come since Sunday morning.

Her tongue pops out and she tickles at a bead of pre-come with the tip. My cock flexes, and I want to tangle my hands in her hair and bury myself deep in her mouth.

Instead I stand perfectly still, letting her be in charge. She takes a long, slow lick from root to tip like it's a fucking lollipop and she's killing me. Such a sweet death.

When she finally takes me into her mouth, she swirls her tongue around the head, then sucks gently.

I can't take any more and I don't want to come in her

mouth. This time I want to be buried deep inside her. I stroke her cheek. "Bed, now. Shoes off."

She scrambles across the room and I follow. I grab a condom from the nightstand and roll it on before I join her on the bed.

"Ellie…" I tangle my fingers in her hair and gently kiss her lips, teasing them open with my tongue. I slip two, then three fingers inside her pussy again, this time savouring the feel of her against my bare skin. She's more than ready for me. Rolling on top of her, I position myself between her legs and slowly press my way into her sweet body. My lizard brain is screaming to hold her down and take her hard and fast. But I won't. I missed her so much and my heart needs slow and gentle.

She wraps her arms and legs around me. I pull my head back and look deep into her eyes. I'm so lost. I don't know how I got here, and I have no interest in finding my way back to wherever it is I was.

My cock is in to the hilt and I grind against her clit before easing back. I adjust my angle a bit and give her a few quick, shallow thrusts before sliding home again.

She tilts her hips a bit and as I pull back, I slide my hand between us. "That's it, take what you need and come when you're ready."

I stay still inside her as she rubs against my fingers. She grows frantic, and soon I feel her muscles gripping my cock. I can't hold back any longer. I kiss her hard and snap my hips forward. My tongue and cock thrust in unison until finally, I let go. Electricity arcs down my spine as I fuck into her, driving against that spot inside her that makes her scream. I swallow each of those cries as she rocks helplessly beneath me, taking my brute force and begging for more. My balls pull tight, desperate to spill inside her, and as soon as she explodes, I bury myself deep.

Ellie's legs wrap around me, holding me close. I need to deal with the condom that's probably overflowing with a week's build-up of come, but she and I want the same thing. A minute where we're just connected. Nothing more.

I start to move, but she holds me tighter. "Not yet."

"God, Ellie," I whisper, kissing her roughly. "I missed you."

There it is. The truth, out loud. One week into dating her, and I'm a hopeless mess. I've never felt this strongly about a woman, not after a week or a month or the entire duration of a relationship.

"I missed you, too," she says sweetly, running her fingers through my hair. "But what a way to reconnect, eh?"

I laugh. And just like that, she pulls me forward, into the light. I slide out of her and get rid of the condom. What a way, indeed.

22

ELLIE

SASHA'S GONE to the cottage again for the weekend, so I don't need to worry about the fact that for the second weekend in a row, I've spent an entire day wearing nothing but one of the PM's dress shirts.

We're doing this weird thing where we bobble back and forth between dirty lusting for each other and something that approaches a totally normal relationship. Last night started out as a kinky role-play, but it got emotional pretty fast. Even faster than last weekend, and I worry about the speed at which we're racing toward something big and serious.

But then we have a light, teasing morning together, and that niggle fades away.

Now I'm lounging on Gavin's bed, waiting for him to finish a meeting downstairs. I love the secrecy of being up here, naked except for his shirt, and he's down there running the country by way of meetings in his library with a visiting environmental science expert, the governor of the Bank of Canada, and a couple of guys in suits that he didn't tell me anything about.

CSIS, probably. My boyfriend is meeting with spies right now.

While I'm his kept mistress, locked in his bedroom.

Well, not locked. The door is actually wide open. This sounds way more sordid than it really is—I got to finish reading that book I started last weekend, and then I started making the list of dirty things I might like to do with Gavin.

At first I thought about writing down an actual list, but when I put pen to paper, I started to freak out. What if Gavin's housekeeper did that trick of rubbing a pencil over the blank page to find out what had last been written on it?

Nobody needs to know that someone in Gavin's bedroom wants to be tied to his bed, even if anyone with half a libido would look at that gorgeous four-poster and have the exact same thought.

So instead I make the list on my phone. Not the burner phone Gavin gave me, but my regular phone, which is in no way connected to the PM.

I type out **tied to the bed**, but I don't know any specifics. So I flip over to Tumblr and search for bondage pictures.

And that's when Gavin finishes his meeting.

I'm staring intently at my phone and maybe squirming a little when he clears his throat. I jerk my gaze up and find him leaning against the doorframe, hands in his pockets. He's wearing jeans and a dress shirt, and his feet are bare.

He's totally, completely fuckable.

"What are you doing?"

"Uhhh…" I grin. "Hi."

"You're all flushed," he says slowly as he paces around the bed.

I have plenty of time to close the tab on my phone screen. I don't.

"Shift forward. Let me sit behind you."

I rise up on my knees and as Gavin settles against the headboard, he takes the opportunity to strip me of his shirt.

Now I'm naked as he settles me back against his chest. I'm naked, he's not, and he's just caught me looking at porn.

"Show me, Sprite."

Heat rushes across my chest as I lift my phone, showing him the woman lying face down on a bed, her legs spread and bound to the corners of the footboard.

"Do you like that?"

I nod. "I'm making that list we talked about. Of things I'd like to try."

"You'd look so pretty tied to this bed," he says gruffly, his hands settling hot and heavy on my shoulders. "What else have you looked at?"

"I just started. And some of these photos are intense."

He laughs. "Yeah. There's a kink for everyone, but they're not all for me."

"What is for you?" I glance sideways at him. "What kind of porn do you like?"

He hesitates for a minute. That's a loaded question, probably. Like what he asked me last weekend, if I was testing him about other women. I wasn't then and I'm not now.

"I like GIFs," I whisper. "Not full video clips, just one action repeated over and over again. Somehow it's hotter."

His jaw flexes. So does his cock. I can feel it even through his jeans. "Show me."

I scroll up and stop on a spanking GIF I'd spotted. "Like this."

He exhales, a rush of air that slides under my skin and licks at me from the inside out.

I click on the blog that originally posted that one. Jack-pot. Gavin shifts and his hands slip to my torso as I scroll slowly. Spanking. Light bondage. All black and white images, still pictures and moving GIFs. Sexy and classy and who needs a list when you can just point at it and say, "Yeah, wow."

"You like that?"

I nod. "And…that." A man's hand around a woman's neck. More caress than hold. His thumb rubs back and forth along her jaw. Gavin takes my cue and collars me with his fingers.

I shudder.

"I haven't looked at porn in…ages," he says roughly, his voice low my ear. "And not because I don't like it."

My eyelids flutter shut as he strokes my throat. I swallow against his touch. "Worried someone might hack your internet?"

"And my phone…" He trails off as he rubs his other hand against the trembling flat of my belly.

I'm so slick between my legs. I want him to touch me there. I want him to get me off, and I know he won't for ages yet. Not unless I drive him crazy. "But you've got my phone now. Perk of being a private citizen. We could watch anything you like."

"I like watching you."

I think about the fantasies he teased me with via texting last week. "What about some naughty school girls? A french maid?"

He laughs, then groans. Like he wants to share something with me but he's trying to be good.

Fuck that. I want him to be bad. "Come on," I pant, arching my back. I can practically feel his gaze on the hard points of my nipples pressing into the air. "Tell me what to put into the search engine. Show me something dirty that you can't watch anymore because you're the prime minister."

"Threesome," he growls. "Two men. One woman. Submissive."

He cups my breasts as I type it in. There are a bunch of results. He makes dismissive noises about the first two, but the third one makes him grunt.

I like the grunt.

I click on the GIF and it fills the screen with a never-ending loop of a woman in lingerie, on her knees, bobbing back and forth between two men. In the blurry background, a third man is watching.

"Oh…" I sigh.

His fingers tighten, squeezing my flesh. I sag back against him. *Yes. Touch me.*

I want to touch him, too, but I need both of my hands to hold the phone without dropping it.

"That third guy should be underneath her, biting her nipples," he says in my ear as he pinches me, mimicking what that would feel like. "Every inch of her being pushed to the limit."

"That's your fantasy?" Not two chicks? I'm skeptical.

Even when talking about sex, he gives the question serious consideration. "Not exactly. I like orchestrating a woman's pleasure. Giving her the release she seeks. The power of that turns me on."

"But you wouldn't…use the word fantasy…?" I'm breathing so hard I can't talk, and I wonder if maybe he can make me come just by flicking his thumbs back and forth across my nipples.

"My fantasies now involve you. And my sharing days are done. Do another search." He slides one hand through my curls and swears under his breath when he finds me drenched. "Dirty, dirty girl."

"That's what you want me to search?"

"No." He smacks me lightly on the inner thigh. "Type in **anal**—"

"No!" I laugh nervously.

"Okay." He waits a beat. "So what do you want to watch?"

God. I have no idea, and my knee-jerk protest there has faded. "Okay, anal what?"

"Well, anal by itself is probably a decent term. Anal play, anal sex…" His voice deepens. "Anal fisting."

My eyes are like saucers and my voice squeaks a little as I veto the last one. I'm pretty sure he's kidding, but just in case… "Hard limit."

"But not the first two?"

I blush. "No. You already know that."

"I do. That's why I suggested it." He slides his fingers through my wetness one more time, then lifts his hand to his mouth and sucks them clean.

Has he picked up on how hot I think that is? It's ridiculous what that act does to my insides.

He brushes my hair off my shoulder, tucking it behind my ear. His hand lingers there for a minute as he traces the edge of my ear with his finger. "I want to see how wet it makes you to watch someone take a big, hard cock up the ass."

I whimper and drop the phone, turning in his arms. My pulse is pounding in my ears as I fumble with the buttons on his shirt. He pulls a condom and a packet of lube from his pocket.

I rip open the foil on the condom while he shoves his jeans down, then I'm sinking on to his length. I'm not quite ready yet but I need him, *need* him, and it's worth the ache as I stretch around his erection.

"You want me to tie you down and fuck you hard?" He's touching me everywhere as he talks. A hard squeeze to the ass as he pulls me down. A whisper light tease against my nipple as he strokes up my body to circle my neck again.

I clench around him as he presses against my throat.

"We didn't get very far on that list making, Sprite."

"I'm sorry, Sir." I'm not really sorry. This is crazy hot.

"Are you? I think you wanted to be fucked and you're getting that."

"Ahhh," I breathe, smiling as he pumps into me again. "You're giving it to me."

"Yes I am." He rips open the lube and coats two of his fingers. My eyes go wide and he grins. "And you can take more."

He starts with one, easing into me from behind, and my thighs shake as I fight the urge to leap away from his touch. His cock swells inside me. He loves pushing me to the edge, I've already learned this, but the threesome thing has me thinking.

It also has me turned on. I grind against him as he slowly fucks his finger in and out, just to the knuckle again, getting me used to the invasion.

"You're all done sharing?" I ask, bracing my hands on the headboard on either side of him. He presses his face into my neck and rubs me with his second finger instead of answer.

No way is that going to fit.

"Shhh, Sprite. You can take it."

I can't. I'm twitchy and achy and God, I just want to fuck him. And find out more about how he used to share women with dozens of faceless men. Or something.

"Good girl," he growls, his voice on the edge of losing control. "Ease back on my fingers. Yes. Fuck, that's so unbelievably sexy."

I make an indecipherable whining noise that I force into

a pant as he finds a new rhythm, pumping in and out of me in opposite timing to the slow thrusts of his fingers.

"I'm going to kiss you now, Sprite. And you're going to come with my fingers in your ass, my cock in your pussy, and my tongue in your mouth. You're mine in every way."

"Yes..." I breathe, our faces close enough that he's all blurry. Or maybe that's because I'm lost in the sensations and my other senses have been subsumed under the pounding need.

"Say it." His free hand twists in my hair.

"Yes, Sir. I'm yours. In every—"

He crashes his mouth against mine and I come hard and fast, the climax wracking my entire body. As the after-shocks ripple through me, he slides out of me, holding me tight at first.

Then he folds me, still limp and wrung out, to the side and disappears for a moment. I hear the sink, then more water running. When he comes back, he hovers over me for a second before his arms scoop under me. "Bath," he says simply.

He sets me in the tub by myself, then disappears again. This time it takes him longer, and when he returns, it's with supplies. A bottle of wine, some fruit. Cheese and meat and crackers.

He dries me off and we settle together in one of his big arm chairs. He loves holding me in his lap as he feeds me, and I love letting him. Once I'm full, he entwines our fingers and gives me a serious look. "How did you enjoy that?"

"Watching the dirty GIFs together?"

He nods. "That. The rest."

"I liked all of it. You're...amazing. You know just what to do with my body."

"I'd like to do more." He searches my face. He's not going to find any concern there.

"Yes, please." I grin. "I trust you."

"Your bottom's not too sore?"

"Not at all." Two fingers weren't that bad.

He squeezes my butt cheek. "Ready for more there?"

"Maybe." I lick my lips. "You're all kinds of prepared, eh? Individual packets of lube? Fancy."

"Max did all my shopping in anticipation of our first night. He went a little overboard."

"Excited that his best friend was getting laid again?"

"It had been a while."

"You keep mentioning that."

"I'll stop."

I kiss his neck. "You don't need to be anything other than your real self with me, Gavin. Your preferences, your history, your…work hours. They're all a part of you. And I…" I trail off. "I'm all in. If you want me to be."

"I do."

"But…"

"No buts."

"Hear me out."

He gives me a grumpy look. He really doesn't like not being in charge of a conversation.

"Here's the thing." I soften my voice as much as possible and stretch my body out against his. "My boss's boss was away last week. Now he's back and I only have this job for five more weeks. I want to give it my all."

"We can keep it professional. This has nothing to do with that."

"Of course it does. That's why you resisted."

"That was before."

"Let me just finish this. You're insanely busy. You always will be. So finding time is going to be a challenge.

I'm okay with that. Because at the end of the summer, my schedule will get lighter. I'll have a lot of work to do, but I can do it mostly on my own schedule."

"What are you saying?"

"Just...let's take it easy. Slow. Serious." I kiss him lightly, my lips dusting against his. "But slow. No expectations about time and availability."

His face tenses up, but he lets me keep talking. And maybe that's why I trail off, until silence hangs between us.

"That was it, really. I just want you to know that I'm easy." I don't mean it like *that*, but it still cracks me up. I'm still laughing when he gives me a look I can't quite parse. "What?"

"Nothing easy about you, Sprite. I say that in the best way possible. Everything about you is different for me."

"I'd say the same thing about you, but that's not a surprise. I don't have that much experience." *And you're rather unique*, but I don't add that part.

"You don't need to worry about my history," he says with a frown.

"I wouldn't say I'm worried. More...curious."

"Really?"

I nod. "I want to know more about the whole threesome thing."

"That was just..." He takes a deep breath. "Okay, here's where I feel a little on unsteady ground. I want to say that was just porn preference, but I don't want to accidentally lie to you. So it's porn preference and a reflection of some things I've done in the past."

I squirm in his lap. "Tell me more."

"No."

"Please? Pretty please with a cherry on top?"

"You're not letting this go, are you?"

"I will if you tell me to."

His eyes soften. "No. I don't mind your curiosity. Let's get into bed."

He gets me to stand up, then leads me over to the bed. While I was in the tub, he'd re-made the sheets and turned back the blankets, and we slide under the covers together.

I curl up against him, both of us naked, and he plays with my hair as he talks.

"My first threesome, I was the third. I was a young guy, new to the kinky scene, and I went to a sex club where they encouraged mentoring for anyone…fresh. It's a safety thing, mostly. You don't want anyone to get too into a scene and hurt a sub. So I was paired with this couple who were into sharing. He taught me how to safely use impact toys on his wife. When I was done working her over, he'd fuck her. And after the first time, he got me involved. Hold her down, that kind of thing."

"How old were you?"

"Twenty, twenty-one? Still in undergrad. Max had introduced me to the scene, but we have different tastes."

"Did you ever share with him?"

Gavin laughs. "No. We're both too dominant. And he's like my brother. I've seen him have sex with someone, but I don't have any desire to be a part of it."

"So is it more than just…Have you ever… with a guy?"

"I've never had sex with a guy. I don't swing that way. But if you're doing it right, there's touching and that feels good, it doesn't matter who it is. Max isn't on the list of people I want touching my cock. Too weird."

"Too bad. He's cute."

"I will kill him if he touches you."

I laugh gently and stroke my hand up and down the firm, ridged muscles of his abs. "It's kind of weird, how you've had all these experiences and I haven't. But I don't feel like right here, right now, we're all that different."

"We're not. I just have more experience saying what I want and how I want it. But with you I feel like it's all new again." An impossible, crazy warmth floods through me at his words and I wiggle closer. His eyes are bright, endless pools I just want to get lost in forever as he keeps going. "You challenge and push me, Sprite. I like it. A lot."

"I like it, too." I hesitate. "But as long as we're together, I'm never going to go to a sex club, you know? Not that I want to do that, exactly, but I don't want to have what-ifs, either."

"I've opened your eyes to all manner of kinky fuckery and I'm no longer enough?" He's kidding, but not entirely.

I've really put my foot in it. "No! Not at all. You're… you'd be enough for a lifetime of fucking, Gavin."

"But?" Now the grumpy edge is back. Men. So sensitive.

"No but this time. You're enough. Let's pretend I didn't say anything."

"That's not how this works, Sprite."

"Then you can't get hurt feelings when I try to talk about it, *Sir*."

He's silent for a minute. "Okay," he finally says. "That's fair. I apologize. So what does my little fuckerette want to explore?"

"Fuckerette?"

"A girl into kinky fuckery." He grins. "A woman after my own heart."

"I am that," I say softly. *I love you.* If I could just say it out loud, it would probably ease a lot of his doubts, but even though my heart is bursting with that, my head says it's too soon. So I focus on safer ground. "What you were describing. The threesome. You dictating what people do to me. Being…fully taken. I'm not saying that suddenly I want a threesome, but—"

"I want to eliminate that word from your vocabulary."

"Oh."

"There's nothing wrong with wanting a threesome." Right. I know that, intellectually. But I still feel like I should feel guilty about it. Even when I don't. I tell him as much, and he gets a curious look on his face. "There are other ways to satisfy a fantasy. Watching porn together, for example. We got to have that bit of voyeurism without risking the public exposure of going to a sex club. There are toys we can use to…fully take you, as you said."

I shiver at the thought of that.

"And if you wanted…"

I hold my breath. Do I want him to finish that sentence?

He looks at me long and hard before continuing. "I'd give you anything you want, Sprite. There's always a way to make it work."

"How?" My breathlessness is totally giving me away, and he gives me a knowing look.

"You let me worry about that." He pulls me close and kisses my forehead, a tender gesture that is actually way hot. He's way hot. I'm the world's luckiest girl. "We're still figuring out what this is between us, Ellie. But whatever it is, it's special to me, and I'm going to take care of it. I'll take good care of you. I promise."

"I know that. Without reservation."

He gives me a long, calculating look that makes my toes curl. "So you want to be taken, eh?"

"It's your fault," I whisper, sliding into the fantasy. "You've given me a taste…"

"Give a girl an inch," he growls.

I blush. "And now I'll be fantasizing about taking a mile. Maybe. Yes."

"And if we did include someone else…it would still be

me in control. Me orchestrating your pleasure. You understand that, right?"

"That's the whole turn on. I'd never imagine wanting to do it with anyone else."

"Good. Get your phone. Show me what you like. Maybe I can find a way to recreate that in another way."

23

GAVIN

I WAKE up with my hand curled possessively around Ellie's breast, and my cock half-hard, rubbing against her ass.

When my alarm goes off, I turn it off. I don't need to do pushups this morning. I got plenty of exercise last night, and if I can pry myself away from Ellie, I'm going to try to make it to hockey again today.

"Morning," she says, and the soft, sleepy huskiness in her voice takes my dick from interested to demanding.

I reach for a condom. Wake-up sex is a fucking awesome tradition.

After she comes twice, both times with her cunt milking my cock for all it's worth, we shower together and that's just nice, but damned if I don't like it almost as much.

I don't tell her about hockey yet. Either I'll get an opportunity or I won't go. And I'm rewarded for my patience when, after we dry off, she pulls yoga clothes out of her bag.

"After last night, I need to do some major stretching," she says as she glides past me. "So once we make some breakfast, I might head to yoga."

189

"Is this some of that taking things slow plan?" Because I want to invite her back here after, but I don't want to push.

She lifts one delicate shoulder. My gaze hooks on a trio of freckles that decorate her bare skin there and I loop my arms around her waist, holding her tight so I can kiss them.

"Come back here once you're done?"

"Okay," she whispers.

"I've got a thing, too, so I'll drop you off and pick you up."

She turns in my arms. "What are you off to do?"

It's damn hard to hold her in my arms and just have a conversation. I want to lose myself in her mouth, but I settle for a light kiss before I tell her about the new team. "When I was trying not to want you quite as much as I do—trying and failing—I asked Lachlan to find me a hockey game."

"To watch?"

"To play. A pick-up team, casual but organized enough that the participants can be screened. I missed last week because I had to prep for the summit."

"You play hockey."

"Used to play every week. Now I don't know how often I'll get to do it, but there's a group of guys that Lachlan trusts, and…it's fun."

"Stop it with the perfect."

She means it lightly, a compliment, but it's damn close to the whole pedestal thing that makes me uncomfortable. I shrug it off. "I love hockey."

"That's because you've got maple syrup in your veins." She gives me an amused look. "Can I come watch you play sometime?"

"You'd want to?"

"Of course."

"Sure. But I need to warn you that Tate Nilsson plays

on my team, and if you drool over him, I'll get all jealous and beat my chest like a caveman."

"The captain of the Ottawa Senators plays on your pick-up hockey team?"

"There are some perks to being the prime minister."

"No kidding."

TODAY I WATCH my teammates through a new lens. Of course, once you're looking for it, the signs are there. Tate's so alpha it hurts, but he's a maverick. None of Max's rule-bound Dominant persona for him. He's more like me, and just wants to be in charge. Gets off on the extra dirty stuff, maybe.

And Lachlan… I think back to how many times Tate has said my security chief is the go-to guy for setting things up.

Fuck. Lachlan probably spends his free time being a monitor at a local BDSM club. He's got exactly the right personality for serving as the DM, disarming and calm, but with a natural authority that people can't help but respect.

And like.

Ellie likes Lachlan, for example.

My dick is so busy thinking about that little ping in my head—Lachlan, Ellie…Lachlan and Ellie. How much I trust him, and maybe only him, at least in this regard.

I'm thinking so hard, I miss a turnaround at the far end of the rink and suddenly one of the forwards from the other side is shooting up the rink toward our net.

I skate backwards as fast as I can, hustling to get between him and Corinne in goal. I'm not going fast enough to intercept, but he veers to the side and that's enough that when he shoots, she catches an edge of it and dumps the puck into the corner.

"Lucky," Tate yells at me as I hook it with my stick and pass it behind the net to our other defenceman.

Sometimes, that's my middle name.

"Turn-up!" I holler and he dekes out of the way as their right winger charges in, feinting to the left before spinning toward the boards and getting the puck back up the ice where it belongs.

I keep my mind on the game for the rest of our ice time, but the spark of the idea I had out there doesn't want to leave me alone.

As soon as Lachlan and I are in the car and the doors are shut, I start talking. I need to take advantage of the absolute privacy before I lose my nerve. "So…what do you think of Ellie?"

"She's lovely." Not hot, cute, sexy, gorgeous, fuckable. He gives me a careful, diplomatic answer.

Jesus. How the hell am I supposed to ask my head of security to help me fuck my girlfriend?

I try again. "Do you find her…attractive?"

"Where's this going? Because, I sure as shit know you're not looking for approval."

"Can we talk in hypotheticals for a moment?"

"Whatever it takes."

"Okay, if someone you knew had a girlfriend who's shown a little interest in…an extra set of hands, among other things, in the bedroom and has maybe hinted that she might like that second set of everything to be you…"

"And, you're wondering whether my level of kinky extends to threesomes involving more than one dick."

"Yeah, I guess that's kind of where this is headed."

"Kind of? Are you fucking kidding me? This isn't some

harmless kid's game. There can be serious repercussions from this kind of activity."

"I'm well aware. Not my first rodeo."

"Maybe not, but this time, it would involve someone you care about."

I let that sink in for a minute. "True. But part of caring about her is fulfilling as many of her fantasies as I am able."

"Not all fantasies are meant to become reality."

"Are you saying no?"

"I'm saying there would need to be ground rules."

"Of course. First and foremost, her pussy is off limits. That's mine."

"Fair enough. Second—no mouth kissing."

"Definitely no mouth kissing."

"What about her ass?"

"Also mine."

"Breasts?"

"They're yours to do with whatever she lets you."

"You're sure about this?"

Not really, but as Dan Savage would say, I'm good, giving, and game. "Let's go pick up Ellie and take her home."

"Well, that escalated quickly," Lachlan says under his breath.

Yeah. I can't explain the urgent drum beat deep inside me, but this is a now or never thing, and I don't ever want to say never to Ellie.

24

ELLIE

GAVIN'S HOCKEY games are at the Sensplex in the suburbs, so I've got time after my yoga class to take a long, hot shower and browse through the shop at the front of the store. When his car pulls up, I dash out.

Lachlan barely makes it around to get the door for me.

"In a hurry?" he asks, his eyes lingering on my face as he waits for my answer.

I laugh. "Shush. Secrets, remember?"

"Indeed."

"You're working non-stop lately," I say as he pulls open the door and gestures for me to get in.

"I wouldn't call today work, Ms. Montague."

Weird.

Gavin reaches for me and tugs me in close as Lachlan closes the door behind us. We're alone for a second and his mouth covers mine, his fingers tracing the shape of my face as he gives me a searing kiss hello.

"Good game?" I ask breathlessly when Lachlan takes his place in the driver's seat again.

Gavin nods. "Yeah. How was your yoga...game?"

"Practice." I lace my fingers through his and lean back against the seat. He reaches across me and grabs my seat belt. I could do it myself, but somehow he makes this hotter.

Lachlan is watching in the rearview mirror as Gavin tugs the belt across my torso, buckling me up before he runs his hand back up the part that crosses my chest. He settles the canvas right between my breasts.

"What are you doing?" I whisper.

He grins. "Is Lachlan watching?"

I glance at the front again. Our gazes meet in the mirror and Lachlan winks.

"You know he is," I whisper to Gavin.

"Good. Let's have some fun."

Fun. That's a loaded term.

I want to tell him this is a mistake. He's misread me or I was just talking last night, but beneath my light top, my nipples are hard and the thought of Gavin's chief of security watching us do something, anything...it turns me on.

There's nothing wrong with this.

Doubt wars with hot, hungry desire as I search Gavin's face for that reassurance. But it's really gotta come from inside me. My hands slick with perspiration and I press them to the skirt I changed into after my shower.

Easy access for Gavin.

Now the way his fingers are circling on my knee and onto my thigh, I'm realizing the error in my judgement.

Too easy.

I'm too easy.

God, I'm going to let him touch me and Lachlan's going to watch, and no, that isn't making me wet.

I'm soaked.

Like, these panties are toast.

I'm easy and a liar.

"Fun?" I ask on a quick exhale, turning my face toward Gavin.

"We've got some ground rules," he says, but not quietly. He's not hiding this conversation from Lachlan.

They have ground rules. For me. The *we* in that sentence is my boyfriend and his security officer.

"Do you?" I arch my eyebrows, but I'm not kidding anyone in this car. My nipples are on board, my panties are soaked, and I'm pretty sure both of them can smell my arousal. My red cheeks are totally betraying my lofty questioning of this plan.

"You've got your safewords, Sprite."

I nod my head. "You're in charge?"

"Always."

"Then I'm yours, Sir."

His palm glides up my inner thigh as his lips caress the outer curve of my ear. "Think you can come by the time we get home?"

We're only two blocks away. "Ahhh…"

"Imagine Lachlan's hands on your breasts as I lick your pussy. His cock sliding into your mouth as I fuck you from behind, just like that video we watched last night."

My eyelids flutter shut as he rubs his thumb over my clit through my panties.

The car slides to a halt.

My eyes snap open and I see we're pulling through the gates at 24 Sussex.

Gavin tugs my underwear down my hips. My gaze flies to the rearview mirror, but Lachlan's busy driving.

Am I disappointed? I don't have any time to process that before Gavin smooths my skirt back in place. Then he brushes his mouth against my ear. "Time's up, Sprite. Now you have to wait."

Lachlan smothers a laugh from the front seat—so he'd been paying attention even as he was parking the car—and Gavin takes my hand, kissing my knuckles as I glower at him.

"I'm sorry. There wasn't enough time." His eyes glint with mischief, though. He doesn't mean it. He could make me come in ten seconds if he wanted to.

He presses my palm to his erection, and I stroke the length of him. He's rock hard. He wants this as much as I do.

I give him a flirty look from beneath my eyelashes. "Maybe I'll torture you when we get inside."

"Please do."

He holds me close as Lachlan lets us in and turns off the alarm.

Then Gavin leads us upstairs. Not to his room, but the other end of the second floor, to a room I've never been in before.

It's a space designed for entertaining, with couches and chairs on every wall, even in front of the bookcases that line one end and around the fireplace at the other.

Has 24 Sussex ever seen this kind of entertaining before?

Probably. My world view is rapidly morphing.

Lachlan sits on a wide chair. Gavin points me to a couch on the opposite wall, but stays standing. He looks back at our guest. "Drink?" Lachlan gives him a look and Gavin rolls his eyes. "*One* drink. To be social. We all know the limits here."

"Sure, I'll take a beer."

"Sprite?"

"A beer sounds great. But I can get it."

"Stay, please." He leans over and kisses me, a rough and possessive burn across my mouth that leaves my lips tingling. "Be right back. And while I'm gone, I want you to keep your thighs spread. Just enough to make Lachlan's mouth water, wondering what's under your skirt."

"Gavin…" I touch his cheek.

His gaze is steady. "Yes, Sprite?"

Maybe if he'd used my name, I'd have questioned him here. Is this insane? But everything about us is insane. So I just smile and say, "Hurry back."

"This is still you and me." He rubs his thumb against the corner of my mouth and I lick at it. He groans. "Lachlan's game to be an extra pair of hands to help me blow your mind. That's all."

I watch him leave. He changed into jeans and a t-shirt after the game, and both fit him like a glove. The sight of him leaving a room is very distracting.

It takes me a minute to turn my attention to the other man in the room. When I do, Lachlan is just watching me.

"What?"

"The PM has taken me into his confidence with this, and I will never betray that, Ellie."

"Thank you." I twist my fingers together. "You've done this before?"

He leans back in his chair. "I have."

"That's good."

He grins. "I hope it is. I'll do my best."

Before I can answer, Gavin's back. He hands Lachlan one of the three bottles of beer he's carrying, then crosses to me and gives me another kiss before pressing my own beer into my hand.

"Talk about anything interesting while I was gone?" He winks at me as he paces backwards toward the fireplace.

We've got a triangle going on now, and the electricity is arcing back and forth. Mostly between Gavin and me—I want him back over here, beside me. I'm always greedy for him.

And he wants me to be patient.

To take the anticipation and let it brew into something I've never experienced before.

"Lachlan just told me that he's done this before, too." I take a sip of beer, grateful for the cold, bitter liquid sliding down my throat before I look back at the RCMP officer. "I'm assuming Gavin told you this is my first threesome."

"And likely your last," Gavin says. "So I want to make it a good one." I'm still a little surprised, but he set this up. And the bulge in his jeans says he likes it.

I take another sip of beer, watching him over the bottle. "I have no doubt you will."

"Maybe it's not exactly a threesome," Lachlan offers, putting down his beer. I don't think he's touched it. "Think of it as more of a two-four. Two guys, four hands. Double your pleasure."

"But it can't be all about me," I say, restlessly shifting my legs together.

Gavin snaps a look at my thighs and I spread them again. *Good girl*, he mouths. Heat spirals up the inside of my torso.

"Why don't you tell me the rules you both agreed on, then? Touching is okay?"

Lachlan slides his attention down my body. "I can't touch everything. But I can look all you want."

"Show him more, if you want," Gavin says softly from where he's leaning back against the bookcase. "You're beautiful. I want you to feel worshipped. But your pussy is mine."

I blush. He hesitates, and I fill in the rest with a guess. "Lachlan gets the top half?"

They both chuckle and I relax.

Gavin nods. "And we're going to keep this light. I'll give you anything you want, Sprite. But we might need to get creative in how some things happen."

"My…mouth?"

He grins. "We can put that to good use. If you want to. But don't kiss Lachlan there. That's mine, too."

I give him a surprised look and he just shrugs unapologetically. I don't care. I'm kind of blown away that this is happening in any way, shape, or form.

"Enough talking. Show Lachlan what you're hiding under your skirt."

My thighs tense up and I curl my fingers into the fabric of my skirt. Another inch or two and he'd be able to see all of me.

He *will* be able to see all of me soon enough.

I take a deep breath and shimmy the hem all the way to my hips. Gavin groans and I look over at him. His erection is bigger now, pressing against the front of his jeans, and my mouth waters.

"Want a taste?"

I lift my eyes up to meet his and nod.

"Of me?" Always. "Or of Lachlan?"

A flood of moisture makes my legs tremble. "Yes, Sir. Both of you."

"At the same time?" He raises one eyebrow and I blush.

"If you like."

"I just might." He rubs his jaw. "But Lachlan's our guest. Why don't you go over there and thank him for playing with us?"

I take one last sip of beer and stand, my skirt swinging to cover my thighs again.

Maybe they both expect me to drop to my knees when I stop in front of Lachlan, but that's not what I want to do first.

And if this is all about me…I want to tease my boyfriend a little. "You get the top half?" I ask Lachlan as I tug at the bottom of my shirt.

He nods slowly.

I reach out and run my hand through his hair, then down his cheek. I can practically hear Gavin vibrating from the other side of the room. *Come closer. Take me.*

"No kissing," Lachlan he reminds me under his breath.

"Is that your rule or his?" I whisper.

"We agree on it." He gives me an easy smile. "But I'm happy to hold you in my arms. Get my mouth on those nipples that keep teasing me from inside your shirt."

"Want me to take it off?"

He glances at his boss.

I don't. I want to, but I'm going to spend most of this afternoon watching Gavin to make sure I don't go too far. Some things need to be okay because I say they're okay.

"Yeah. Take off your shirt." His voice gets a little husky, and I like that.

I bite my lip and lift one leg, brushing my knee against his as I lean in. I hesitate for a second, then set it on the couch beside his hip. I'm straddling one of his thighs now.

He's different from Gavin. More laid-back, a totally different personality type. But up close, there are similarities, too, especially in their looks, which I never noticed before. His brown hair has fewer gold highlights. His blue eyes aren't quite as piercing.

He doesn't make my heart race.

That power solely belongs to the man across the room.

But he's good looking, and kind, and against my thigh, I can feel the start of an erection. Again, nothing like Gavin's

—and that's okay. I cross my arms between us and grab the hem of my shirt, tugging it up my body.

Lachlan groans quietly as I set my hands on his shoulders and swing my other leg up so I'm fully straddling his body now. Under my skirt I'm naked, but his hands stay on top of the fabric. He touches my hips, my waist, then strokes my bare sides. Up and down. Closer to my breasts on each pass.

"Ellie…" Gavin warns from behind me. He's nearer to us now.

I glance back at him. He's in the middle of the room. "When you said thank him, did you have something specific in mind…Sir?"

He laughs. "On your knees."

"No lap dances?"

He gives me his sternest Dom face and I squeak. It's a role-play in a way, because that's not really us, but I think it works for Lachlan. But being caught between a Dom and his sub might just be Lachlan's happy place from the way his cock is swelling beneath me.

I twist around, pressing back into Lachlan's chest as I perch in his lap and give Gavin the show I think he's been waiting for—his girlfriend, topless in the arms of another man. But a man that works for him. A man who will hold me down, maybe even cover my mouth on his boss's orders…

"You want me to give Lachlan a blow job?" I say with a gasp. I squeeze Lachlan's thighs at the same time. He takes the hint and starts stroking my body again, going around my breasts but not touching them yet.

He won't do that without an express order, I suddenly realize.

"You did say that you wanted to…" he trails off and puts his hands on his hips. "Don't be rude, Sprite."

I turn again, slowly this time. Lachlan catches the fabric of my skirt and holds on as I sink to my knees, baring me from behind for Gavin.

I look up at him. Our co-conspirator in this fantasy game.

His gaze is warm, but not predatory. He's a man, and I'm a woman on my knees for him, so there's a basic chemistry thing going on, but he's no threat to Gavin.

Is that a deliberate thing he's doing? Ensuring that Gavin knows he's the alpha?

"Thank you, Lachlan," I say as I rub my hand against the front of his jeans. I get an eager pulse in response. He's thick and getting thicker. This is promising. I flip open the button on his jeans and unzip him. He's wearing utilitarian white boxer briefs underneath. "You forgot your kinky black leather outfit."

Apparently snarky is one way I cope with being nervous now. It's better than my usual awkward silence. Look at me growing as an individual.

"This was an unexpected turn of events." His lips quirk.

Behind me, Gavin clears his throat.

Lachlan gives me a *you're-in-trouble* look that makes me wiggle my butt. Gavin doesn't take the bait, so I lean in and kiss Lachlan's erection through the fabric. He smells shower clean and totally masculine beneath that.

I loop my fingers under the elastic, then bat my eyelashes at him. "I have my shirt off. You should take yours off, too."

Gavin wouldn't fall for that trick. I can't flirt my way into getting him to do anything. He's always in charge.

Lachlan's eager to please, though.

I grin. This is going to be fun. He peels off his t-shirt and I take a second to admire the hard planes of his chest and the delicious line of crinkly hair running the centre of his torso before I follow it under the elastic and wrap my hand around his bare cock.

He jerks at my touch and I stroke him firmly. He doesn't give up pre-come as easily as Gavin does, so after shooting a quick glance over my shoulder to make sure this is still cool, I lower my head and slide my tongue along his slit.

Fascinating. I shouldn't be thinking this much, but this isn't Gavin, so I can have a bit of distance here. I've never tasted two dicks in such close proximity before. And if I play my cards right, maybe in a minute I'll get to taste them at the same time.

And Lachlan tastes good. His broad head feels the same sliding into my mouth. He grunts when swallowed, too.

Fascinating.

I take my time and lavish him with attention, scraping my nails up and down his jean-covered thighs with one hand while I slowly jerk him against my tongue with the other. I let it get a little sloppy, filling the quiet room with the wet slapping of my hand and the slurp of my mouth.

I feel Gavin's hand near the back of my head before he gathers my hair and slows my movements. "Good girl," he praises me, and I beam up at Lachlan, then at Gavin as Lachlan turns me on my knees.

Gavin's already unzipping. "Cup her breasts," he says. "She likes more of a tug than a pinch, but you'll want to warm her up first."

He slides his cock into my mouth, deeper and harder than I took Lachlan. And I can taste him already spilling his pre-come on my tongue.

Yes. He surges in and out of me as Lachlan holds me tight, not letting me chase Gavin as he pulls away. But he comes back, each time harder and faster, until he spills himself down my throat with more force than I expected.

I swallow every drop, then lick my lips when he eases out of my mouth.

Softly, he smiles down at me at the same time as he reaches for my hand. "Up you get, Sprite. Time to get you all the way naked."

Lachlan's legs spread out on either side of mine as I stand sandwiched between Gavin and the couch. My skirt has an elastic waist and Gavin drops it to the ground quickly, palming my ass as he hauls me against him and kisses me deeply.

Between our bodies, I can feel him thickening again.

"Time to take this party to a bed that I can tie you to," he growls.

His bed? With Lachlan? "Are you sure?"

He swings me into his arms, his cock bobbing heavy and proud against my bottom. "Hell, yes. The more hands the better for what I've got in mind."

I giggle as he carries me to the master suite, but my gleeful laughter turns to eager sighs when he lays me on the bed. He covers me with his body. He's still dressed, except his jeans are undone and his cock is pulsing against my sex.

"Here's what we're going to do, Sprite." He brushes an errant lock of my hair off my face as he gazes down at me. "You wanted me to tie you to the bed."

"Yes…"

He grins at how eager I sound. "So Lachlan's going to put some cuffs on you now."

I gasp as I feel a second pair of hands on my left thigh, but the touch is quick and efficient, and replaced by something soft above my knee. Gavin's kissing me so I can't see where Lachlan's going, but then he repeats the action on the other side. This time, there's a gentle tug, too.

"You'll have to move," Lachlan says to Gavin, clear amusement in his voice.

Gavin just winks at me as he leaps off the bed and tucks his erection away. He has the energy of a twenty-year-old amped up on Red Bull. I don't immediately register the fact that the "cuffs" he mentioned are on my legs—obviously—but they're also attached to the bedposts.

My mouth drops open.

I don't know what I was expecting. Maybe rope around my ankles or something. But when they tighten these ropes, it's going to pull my legs wide apart. Like, too far apart. Unless he means for me to bend my legs, which would be…revealing.

I guess that's the point.

"Uh…guys?"

Meanwhile, they're standing there discussing their handiwork. I shift a little closer to the foot of the bed. Maybe they'll do my arms next.

"What's next?"

Gavin just grins.

Lachlan nods and moves around behind me. "What's next," he says, as he climbs onto the bed, "is I'm going to hold you while the prime minister fucks you silly."

I laugh because it's too much. But he's not kidding. He slides his big body around me, surprisingly gentle and nimble as he gets himself in place, then he puts his hands under my legs and…folds me. Into a V. Gavin tightens first one rope, then the other, back and forth until I'm strung tight between the bed posts and right on the edge of the bed.

Like, if Lachlan wasn't behind me, I'd fall off.

Of course, if Lachlan wasn't behind me, I'd be lying down to prevent falling off the bed. I'm clever like that.

Gavin strips off his clothes and prowls towards us, a perfect specimen of testosterone and masculinity. He steps right up to my body.

Oh. I see. My breath catches in my throat as he dances his fingertips down my torso, over the folds of my belly—this is not a flattering position in my opinion, but from the erection behind me and the one bobbing in front of me, I don't think they agree—and finally, *finally* through the slickness between my legs.

Lachlan's hands slide over my breasts again, his fingers going faster for my nipples this time. I whine a little as he finds that edge of pleasure and pain. He doesn't know my body like Gavin does, but he figures it out quickly, and as Gavin slips a third finger inside me and rocks his thumb against my clit, I slide sideways into an unexpected orgasm.

My legs yank hard against the cuffs, velcro straining—but holding—and Lachlan tightens his grip on me as I shake in his arms.

Gavin doesn't stop. He drops to his knees and holds me open so he can lick me, softly but thoroughly, until I imagine he's sucked up every last drop of my come.

When he stands again, he's got a condom on and he crowds against me, hard. Lachlan doesn't move.

Gavin rubs the thick head of his cock through my swollen folds. I want to rock into him but I can't move—at all. I try, and Lachlan just holds me tighter.

"So, so pretty like this," Gavin says, his voice thick with lust. "Bound and held for me."

I moan as he enters me, just the tip, but every nerve ending is firing off as he pumps his hips, working his way inside. His third thrust feels like he's bottomed out, but when I look down, he's not buried inside me.

"You're too big," I whisper, which is ridiculous. He's big and he fills me up in the most delicious way, but he's not *too* anything. He's perfect for me.

"Just the position, Sprite." He smooths his hands down the backs of my thighs. "Shhh. That's a good girl."

I don't know what he's talking about. I'm not doing anything. But as his hands grip my bottom and adjust my position, he pushes a little further and I cry out, because *ohmygod* he's found the magic button.

"Again," I plead, and he rocks over that same spot as he pulses his body, in and out, in and out. Each time, I beg him to get back inside me and he does.

Over and over again, until a heat starts to build inside me. Restless, consuming heat. I bite my lip and Gavin says to Lachlan, "Give her something to suck on. Your fingers."

Behind me he shifts his position a little so he can keep one arm around my torso. His other hand strokes across my neck, then he rubs his middle finger against my lower lip. I lick at it, greedy and lusty and out of my mind. Yes, I want Lachlan's fingers in my mouth. I want Gavin's cock in my pussy and—

Oh.

Oh, he's magic. Gavin shifts one of his hands and a finger finds my rear hole.

That's rapidly becoming my favourite thing and I don't even think I'm blushing over that realization.

In and out. Here and there, and *there*. Pushing and pumping, filling and sliding, until that fire inside is an inferno and I don't even think there's an end to it, I can't see how I'm going to come like this, it's too intense too much too…

"I've got you," Gavin says, and I'm falling, tilt-a-whirling into space, but he does have me, and it's okay, because his mouth is on mine and Lachlan's moving.

"Don't go," I whimper. I need to thank him again.

I reach for him and he holds my hand as Gavin kisses me, long and slow, laying me back against the bed. Lachlan gets the leg cuffs off me, then Gavin's above me again.

"You okay?"

"I'm fine." I give him a shaky smile. "What happened?"

"You blacked out. It happens sometimes."

"I missed that part of the in-flight safety presentation," I mutter, closing my eyes again.

Gavin tells Lachlan to go get me some juice.

"My beer would be great," I add, but I don't think they're listening again.

I curl into Gavin's chest and he strokes my back and my hair. It takes me a minute to realize he's holding a piece of chocolate for me. "This is better than your beer," he says, and I open for him. He places it on my tongue and I close my eyes, curling into him again.

In the quiet, Gavin murmurs to me. Nice things about how hot that was, how pretty I am, and I slowly calm down.

Lachlan brings an entire snack tray that I'm not interested in, but I grab his hand and pull him onto the bed with us.

"So that was a two-four."

Gavin laughs and kisses my shoulder. "Apparently."

"And I'm a fuckerette."

Lachlan's face is priceless when I say that. It gets even better when Gavin sagely affirms it. "You definitely are."

"We need our own dictionary," I muse, and that's probably the crazy rush of endorphins talking, but I like the sound of it.

Lachlan chokes on a cough. "Excuse me?"

"Can you imagine if we published it?" I say breezily. "Bestseller, guaranteed. Especially with a foreword by the prime minister."

Gavin just laughs, and tugs me close again, holding me until I stop being silly, and then he tells me we should shower.

I tilt my head toward Lachlan. "You want to join us?"

The poor guy didn't even get fully naked. Or come. But he just shakes his head. "You go on without me."

I roll back toward Gavin and slide my arms around his neck. "Okay, Sir. Time to get me all squeaky clean."

25

GAVIN

OUR ROOM IS empty by the time Ellie and I are finished in the shower and I'm relieved. Sharing Ellie didn't sit right with me. But I'd set it up—I had to own it. I could have denied her, but that wasn't right either. It was something I'd experienced, and who was I to refuse her fantasy because of my own selfish feelings?

We both dress, because as much as I'd like her to, Ellie can't stay over on a Sunday night.

Just one of the many inconveniences of a kinky clandestine workplace affair with your subordinate.

"Lachlan will drive you home, Sprite." This makes me uncomfortable, but it's the only realistic option. I should have given this threesome business way more thought.

Her wide grin gives me a glimmer of hope that she's handling this better than I am. "Yeah, I guess a taxi might not be a wise choice."

We head downstairs and grab a bite to eat while we wait for Lachlan.

When he lets himself back in, it's as if nothing

happened. As if he doesn't know what Ellie sounds like when she comes.

And I know that's truly how it is for him, because it's been that way for me in the past. Just a fuck between friends, meaning nothing once it was done.

I've shared women.

I've been the third.

I've never shared a woman that owns a piece of my soul, though. And I think it took sharing Ellie to show me just how stupid I've been.

She has no idea. She kisses me and ducks out the door like our afternoon was a few hours of kinky fuckery.

Well of course she does. That's what I've told her, over and over again.

———

LATER THAT NIGHT, I'm unable to sleep. My bed feels empty—wrong—when she's not in it and I find that worrisome. I shouldn't be this attached. Maybe she's right and we should slow things down.

The threesome weighs heavily on my mind as well. It would have been better with someone more peripheral to our lives. I can't exactly request a new chief of security because I'm regretting my decision to bring him in as a third. It was a poor proximity choice on my part. He's not distant enough to allow us—me—space to process, and not close enough where processing isn't necessary.

My alarm wakes me up at four and I'm a mess. I have no idea when I finally fell asleep, but I was still awake at one-forty-three. I stumble out of bed and head to the kitchen in search of coffee.

Lachlan is already there, sitting at the table. He takes a

sip from the mug in his hand, then sets it on the table. "You look like shit. There's coffee in the pot."

"Yeah, well you're not looking so good yourself. Did you get any sleep?"

"Some. Which is usually worse than none."

I grab a mug from the cupboard and pour myself some coffee before joining him at the table.

"We okay?"

"We will be."

"How was she on the ride home?"

"Quiet. We both were."

I should have called her. Or texted. But what was I supposed to say? Tip-toeing around conversations because they might be listened in on is becoming more and more frustrating. "But she seemed okay?"

"This isn't fucking high school. You want an answer, go to the source."

"I'm sorry, Lachlan. For everything. I put us all in a really awkward position and it was irresponsible of me."

"We were all consenting adults participating in a mutually enjoyable activity. We need to own that and move on. Wasting time on regrets does more harm than good."

"This from the man who had a disturbed night's sleep."

"Who said my lack of sleep was from regret?"

"Was it?"

"No. I'd say it was more…reflection."

"And…?"

"And what? You want to know where I'm at? I'm still figuring it out. But I do know I can keep my professional life completely separate from my sex life." He gives me a pointed look and I get it.

But it doesn't stop me pushing. "If you want to take the day off, I'm sure someone can switch shifts with you."

"Are you taking the day off? Is Ellie?"

"No."

"Then why would I?"

To give me some fucking space. But he's right and I have to acknowledge that. "Fair point."

"Look, I get that you need to sort through your feelings about all this, but I'm not going to make changes to your protection detail just because you're suffering some emotional discomfort."

"I wasn't asking you to. I just thought…"

"You just thought you'd take my shitty night's sleep and use it as an excuse to create some distance. If you want distance, then request a new security chief. Otherwise, trust me to do my job."

"Dammit, Lachlan, I need…" I drag my fingers through my hair.

"Most of your day is already happening in your office. Get Beth to rearrange your schedule so you don't have to go anywhere. That will keep me out of your way for the whole day."

I relax a little. I'm making this bigger than it needs to be.

SHORTLY AFTER TWO THAT AFTERNOON, I stop myself from calling Ellie and ordering her to my office. Same as I've done in between every meeting I've had so far today. I've also ducked three of her calls on my office line. I have no idea if she's used our burner phones, because I left mine at home so I wouldn't be tempted. I'm grateful she hasn't come to my office, because there's no *send to voicemail* option for that.

I'm being a coward, I know. But I don't know how else to slow things down. When I hear her voice, I want her right there with me. And when she's with me, I want to touch and kiss her. Everywhere. There is no slow and easy when we're together. It's all or nothing.

Ellie walks into my office on Tuesday afternoon and shuts the door.

"Did you decide that we were in fact taking things slow and easy?"

"I don't know what you mean."

"Oh come off it, Gavin. All weekend you were all up in my grill, among other places, and couldn't get enough. Then come Monday it's like you've got no time for me. Not, I'm busy being Prime Minister no time, but I've made a huge mistake no time."

"Ellie, I have a lot going on—"

"It's because of the threesome isn't it?" Her face pinches tight. "I let Lachlan touch me and now you want nothing to do with me because I'm—"

Oh fuck. My first thought is she's suffering from subdrop and I did nothing to mitigate it. And maybe she is to some degree, but there's something more going on. "Enough. It's got nothing to do with what went on this weekend. That was consensual, and you were beautiful." And I'll never let her know it made me feel uneasy.

"I did some thinking. You were right. I've been taking risks that neither of us can afford and decided it was best to dial things back." It's not exactly best, but it's all we can do. I hate this, but we don't have time to get into it now.

"You decided? Really? You? Last I checked there were two of us involved, so where do you get off making decisions about our relationship without me? After you got all hurt when I said exactly the same thing."

Exactly. She was the one who originally brought up taking things slow and easy. I don't say that, though.

Because I'm responsible for my own behaviour and I will never turn anything back on her to get the upper hand.

And because I'm so scared of fucking this up—I'm totally fucking this up. I move towards her and she backs away. Not good. "I'm sorry. I had planned to talk about it with you tonight—"

She cuts me off. "How very fucking convenient. You know what? Fuck you. I don't need this."

"Ellie, I—" She rips open my door and I rush after her as she storms out of my office.

I can't stop her and when I burst through into the outer office, Beth is staring at Lachlan, hurt written all over her face as she grabs her purse from her desk. I turn my head. Lachlan's skin is bright red and he looks ready to explode.

He rises from his chair and points to my office.

26

ELLIE

You know you've hit a low point when you hide in a washroom stall.

I can't go to my desk, because I share that space with the other junior staffers. I don't want to leave the building, even to go over to Langevin Block, because that would feel too much like a temper tantrum.

We are not toddlers.

We might be acting like them, but deep down, we're grown-ups and we'll figure this out.

Until *I* figure out how that might happen, I'm hiding.

The door to the washroom squeaks as someone comes in and I silently groan. The only thing worse than being a chicken is being a chicken caught out as a creepy hider in the washroom.

But whoever comes in doesn't use the stall beside me. She just turns on the water for a minute, then turns it off and sighs.

Then she sniffles.

Damn it. Nobody needs me listening to their sadness.

217

"Pull it together, Beth," she mutters, and my eyes go wide. "He's so not worth it."

Beth? My stomach does a plummeting drop to the basement. Oh God.

Oh my fucking God.

I jerk the door open and she whirls around.

"You can't say anything—" I burst out as she gapes at me.

"I didn't know you were in here," she says at the same time.

"I'm sorry. I was hiding. I'm sorry. I'm so sorry. Please don't say anything. I didn't know…I thought your relationship was strictly professional."

"It is." She wipes her nose. "Don't worry about it."

But I do, because the only thing worse than breaking news about the PM and his intern is a sordid love triangle between the PM, his intern and his secretary. "I don't know what to say. I…nobody knows. Stew doesn't know. I mean, Lachlan knows, obviously, but it just happened—"

"Stop. I don't want any details of what you did."

My cheeks go up in flames. "I wasn't going to give details."

"I just never thought that Lachlan…" she trails off.

I blink. "Lachlan?"

She makes a face. "Yeah. Stupid, right?"

"No, not at all." Relief rushes through me, fast and sweet. Oh, Lachlan. *Oh, for fuck's sake, Lachlan, you idiot.* And also, still double-shit on her overhearing anything, but this is fixable. "Not stupid in the least, Beth. I thought you were talking about Gavin."

She gives me an alarmed look. "Gavin. Oh. No."

"Right." Because lusting after the PM…now that would be stupid. Sigh. "I don't know what you heard, but I think you might have the wrong idea about what happened."

Her look shifts to fragile wariness and I want to give her a hug, but now is not the time for assuming any liberties with regard to friendship and boundaries.

"Gavin and me…it's complicated. But it's just the two of us."

"I heard you," she says quietly. "Don't lie to me."

"You heard heated words in the middle of a fight. And that was so unprofessional of me, I can't even begin to apologize. I'm so sorry. Nobody knows. And it's stupid of us, we both know that. But you have to know, we fought it. We still are, hence the fight."

"Far be it from me to give you relationship advice, but a threesome with his security chief is not a great way to start a relationship."

No kidding. The floor could open up and swallow me now, please. But it doesn't and even if she hates me, I need to clear that up. "It wasn't really a threesome. It was probably stupid and a bad idea, definitely, but it wasn't whatever you're thinking."

"You don't even want to know what I'm thinking." She makes a face. "I thought Lachlan was straight-laced. I thought he was too square to have an office romance."

"That's something you should probably talk to him about directly. But…" How do I walk this line without betraying either man? They're big boys. They can handle Beth having a little knowledge. "Beth, I'm going to tell you something that needs to stay between us. I'm trusting you here, because I know that Gavin trusts you. Okay?"

Her lips pull tight, but she nods. "I'd never betray him. Whatever you do privately is your own business."

If only the rest of the world were that understanding. "Gavin's more experienced than I am, and we got carried away. Lachlan's similarly experienced. Gavin trusts him, too. So he asked Lachlan to help him set something up. What we did wasn't for his pleasure."

"That won't make the encounter any less scandalous if it comes out," she mutters, but her shoulders relax.

"I know. But right now, I don't care about a public scandal. I care about the fact that we've hurt your feelings."

"I have no claim on him," she whispers. But she wants to, and oh, I know that ache.

She gives me a rueful smile that doesn't go anywhere near her eyes, then presses her hands together as she glances back at the mirror. A professional mask slides back into place as she straightens her shoulders. "Well, better get back to it."

Inside, I tremble with relief. She's not going to be inviting me out for drinks again any time soon, but she's not going to share what she overheard, either.

I wait another minute after she leaves, then duck out myself. When I get to my desk, there's an email update from Lachlan, sent to the entire PMO staff, that Gavin's left the building for the day.

***

WEDNESDAY I WORK at Langevin Block.

Thursday I work at Centre Block and make it through the seven a.m. briefing without once looking Gavin squarely in the face.

I'm relieved when the student health clinic calls at noon and tells me I can come in to get the results of my physical. I went in last week while Gavin was in Europe, thinking that maybe we could ditch the condoms.

Ha. Now I wish I could seriously consider ditching him.

Love is awful.

But once we get past this, whatever *this* is, ditching condoms will be a fun surprise for him.

I pop my head into Stew's office to tell him I've got a doctor's appointment. He gives me a distracted wave as he's on the phone, so I let his secretary know instead and head out.

While I'm on campus, I stop in to chat with my advisor about the course I'll be teaching in the fall and a conference he wants me to attend in September. Then I run into Sasha and we grab coffee, so it's nearly five by the time I'm back at the office, takeout dinner in hand.

I could have just taken the afternoon, but my summary notes won't write themselves, and the report I'm reading is fascinating. So I dig in, and the next thing I know it's getting dark outside.

People head out, and I try to tell myself that I should do the same, but the truth is that I don't want to go home.

As the last of the junior staffers who I share my space with leaves, I give a half-hearted glance toward my bag, then open another report.

The soft creak of the elevator doors opening grabs my attention a while later. It's followed by footsteps I can hear because suddenly the entire floor is silent, and I find myself holding my breath.

A soft conversation happens between people, then nothing.

I look down at the report I'm supposed to be summarizing a response to and tell myself it's not him. And if it is, I don't want him to know I'm here.

I'm such a liar.

My desk is halfway down the office, a good distance from the door. Two other desks now sit empty, and when he appears in the doorway, that gap between us somehow makes the moment more intimate.

We're extra alone. My pulse picks up.

"You disappeared this afternoon," he says quietly after glancing over his shoulder.

"I had a doctor's appointment."

He moves closer, leaving the door open behind him. "What's wrong?"

"Nothing." I push back from my desk and cross my legs. His gaze tracks the movement. I'm such a total fucking liar. The skirt I'm wearing, the fuck-me heels…at least part of me wanted him to come find me. "It was just a follow-up."

"For what reason?"

But not all of me is ready to forgive and forget. "Maybe that's none of your business," I snap.

A muscle twitches in his jaw. "Is that right?"

No. I hate fighting with him. I sigh. "I had a full work-up last week. Physical. Blood tests." All clear.

He nods, his jaw tightening as his eyes bore into me. "And you got the results today."

"Yes."

He slowly unbuttons his jacket as he looks right into the heart of me. "My office. Now."

"Gavin!"

"No, Sprite. When I tell you *my office, now*, the answer is…?"

"Yes, Sir." The rational part of my brain is screaming right now. Really? We're not going to talk this out like adults? But my inner submissive just let out the breath she'd been holding for like three days, so I'm not taking it back.

I stand up.

"Good girl." He steps closer. His eyes are glittering. "Do you need to see my last physical? I'm sure it's on record around here somewhere."

I shake my head.

"Then you'd best be moving quickly."

I slide past him and head into the hall.

Lachlan is standing at the elevators, facing away from us, and I suddenly realize the entire office suite has been cleared.

Oh. Shit.

Gavin's office door is open and I walk straight in.

He follows, closing the door with an ominous click. My nipples love that click.

"Bend over the desk," he says. The rustle of fabric tells me he's taken off his jacket.

"Gavin…"

"Say stop or no, or bend your ass over my desk."

I walk forward on shaky legs, painfully, deliciously aware of the slide of my skirt against my legs, the slickness already painting the tops of my inner thighs, and his gaze, hot on my back. Setting my palms against the edge of his desk, I hinge forward at the hips, slow and controlled, until I'm bent at ninety degrees and my ass is stretching the confines of my skirt. My heels come off the floor as I settle, and I ignore the stretch across the bottom of my feet as I press onto tiptoes.

"Oh, Ellie, what you do to me…" He paces forward, bumping me into the desk.

I hold still.

He fists his hand in my hair and turns my head, pressing my cheek against the desk. I suck in a shaky breath as he folds himself over my right side, hot and heavy, and nips at my ear. "When were you going to tell me that we don't need to use condoms?"

"When we were actually speaking to each other."

"We're talking now."

"Does this count as talking? Because I have some things to say—"

His hand lands sharp on my left butt cheek. I gasp and drag in another breath as he smooths his palm over the same spot. "Too late."

That one swat against my bottom has my blood churning, and I press my body against the desk, trying to keep control. My breasts ache and my thighs want to spread wide. I bite my lip to keep from begging him for more.

"The last time you were in here, Ellie, you were very rude to me."

"I'm sorry," I pant.

"And now tonight you tell me something that makes it very difficult to take anything—" *smack* "slow—" *smack* "and easy."

"Ahhh!"

"So what should I do to you, Sprite? What will correct this misbehaviour?" He yanks up my skirt, baring my basic white cotton panties. I flush with heated embarrassment as I remember pulling them on this morning.

His fingers trace along the elastic waistband. *Pull them down.* But he doesn't. He just touches me, gently, all the way across my lower back.

Smack.

I cry out again and my legs, now free, spread apart as I press onto my toes, presenting myself shamelessly for another.

"Fifty-four hours since you stormed out of my office, Sprite."

I can see where he's going with this. Eeek. My thighs tighten up. No, no, no…

"Can you take that many strikes?"

"Yes, Sir." What? Who said that?

He's tracing one of the leg holes now, his finger sliding off the elastic and onto my butt cheek as he follows the curving line closer to where my legs meet. "Good girl."

And just like that, I'm eager and pliant again, getting wetter by the second.

He pulls his fingers off my skin before he gets to my swollen sex and rains a series of gentle blows on my backside instead. None of them hurt, and by the tenth one, I'm rocking into them.

I'm warm and ready for more. "Please..." I plead. "Harder."

He presses his hand between my shoulder blades, stilling my body. "Forty more to go, Sprite. You don't want them harder yet."

Yes I do. But I swallow the whine, because I don't want to talk back.

He tugs my underwear between my cheeks, pulling the gusset tight against my clit, and baring more flesh at the same time. "You're strong and brave, though, wanting more."

He slaps my bare skin, where it's already warm and I'm sure quite pink, and the next five taps are sharper.

"Ow," I gasp, but the complaint turns to a throaty moan as he shoves his hand between my legs and rocks his fingers hard over my pussy, holding them flat as he gives my clit the attention it's been aching for since he stepped into my office.

Even through my underwear I know he can tell how wet I am, and he's breathing hard as he pulls away.

"Thirty-five," he grunts. "Thirty-four..." Each whack lands in a different place. Some are softer and others sting, but after each one a lovely warmth blooms deep inside me, each time bigger and brighter than the last.

When he gets to the last ten, he drops to his knees behind me and tugs my panties down my thighs. My shoes slip off my feet as he discards my underwear and my toes barely touch the floor without them.

Gavin doesn't give me a chance to find my balance again before he leans in and licks through on my soaking wet pussy, swirling the tip of his tongue around my clit twice before sucking it into his mouth. The sweet tug is almost more than I can bear.

"Ahhhhh!" I cry out, so close to coming, but I can't, I can't, I can't…

Then his mouth is gone, and I don't. Disoriented, I scramble to catch my breath.

"So good, my Sprite," he says as he kisses the back of my shaking thigh, right below the first of his many marks that start right at the top of my leg and fan across my entire backside. "Thank you for controlling yourself."

A shudder wracks through me at his praise and I grin to myself.

"Ten more, baby. Then you can come."

His fingers trail over my sensitive skin, then lift away for just a second before flicking back. Barely a tap, but it's overwhelming now. Ten.

Nine is harder, but eight is soft.

Seven makes me scream and six and five happen together.

I'm buzzing for four, and it's like the countdown has a direct line to my clit. Three, two.

The last one is hard enough to make my eyes water, but then his fingers are inside me, curling against my g-spot, and pleasure vaults through me, boosted by the sting and the burn, reaching a new, unbelievable height.

I come hard, clamping down on his fingers, and he strokes me through the orgasm until I'm temporarily sated.

When I finish quivering, he stands me up and roughly unbuttons my blouse as I stand boneless, his doll to do with as he wishes. My skirt joins my blouse and panties on the floor, but he leaves me in my nude bra as he turns me around.

His eyes roam over me, hungry, like he hasn't seen me naked in ages instead of just four days.

But the last time I was freshly fucked in front of him, we weren't alone. And he looks like he's been made to wait a lifetime to reclaim what's his. Suddenly I feel like I have so much more to say sorry for than a simple tantrum.

"Gavin," I start, but the look on his face has me stopping and trying again. "Sir?"

"Yes, Sprite?"

I carefully lift myself up onto his desk, scootching myself back just enough to keep my balance on my oh-so-sensitive bottom.

Good. I deserve that sting.

I spread my legs and run my hands up the insides of my thighs, stopping just short of my still swollen core. "I should have told you sooner that I'd gone to see the doctor."

He steps closer, his fingers chasing the path I'd just blazed. "You should have."

"What would you have done?" I ask breathlessly.

"What I'm going to do right now." He skirts around my pussy and grazes his knuckles up my belly. When he reaches my bra, he hooks his fingers into the stretchy mesh fabric and plumps up my tits as much as they allow, spilling my nipples out onto a makeshift platform.

"And that is…?"

"What do you want me to say, Sprite?" He squeezes the nape of my neck, using his thumb against my jaw to tip my head up. He pinches my nipple as he gets so close he goes blurry. I try to pull back but he doesn't let me. His hold on me tightens to the point of pain as his breath puffs against me, raw and ragged. "You want me to say that I want to claim you?"

"Yes," I whisper.

"Then tell me that. Don't play games."

"I want you to take back what's yours," I say, my voice cracking. "In a way that nobody else ever has. Just you and me, skin on skin."

"Ah, Ellie." He crushes his mouth down on mine and I pull at his tie. I need to feel his muscles play under my fingers without anything in between.

He breaks off the kiss and strips out of his shirt.

I reach out to touch his skin as he toes off his shoes. His muscles bunch against my fingers, hard and unyielding as he strips in quick, efficient movements. He's never out of reach and the way he's acting tonight, I think I might not get many more chances to touch him again until he's left his mark on me. So I stroke and squeeze his arms and his chest, memorizing this moment with my hands as much as my eyes.

Once he's completely naked, he spreads my legs wide and moves between them.

The tip of his cock drags through my folds, grazing over my clit until he's pressed against my entrance.

My heart is beating a mile a minute. I've never fucked without a condom before and there's something base and primal about the sight of his erection sliding against my sex, stretching my pussy open without any barrier between us. Only Gavin gets this part of me.

Grasping my hips in his hands, he squeezes them hard. As he leans in, gently touching his lips to mine, his gaze locked on my face, he snaps his hips forward and buries himself so completely, I think it could be permanent.

"Mine," he growls.

He kisses me again, this time more insistent as his tongue teases my lips open and swirls around in my mouth.

His hips ease back until he's barely inside me, then he

thrusts again, stretching me to the limit. He fucks me with his entire body, his pubic bone finding my clit with each snap of his hips, his thighs spreading my legs wide, making sure I take every last inch of him.

And still I want more.

I let out a little whine when he lets go of my hips and withdraws from my body.

"Don't worry Sprite, we're not nearly done. But I can't be as rough with you as I'd like when you're on that hard wood."

Rough. The word sends a violent shiver through me, a tremor of want the likes I've never felt before. Yes. Use me. I'm yours.

He picks me up from his desk and carries me across the room to the black leather chesterfield. "After my desk, this is the piece of furniture I've most wanted to fuck you on."

I yelp at the cold leather against my skin as he begins to arrange me like his own personal fuck-doll. Which I am. My right foot on the floor. My left leg along the back of the sofa. My head propped up on the arm.

He climbs onto the sofa, looming over me as he repositions my left leg so it's over his shoulder. "Make sure you keep doing yoga, Sprite. I love having a bendy babe."

He traps my wrists above my head, anchoring them to the side table, then plunges into me, reaching so much deeper than before. This position keeps me pinned down and I can't even grind my clit against him.

My pleasure is completely at his mercy. And I'm so good with that. Bad feminist. What happened to being responsible for your own orgasm? Gavin: the man who makes me come harder than I've ever managed on my own, no matter how powerful the vibrator.

He drags his cock out and rams it home, again and again. The sofa shifts slightly with each thrust and just as

I'm about to beg him to let me come, there's an almighty crash behind me.

Instead of slowing or stopping, he speeds up, fucking me harder. Like he doesn't give a fuck that he's literally destroying the room around us. Like nothing else matters beyond being inside me, deeper and harder than anyone else ever has. "Come now, Sprite, or you're going to have to wait until I'm feeling benevolent."

His words send me spiralling out of control. I'm like one of Pavlov's dogs, except instead of salivating at the sound of a bell, I'm conditioned to come when he tells me to. His dark promise of withholding unless I come *now* works like a charm, and the coil of desire that's been winding tight inside me unspools. Faster, faster, higher, higher I spin, until I don't know which way is up and there's no safe way to fall.

I'm still spasming around him as he pumps his hips two last times, jerkily now, before he freezes above me, all his muscles clenched in stark definition as he comes deep inside my body, marking me as his.

It takes me a minute to return to reality. I don't want to let go of this moment, of the way he's looking at me. Then I remember the crash, and panic starts to build in my chest. "What did we break?"

"A lamp." His chest is still rising and falling and he's covered in a light sheen of sweat. I want to lick him all over.

No. Fuck. Focus, Ellie. "We need to get up. Surely someone heard that and will come and check."

"Don't worry." His voice is rough and low, drunk on sex like we don't have a care in the world. "Nobody is coming in to check anything. Now, let's get you cleaned up."

I don't care what he thinks. That was a loud crash and even if Lachlan doesn't come through that door, someone downstairs may have heard and come looking.

Gavin being caught with his pants down with an intern would be political suicide.

"I need to go." I push at him to let me up.

He strokes my cheek and I just want to lay there and let him do that all night. "Ellie, it's fine."

"No. It's not. Gavin, let me up. Now."

His gaze locks with mine for a moment, then he nods and shifts off the sofa.

I can't breathe and I need to get out. I stumble across the room for my clothes.

"Ellie…"

I don't answer. I pull on my underwear and skirt. I forego the bra, folding it into as small a square as I can manage. I'll shove it in my bag when I get back to my desk. Gavin tries to help me as I fumble with the buttons on my top. I shrug him off. "Don't mind me, just get yourself sorted out."

"Ellie, slow down. We need to talk about this."

His words have the opposite effect. My heart is beating a mile a minute as I slide my feet into my shoes. I finish with the last button on my blouse, my hands shaking and slipping as I smooth the fabric. "No. I need to get out of here right now. And I suggest you get your clothes on lickity split."

My voice speeds up, catching and twisting as I spit out the last sentence. Then I open the door just enough to slip through, careful not to look towards where I know Lachlan is standing near the elevators. I dash to my desk, grab my purse, then make my speedy getaway down the stairwell.

I'M SO over waking up at four in the morning. Although waking up is a generous term for still being awake after a night of drifting in and out of quasi-consciousness, bumping into worry and panic every time my eyes close for more than a second.

Every muscle in my body aches.

I feel like a failure. Last night is proof that our relationship has undermined my professionalism—and his, too. That's on him as much as it's on me.

We both fucked up, royally.

But the internship was always temporary for me. I'm the one who can walk away and nobody will notice.

Nobody except Gavin.

I numbly shower and get dressed. Go through the routine I'd come to love and hate at the same time. Normally I'd pack a lunch, but I'm not going to be there that long. Just my coffee to go in a travel mug this morning, and even that sits like battery acid in my stomach.

I go to Langevin Block. I can't even look across the street.

I love him. And if we keep this up, I'm going to destroy his career before he gets a fighting chance.

I log in to the internal network and open an email to Stew.

If I got spanked for storming out of his office, what will he do when he finds out that I've just quit?

27

—————

GAVIN

THE NEXT MORNING, Ellie is noticeably absent from my briefing. She was supposed to be there—she was included on the meeting invite list in my schedule. I know this because I checked. I'm bothered, but I can't address it until the meeting is over. Thankfully it's only fifteen minutes. I can hold out that long. Barely.

I know something's very wrong. Through the entire briefing, Stew looks everywhere but at me.

By the time the last of my staff files from the room, I'm in full-blown panic mode. My heart is racing and my head feels wonky.

"Where's Ellie?"

"She quit."

"What do you mean she quit?"

"Quit. As in no longer works for me." He's furious, and no longer trying to hide it.

Fuck. I ask what is probably the stupidest question ever. "Why would she quit?"

"Really? We're going here?"

"For fuck's sake, Stew. Why?"

233

"Well, she *told* me it was because something came up and she had to return to the university early."

"That's bullshit."

"Yeah, I know. So how about you tell me what the fuck is going on."

It's killing me that I cost Ellie her internship, and I need to find a way to fix it. Coming clean with Stew is the first step.

"I'm dating Ellie Montague."

"Jesus."

"Thanks, I'm glad you're thrilled that I've finally found someone special."

"This is why she quit."

"Most likely."

"Jesus."

"You already said that."

"Okay, so she's not quit, exactly. She's finishing up the internship at the university. No, I'm not fucking happy about that because she's smart and we were lucky to have her for the two months that we did before lust got the better of you."

He should be grateful there's a desk between us. "It's not like that."

"Give me a break, Gavin. You think I'm blind to—"

"It's. Not. Like. That."

He chews on his bottom lip instead of responding.

I don't want to have to explain anything to him, but I do trust him even if he's callous. And in order to get ahead of the story it will inevitably be, he needs to know the truth. "Not that it's any of your business, but lust got the better of me on her first day on the job. And since I took six weeks to think about it, try and talk myself out of it, and do everything in my power to push her away, I also discovered in that time that I love her."

Silence fills the room as the words crack out of me. Stew stares at me, shocked. I know the feeling. That's the first time I've admitted just how serious my feelings are, even to myself.

And I fucking told it to Stew, instead of Ellie.

Fuck my life.

Thankfully, Stew shifts gears pretty damn fast. "So this isn't a lawsuit waiting to happen?"

"From Ellie? No."

"From anyone else?"

"That's your job to worry about. I'm giving you the heads up so you can craft a message for when our relationship becomes public information."

"And when will that be? Are you planning on eloping to Niagara Falls?"

"We haven't talked about a wedding yet."

"I should hope not."

"I can take it a bit slow. Get your ducks in a row, though, because I'm not going to deny how I feel about her if I'm asked. I'm never going to lie about her, Stew."

"Your principles are damn irritating sometimes."

Early that afternoon, instead of working things out with the woman I love—yeah, my heart skips a beat every time I admit that—I'm on a plane heading home to Vancouver to make a bunch of announcements. And for the first time since becoming Prime Minister, I'm resentful as fuck about fulfilling my official duties.

At least I get to spend some time with Max this weekend. He's supposed to show up at my place for pizza and beer at seven. Then spend the evening listening to my tale of woe.

Meanwhile, things are still a bit strained between Lachlan and me. I had no idea he and Beth had been circling around each other. If I had, I sure as fuck wouldn't have involved him in my kinky game.

I spend the flight going over my speeches. I'm really going to miss having Ellie's fine-tuning.

When we land in Vancouver, I decide to drive the car back to my house. I want to talk to Lachlan and I figure I'm more in charge if I'm behind the wheel.

"Why didn't you tell me you had a little thing for Beth?"

"With all due respect, not your business."

"It is my business. Strip away all the professional capacities here for a moment, and it's still my business. When I asked you to participate with Ellie and me, I was under the impression you were free of…entanglements."

"I was—am. I'm single. Not dating. Hell, I don't even have any friends with benefits."

"What is Beth, then?"

"Not your business." His jaw is set and his eyes say don't fucking go there.

"Okay, let's bring the professional back into it. My chief of security has some kind of interest in my assistant, yet he participates in a threesome with his boss and his boss's girlfriend, who also happens to be an intern. See where this is going yet?"

"Like I said the other night—no point in wasting time over regrets."

"So there is regret?"

"Not exactly. I'm coming to terms with my choice and how it affects me and those in my sphere. And I'll be honest, if I had a do-over? I'm not sure I wouldn't make the same decision."

I'm surprised. Lachlan had to have seen the same stricken look on Beth's face the other day as I did. It makes me wonder if he's even clued in that she has a thing for him.

"So now what?"

"We move on."

I agree with him and offer an olive branch. "Max is coming tonight with pizza and beer. Would you like to join us?"

He hesitates a moment. "Yes, on the pizza, but I'm still technically on duty, so I'll skip the beer."

"Excellent. What kind of pizza do you want?"

"Meat lovers."

"Why am I not surprised? I'll call Max when we get home."

Max arrives shortly after seven, loaded down with three large pizzas and a half-sack of beer.

"Seriously, only six bottles of beer?"

"It's just you and me drinking, and I know *you* have to work tomorrow."

I sigh and lead the way to the living room.

Max sits down and starts dealing pizza boxes. "Hey Lachlan, against my professional better judgement, I've got your artery clogger right here."

Lachlan smiles wide as he opens the box and pulls out a large gooey piece of pizza, using his fingers to sever the strings of cheese and add them to the top. "Just what I need, cheesy, meaty goodness." Folding the slice over, he takes a massive bite. Cheese trails down his chin and he uses his thumb to sweep it into his mouth.

I don't know whether to be disgusted or impressed. "You are a total pig."

He flips me the bird while he finishes chewing.

"Shall I get you a knife and fork, Prime Minister?"

"Fuck you, Lachlan." And right there, we're good.

Meanwhile, Max has been sitting back in his seat chuckling away as he consumes his beer and pizza.

"Max, did you know that our whole hockey team is kinky?" This is the first opportunity I've had to mention anything since I found out because that's not something I wanted overheard on a cell phone.

"Oh, really?" He looks at Lachlan, who nods while continuing to stuff his face like it's his first meal in a week. "I just got more excited about the move. Tell me all about the Ottawa kink scene. Are there any decent clubs?"

Lachlan swallows his mouthful and chases it down with a swig of Coke. "There are clubs, but access isn't restricted enough to ensure privacy. Therefore, not what I would consider appropriate for high profile individuals—and make no mistake, as the Prime Minister's closest friend, and an eligible bachelor, you are most definitely high profile. Occasionally, there are private parties. But they are very select and don't happen often."

"Then how do kinky high-profile birds of a feather manage to flock together?"

"Connections, mostly. Friend-of-a-friend type stuff."

"Or a hockey team."

"Yeah. Or that."

"But no secret dungeon in the bowels of the Parliament Building where all the kinky politicians gather to let their freak-flags hang out, then?"

"Afraid not."

I have a vision of that West Wing episode where Leo discovers there is an alcoholics anonymous meeting for prominent politicians and administrators. The idea of Parliament Hill Kinksters Anonymous tickles my funny bone, but I hold back my mirth. I want to see how this conversation plays out.

"So...if I built a dungeon in my new house and knew the right people..."

"You'd probably become very popular in certain Ottawa circles."

"Do I know the right people?"

Lachlan snorts. "You play hockey with enough of them. You're golden."

I'm touched that Lachlan trusted both Max and me enough to bring us into his private world. Max, in particular, was a relative stranger, even if he had been so thoroughly vetted, no closet held an undiscovered skeleton.

Considering it was technically a business trip, it turned out to be a halfway decent guy's weekend. Which was the only thing that made being away from Ellie remotely bearable.

Lachlan and I are in the car, well on our way home to 24 Sussex when I change my mind and give him a different destination.

28

ELLIE

WHEN I GOT HOME Friday morning, I took the burner phone out of my purse, turned it off, and put it in the top drawer of my dresser. Then I changed into my pyjamas.

Now it's Sunday afternoon and I'm still wearing them.

Sasha's given me a wide berth all weekend. I told her that the hours were too much, that the internship had slid way beyond the original scope of the position—a painful understatement—and that I've decided to return to the university. I'll complete the position paper reviews from there and submit them to Stew electronically.

Like the ten blocks and a bridge that separate the university from Parliament can somehow protect Gavin from the risk that I pose.

We're not going to last a month. God, even that isn't long enough. If either of us had any will power, we'd walk away from each other and reconnect in a year. Two years. When the fact that I was an intern in his office is nothing but a titillating note from the past.

The truth is, I don't have a plan here. I'm pretty sure that one day I'm going to wake up and find my apartment building surrounded by press, and that's going to be humiliating.

It might even destroy my career. Who wants to hire a Women's Studies professor who slept with the country's leader while interning in his office? It's the worst kind of cliché. The boss and the secretary. He's basically the CEO of an entire nation. And I shimmied into pencil skirts and bent over his desk.

Worst of all, I loved every last dirty second of it. I wouldn't change a single thing about this summer. I'll never regret our secret affair, even if it becomes my public shame.

I roll over and glare at the top drawer of my dresser.

Then I force myself to go have a shower and pretend for another hour or two that I can do this.

———

AFTER MY SHOWER I dig through the fridge looking for something healthy to eat.

I pull out everything to maybe make a salad, if said salad doesn't have any lettuce and is served on top of cheese-covered tortilla chips.

Yes, I'm making nachos for dinner and I'm not going to feel bad about it for a second.

Besides, our lettuce is looking a little wilty.

"Sasha?"

She pops her head out of her room. "Yeah?"

"Do you want nachos?"

"For dinner?"

"Is that a no?"

"Only because Kyle's going to be here any minute." She's heading out with a friend—not a date, she swears up and down, except she's been getting ready for an hour, so it's totally a date.

"You're missing out," I holler at her as she disappears, probably to change her outfit again.

I'm spooning salsa into a bowl as a knock sounds at the door.

"Ellie?"

I roll my eyes. "Yeah, I'll let him in."

I dance over to the entrance way, licking salsa off my thumb as I pull the door open.

It's not some guy named Kyle who's totally going to get lucky in the stacks.

It's Lachlan. And behind him looms Gavin, hands shoved in his pockets. His jaw is set firmly and covered in a few days of scruff.

He looks tired. And determined. His eyes are bright and laser-focused in on me. My heart lurches toward him, just leaps right out of my chest and pads across the faded carpet to rub against his leg.

Stupid heart.

"No," I say firmly. "Go away."

Lachlan just raises one eyebrow at me and I sigh.

"Fine, come in, check the place out. I've got bras hanging in the bathroom, fair warning."

He smirks at me as he moves into the apartment. Gavin steps over the threshold, right into my bubble, and my front door swings shut behind him.

I want to touch him so badly it hurts. I squeeze my hands at my side instead and glare at him, my voice managing to stay a stern whisper. "You shouldn't be here."

"And yet I can't stay away." His voice isn't stern at all. It drips with an all-too-familiar ache.

I try again to summon callous indifference. "You've really interrupted me at a very busy point in my evening. I'm making nachos."

He gives me a hopeful smile. "Black olives?"

I'm a goner. "And chicken."

"Delicious."

I shake my head, but now my voice is soft and pleading. "You can't be here."

"You quit."

"I'm officially finishing my internship from the university."

"Isn't that the kind of thing I need to sign off on?"

"You're making light of this?" I snap. "I had to quit my job because of you."

"You didn't have to do anything. And you said you're finishing it at the university."

"That's hardly the same experience."

"Then you should have told me what you were thinking about doing and I'd have talked you out of it."

"And that's exactly why I didn't. We don't have any boundaries, Gavin. We *need* boundaries. Distance. Restraint."

"I won't apologize for wanting you. I've needed you from the moment I laid eyes on you, so I'd say my restraint is pretty fucking admirable."

My heart leaps into my throat, but I'm not prepared yet to accept all that comes with admitting he's right, so I whisper, "You don't need me."

"I damn well do. You're my Sprite."

From behind me, Sasha gasps, and from the other end of the room, Lachlan groans. I wave my hand at both of them. "Sasha, this is Gavin. Anything he says is a lie and also top secret."

"Nice to meet you," she whispers.

Sasha might have a crush, too. It's a national epidemic. I can't fault anyone for it.

Behind Gavin, someone else knocks on the door. I roll my eyes. My apartment is suddenly visitor central. I reach out and grab Gavin's hand and pull him toward the kitchen, but that's open to the living room.

I point to the oven. "Lachlan, I've got nachos in there, can you pull them out?"

"Of course," he says, and I swear he's trying not to laugh.

This isn't funny.

I'm mad at Gavin. Mad at myself, too. But that doesn't do anything to mitigate the duelling facts that I'm excited and freaked out about dragging him into my bedroom.

I'm just hiding him, of course. Because he came over to talk and Sasha's got a friend who doesn't need to see him here.

"They're heading out shortly," I whisper as I click the door shut. "We'll just—"

Gavin's mouth crashes over mine, his tongue shoving into my mouth at the same time as he tugs down the waistband of my sweatpants so he can palm my ass.

No. Yes. *No*. This is…Oh God.

This is unbearably good. He's kneading my skin, hard, and I'm whimpering against his mouth as he mauls me.

"Stop."

He freezes.

I fist my hands in the front of his dress shirt and thump my head against his chest.

With a heavy sigh, he kisses the top of my head.

"I can't be your sordid affair," I mumble into his shirt.

"Then we have a problem. Because three days away from you, three days of not knowing what the hell is going on with us…that's my limit." He drags in a ragged breath as he lets me slump back against the wall.

"We can't do this."

"We'll be discreet." He shakes his head when I open my

mouth to protest. "And after a reasonable amount of time, we'll start dating."

"We weren't discreet enough when I was an intern in your office. No offense, but I don't think either of us is capable of discretion when it comes to the other."

"Then we start dating sooner than later. I've already got Stew thinking about how to spin it. You're a doctoral candidate at the university. We'll find some other language to describe your consulting in the PMO."

"It was a formal *internship* program."

"That will be a day's news story, nothing more. We'll manage it."

Now it's my turn to shake my head. "And what will that look like? How does this not end with me being a joke?"

"I don't follow."

Of course he doesn't. He's going to be the wink-wink, nudge-nudge sex machine that banged an intern.

I'm the young hussy who couldn't keep her panties on.

"Is Lachlan standing outside my bedroom door right now?"

"He'll wait out on the landing when your roommate leaves."

"That's subtle."

"This is why you need to come to me, Sprite." His voice turns gruff and he cups my face.

I press my cheek into his palm, achy relief coursing through me at his touch. Why does this feel so right when I know it must be wrong?

I can't keep sneaking around with you. It's right there on the tip of my tongue, and I can't say it.

I'm weak.

I called it. There's no keeping us apart, and we're going to keep crashing together until it all comes crumbling down.

He groans again, and I close my eyes and tug him toward me. Fuck it. We'll be grown-ups in the morning.

His nose bumps against mine and I tilt the other way. Our mouths slide against each other. Wet, hot breath. Dizzying need and dangerous hunger. A silent kiss that goes on forever and ever, and when we break apart, I want more.

I always want more.

It will never be enough.

His hand shoves hard against the wall as he breaks away from me. "Damn it."

"What?"

"This isn't how this was supposed to go."

I laugh weakly. "This is how it always goes with us."

"I know. But that's gotta change."

Now he gets it. Hot, prickly disappointment surges through me. "Right."

His jaw sets again, the same way it was when I first opened my front door.

Right. He came over here to say something else and I threw him off track. Of course I did.

"Ellie…"

"It's fine, Gavin." I can crawl back into my PJs for another three days. No biggie.

He shakes his head. "Let me try again. You're right. I can't be seen making a booty call to an intern's apartment. And I can't ask you to sneak into 24 Sussex any longer. It's not fair to you. So there's only one thing to do."

I frown. I'm not following.

He reaches out and cups my cheek. "Ellie, I love you."

"Oh, Gavin…"

"Let me finish."

"But I—"

"I love you, and I need you, and I want to take you out

on a date." His eyes light up and his face softens as he gazes at me. "A real one this time. An official first date. And I don't want it to be a secret."

My head is spinning. "I love you, too," I whisper. It's the least I can say. "But what about…?"

What about everything? The optics and the party, the media and the scrutiny?

"Nothing else matters." He strokes my cheek. "You're mine. And we'll deal with the rest of it together."

29

———————

GAVIN

I DON'T THINK I've never been so grateful for Lachlan as I am now. He's pulled all kinds of strings and arranged a number of distractions for the press so Ellie and I can have our first date in peace.

Lachlan gets us to Ellie's with ten minutes to spare. My palms are sweaty and my pulse is erratic. I have no idea where these nerves came from. It's not like this is my first date ever. Except it is. It's my first date ever with Ellie. It might even be my first date ever with someone I've already had kinky sex with. And it's definitely my first date ever with someone I already love to distraction.

Sasha answers the door and says, "Have a seat. She'll be out in a few minutes." Then disappears down the hall.

I don't want to have a seat. I want to storm down that fucking hall to Ellie's room and drag her off to bed so I can do all the bad things that make her feel so good. But I behave. Because I've done it all backwards and I need to make it up to her. Ellie deserves proper courting and romance to go along with all the dirty, kinky stuff.

I wonder if she's as anxious as I am. I assume the

248

answer is yes when she comes into the living room five minutes early, looking absolutely gorgeous in black capris and a silky green t-shirt that makes her grey eyes pop.

"Does this work?" she asks softly, searching my face. I'd given her vague instructions—we're going out for dinner, but she should plan to dress comfortably all the same. And while I didn't spell it out, we both know that our photograph might get taken tonight.

"You're perfect." My voice is husky and I don't care.

I wanted to take her on a picnic, but add in the required security detail, and that would have drawn too much attention. Instead we'll go to a nice little bistro on the Quebec side of the Ottawa River.

I walk across the room to meet her. Taking her hands in mine, I buss her cheek and start to lead her out of the room.

"Not so fast," Sasha says, her arms crossed. "What are your intentions towards my best friend?"

Ellie does a slow head shake and rolls her eyes. "You can't be serious?"

"You hush up. This is between me and *Mr. Prime Minister*." Jesus, the way she says it sounds like an insult.

"My intentions are to do whatever is within my power to make her happy."

"Sure, until the next bright, shiny new intern with the right equipment shows up in your office."

Right now, I'm thinking I'd rather have an irate father waving a twelve-gauge in my face than Ellie's razor-tongued roommate.

And Lachlan's unrestrained smirk is only making it fucking worse. I need to reel this in.

"I get that you're concerned—that's fair and reasonable. But the only person I need to prove myself to is Ellie. And that starts here and now."

Sasha pauses for a moment, her shoulders sag a little.

Resignation. "See that you do." The threat may be left unsaid, but there's no question there's an *or else*.

As we walk out the door, Ellie pulls me close and whispers, "I'm sorry."

"Don't be. She's worried about you. And I respect that."

The bistro is just across the Portage Bridge, on Rue Laval. The thirty minute drive from Ellie's is exquisite torture. I'm hard as a rock, and Ellie keeps snaking a hand across my thigh.

I take both her hands in mine. They're warm and soft. I love these hands, but they need to stay well away from my cock tonight. "Enough, Sprite. This is our first date, so we need to act the part."

"Are you really going to hold us to that?"

"Absolutely. I want there to be more than just sex between us. Don't get me wrong, I want lots and lots of raunchy, dirty, mind-blowing sex between us. But relationships can't survive on that alone."

"But what if I'm a sex on the first date kinda woman?"

"I guess you'll just have to wait. Same as me."

"You're actually serious about this?"

I nod. "I am."

"Wow. I thought this was another game."

"I told you last week—no games."

When we arrive at the restaurant, Tim is there waiting with a parking spot cleared out front. He and Lachlan escort us in and we are met by the owner, who leads us through to a quiet corner.

Tim leans in and whispers in my ear. "This guy is awesome. He rearranged the seating to allow you and Ellie extra space and privacy from the other patrons and still seat us at a table near enough to maintain security."

"Good to know. I'll make sure to come up with an appropriate way to thank him."

The owner himself waits us, filling our water glasses as he explains the specials. Then he leaves us alone for a few minutes.

"This place is nice," Ellie says.

"I discovered it when I was a new MP, suddenly thrust into the spotlight. Cross the river and nobody cares."

"Smart." She takes a sip of her water and I just watch her because I can. I don't know how many of these moments we'll get before the entire country is watching. I want to savour the experience of wooing Ellie Montague for as long as I can.

"You're from Montreal, right?"

She nods. "Born and raised."

"Do you miss it? Montreal is an amazing city. I did a semester just outside the city in high school. A language exchange, because we didn't have French Immersion yet in BC."

"No?" She gives me an appalled look. This might be the first time since we met that I've been acutely aware of the fourteen years between us.

I laugh. "When I was a kid, the value of a bilingual education wasn't as widely understood as it is today."

"And yet you're fluent. That's amazing."

"It helped that my mother knows French. She was one of the pioneers on the west coast who pushed for French Immersion to be available through the public school system."

"Your parents are quite the force."

"Now they spend most of their time at a place in the mountains and limit their politicking to phone calls."

"Convenient to have a direct line to the PM." She grins. "Your mother must like your Children First initiative."

"She thinks it doesn't go far enough." She's not wrong,

and I have plans. I tell Ellie some of them, and she listens more attentively than any of my advisors.

"Was it intense growing up a child of Vince and Barbara Strong?"

I shake my head. "I think more so for my sister Pia. She's the oldest, and she did well at school out of the gate, so they piled tutors on her. I got some of that when I showed an aptitude for languages, but she had a tutor for absolutely everything. Math and music and science. It was intense."

"I saw her TED talk last year. It was fabulous."

That's my sister. "I always say she's the one who should have gone into politics."

Ellie laughs. "That seems like the last thing she'd like."

"Indeed. She's more like you." Pia's a scientist and a writer. She had a TED Talk on sexism in science go viral last year, right around the release of a non-fiction book she wrote on the same topic. "I get phone calls from her, too."

"I bet."

"I welcome them, you know. And the ones from my mother, too. They're incredible women."

This time her laugh is longer, lower, and totally contagious. "You don't need to impress me, Gavin. You've already done that in spades."

"So I don't need to pretend that I know what wine goes with what on the menu?"

She shakes her head slowly, her eyes glued on my face. "Not at all."

We order food. I'm hardly aware of what it is, but it's tasty and Ellie likes it. That's all that matters. She kicks her feet under the table at the first bite of her pumpkin ravioli and my dick chubs up. Those sounds should only be made in the privacy of my bedroom.

But then she smiles at me again, her eyes lighting up,

and I think damn, she should make those sounds and give me that look wherever and whenever she wants.

"How's your food?"

Zero clue. "It's good."

"You've hardly touched it."

"I'm watching you."

She rolls her eyes. "You'll be hungry later."

"They do a very nice doggie bag here."

"You really like leftovers, don't you?"

"I do." I take a bite of my steak and think about that. It's not like I wanted for much growing up. But my parents were constantly on the go. "Sometimes my mother would bring back some of her dinner from an event, and I'd sit on the stool in the kitchen and eat it—because it was always better than whatever the babysitter had made us—and she'd tell me about the important thing they'd gone to support. I learned a lot over those leftovers. And I also learned that most working dinners are more about working than actual dinner."

"Fascinating."

"What was your childhood like?"

"The complete opposite of that." She pushes her plate forward a bit and rubs her fingertips against the edge of the table. I reach my hand across the tablecloth and offer her fingers to hold instead. Her smile is the sweetest bit of sunshine I've ever seen. She relaxes back against her chair as she continues. "My mother makes dinner every night at half past five. The only excuse for missing is if you're literally not in the city. She hated my night classes in undergrad because they didn't fit into her suburban paradigm."

"How often do you go home to visit?"

"A couple times a year. I love my parents, but we're not super close. I have an older sister, too, and she's provided them with two adorable grandchildren to dote on. They barely miss me."

"I'm sure that's not true." I miss her right now because she's not in my lap. "Nieces? Nephews?"

"One of each. A six-year-old boy, Robert, and a three-year-old girl, Amie." She pronounces them with the French pronunciation.

"They're not Anglophones as well?"

"No, my sister married a man from the Quebec countryside, although they live in Montreal now. The kids will be bilingual, of course, but they're being raised in French."

"Good that I'm fluent, then."

"You want to meet my niece and nephew?" She blinks at me in surprise.

"I want to meet your entire family. And introduce you to mine, of course. They will adore you."

Her cheeks stain pink and she takes a sip of wine. I can see her mind whirring. She knows more about my family than I do hers. My entire family tree is detailed on Wikipedia. "Pia's intimidating."

"Does it help if I tell you that she constantly worries she's a terrible mother?"

"No!" But she grins. "Her kids are older, right?"

Didn't see the tiger trap until I was falling into it. I answer carefully. "The youngest, Jamie, is....thirteen? Fourteen maybe. I'm a terrible uncle, clearly."

Her brain is still whirring. Damn it. "So the older ones are closer to my age."

I think Sabrina is probably six months younger than Ellie. "Yeah, something like that."

"And you think your family will adore me?" She winces. "Maybe we can hold off on the formal introductions for a bit."

"My niece is a Rhodes Scholar and I was practically a

kid when she was born, so I don't think they're going to come to the same salacious conclusion you've gone to in your head, Sprite."

The pink stain grows and she takes another sip of wine. "Maybe."

"We're more like siblings."

"I'm sure your sister, the feminist flag-bearer, will see it just like that." Ellie's brow knits together.

"If she doesn't like it, she'll talk to me and I'll set her straight."

"Does mansplaining go over well with Pia?"

Ha. "No, fair point. But she's more understanding than you'd think. Pia was a very young mother."

"We can stop talking about this any time now."

I'm not stopping until she's laughing and having a good time again. "Plus I'm terribly immature."

She rolls her eyes. "You are not."

"I am. Six weeks ago I was in my morning briefing with my staff and this intern was talking about what I'm sure was a really great idea, and all I could think about was getting her naked and spreading her out on my desk."

Her mouth drops open in outrage, but her eyes are twinkling. "You didn't hear anything I said?"

"You were fidgeting. It was irresistible."

"I do that a lot."

"I know. I spend a lot of time with a hard-on around you."

Her hair falls around her face like a curtain as she ducks her head, and I'm about to change the subject when she says, "It's for the best that I've gone back to the university."

"No."

"Yes."

"We could have controlled ourselves," I say firmly. "But—"

"We didn't want to," she says, finishing my thought. "I didn't, anyway."

"I've been waiting for you a long time, Ellie. I could wait longer."

"That sounds terrible. Waiting longer, I mean." Her tongue peeks out the corner of her mouth as she pauses for a few seconds. "The rest makes me melt."

"Good. That's my goal tonight."

We finish eating, then get the rest packed into doggie bags and head for the waiting car. None of the bistro's clientele give us even a second glance, and as we settle into the backseat of the town car, I think this is actually going to work.

Ellie tangles her fingers in mine as we start the drive back. I watch her quietly for a minute before asking, "Are you ready to officially be the PM's girlfriend, and all that entails?"

"Are you giving me an out?"

"Not really."

A smile curls up her face at that. "Yes, I'm ready. I don't really have any other choice—and not because you're bossy —but because I tried, Gavin. I tried to save you from me, and maybe me from you a little too. But I don't want to be a martyr. I want to be with you, whatever the cost."

Alarm grows inside as the words spill out of her like water down a mountainside in the spring. Slippery and fast. Dangerous, too. "What do you mean, save me from you?"

She gives me a little shrug. "I'm a liability."

Jesus, no. "Is that what you think? Ellie, you're one of the smartest people I've ever met. Accomplished and kind, funny and sexy as hell. There will be a storm of interest in you once our relationship is out in the open. And Canadians are going to love you just as much as I do."

"Well, that's probably an overstatement, but that's not

what I mean. Yes, I worry about being called names and having my identity reduced to a woman who had sex with a powerful leader. But I'm more concerned about your mandate. I don't want what you did with an intern to derail the fall session of Parliament. The climate change push, the Children First initiative…the entire platform will suffer if the government needs to go on the defensive."

"Oh, my little policy wonk." I weave my fingers around hers and squeeze. "Do I look like someone that goes on the defensive?"

She blushes, and with the setting sun backlighting her hair through the car window, she looks like an innocent angel. When it comes to the game of politics, she is.

I am not.

Wonks care about policy. Hacks—that's me—we obsess over how to get that policy *done*. The game, the players, the manipulation. It's why lawyers make such excellent politicians—and if we go too far, why the public ends up hating us. I never want to violate anyone's trust in me, but I'll do whatever I have to do to make sure that the right thing happens at the end of the day.

"Anyway, enough of that worry for tonight. I only asked because we'll wait until it's dark to join the crowd, but there's a chance we may be seen."

"The crowd…" She swivels her head around, returning her attention to where we're going. We're a block away now, and understanding dawns on her face. "The Sound and Light Show? We're going to end our first date on the lawn in front of the Parliament buildings?"

I grin at her. "The best defence is a good offense."

30

ELLIE

WE GET DROPPED off at Centre Block, but we don't go upstairs to Gavin's office. The sun's rapidly setting, and there's a small bag waiting for us, so we just wait inside.

The security detail gives us enough privacy that we can keep talking about family and work, until Gavin points out that we only talk about family and work.

"Hopelessly uninteresting, aren't we?" I whisper as he pulls me into his side.

He kisses my forehead. "What was the last movie you went to see?"

I can't remember. "Maybe Star Wars."

"Me too."

"Maybe I should take you to the movies. Sneak you in or something."

"Dating me isn't *that* complicated. The hardest part will be me finding the time you deserve."

"Oh, that's not…I'm going to be busy too. I have a conference in September, another one in November. I'm not going to be needy about your time."

"You could be if you wanted. Throw a little tantrum in my office late at night…"

Desire pools low in my belly. "You looking for an excuse to punish me, Sir?"

"Not tonight. But soon. And I don't need an excuse—"

"And it's not punishment. I know."

"Back talk?"

I grin wickedly. "You already told me you won't be doing anything to me tonight."

"I have a long memory." He winks and glances at the door, where a guard has surreptitiously moved into place. "That's our cue."

He grabs the bag and laces his fingers through mine, leading me out onto the lawn. We go around the crowd, about halfway back, and we stop next to two men in suits sitting in lawn chairs.

I try not to laugh as Tim and Lachlan get up in synchronized fashion, fold up their chairs, and get out of our way—leaving a perfect space for Gavin to spread a blanket for us.

"That wasn't very subtle," I giggle as he settles me in front of him, between his bent legs.

He wraps his arms around my waist and sets his chin on my shoulder. "I'm not trying to be subtle. I'm wooing you."

Warm, sizzling pleasure zips through me at his words. "I'm pretty wooed."

"And the sight of two men in suits carrying their lawn chairs away is heaps more interesting than a couple on a date, right?" He kisses the curve of my ear. "See? Nobody's watching me right now."

And he's right. Now that the show has begun, we're totally anonymous. I relax against his solid, broad chest and let myself enjoy being wrapped in his arms, surrounded by his scent. At least for tonight, I'm just a girl on a date with a guy who really, really likes her.

For the next thirty minutes, the history of our country plays out in a spectacular light show that uses Parliament as a movie screen of sorts. The building adds texture and an unexpected emotion to the display, and we're both completely absorbed. When the national anthem begins to play at the end, we stand together, and as the last notes fade into the crowd's applause, Gavin snatches up the blanket and takes my hand.

Lachlan's waiting a few feet away, and points us to the car. Nine minutes later, we're pulling up to my apartment and I'm still grinning.

"Thank you," I start, and Gavin silences me with a press of his fingertips against my mouth.

"Upstairs. I'm walking you to your door."

"Okay," I mumble against his fingers.

He grins.

Lachlan goes first, and when we get up to my landing, he heads back downstairs, leaving us alone.

"I had a wonderful time," I say, glancing up at him from beneath my eyelashes and try to see him as a real first date. Imagine the will-he-or-won't-he question of a goodnight kiss. I've got butterflies, all right, but they're more about how long it's going to be until our second date, our third, our tenth, and when he's going to tie me to his bed again.

But this man in front of me is also lovely. He'd take my breath away even if he was a stranger, a blind date, or a guy from work. He's tall and handsome, attentive and smart. He likes his mom and his sister, and cares passionately about his job, which just happens to be pretty intense.

This is a side of him I didn't really get to see when I was working with Stew. I was too close. Coming at him from the wrong angle, so I saw the fighter, the raw underbelly of the caged tiger. The secret, buried needs of a man locked up tight.

That had been hot as hell.

This is something else. Something infinitely more dangerous than the risks of a forbidden affair.

I already love him. So why is the idea of Gavin being a forever kind of guy so frightening?

Because you're so simple compared to him. His sister is famous in her own right. His mother changed an entire education system. His niece is a Rhodes Scholar.

And I'm a yoga enthusiast who can't cook.

I suddenly need a hug quite desperately. Gavin's right in front of me, shifting closer, and I close the gap, pressing myself flat against his body.

"Hey," he says gently.

"Really wonderful time," I repeat.

"Ellie."

I don't move.

"Sprite." His voice deepens and I step back like I've been zapped by a gentle electric current. One that's hot-wired to my erogenous zones. He gives me a warm but firm look. "Where did you go just now?"

"I just realized this is different. A little overwhelming."

"Than what?"

"Than before."

"Dating is scarier than…" He lowers his voice and leans in, backing me up against my apartment door. "Kinky fuckery?"

I lick my lips. "Maybe yes."

"Why?"

Because when it comes to sex, I don't doubt my appeal. "You're on a whole other level," I whisper. "This isn't a conversation for my landing, I guess."

"Ah, whatever." He gives me a lopsided grin. "But it's not where I want your head at on our first date. Because you're everything I want. Never doubt that. That bullshit your roommate said…I've never had a workplace affair before, and never will again. It's entirely incidental that you were my intern. It was *you*. Your wit and your sweetness, and yes, your beauty. I'm captivated, Ellie."

"But I'm just me and you're…perfect."

"Did you ever consider that maybe I'm just perfect for you?" He exhales roughly and twists his fingers into mine. "I do a good job of being a persona, Ellie. But I'm just a regular guy, with weaknesses and failings. You've seen that more than anyone else. I don't even know that I am perfect for you. I worry that I'm too old, too risky, too busy."

"No." I press my hand against his chest and his muscles flex beneath my touch. So I'm not the only one who's feeling unsure. "We're a pair, aren't we?"

He nods, then his face shifts again. Determination is incredibly sexy. My breath falls into a shallow, anticipatory rhythm. "I'd like to see you again, Ellie."

It should sound formal and stiff. Instead it's sexy, dripping with intent. "Yes. Absolutely."

"Lunch tomorrow."

"Aren't you going to Washington tomorrow?"

"In the afternoon." He brushes a lock of my hair off my cheek. "You want to come with me?"

I laugh. "That would be an inappropriate use of a government plane."

"It's going there anyway. I could pay the Bank of Canada for your ticket."

"Are there actually tickets?" A crazy, fluttery feeling has taken over my entire body.

He winds his hand tight into my hair. "I'd make one for you."

Now his face is right over mine and he's holding me still, my hair wrapped around his fist, and I want him so much it hurts. A physical, heavy ache that only intensifies as he brushes his lips against mine.

"Until tomorrow, then," he murmurs, and the ache turns to actual pain. "You can wait that long, can't you, Sprite?"

"Yes," I breathe. I really need to get control of my vocal cords—they don't know what they're talking about. But as I say it, I believe it. The pain inside is like the burn of him spanking me. Once I know rubbing it away isn't an option, that it can't be replaced with something sweeter and easier, I realize I want more. I want to lean into the sharpness of my longing for him.

"Good girl." He tugs my lower lip into his mouth, sinking his teeth into my flesh until I gasp, then he covers my mouth with his and I'm lost. His tongue is slick and clever as he slides inside. Want rushes through me, a harsh current of dirty thoughts. His exploration slows, turns leisurely, as he tastes every last inch of my mouth. I push up on my toes, needing to do the same to him, but he tugs my hair.

Hold still, the command is clear.

My thighs start to shake. My breasts are swollen and if he rubbed his thumb across my nipples, I think I'd probably spontaneously combust.

This is a hell of a state to leave me in, but that's exactly what he's going to do.

He eases back, his mouth lingering on mine even as his body shifts away from me. When our lips finally slide apart, he grazes his thumb across my lower lip. I open a little more, and he groans.

He dips the tip into my mouth, just enough for my tongue to swipe at it, then he takes a big step back.

I look down at his erection and bite my lip in a failing attempt to contain my glee.

He rubs his jaw as he chuckles. "Okay. Good night, Ellie."

"Night, Gavin."

"Until tomorrow."

"Sweet dreams," I say softly.

His gaze lingers on mine as he nods. "Most definitely."

31

GAVIN

I DIDN'T TELL her not to touch herself, mostly because there's zero chance I'm going to abstain. When I get home, I jerk off in the shower, the memory of her hair wound around my fingers taking me over the edge.

I'm hard again as I get into bed. I want her waiting for me right here when I get back from Washington.

Four and a half hours later, my alarm goes off. I jack-knife out of bed before my inner lazy guy has a chance to suggest otherwise, and push myself through a ten minute high-intensity workout that both wakes me up and justifies the cold pizza I eat for breakfast.

I have Tim do a loop through the grounds of Rideau Hall, across the road, so I can tweet a picture of the first rays of the sunrise over the Governor General's official residence.

@therealgavinstrong Beautiful morning to be in service to Her Royal Majesty. Off to work. #morningperson #atleasttoday

By the seven a.m. briefing, **#morningperson** is trending. Stuff like that has zero to do with the job of running the country, but it makes the new communications director happy.

After the disaster of our last speechwriter leaking the fundraiser speech, Stew quietly moved the last communications director into another role and hired someone from BC, Caroline Miller-Best. She and her husband have a PR firm in Vancouver, and she's only promised us six months of her time, but that's all I need.

Caroline has made a **#morningperson** sign and has it propped up on my desk when I walk in.

"You liked that?"

"I loved that. Can we have a minute before the briefing?"

I shake my head. The briefing doesn't start late for any reason. "But you can have five after."

"Deal."

Stew gets us started thirty seconds early, and we finish with forty-five seconds to spare. This is why he's my CoS.

"Thank you all," I say, standing as they start to leave.

Stew glances at Caroline, who remains seated. I shrug. He can stay if he wants. He closes the door and starts to pace back and forth.

I laugh. "God, you're such a fucking pessimist."

Caroline keeps a neutral face. "Is he pacing because of a blind item about you on a date last night?"

"Probably." Well, that didn't take long. "Do they have her name?"

"No. I think it's truly blind for now. There's a Snapchat video of you holding someone's hand and carrying a blanket. It's a few seconds long. Any chance this is the real reason I've been hired?"

"Yes. Every chance."

"Who is she?"

Stew doesn't let me answer. "She's a PhD candidate at the University of Ottawa's business school. They met earlier this summer, through work."

Caroline's face doesn't change. "Here?"

I nod.

"What's the most important thing I need to know about your relationship?"

"I love her."

"Okay. Stew can fill me in on the rest?"

"Yes, but I want to see anything and everything that's drafted on this. Nothing comes out of this office on the topic of Ellie without being approved by me first."

"No problem." She stands and gives me a little nod. "It's smart to do this now, before the House is in session."

I give her another terse nod and they leave. I've got two minutes before Beth bustles in with the next thing on my agenda. I spend every second of it wondering if Caroline's right and I've decided to shove Ellie into the limelight because it's politically advantageous to get this scandal over with sooner than later.

32

ELLIE

Our second date begins the way our first one ended, with a kiss that leaves me distracted beyond measure.

Gavin picks me up at the university this time. I get a single knock-at-the-door warning before he's inside my office, the door closed and locked. Within two strides he's got me backed up against my desk, his hands in my hair and his lips pushing mine apart.

"I was going to meet you downstairs," I say, my voice hitching as I try to think about something other than getting him out of his navy suit. My hands aren't cooperating.

"I've been hungry for you since I left last night, and this is our only chance to be alone today."

I should have taken him up on the offer to fly with him to Washington. "Let's send your security detail down to the cafeteria for sandwiches and stay here until you have to go. I've never used the lock on my door. This would be an excellent opportunity to break it in."

"A virgin lock," he says, groaning as he lifts his hands off my hips and tries to back away.

I'm having none of that. I grab his hands and slide them down my thighs. "And I wore stockings today."

"You're killing me." He kisses me again. Ruthless and possessive. God, I love him. I'm out of my mind, head over heels in love with him.

"No panties today, either." I'm lying. I wore those to work. I just took them off ten minutes ago.

"Fucking hell, Sprite." He lifts me up and shoves me back on my desk. "Feet up."

I kick off my heels and bend my legs, resting my silk-covered soles right on the edge of my desk. The dress I'm wearing today has a full, twirly skirt, and it falls away from my body, leaving nothing hidden from his hungry gaze. "I want you inside me," I whisper. "Every minute of every day."

He shakes his head. "Just kissing I said. For the first few dates."

"I know you did…"

He leans over me, bracing his hands on the desk on either side of my hips. "But?"

But nothing. "You're right. I'm sorry."

"So what's the rule?"

"Just kissing."

"Is that a problem?"

I shake my head. "I love kissing you."

He smiles. "Good girl. I love kissing you too, Sprite." He pushes himself up again. He smooths his tie, then adjusts his erection before smoothly dropping to his knees. "Everywhere."

Heat shoots through me as his head obscures my view between my thighs. I feel his breath next, on my thigh, then the tease of his tongue along my slit. Like we've got all the time in the world instead of just an hour, and oh my God all the things I want to do to him. If he'll even let me. He might not.

His next lick is slower, dirtier, his tongue wide and flat, and I want to shoot off my desk from the pleasure of it. He's so unbelievably good at this I want to cry and scream and kick my feet. Instead I press my heels harder against the desk and swallow a moan. Lips tight together, eyes closed, I give myself over to him. My body is his to tease and devour, light up and set aflame however he sees fit.

Devour.

That's the right word for how he's going down on me, but it's soft at the same time. Hungry and insistent, a gentle but thorough dismantling. He's everywhere, licking and sucking, his fingers holding me open so he can explore every last inch of my flesh with his tongue and—sometimes, carefully—his teeth.

Consumed. That's another good word for how I feel as he tugs my clit into his mouth and suckles on it until I climax in a shuddering, whimpering, happiest-girl-ever-who-maybe-bit-her-tongue kind of way.

My eyes are still screwed shut when I feel the blunt, swollen head of his cock rubbing against my entrance.

I bite my lip harder to keep from moaning at how good that feels—rub, rub, oh God, put it in already, rub—and ask, "What about just kissing?"

"Rules are stupid." He bottoms out inside me and holds still there as he presses his forehead against mine. It feels incredible—better than I ever imagined. "I'm going to miss you tonight. I want you in my bed tomorrow when I get back."

"Okay."

"It'll be late."

"I'll be there."

He rocks his hips back, then pistons forward again,

hitting the sweet spot on the first thrust. "Do I have to pull out? This could be messy for our lunch date."

He can't be seriously still thinking about food. I kiss him breathlessly. "I've got wipes, it'll be fine." I lick his lower lip with the point of my tongue. "You taste like me."

"Then I taste fucking amazing."

I gasp as he fucks into me harder, his hands tightening on my hips.

"Gonna come again? Come on my cock, babe. Let me feel that sweet pussy tighten up all around me and I'm going to fill you up."

Those words shouldn't work on me as well as they do, but I'm just as dirty as he is, because yes I want that. I want it all and I want it now and if he just keeps it up— "Yes, there."

He holds himself buried inside me. "There?"

A grind of his hips tests it out and I throw my head back. "Yes."

His hips pump, barely moving but doing all the heavy lifting as far as my G-spot is concerned.

I'm whisper-chanting his name now, *Gavin yes Gavin yes Gavin yes*, and I'm pretty sure I'm being quiet, but he folds himself over me again, this time whispering that I need to be quiet. I am, I think. And in the silence he does it again.

"Shhh. Be a good girl and come for me."

I shatter. He follows me into the orgasm, fucking me roughly again for the last few desperate strokes, then he groans as he spills himself inside me.

Messy. Perfect.

"Shhh," I tell him as he buries his face in my neck.

He laughs.

"So we can make it one date without sex," he says a few minutes later as I pass him a wet wipe from my emergency stash in my drawer. It's previously been used to erase evidence of me devouring a donair before my office hours and scrubbing white board marker off my forearm when I got a little hyper in a lecture about microaggressions in the workplace.

I shrug, too blissed-out from two orgasms to worry about the fact that we're clearly sex addicts. "Well, that's longer than some people."

"You're shameless."

"You made me so. I used to be such a good girl."

"That is not a complaint, I assure you. And you are still a very good girl."

"How much time do we have now?"

"An hour. How about we go to the cafeteria?"

"That's not exactly low-profile."

"Yeah." He gives me a level look. "About that."

"Gavin…"

"Someone took a video of us last night at the Sound and Light show."

The bottom drops out of my stomach. "Oh."

"It's just me. The video shows your arm, the back of your head, and it's dark, so right now it's just a non-story, the PM went on a date."

"For now."

"I'm not hiding you."

I frown. No, he's not. Suddenly he's ruthlessly *not* hiding me, and I point that out. He has the good grace to look a little chagrined, although I don't think for a second that he's using me. "Is this because we've still got four weeks until the House comes back and you're hoping it'll blow over by September?"

"That's what our new communications director suggested this morning." His face tightens up. "It wasn't my deliberate thought, no."

But it's convenient. I sigh. "That better not be what the sex was about."

His eyes flare. "No. Never. That was because I can't keep my hands off you."

I sigh. "Okay. Let's go have lunch and have our picture taken."

"Just like that?"

"I think our second date is a little early for me to turn into a shrew. I'll save that for date five. But when you get back from Washington, I want to meet this communications director. If we're going to do this, I don't want to be in the dark about it."

Gavin does one better. After lunch—where he did a quick glad-hand around the cafeteria, and then we were left pretty much alone—he calls Stew and advises him that I'd like to meet with Caroline Miller-Best. *The new communications director*, he mouths. I make a mental note to Google her and make sure she's not hot or single.

Although Beth is both hot and single, and I'm not jealous of her—wasn't even in the nano-second that I thought maybe she might be crushing on him. But she has a sibling-esque vibe with Gavin, like she'd rather gouge her eyes out than see him naked. She might be the only person in the country, so that makes her special.

Yeah, I was kind of crazy to think she had a thing for him.

I should buy Beth flowers.

After I google this Caroline person, and give myself a talking to, because crazy is not cool.

"Perfect. I'll let her know." He hangs up. "Tomorrow, four o'clock, Stew's office."

"That's not going to be awkward at all."

"Do you want to wait until I'm back?"

We don't really have that kind of time. "No, this is fine."

He gives me a quick kiss and ducks into the car.

I'm left standing on the curb, wondering how many hours I have left before I'm surrounded by photographers and reporters throwing questions at me about sexual harassment in the workplace.

33

GAVIN

FROM THE SECOND I step onto the plane until I crash into my hotel room bed after midnight, the rest of my day is non-stop work. I get to sleep in until six, which should feel like a luxury, but I wake up at half past five with a hard-on that won't quit.

I look through my burner phone, eating up Ellie's PG-13 texts about yoga like they're porn.

It's too early to call her, and she's not as practised as Max is at the careful double-speak of a burner phone call. I'd wake her up and she'd be all breathy and half-asleep, and she'd say my name…

That does it. Just the imagined echo of my name in her sleepy, sexy voice, and I come all over my stomach.

Fucking teenager.

I scrub myself clean with a washcloth from the bathroom, then push myself through a quick but painful workout.

Time to suit up.

Rick Stupes tried to get in the elevator with me last night. He got a face full of Lachlan's chest, but Caroline already gave me the heads-up from Ottawa that CAN News has requested a one-on-one interview, and I don't have a great reason to say no, other than I don't like the guy.

"I don't have time on the trip," I hedged.

"No, of course not. When you get back."

"Right."

"But they'll want some footage of you at the Embassy."

"Fine. But someone's gotta be in all that footage with me so we have something to talk about. I can't just ignore the guy's questions for however long the camera is following me around."

We settled on footage of my working lunch with the Ambassador and some meet and greets with American guests in the garden.

I pack up my bag. Yesterday's suit, my book for the plane, my briefing notes. Normally I slide my burner phone into my carry-on, too, but today I want it on me. Elle's sweet texts, right next to my heart.

I'm such a goner for her, and not embarrassed at all.

I never thought I'd be one of those sentimental mooners who saves every little dating memento. Okay, I'm not quite that bad, but Max is going to get a lot of mileage from this. And I'm going to let him, because apparently, love does crazy things to your threshold for humiliation.

The morning speeds by and lunch is productive. I like the ambassador to the United States. He was appointed by the last guy, but our philosophies align and I'm confident he'll continue to represent our government well and advocate for the issues that matter most to Canadians.

After lunch, we head outside for a meet and greet with business people who have significant investments crossing the border on a regular basis. Trade is the primary reason for this trip and I'm intent on fostering an excellent relationship with all involved, no matter how our personal and political beliefs may be at odds.

I'm in the middle of a conversation with an import/export dealer from Montana when my pocket starts crooning.

"Excuse me," I mutter, pulling out my phone as Jann Arden asks "Could I Be Your Girl" … a ringtone I never thought anyone would hear.

As much as I hate sending Ellie to voice mail, there's no way I can take her phone call on camera.

I return to our discussion of the North American Free Trade Agreement, nodding noncommittally as I silently scream *hell no*. All I really want to do is tell the guy to stop thinking of that expensive new toy he wants to finance on the backs of ordinary folks, then lock myself in a room and have phone sex with my girlfriend.

And my head is spinning as I try to figure out who heard the phone ring—and picked up on my choice of ringtones for Ellie. I catch Lachlan's eye and he gives a slight sideways nod. I slide my gaze over and my belly hits the ground when I see Ricks Stupes and his camera operator standing well within hearing distance.

I am royally fucked sideways with a two-by-four. My selfish desire to carry some semblance of Ellie with me has jeopardised her privacy, and now I'm going to have to shift my communications staff to damage control.

34

ELLIE

I SHOULDN'T HAVE CALLED Gavin. I'm kicking myself as I dash into Centre Block and stand in the visitor security line, just like I did the first day we met.

Lachlan texted me a few minutes later.

Lachlan
BJ's busy. Will call soon.

Now I'm second-guessing this whole thing. This meeting could wait until he's back.

We could just hook up under the cover of darkness at 24 Sussex. Nobody needs to know I'm banging the PM.

Except as I hold out my purse for content inspection, my phone vibrates again. This time it's Gavin himself.

BJ
So my phone just went off on camera. Did I tell you that my ringtone for you is set to a Jann Arden song?

I guess we're not talking in code any more.

Lee
Oh, my!

BJ
Yeah.

Lee
Sorry.

BJ
My fault. I must have accidentally turned the
ringer on this morning. Did you need
something?

Lee
Not really. And now I've arrived…where I'm
going. Your office.

BJ
Noted. Will call you soon.

It's weird coming back to Centre Block with the visitor
badge around my neck.

Even weirder when I bump into Beth, but she gives me
a genuine smile and whispers that Caroline's waiting for me
in Stew's office and Stew's about to have a coronary.

On one hand, that's seriously eye-roll worthy.

On the other, Stew having a fit is something I can totally
handle.

I take a deep breath and knock on my former boss's
door.

CAROLINE MILLER-BEST IS HAPPILY MARRIED, and very
smart. I like her mostly for the latter reason, but the former
is good, too.

I'm also greatly relieved to discover she doesn't seem to care in the least that I was briefly an intern in this office. One woman down, fifteen million to go.

She's done a masterful job of crafting a narrative that highlights my education and frames the internship as more of a reward opportunity than a true employment situation.

It's seventy-three percent fibbing, but I don't care because it sounds plausible, especially coming from a woman. And it's something I can repeat, over and over again.

"Thank you," I say, feeling full of gratitude.

She gives me a bullshit-free smile. "You're welcome, but don't assume that this is going to go that easily."

"No, I know it probably won't. But I couldn't find the words the way that you did. Because…" I trail off. Stew doesn't need to hear that a lot of my rationalization about my relationship with Gavin is dirty at its core.

It just feels good.

He looks at me like he looks at nobody else, ever.

I think I might believe in soul mates now.

No, I can't say any of that.

"Because I'm too close to it," I say instead, and that's true, too.

"You need to brace yourself for lies," she says, glancing back and forth between me and Stew. "You all do. This may be used as cover for a smear campaign. The key is to never waver from the core narrative and stay on message. That goes for questions about your relationship along with questions about Ellie's brief employment here, and any policy that gets connected to Gavin…being human."

That's not how his political opponents will put it. But it's the truth, and I'm glad she gets it. "Okay."

"We're still planning on not saying anything until we're asked outright, but since you're going out in public together, I'd expect the story to break—and your name to be out there—by the end of the week. So if there's anyone at the university that you want to warn, or a roommate to prepare..."

"Thank you. My roommate already knows, and has family experience with keeping her head down."

"Oh?"

"Her father manufactures car parts. Brewster Automotive?" Sasha's father is a legit business magnate. He always wanted her to join the family business. She got her MBA, but instead of going to work with him, she applied for her PhD instead. I'm pretty sure that when she finishes this degree, she'll find a post-doc on the other side of the planet.

Telling her dad she wants nothing to do with the family business would be easier, but he's the one man Sasha has a hard time telling off or letting down.

"Sounds good. But let me know if you run into any problems. There's a limit to what I can do from this position, but Gavin will hire a private PR firm if needed."

I shake my head. That's kind of insane. "We'll manage just fine."

Stew moves the conversation to the more political considerations, which I'm interested in but don't directly affect me anymore, so when Beth knocks on the door and asks if she can steal me, I duck out.

"There's a call for you in Gavin's office," she says as she leads me over there.

Seriously? I'm smiling despite myself. That can only be one person. She lets me in and points me to the desk.

I notice the lamp is missing from the table next to the couch, and my cheeks flame red as she closes the door, leaving me alone.

I pick up the phone. "Hello?"

"Sprite," Gavin says warmly in my ear. "I'm returning your call."

"Isn't that what one of the two phones in my purse might be useful for?"

"I'm at the Canadian Embassy in Washington. I might as well take advantage of the secure line."

"Okay. I don't have any state secrets, though."

"You know a few." His voice has dropped. I recognize that tone.

"No. We are not having phone sex while I'm in your office and you're at an embassy and I don't think secure line means CSIS isn't listening."

"They're really not listening. What are you wearing?"

I lower *my* voice, because two can play this game. "A burlap sack."

"Daring choice. Take it off."

"Oooh, it's so rough on my skin."

His laugh is bright and unrestrained. "And underneath it is a full body black leotard?"

"How did you know?"

"Magic."

"Are you sure you aren't watching me? Where are the cameras?"

"I told you. No cameras in my office."

"That's a relief. I noticed the lamp is gone."

"I disposed of it."

"How heartless. What did that lamp ever do to you?"

"Scared off the woman I loved."

"Ah, but I came back to you."

"So you did." He clears his throat. "I gotta go. I'm being summoned."

"Love you. Wake me up tonight."

"You can count on it."

Beth stops me on my way out, holding up her hand. "Gavin's arranged for a car to pick you up at eight."

Oh, no. "He can't do that."

She shrugs. "And yet he has."

"Call it off. I'll find my own way there."

"Ellie, that's not how things work. My boss tells me a car has been arranged, I pass on the message. I don't cancel the car."

Her phone rings and she turns back to her desk.

Oh, no no no. I don't want to have this conversation with Stew. But I pull up my big girl panties and march back to his office. Caroline has disappeared.

The RCMP *cannot* chauffeur the PM's girlfriend everywhere. Gavin's probably going to freak about me taking the bus to 24 Sussex, but a cab would be too obvious.

So I sit down in front of Stew's desk and start what proves to be a terrifyingly awkward conversation. "So I need to tell you something and don't want you to freak out, because there's an easy fix."

He groans. "I'm scared to say this, but yes?"

"Gavin has arranged for a car to pick me up tonight and take me to his residence." Stew groans again but I keep going because I don't need him to lecture me on what I already know. "Which of course can't happen."

"Right. So just tell him that you won't be waiting for him when he lands."

I roll my eyes. Of course I'm going to be waiting for him. I'm just going to get there on my own. "I'm still going there, Stew. I'm just taking the bus. Can you put me on the approved visitors list?"

He swears under his breath. "I'm sure you're already on it, but yes, I'll check."

"Thank you."

"The bus?"

"It's how I get around."

"Well when this blows up in our faces, that will at least please the environmentalists."

"Glad I could be of some service."

"Let's pretend we never had this conversation."

"Deal."

35

GAVIN

I'M FREAKED out over the ring-tone incident and need to get some perspective, so I pull out the burner and call Max.

He answers on the second ring. "Shouldn't you be wheeling and dealing with a big-wig right now?"

"Fuck!" Not the most cryptic response.

"Oh, that sounds serious. What's up?"

"I'm sure it'll be national by morning."

"What will? Can you be more specific?"

Oh fuck it—it's gonna be everywhere in the morning, anyway, so why worry? "I left the ringer on for my special phone and Ellie called."

"Did you say anything embarrassing that was overheard?"

"I didn't, but my ringtone may cause me a little discomfort."

"Was it *Fuck the Pain Away*, by Peaches?"

Only Max would go straight there. This explains so many things.

"Nope. Jann Arden's *Would You Be My Girl*."

"Well, at least it was CanCon."

The fact that it's Canadian content makes it all okay? Sure. "I've just complicated everything."

"With...?"

"This wasn't exactly the plan."

"That's life."

"That's all you've got? I call you to vent and you tell me to suck it up?"

"Meanwhile I've got a kid arriving in five minutes who might not see his fourth birthday."

Point taken. I glance at the clock. I've interrupted Max in the middle of his afternoon clinic at BC Children's Hospital. Maybe I'm the asshole after all. "Perspective shift achieved."

"That's why you called me. I'll see you in a month."

"Can't wait." I hang up the phone and look at it. Yeah, I really can't wait, actually. Max is a unique counsellor in my life—no sugar coating, no bullshit. I can always count on him to give it to me straight.

Now I need to go impress the leader of the free world.

<hr>

WHEN I RETURN to the hotel from a gala at The White House late that night, Tim stops me as I head for the elevator to go to my suite. "You've got a visitor you need to see first."

"Who?"

He gives me a stone-faced look that says he's just doing his boss's bidding. "Lachlan just told me you need to go to a conference room first."

Bullshit. He knows more than he's telling me. "Who?" I ask more insistently.

He points me toward a room marked private. "A reporter."

I steel myself and stalk in. The last person I'm expecting is Rick Stupes. We had an agreement and all.

"Mighty late, Rick," I say quietly as I slide Lachlan a WTF look.

"Ellie Montague," he says, cutting to the chase.

"What about her?"

"Do you have any comment for a breaking news story that you had an affair with an intern who has since left your office?"

Ten, nine, eight... Lachlan would have frisked him. That would have been the deal. He got in to see me, but he's not wearing a wire. Of course, you can never be too sure about these things, so my answer can't be my fist through his face, no matter how much I want it to be.

I pull out my phone—the official PM phone—and dial Caroline. My teeth are clenched so hard that when she answers, my jaw cracks as I start to talk. "Pull the CAN News interview. Bullies don't get any attention from this government. And set up a live interview with as many of the other stations as want one. They each get three minutes of my time tomorrow, live to air on their morning shows."

"Bullies?" She clears her throat. "Of course. Consider it done."

I hang up the phone and toss it onto the table. Then I take off my jacket and loosen my tie.

Rick shifts restlessly on his feet. Clearly this is not how he thought this would go.

The best defence is a good offense. I cross my arms and sneer at him. "I will not be threatened. Run whatever you want, but in the morning your competitors are getting an exclusive quote that makes your story look like something the National Enquirer would be ashamed to print. Get the hell out."

"Is that on the record?"

"Fuck you, Rick. And tread carefully with how you treat Ellie. You don't want to end up on the wrong end of this story."

"Is that a threat?" Sweat beads on his temple, just a spot here and there, but he's fucking nervous. Good.

I crowd closer, herding him toward the door. "When I threaten you, you tiny little shit, it won't be in a private hotel room. It'll be on national television. Tune in to any station other than your own in the morning to hear it for yourself."

His face is ruddy with frustration and he clearly wants to say something else, but I'm done talking. I stalk closer and he pulls the door open, scurrying away like a scared mouse.

"That didn't go quite as I planned," Lachlan says, and I don't fucking believe him for a second.

"No?"

He shrugs. "I thought you'd plow him in the face."

"Wanted to."

"Being a grown-up sucks sometimes."

"Tell me about it." I sigh. "Let's get my bag and head to the airport."

I have a sweet woman to wrap myself around. And in the morning...well, we'll worry about that in the morning.

36

ELLIE

I'VE BEEN DRIFTING in and out of semi-conscious sleep state for hours, so when the mattress shifts under his weight, I immediately turn and reach for him in the dark.

He's naked. My fingers skate over his warm skin, working their way down to the erection I know is there. Because it's always there when we're close.

He grabs my wrists, trapping them above my head as he takes my mouth hard, his tongue insistent. I open for him in every way, pliant and soft still from sleep, but that's not the only reason. There's a tension running through him. He needs this from me right now, and he can have it.

He can take anything he wants.

But even as his grip tightens on my wrists, as his body flexes above me, he's still gentle as he climbs between my legs, nudging them apart with his knees. I'm slick and ready for his cock to slide deep inside, filling me completely.

Hard and thick, he stretches me to the point of aching. I try to rock my hips to adjust, but he's already dragging his cock out of me again, and his hands shift, pressing me harder against the bed. Be still, he's telling me. Take it. He thrusts his hips hard and fast, his lips devour me, and all I can do is lay there. But that's okay. I'm giving him exactly what he needs.

It's rough and fast, a whirlwind of heat and motion. He's bigger in the dark, and heavy. His touch is coarse—a hard squeeze of my breast, a bruising press against my hip. Every flex of his body moves me closer to the head of the bed as he fucks into me, grinding his pelvis against my clit.

I don't say anything, but we're both breathing hard, shaky, desperate sounds in the quiet of the night. He's shaking now, and I know the feeling. Inside, I'm so close. I want to fight for it, but I know it will be better if I just give in.

And it is. He doesn't last much longer, his last few thrusts wild and uncaged, but even in his need, he makes sure I'm coming before he lets himself go.

I wasn't expecting a nice little orgasm tonight. I wasn't expecting anything like this, and I don't know what it's all about, but the endorphins are racing through me and I'm so tired, I can't keep my eyes open. Gavin settles his weight on top of me again and alternates between peppering my face with gentle kisses and nuzzling my neck.

I feel like a lioness after mating, and I'm grateful we've moved on from condoms, because they are not conducive to blissing out after sex.

Eventually, he pulls out and shifts to the side before rolling me over on my side. He snuggles up behind me, wraps his arms around me and holds me tight to his body.

Now I can sleep.

37

ELLIE

GAVIN'S UP AT FIVE. He whispers for me to go back to sleep and I do because I swear we only fell asleep an hour ago. When I wake the second time, there's a note on the pillow that says he's left me breakfast—a travel coffee mug and a muffin—and if I'm up by eight, I should turn on the TV.

It takes me a minute to find the remote for the small flat-screen mounted on the far wall. I've never noticed it before.

When I turn it on, it's already tuned to a morning news show. The anchor is doing a summary of the day's headlines.

I pick at the muffin as I slowly wake up. I'm thinking about having a quick shower while I wait for whatever I'm supposed to see on TV when my phone rings. It's Sasha.

"Hey," I answer.

"What is going on?" She's out of breath. "I got a breaking news alert email that the PM is doing an interview in half an hour, addressing questions about his personal life."

"No clue," I whisper, my eyes huge as I watch the same

teasing headline suddenly scroll across the bottom of the screen.

"He didn't tell you he was going to do this?"

No, he didn't. I don't know how I feel about that. "We didn't talk last night. He came back in the middle of the night and left again before I was up for the day."

"He didn't wake you up?"

He did. Just not to talk. I press my thighs together. "It was really late."

"What is he going to say?"

I huff out a breath. So this is really happening. "I think he's going to say that we're in a relationship and point out repeatedly that it's not news until they believe him." Something must have happened. I flash back to the night before and the urgency with which he took me.

"Is he going to name you?"

"I don't know. Maybe."

"Have you told your parents?"

No. "You think I should call them?"

"I think your mom watches the news every morning."

She's right. I groan. "Gotta go."

I glance at the clock. It's half past seven. My father won't have left for work yet. They might be in the kitchen having breakfast, or they might be done by now and reading the paper while they finish their coffee.

My mother picks up on the second ring. "Hello?"

"Morning, Mama."

"Ellie!" She makes a sweet humming noise. "Oh, it's good to hear from you, sweetie."

Oh, Mama. Just wait. I wince as I grip the phone tighter to my ear. "How's Daddy?"

"He's good. Just getting ready for work."

"Good."

"Is something the matter?"

"Well…no. Nothing's wrong. I just have some news."

"What is it?" I can tell she's sat down. In the kitchen, maybe? I try to picture it. Orderly and neat. Everything in its place and as it should be.

I'm so the odd duck in our family. Wild and free, and now about to cause a ruckus on the national stage. "I'm seeing someone. And it's serious."

"Oh! Are you…" She trails off. "In a family way?"

Oh, God. "No. I'm not pregnant, Mama."

"Okay. Good. Although, you know, you're not getting any younger. But make him marry you first."

"Yeah, we're not that serious yet."

"Well, that's exciting anyway. When will we get to meet him?"

A hysterical giggle burbles up in my throat. "You already have, actually."

My mother doesn't update Facebook very often. I think the picture of her and my father meeting Gavin on the campaign trail is her most recent photo.

"Is he someone from school?"

I glance toward the TV. The anchor is now setting up the interview. "Are you watching the morning news?"

"It's on in the other room."

"Go put it on CTN."

"Why?"

"Just…do it. I'll stay on the phone."

She calls for my dad, and I hear the TV change. My father mutters something about Gavin looking…I'm not sure. Too pretty for so early in the morning, maybe. He's never been as much of a fan as my mother has been, although they both voted for him.

"Mama, maybe send Dad to work."

"It's not time for him to go yet, sweetie."

Kill me now. "Right."

"So what are we watching for? The prime minister is on there now."

I know. He looks stern, a muscle flexing in his jaw as he adjusts the earpiece so he can hear the interviewer. "That's him."

"That's who?"

"That's who I'm dating."

Silence is the only response from the other end of the line. I wish my mother would say something. In stereo, both from the TV on Gavin's wall and over the phone from my parents' living room in Montreal, I hear the reporter wrap up the introduction and lob a first, easy question. "Mr. Strong, you were in Washington yesterday talking trade deals. You've spoken publicly before about needing to undo a lot of messy deals that were negotiated by your predecessor. Did you make any progress on that promise yesterday?"

In my ear, my mother clears her throat. "Ellie?"

My mother hates lying above all else. Although maybe she just thinks I'm delusional, not lying. I don't answer her. My attention is locked on Gavin as he pours his attention into the camera, answering the question masterfully. That would be the trade—he gets to talk about trade first. Then the next question will be...

"And we understand that you got a phone call yesterday in the middle of a meeting?"

He flashes a quick grin. "My phone rang. I wasn't able to take the call, because of that meeting."

"Your ring tone drew a lot of attention. The reporters that have followed you on the campaign and as you've settled into office have never heard Jann Arden come out of your phone before."

"She's a national treasure."

"Indeed she is. But coupled with the reports that you

were seen on a date earlier this week, and we doubt that the caller was actually Ms. Arden—"

"That's quite the presumption," he says with a chuckle.

"The fact remains that you are an eligible bachelor and people want to know, Mr. Strong—who is the lucky lady?"

It's a total softball question. I wonder what else he had to trade to get it pitched like that, and my chest pulls tight with worry. How much am I costing him?

"In an ideal world, I wouldn't have to answer that question. Let's be honest here for a second—this is good gossip, nothing more. But yes, I am in a relationship. It's new and getting serious. It's also private. I think most Canadians can appreciate that I'm not the easiest man to date, and it would be great if I was allowed to fumble my way through impressing this woman on my own terms."

"When will we get to meet her?"

"When she's ready. She's a private citizen, and I hope everyone continues to respect that fact."

"How did you meet?" This question is less soft. This is what they get.

He doesn't flinch. "She's a PhD candidate at one of the universities here in Ottawa. We met through work."

"She worked in your office?"

"Briefly. She's an incredibly bright woman, and I was lucky to benefit from her input on a number of issues for the short time she worked with my chief of staff."

I let out a breath that I hadn't realized I was holding. In my ear, I hear my father talking about going to work. My mother, like me, is still totally silent.

The interviewer wraps up the interview with one last question about trade, then they cut to a commercial.

"The prime minister?" my mother gasps in my ear.

"Yeah. Yes," I repeat, because my mother hates casual answers.

"The prime minister what?" my father asks, and I thunk my skull back against the headboard.

"Is Ellie's new boyfriend."

I can see it now. My father's brow furrowed as he bobble-heads back and forth between my mother and the TV as he slowly processes what he just saw.

"Ellie's the incredibly bright woman?"

"Seriously?" I exclaim, jerking upright. "That's what he grabs on to? I have a Master's degree. I'm ABD on my PhD and—"

"Sweetie, you know we don't know what those letters mean."

"All But Dissertation. Seriously, Mama, we've had this conversation."

"I can't remember those things. Well, I hope you don't get hurt."

And this is why I don't go home more often. I'm used to her missing the point like this, but it still stings a little. I bury that deep. "Thank you."

"He's a good catch," she adds, trying to soften her response, but that's really not the right approach.

I sigh. "Tell Daddy he should have a good day at work."

"Will we see you on TV later today?"

Not if I can help it. "I love you guys."

I CALL Sasha after I finish freaking out and we agree I can legitimately avoid campus for at least a day. I don't have any posted office hours right now anyway, so she doesn't even need to put a note on my door. Which is good because the last thing I want is video footage on the news of my office door with a note posted on it, practically screaming that I'm hiding.

Because I totally am, but I'd prefer to hide in secret.

Lachlan shows up mid-morning and asks me if I want to go back to my apartment. He claims he can get me out of 24 Sussex without anyone being aware—and I don't even have to get in the trunk of a car. But I'll have to come back sooner than later because if I don't, Gavin will come to my place and that can't happen. **The Prime Minister's Booty Call**, the headline would scream. No, no, no.

So I'm staying put. Instead I have Sasha pack me a bigger bag and pick up some of my work from my office, and she meets Lachlan a few blocks from our place. Fancy spy work, I tease her, but it works.

Really, hiding out at 24 Sussex isn't that bad. And it seems that nobody is aware I'm hiding in the prime minister's residence, which is even better.

I poke about in the kitchen and discover Gavin has the makings for the most epic sandwich ever. I make myself one for lunch, then text him a picture of it.

BJ
I want one for dinner.

Lee
Awww, the first meal I've ever made for you.

BJ
You made me nachos.

Lee
No, I made myself nachos and you came over uninvited and helped yourself. Not the same thing. This sandwich will be crafted with love.

BJ
And the nachos were...

Lee
Built from tears of sadness.

BJ
LOL

Lee
My tears of sadness aren't funny

BJ
Sure

Lee
No sandwich for you

BJ
We'll see

Lee
I'm holding strong on this

BJ
Sure

Lee
Stop it

BJ
What? I'm not doing anything.

Lee
Don't you have work to do?

BJ
Doing it right now. Multi-tasking.

Lee
I love you. You can have a sandwich.

By the end of the day, the media has my name and the

internship details, but not much else. They have zero footage of me or Sasha, or even our apartment. A few nice photos are lifted from my social media pages, but those are mostly locked down thanks to my teaching time as a grad student, so the ones they take are the ones I intend for public consumption anyway. The rest of my much-discussed biography is culled from my academic curriculum vitae which they must have grabbed from my very sparse university web page.

When Gavin arrives, I'm in the living room, and the TV is on but I'm ignoring it because I've gone back to my work. My laptop is open and I'm surrounded by a stack of journals on one side and a couple of confidential reports I'm summarizing for Stew on the other.

"We should probably stop using you for those position papers," he says from the doorway.

I glance up at him, then back to the report in my hand. "What? No, I love doing these. And if or when I get asked about what I did for you, I want to say it was more than fetch your coffee."

"Did you ever fetch my coffee?"

"No."

"Then..."

"I like these," I say again, clutching the report to my chest. "Don't take them away from me."

He strolls over and leans in, kissing me lightly before tugging on my hair—a little not so lightly. "Okay."

"I'll make you that sandwich in a minute."

"I'm going to go take a shower and change. Finish your work. Or I can make my own sandwich."

"This might be the one and only time I ever offer to cook for you."

He can barely suppress his smirk. "Cook?"

I laugh. "Prepare something."

"I should've locked you up in my gilded tower sooner," he murmurs, then swears under his breath when my face crumples. "No, sorry, that was a shit thing to say."

"It's okay." I school my features into something more understanding. "We can play kidnapped princess another day. I'll regain my sense of humour about it soon enough."

"It's just for a little while. And I'll arrange for private security for you if you want to go back to your apartment and the university. We can make that happen tomorrow. Just say the word."

"Not the RCMP."

He shakes his head. "No. Private security, paid for out my own pocket."

"I can't let you —"

"You can, and you will, Sprite."

His tone works where his words didn't. "Okay."

"Excuse me?"

I smile. "Yes, Sir."

"You're mine to protect, Ellie. Never forget that."

"I won't." I take a deep breath. "I'd like to go to campus next Monday. I have a meeting with my advisor. But I don't need to go anywhere before then."

"We'll make sure that happens. And until then, you can roam around here wearing nothing but my dress shirts. Or just...nothing. Either would please me immensely."

I set aside my work and stand, carefully stripping him out of his shirt. My hands slide beneath the cotton, touching him for no other reason than the warmth of his skin brings me joy. Hard muscles, tight planes, soft fur down the middle...I bare it all. Then I quietly strip for him, taking off my tank top and lounge pants. He watches me through hooded eyes as I pick up his dress shirt and wrap myself in the soft cotton that smells just like him.

"Now I can make you that sandwich," I whisper, and he

picks me up instead. My legs wrap around his waist and he kisses me hungrily.

"After," he says.

"Later?"

"Much later."

3 8

___

GAVIN

ELLIE'S BIRTHDAY begins with me on the other side of the country, wrapping up a three day hop through the Prairie provinces, talking trade on this side of the border. But by mid-day I'm jetting back across the country to see her, and I can't wait.

Last week she was totally fine with laying low.

This week she's going nuts and I can't blame her. Her first outing with her private security guards went just fine. But when she tried to go to yoga the next day, two photographers blocked her entrance to the studio until the owner came out and escorted her inside.

I lost my shit over that one, and Lachlan had to stand between me and the press bus at our event.

"This will blow over," he insisted, and he was right.

I fucking hate to admit that. I really wanted to bust some heads that day, but the guilty parties weren't on that bus. They were three provinces away, and losing my cool would only make the story bigger, not help it fade away.

So she's back to spending most of her time at 24 Sussex,

302

although this time people know that's where she is, so leaving is harder.

But it's not impossible, and tonight I'm taking her out for a private birthday celebration. Her roommate agreed to go shopping for a surprise birthday dress for Ellie—through Beth as my proxy, because despite officially not being afraid of anything, I'm still a little scared of Sasha.

Beth is waiting for me at the airport when we land. The first thing she hands me once we're driving to Parliament is a stack of letters to sign. The next is a long, slim velvet box. "This arrived for you while you were gone."

Thank God for overnight shipping and online shopping. "Thanks. And the other gifts?"

"There's a boxed up dress and shoes from Sasha in the trunk. And the big gift is at the Hill. Do you want to take it over?"

I glance at Lachlan, who is studiously staring straight ahead. "You think they'll let me?"

She sniffs frostily. "It's her birthday. If *they* don't, there's no hope for *them*."

"I can hear you," Lachlan says gruffly from the front seat.

I smirk. Of course, I'm in the smug position of being very much in love, and these two are still circling each other like idiots, so I'm just being mean, but whatever. It's my girlfriend's birthday and I'm about to spoil her rotten. "So that's a yes?"

He sighs. "Sure. You can take Ellie's present to 24 Sussex."

I ONLY MEANT to go into the office for a few minutes, but that's never how it goes, so it's already five o'clock when I arrive home. Early by any measure, except for when I haven't seen Ellie for a few days and it's her birthday and I know she's waiting for me.

I find her in my room, fresh from the shower and wrapped in a towel. I toss her gifts on the bed and wrap my arms around her from behind. "Missed you," I whisper as I kiss her neck. "Are you wearing makeup that I'll mess up if I kiss you properly?"

She shakes her head and I spin her around, cupping the back of her neck as I pour just how much I missed her into one hot kiss after another. She tastes like sunshine and berries, the sweetest woman I've ever kissed, and it takes all my will power not to tug away the towel and drop to my knees.

Later. There's time for me to lick up every last inch of her later. Maybe while she's tied to my bed and begging me for yet another orgasm.

"Finish getting ready," I whisper against her lips as I release her.

"I'm not sure what to wear," she whispers back. "I don't have any nice dresses here and Sasha was too busy to meet up with Lachlan."

I grin. "She was too busy running an errand for me — picking up your first present."

"What?" She presses her hands against my chest and pushes me lightly out of the way. I gesture toward the bed. Three presents.

I've never wanted to lavish a woman with gifts as much as I want to spoil Ellie. But I've contained myself today to practical gifts — if we're going by the literal definition of practical, and ignoring that one of them is a pearl necklace. Mostly practical.

She lifts the lid on the largest box and gasps. I'd given Sasha some parameters. Strapless, like the dress she wore to the fundraiser. Green or blue, to set off her colouring perfectly. And nothing too stiff.

What Ellie lifts out of the box matches what I saw in my mind almost exactly—and the one way it's different is even better than I imagined. My dick slams into gear as she drops her towel and slides her naked body into the gauzy, ethereal layers of chiffon. It's not strapless, exactly. The top layer of fabric floats over her breasts and glides over her shoulders, twisting behind her before falling into the skirt. But it's see-through, too, an illusion of skin that I can see but can't touch, and it's perfect.

"Open the next one," I say roughly. She reaches for the jewelry box and I move behind her. Her zipper's only partially done up, and I zip her closed, rubbing my knuckles along her spine as I go.

She shivers and her fingers pause on the still-closed box. "You're spoiling me."

She's left her hair loose tonight, her waves spilling down her back. I gather them in my fist and move the long, soft locks to one side so I can press my mouth to the bare skin of her neck before answering. "Yes. And you will accept all my gifts. Understand? It's your birthday and I love you. Let me do this."

She takes a deep breath and snaps open the lid, revealing the necklace. "Oh, Gavin…" She lifts it out of the velvet case and exhales. "It's stunning. This is—"

I cut her off. "The only finish to that sentence I want to hear is beautiful. 'Beautiful just like me,' would also be acceptable."

She smiles. "Fine. This is beautiful just like you."

I laugh under my breath. "Brat."

"Put it on me?"

"My pleasure." Our fingers tangle more than necessary as I take the two ends of the strand from her. I will never tire of touching her, in big and little ways. It fits her perfectly, falling just below her collarbone, and I trace the entire length of it with my finger. "One more gift, Sprite."

She gives me a little look. Yes, on this last gift, there will be no debate. *Yes, Sir* is the only answer I want to hear from her when asked if she understands why I'm giving it to her.

This box is deceptively small. She lifts the plain white cardboard lid and then just stands there, stock-still.

I wait for a protest, but one doesn't come.

"Ellie?" I turn her around so she's facing me, but her head is still bent. She's staring at the set of car keys nestled in the white cotton batting.

"Why?" she asks, her voice breathy and full of emotion.

"Because I want you to be able to go anywhere, anytime, and the fact that you can't just hop on the bus anymore is all on me." I gently lift her chin up so she can see my face and I can see hers. "Because I love you. And I want you to be safe and *feel* safe at all times."

She blinks up at me, her eyes bright and shiny with unshed tears. "It's too much."

It's not enough by a million miles. "It has tinted windows and Bluetooth everything. You can summon Lachlan at the push of the button."

She frowns. "Did you get me the Batmobile?"

"Sadly, no." It's not even the fancy Lexus I wanted to get her. Sasha convinced Beth that I should go for something more mid-range.

"Is it made in Canada?"

God, this woman. I couldn't love her any more than I already do. "Yes. First thing I thought of."

She does this whole little processing thing in front of me as she nibbles on her lower lip and looks at me so intently I want to tell her it's no big deal—but it is, for her, and for that reason, it is for me.

I want to take care of her on an epic scale. But she has to be okay with that, too.

When she smiles and twirls the keys around her index finger, I know I've done well. She throws her arms around my neck. "I love you," she says in my ear, and those three little words make my heart explode. "Best birthday ever."

"It's only just begun." I squeeze her against me. "I'm going to quickly jump in the shower, then we've got dinner reservations."

"What time?"

"They're expecting us at seven, but it's a bit flexible." I kiss her once more, then wave her back to the dressing table where I found her when I came in. "Finish getting ready."

"I won't take long. A bit of makeup and I should probably put on some underwear."

I clear my throat. "No, that won't be necessary."

"Oh, come on…really? In public?"

I grab her hand and tug her back against my body. "Who said anything about going out in public?"

ONCE I SHOWER and change into a fresh suit, we head downstairs. Ellie spends a bit of time getting to know her new compact SUV, which she's already named Gladys, then I make her get into the back of my official town car.

"I can't drive to my birthday dinner?"

"Sure you could. But I've requested a bottle of champagne be waiting for us on ice, so you'd have to leave Gladys behind at the end of the night."

She gasps. "Oh, no!"

"Exactly."

She settles into the crook of my arm and sighs happily. "So where are we going?"

I just smile at her. It won't take long.

Lachlan turns left out of the gate and follows the street along the river until we reach our destination. Ellie does a double take. "The Aviation and Space Museum?"

I give her a broad grin and leap out. She waits for me to open her door, then winks at me to make sure I know she did that for me.

I offer her my arm and she rolls her eyes before sliding her fingers through mine, and that's even better. Give and take. That's the foundation of our relationship.

Hand in hand, we walk toward the door. I don't know if she noticed that the parking lot was empty, but she definitely notices that we're all alone when we step inside.

"What have you done?" she says quietly, her eyes big.

"This way." I guide her past the airplane in the lobby and into the main exhibition hall, a massive space filled with aircraft from all points in modern history.

Her heels click on the floor and echo in the oversized space, but as we curve past the Avro 683 Lancaster X, the string quartet starts playing Strauss's *Emperor Waltz*.

Ellie slows her steps as she sees the table for two set up in the middle of the exhibition hall, an ice bucket standing next to it with a bottle of champagne waiting for us. "Oh, Gavin."

She turns in a circle, wonder painted all over her gorgeous face, and I want to take her right here. Against the side of a fighter jet. Claim her as mine, over and over again, surrounded by history.

I shove my hands in my pockets instead. "Happy birthday, Sprite."

"This is crazy." But she says it softly, in a good way, and

when she twirls again faster this time, I catch her in my arms when she's done and we start dancing.

It is not in my nature to dance, really. I know how, I make it look passable—it's not that different from hockey, I suppose. But until this moment, I wouldn't have said I had the romantic nature for it.

But holding Ellie close, moving my hips against hers as she holds my gaze, her lips parted and her eyes bright…I want to do this forever. She softens in my embrace, letting me lead with ease, and I spin us around and around slowly, my legs following the cue of the music. Wide step, pull her in tight. Turn. Hips together. And again, more because it feels good than anything to do with the music. Another step, another brush of her belly against my thickening erection. Fuck me. She sighs and I tighten my arms around her.

My Ellie. My Sprite.

"Shall we have a toast to your twenty-sixth birthday?" I ask as the song fades, my voice husky.

She nods and the musicians slide into another song, this one quieter. I pour us each a glass of sparkling wine as a waiter appears from around one of the dozens of airplanes surrounding us.

"Dinner will be served in a few minutes. Feel free to explore the gallery, or make yourselves comfortable."

Ellie's already heading for a helicopter. I grin as I follow, but while her eyes are on the Boeing Vertol in front of us, my eyes are on her ass. It's the most spectacular view in the place.

Besides, I already had a personal tour of the collection from the museum director when I first moved to Ottawa. He's an old family friend.

"You want to try out the flight simulators?" I ask as I stop right behind her.

She glances at me over her shoulder. "We can do that?"

Oh. Can we ever.

Dinner waits another thirty minutes for us, and when we finally sit at our table, we're both a little silly. I'm so fucking proud of myself for nailing this birthday present.

Which makes it all the more disappointing when my phone rings halfway through our meal. Only one phone number is set to ring through right now, and I need to answer it. I kiss Ellie's hand quickly and step away from the table.

"I'm terribly sorry," Stew says, and he sounds it. Duty calls. "There's been a bombing at the Embassy in Sudan. No fatalities yet, but—"

"I'll be right there." I turn back toward Ellie and she's already walking toward me, her game face on. "Something's come up," I tell her, but I don't need to. She knows, and she gets it, because she's perfect.

"Of course. Tell me what would be most helpful— should I come with you?"

Ahead of us, Tim steps into view and gestures for us to follow him. My car is already waiting, but another one is fast approaching across the parking lot. I recognize the SUV that Ellie's private bodyguards are using, and say a small thanks that Lachlan knows to both take care of her and make sure it's not on the public dime.

"Don't wait up for me," I tell her as she squeezes my hand.

She shakes her head. "I won't. But wake me up when you get back."

I'm so blessed that she understands. And if I wake her up, it'll be to give her one last birthday present. Maybe just belated by that point.

39

ELLIE

IT'S ALMOST MIDNIGHT, four hours after Gavin was whisked away. An hour after we were dancing like carefree lovers, he made a terse statement against violence and terrorism on the steps of the House of Commons.

Now I'm curled up in his bed, wearing one of his t-shirts, and I stare at the television screen in horror. I knew it must be something serious, but a series of bombs at a number of embassies of G7 nations…There's been a deliberate, orchestrated terror attack. Hundreds of local Sudanese and dozens of international staff have been injured. There are fatalities, but not at the Canadian Embassy.

This is the first military strike of Gavin's term, so he needs to make a strong statement, but he ran against the rabid lunacy of the previous government. This is a test. The entire country will be watching, judging, how he handles this—and measuring him against his NATO allies.

As an academic, my areas of interest lie within domestic politics, but as a citizen, my hopes and fears don't stop at the border.

Dawn has broken now in Sudan. It will crack across the skies of the UK shortly, where the British Prime Minister will surely be calling for blood. And on the television screen in front of me, the Australian Prime Minister has just pledged ground forces if needed.

The French and the Russians are in. The Germans are so far the only ones calling for calm. I can only imagine the phone calls in and out of Washington right now, and as a brand new leader with little history with the US President, Gavin's playing at a disadvantage.

I'm not going to sleep tonight.

I know that's ridiculous. There's nothing I can do. No chance he'll be back, and I can't go to him.

So I set up the coffee maker with a filter and freshly ground beans and water, just in case. I look in the fridge. He doesn't have any leftovers, so I order a pizza.

Or at least, I try to order a pizza. I dial the number Lachlan gave Gavin—it's also posted in the kitchen.

It seemed straightforward when Gavin did it, but he must have a magic code or something, because I get a runaround about how it's not cool to prank order pizzas to 24 Sussex. I do my best to stay polite, and after explaining for the third time that yes, I'm actually calling from where I'm saying that I'm calling, and they could check with the guard house if they really don't believe me, they take my order.

I'm a little surprised when, forty minutes later, the delivery car actually shows up. And then the guard at the gate doesn't want to let him in, proving that no good deed goes unpunished. I step outside and wave, and only then does the guard let him through, watching suspiciously as I pay the driver.

It's a constable I haven't seen before, but he knows who

I am. "I'm sorry, Ms. Montague. I thought for sure it was a trick to get in. I didn't think…"

"It's fine. I just thought…the PM likes pizza. And in case he comes home tonight. You know?"

"That's a nice idea."

"Thanks."

We say an awkward goodnight before I duck back inside. I carry the pizza into the kitchen, where I pick at a piece while reading news on my phone. No updates, really, but there's a lot of chatter on Twitter that makes my head spin.

I put the rest of the pizza in the fridge and write a big note to stick on the front.

Leftover pizza inside! Loaded with love. And pepperoni. Ewww.

I draw a heart beneath it and slowly climb the curving staircase up to the second floor. It takes me ages to fall asleep and I wake up before dawn.

The bed beside me is still empty, and when I turn my bleary attention to the TV that I left on all night, there's still no real update.

40

GAVIN

WHEN I WAS IN WASHINGTON, I had the briefest of meetings with the President. His daughter was sick, and I'm going back again in another month for a more focused leadership visit, so it didn't seem like a big deal at the time that our planned one-on-one sit down had turned into a five minute handshake and photo-op.

After a night of waiting in a queue to talk to the guy, and then after we talked—which was good, but short, because the Russian President called him, and I get bumped for that call. I get that.

But *fuck* it's frustrating when I think we might be aligned in how to deal with this situation and I spend most of the night sitting on my hands. Figuratively, of course. I've actually spent most of the night pacing, tearing at my tie, kicking things, and yelling at Stew.

"We need an action statement by the morning," he says for the third time.

"I'm not going to say something that we walk back from. And I'm not going to say something that doesn't go far enough if we decide to go fucking further."

"We can't commit to much. Our defence budget is in shambles."

That just makes me yank at my tie again. "When is the defence minister's plane landing?"

"Two more hours."

My cabinet is so junior it hurts. I chose my ministers carefully, and they all have relevant experience, but governing is its own thing, and tonight that thing is a powder keg.

"When he lands—"

"He's coming here."

"And the Chief of Defence?" I've only asked for this update a half dozen times. Stew glowers at me, because I know that General Finnette was an hour away half an hour ago, and I can do math.

"Thirty minutes out of the city. You can get him on the phone again, but it's not going to do any good. He has to stop at DND HQ and get the options from the analysts. He'll be here as soon as possible."

And on it goes. By six, we have an idea of what we can do—not much. We could contribute planes to a bombing campaign that won't work. We could send our special forces to train African peacekeepers. And we could immediately rejig the budget and find a way to finance just about anything else...if we wanted to.

I don't want to, and it's not because I'm a pacifist.

At the moment, I'm feeling downright murderous. But that's the battle of terrorism. It's not at the gates of an embassy or six embassies. It's in the hearts of the leaders that feel that wound like it was on their own skin, and retaliate.

These terrorists *want* our retaliation. It will contribute to the chaos that makes them stronger.

I don't want them stronger. I want them choked out,

obliterated from existence. They're spineless, pathetic monsters.

And I don't have the first clue how we're supposed to deal with that.

Beth steps into my office and hands Stew a new call sheet. She came in to work last night and like everyone else has been here ever since. At some point, we're going to need a backup crew of staff from the PMO to give these guys a break.

"The British Prime Minister," Stew says. "In ten minutes. And then the American President after that."

Thank Christ. "Okay. Can I have the room for these calls, please?"

I roll my shoulders as everyone files out. I wave at Stew that he should stay, then I redo my tie.

When I accept the call from the UK, I do it standing up, my shoulders back, and my best listening ears on. The only way I'm going to convince anyone that today is not a good day to declare a new war is by finding the part of their argument that makes that point for me.

41

***

ELLIE

I TAKE Gladys for her inaugural drive midmorning. I'm feeling crazy restless and I need to get out of the rambling mansion. And with the entire country watching and waiting for news on what the G7 leaders are going to do, nobody is paying any attention to me driving my shiny new RAV4 out the gates of 24 Sussex and over to the university.

I find Sasha in her office.

"Who are you, strange person I haven't seen in days?" She stands up and gives me a hug. "I'm guessing your birthday was interrupted?"

"A little bit. It's fine, of course." I wave my hand aimlessly in the air. "Thank you for the help you gave him. Sneaky girl."

"Just doing my best friend job."

"I know you're not sure about Gavin…"

"No. It's fine. I mean, I don't think any man is good enough for you, but he genuinely seems to care about you."

"The feeling is mutual."

She gives me a careful look. "You scared about what's going on?"

I nod, desperate to talk about it. "Really scared. Too much so, considering he's safe and I know he's going to make the right decisions."

She presses her lips together. We don't always share the same politics, and I'm not sure if we agree on what Gavin should do today. But instead of going there, she turns the conversation to our own work, filling me in on department gossip that I've missed in my absence, and then we go and get coffee, and for an hour, my life is almost normal.

WHEN I GET BACK to 24 Sussex, Gavin's returned. He's in the shower, and I strip out of my own clothes and join him. He holds me close for a minute, then I turn him around and slowly scrub his back with a washcloth.

"Thank you for the pizza," he says as he leans against the tile, letting the water beat against his muscles.

"I thought…just in case you got a break…"

"It was perfect." He sighs. "I'm only here because the water pressure at the Hill is brutal. But I need to get back. I've got a caucus meeting in an hour and then I'll be making an announcement tonight."

I don't ask him what it is. If he wants my counsel, he'll ask. And right now, he needs a few minutes of quiet.

"I drove Gladys today," I tell him as we dress again.

"I noticed. Did you enjoy your freedom?"

"Very much so."

"Good." He kisses me, hard and fast, then just looks at me as he tugs on my hair. "Good," he says again, and my heart aches for him. "But be safe, okay?"

"I will. Nobody even noticed me today. I just went to campus."

He nods. "Yeah."

I'm confused for a minute, then it dawns on me. "I was followed?"

"You have a security detail, Sprite."

"I thought you got me the car because they were glorified chauffeurs!"

"One has nothing to do with the other."

Today is not the day to tell him he doesn't need to keep paying for bodyguards for me, so I let it go. "They were good, then. I had no clue."

"That's how it should be."

"But I'll keep that in mind if I'm trying to plan you any surprises." I stick my tongue out at him, but then he hauls me close to him, roughly, and I gasp as his palm lands flat on my bottom. "Oh."

"No sneaking around, Sprite."

"Or there will be consequences?"

He grins. "Or there *won't* be consequences."

"I'll be good."

"And then you'll be rewarded." He gives me one last kiss, then swears under his breath. "Gotta go. Back late tonight."

"I love you." I follow him down the stairs to the central hallway.

He grabs his briefcase and gives me a quick wave over his shoulder as he heads out the front door.

"I believe in you," I say in the silence. I should have said that sooner.

BUT GAVIN DOESN'T NEED to hear that—he's got this. I watch on the news as he strides from the caucus room, his party streaming out behind him. He looks hard and commanding, and when the news breaks away for an announcement from the American President, I know it's going to be good news.

"Early this morning, an elite group of American operatives captured two key members of the leadership of the terrorist organization responsible for last night's bombings. They will be transported to The Hague in the coming days. This was not our only response to the devastating events of the last twenty-four hours, and I assure you, it will not be our last.

"We will not be invading a foreign country to rain down our anger, however. We will work harder and smarter with our allies to choke those that wish to plunge this world into anarchy. We will shut them down at every possible turn. But we will not give in to their attempts to engage us in all out warfare played out on top of an innocent civilian population.

"I have spent much of the last day and the previous night on the phone with my counterparts in Canada and Germany. Soon you will hear from Prime Minister Strong and Chancellor Wagner, and they will reiterate our common affirmation. Terrorism is criminal and should be punished at the highest levels, and that is where our response will be focused. These are common thugs, petty gangsters. They don't control us. It is time to lay down the law, and we will do that in a way that best protects the world's citizens."

I'm stunned. Impressed. And crying.

I wipe away my tears, but they slide down my cheeks as the Canadian news channels break away for Gavin's speech. He covers a lot of the same ground, and then adds, "Canadians are divided on the best way to fight terrorism. I understand that. In the coming months, we're going to have a national dialogue about fear and aggression. I'm going to bring in experts to help us all understand the best way to keep ourselves safe. But bullies don't get to push us around.

And that might sound juvenile to some of you, but that's the narrative they want to trap us with. I am not afraid to ask our Parliament to use force when force is needed. Tonight I announce the funding of a new special task force for rapid response..."

I lose the rest of his speech because my face is wet and my heart is pounding, but I get the gist of it.

My boyfriend is a superhero, and I think he just saved the day for the entire planet.

42

ELLIE

LIFE RETURNS TO A NEW NORMAL. The last few weeks of summer slip by with simple dinners, amazing sex, and lots of work for both of us. Gavin's gearing up for his first full session of Parliament as PM, and there's a new, restless energy radiating from him at all times, but he locks it down when we're together. I spend more nights than not at 24 Sussex, but I ignore the little voice inside me that has started to ask what exactly we're doing.

We're happy. That's all that matters.

Labour Day weekend is the last chance Gavin has to play hockey for a while, because Tate's on pre-season work-up already, with less time to play for fun, and the team will be disbanded until next summer after this game.

Of course, he could play pick-up hockey with anyone else. The fact that the PM is playing in a beer league of sorts is getting a lot of buzz, and at the last game, there were a few people who'd snuck in to watch.

"You have puck bunnies," I tease him as he gets ready. I've come to the Sensplex to watch him play, and the women across the way are giving me dirty looks.

He gives me a lazy, sexy smile that makes me instantly wet. "They're just fans. Probably here for Tate more than me."

Nope. Doesn't look like it from my vantage point. "Super-eager, wanting-to-get-in-your-pants kind of fans."

He double-checks the tape on his stick one last time. "The only puck bunny I have eyes for is you, Sprite."

"Don't distract me from my rant."

"Okay. Rant away."

"They're practically advertising themselves as breeding partners."

"Breeding?"

"Don't mock me. They're....frisky beavers."

He snorts. "I have to get on the ice."

"Don't get too close to them when you do your charming skate by."

"To the frisky beavers?"

"Yep. That's what I'm calling them now."

"So what does that make you?"

"Wait, I take that back. They're eager puck bunnies. Boring name. Pffht. I'm the frisky beaver."

"The most special of all the rink-side cheerleaders."

"Exactly."

"Mmm. I like the sound of that."

I grin the entire way through his game, which is even more fun to watch than I expected. Gavin's good. This doesn't surprise me at all, but it's still thrilling to see him be awesome at yet another thing.

At moments like this, it's hard to remember that he's mortal. I know he's slightly uneasy about being put on a pedestal, but he makes it so damn easy.

I cheer myself hoarse, and when he comes off the ice, I plaster myself against him and kiss him senseless.

"I'm all sweaty," he says under his breath, and I make an appreciative sound. "Really? You like it?"

I. Love. It.

I'm coming to hockey more often.

As we leave the rink, Tate's ribbing Gavin about constantly kissing me.

Gavin tugs me close and lays a relatively chaste peck on my lips. "When it comes to Ellie, one kiss is never enough," he says with a laugh.

And that's when we see the cameraman. There's a videographer and a reporter here from a news station, and it looks like they're getting ready to go inside for something not related to us, but the camera is up on the guy's shoulder and pointed our way.

Gavin tenses and I press my hand against his side. "It's okay," I whisper. "That was pretty tame."

His muscles ripple under my touch but he nods and turns us around, so his back is to the camera and I'm in front of him.

"See you guys later!" he calls as he moves us toward the car. Lachlan's got the door open, and I hop in and slide right over so Gavin can join me.

He swears under his breath as we pull away, then turns toward me. "I'm sorry."

I shrug. I've been waiting for something like that, and in the grand scheme of things, it's no biggie. I tell him as much and he settles down, but it's still bugging him.

OF COURSE, that off-the-cuff comment to Tate becomes tomorrow's headline and we wake up to **One Kiss is Never Enough** on the front page of the Ottawa Spectator. I convince Gavin we should head out to the country house for a day and ignore it while it dies over the holiday week-end, but on Tuesday, the first day back to work and school and news for most Canadians, it's still getting some play.

CAN News spends a solid ten minutes on it on their morning show, which is ridiculous.

I'm at the university, watching Gavin at a press conference on my laptop—love streaming video, oh my God—when he finally snaps.

The press conference is supposed to be about federal support for provincial funding of childhood vaccines.

Rick Stupes stands up and asks Gavin if being involved in a new relationship is interfering with his job.

My coffee mug lands hard on my desk as my jaw drops open. He didn't just say that. He didn't just—

"Oh my *God*," Sasha yells, running into my office.

"Are you watching it?" I ask her. I keep my eyes glued on the screen. Gavin just ignored question and moved on to the next reporter.

"I was on Twitter and saw someone mention it." She leans over my shoulder. "Was that it? Will they replay it?"

"I dunno."

Suddenly Stupes stands up, interrupting his colleague—so rude—and asks, "Does that mean you don't always kiss her twice?"

I think Gavin would have ignored him again if the room didn't laugh. But there was a faint tittering wave that rolled through at least some of the people present, and I can see that get under his skin. Because it's not funny—it's cheap and baseless. Gavin's a damn hard worker and our relationship has never impacted on his work.

Much. Other than the lamp. And I distracted him through a few meetings. But in general, it's a stupid question.

Gavin waits until the room goes silent. Everyone's realized that he's going to respond, but when he opens his mouth, it's pure perfection and a complete slap-down instead. "It means, *Rick*, we have a serious problem with preventable childhood illness in this country and that's what I want you to ask me about."

The reporter huffs and squares his shoulders. "We'll ask the medical experts about that. But since we have you here, and everyone wants to know—"

Gavin's got no time for that shit. "I'm not a doctor, but I can tell you that vaccines save lives, and when we fail to protect at a population level, there are devastating consequences. I know this because I went on a student exchange program to Russia in 1997. And the first question on the application form was, *Are you vaccinated against diphtheria?* I'll tell you, nothing puts the importance of vaccination into perspective like being told you're walking into the remnants of an outbreak." My heart skips a beat as Sasha claps behind me. "Our goal is that no Canadian community should face a preventable outbreak. Our standard should be that no Canadian parent has to make the call to keep their child home from school or avoid the playground because they don't know if it's safe. And those are the questions I'm going to take today, *Rick*."

Cameras flash as the room is silent for a minute, then someone claps, and everyone else joins in. The press conference continues, and Sasha sighs. "Okay. I'm done being suspicious of him. He's perfect."

He's damn near close to it. "Yep. That's my man."

43

ELLIE

ALL SUMMER LONG, I couldn't wait to get back to my research and teaching. It just takes one class for me to be second-guessing that decision.

One of the down-sides of being a grad student at the biz school means having to teach...biz students. Some of them are incredible. All of them are smart.

But there are a few complete jackasses. Self-entitled spoiled brats who I'd like to strip of their platinum credit cards for just a few weeks and make them live on the street so they could have even half a clue about how good they have it.

And since I'm not a professor, but an instructor who's learning about teaching as part of my graduate studies...I can't even bitch about that to my advisor, because it's unprofessional. And I can't really complain to Sasha, either, because it's kind of awkward. She was that kid in a lot of ways, and she gets prickly about it.

So I go to the advanced yoga class after work and try to work it out there, but I'm still on edge when I leave the studio and start walking down Bank Street. My mood doesn't lighten when Gavin calls and tells me his dinner meeting has been cancelled.

The invitation is wide open, but I'm not sure I'll be very good company tonight. "Maybe later? I need to go home and decompress for a bit."

"Turn around, Sprite." I do a slow one-eighty, knowing I'm about to see a big, black armoured car behind me. He rolls down the back window. "Had a bad day?"

"Something like that." I open the back door and join him. Tim is driving tonight and I give him a little wave. "Hey."

He nods. "Ms. Montague."

I turn my attention back to Gavin. "Did you consider that I might want to go home?"

He leans forward. "Tim, we're going to Ellie's apartment."

I shake my head. "No, 24 Sussex is fine."

"But you said—"

"I…never mind." I swallow my frustration. It's not his fault that we can't just go back to my place, and I'm not going to make a big deal out of it. "Your place is better."

He tugs my hand into his, settling it on his thigh as he rubs up and down my arm, his thumb pressing into my muscles. Over the wrist and up onto the forearm. Back down to my fingers. He pinches and twists the flesh here and there, and the tension starts to ease out of me. I close my eyes and sigh.

"Do you want us to drop you at your place?"

I consider it. But the fall is looming ahead of us, busy and with crossed schedules on every other week. In another month, I'll regret not spending as much time as possible with him. "No."

"When we get back to my place, we'll do something about your mood."

I shrug. "Okay."

But there's really nothing to be done about it. I've got eight months of teaching to survive, plus a heavy research schedule, and I'm dating the most intense man—and sharing him with an entire country. There are just going to be some days where I want to pout for a while.

When we arrive, Gavin keeps a firm hold on my wrist, cuffing it with his fingers.

"Are you hungry?"

I screw up my face, trying to remember the last time I ate. "Maybe?"

He sighs and leads me into the kitchen, where he props me against the counter, kisses me quickly, then starts to pull stuff out of the fridge. Basil and tomatoes, a wedge of white cheese, and a package of fresh pasta.

"Are you cooking?" Two months into our relationship and this is a weird turn.

"You made me a sandwich once. This seems like fair turnaround."

"You've got real food."

"And you're super lippy tonight." He gives me an amused look. "Zip it and let me cook for you."

"I'm just curious—"

He thumps the package of pasta against the counter. "Okay, dinner can wait."

My cheeks flame as I realize I've crossed the line from bratty to rude. "I'm sorry. I told you I was in a grumpy mood, and…yeah. I'm just going to zip it."

His eyes flash as he rounds the peninsula and grabs my hand. "Come on."

He's moving so fast it feels like he's towing me toward the library. He sits in his chair and I move to fold into his lap, but he puts his hand on my hip, stopping my movement. "Just stand for a minute, Sprite. Let's focus on what's wrong before you curl up in my lap and I get distracted by how good you smell."

I shift restlessly in front of him. "It's just work stuff."

"As your boyfriend, I'd like to know about it."

"It's seriously nothing."

He huffs out a frustrated breath. That was the wrong thing to say.

I backtrack. "I mean, it's only a small thing. An adjustment to spending time with a certain kind of student. That's all. It's mostly just something I need to deal with in my own head."

"But it gets you quite worked up."

I'll have to do a better job of hiding that in the future, because he doesn't need to worry about me. "I think we've already spent far too much time talking about my students and their over-inflated sense of importance. Maybe I need something more intense than yoga to get it out of my system."

"Maybe you need a good spanking." He says it so levelly that I almost move right past it in the conversation, only to trip on it as I double back.

My mouth drops open as I stare down at him, and the mood between us shifts. Darker, more intense on his part. A slide into...oh. Something that feels quite nice on my part. Calm. Docile. A place where I might give zero fucks about any work drama. I lick my lips as I look at him again, seeing not just the look on his face, but his entire body language. "Sir?"

His cock is thick and straining at the elegant fabric of his suit pants. How does nobody else see him for the delicious pervert that he is? And how lucky am I that the monster is all mine?

"You want to spank me?" Just like that? Not in the heat

of the moment, but…calmly proposed, as an equal alternative to him feeding me dinner?

I guess it's not dissimilar to looking across at your partner and suggesting going upstairs to have sex, but…it's totally different somehow.

For all my open-mindedness, I still feel like such a kink newbie. And sometimes a bit of a kink fraud, like I'm really vanilla and Gavin's going to realize that any day now.

But this doesn't feel wrong or weird. Just unexpected. And good. So good.

"I want you to relax so, after I make you dinner, you'll be of a mind to suck my cock like a good little Sprite. To that end, I think you need a spanking."

"To relax." I say it with incredulity because seriously? But I'm already wet and achy at the promise of his hand on my ass. *Yes.* So much better than yoga.

"To relax, to re-center. A release." He takes one of my hands and guides me to his left side, then folds me over his lap, carefully arranging me. The calm detachment is a total ruse, because his cock is hard against my belly and his hands are big and strong, and it's taking all his effort not to use them to rip my clothes off.

That sounds so conceited, but it's the truth. We're crazy for each other. And maybe just crazy. But the little niggle of doubt that I'm enough is way outshouted by all the evidence that yes, I'm exactly what Gavin wants.

His hand rubs against the curve of my butt, through the summer-weight trousers I'd worn to work today. The layer of clothing adds just as much as it takes away.

This is really just a spanking.

Not a punishment, exactly…

But not *not* a punishment, either. *Bad girl, bringing work home when Sir wants a blow job.* My pussy clenches at the sudden ache the thought creates.

The first blow is hard enough to pop my eyes open. "Ahhh," I say, not quite crying out.

"Tell me about the best part of your day." He says it calmly, like we're still in the kitchen and he's waiting for water to boil.

"Uhhh…" Another blow and the sound catches in my throat. I tense my thighs against his legs, and he kicks his foot sideways, unbalancing me.

"Don't clench up. I don't want this to hurt—much. Your day?"

"Right now?"

"Yes, right now." *Thwack*. "You can't stop thinking about the shitty parts. I want you to tell me—" *Thwack*. He rubs the flat of his palm over that spot, smoothing out the heat. "About what was amazing."

I think about my lecture. No, earlier, when I got the email from the conference chair about the poster I'm presenting in Colorado. "I've been invited to speak in front of the entire conference about my project."

Gavin makes an impressed sound as he slides his hand between my legs. A dirty reward for positive thinking—I like how his mind works.

But I spend too much time thinking about what a good plan this is and not enough talking, because he pulls his hand back and spanks me twice more.

A rush of heat floods through me, starting at my upturned ass and spilling to every last inch of my body.

"It's a short mini presentation, but it's quite an honour for someone at my level," I say quickly, lest he think that I'm minimizing it. "And it should help move that project closer to publication, or lead to future collaborations with some of the attending academics."

"You didn't tell me about that earlier."

"It slipped my mind."

"You let the students not only take over your day, but consume your good news as well."

"I did."

"Don't do it again."

"I won't."

"Good girl." He shifts under me, his cock harder than before, and when he spanks me again, it's slow and lazy. Hotter, and his hand spends more time easing the sting and rubbing between my legs than it does doling out my punishment. *Bad girl. Good girl.* Turned on girl, definitely.

I run my hand up and down his calf as I relax even further, the strength of his coiled muscles a delicious contrast to the boneless feeling of my body now. My head is resting on the edge of the wide seat, facing out in the library, but I slowly turn my face toward him, wanting to show him how happy I am. Relaxed, re-centered, exactly as promised.

He's staring down at me with barely-contained lust painted all over his face. He liked that even more than I expected, and his reaction takes my breath away.

"Thank you, Sir," I say with a whisper, and he shifts faster than I can process what he's doing, pulling me up into his lap. His hands tangle in my hair as he kisses me. His teeth tug on my lower lip, his tongue spears demandingly into my mouth. *Bad girl. Good girl.*

My blouse falls away from my body.

One of his hands roughly cups my breast, his thumb rolling over my nipple. I arch into his touch. More, I want more.

He lifts me in his arms, his large body flexing as he carries me across the room and spreads me out on his desk.

We've fucked in that chair a few times, but never this desk.

There's a bucket list. All his desks. "How many offices do you have?"

"What?" He unbuttons my pants and peels them open, revealing the bare skin of my lower belly and skimpy black cotton panties. They're soaked and his eyelids are heavy as he glances back at my face for a second before burying his face there.

"Remind me to ask you later…" I breathe. Intense waves crash over me as he tongues my clit through the fabric, licking down, stroking over the crest of my engorged nub, then swirling around to do it again.

"More," I beg, and he wrenches the fabric down my hips, trapping my legs together but baring the top of my cleft. His tongue slides through my curls and teases me again, differently this time. Just a glancing edge. I smack my hands on the desk in frustration. "More…."

He looks up at me, his lips swollen and red, and asks hoarsely, "What do you say?"

"Please, Sir…" My voice cracks and he yanks my trousers and underwear off, finally spreading my legs wide so he can touch and lick and suck my pussy.

I come apart quickly, thrashing under his wicked tongue, and then he's inside me, full and thick. He moves slowly at first, possessive thrusts that remind me I'm his, inside and out, and when I finish trembling and start rocking against him, he picks up his pace. He tugs my hips right to the edge of the desk and hammers into me, his rhythm blistering now as he watches me twist higher again.

"Tighten your legs around me," he orders, his voice hard and clipped. I grip him with my thighs and he shifts one of his hands to my belly, stroking above my mound, then lower. He covers my curls with his hand, his thumb pressing over the top of my clit as his fingertips press into the quivering flesh of my lower abdomen. "Come for me. Let me feel it, Sprite."

"Ahhh…" I roll my head and close my eyes. So close, but I've already come once, and this time it's harder to get there.

He slows down, leaving his cock inside me longer, but at the same time his thumb moves faster, stroking my clit back and forth, back and forth.

"Yes, there, don't stop." I'm babbling now.

"You've got the prettiest cunt," he growls. "I want you all the time, Ellie. I want to be inside you. I want to lick you. I want to hold your pussy and feel it tighten around me. My fingers. My cock. My tongue. So gorgeous."

The rush of dirty talk sends me spinning again, out of control and free-falling. He keeps talking, single words grunted between thrusts as he follows me to a grinding climax. "Mine. Fuck. So tight. God. Ellie, yes."

He holds himself inside me, so deep my hips are stretching to their limit, then he slowly pulls back. But not all the way out. Even though we've both come, he's still looking at me like he could go again.

He slides back inside, sloppy now, and I whimper because it's so sensitive.

"Shhh," he whispers. "Just another minute. Just let me feel you like this. Full of my come."

I gasp and roll my hips, wanting to come again at that single, filthy image. An aftershock ripples through me and he groans, burying himself one last time before easing away.

He cleans us up quickly, then pulls me up off the desk and swings me up into his arms. "Shower, then dinner, then we're doing that again."

Who am I to argue with such an obviously clever plan?

44

GAVIN

I'VE BEEN DODGING calls from my sister Pia for weeks now. We talk, but always when I'm on my way into a meeting. That's a deliberate choice on my part, because I'm not ready for her counsel on my dating life. Politics, absolutely. Whether or not I'm handling a relationship properly…not at all.

My mother's calls, though, I can't dodge. And she waited plenty long, so by the time Beth adds her to my call sheet, the sight of her name spears guilt through me.

"Let's do that one last," I say, and when Beth narrows her eyes at me, I hastily add, "So I'm not on a time limit. We'll do them right before lunch."

The morning's meetings are all productive, so I'm at a minimal level of snarling when I sit back behind my desk. I get through the other calls I need to make quickly, then I dial the number for the mountain cabin myself.

She answers on the third ring, laughter in her voice. "Hello?"

"Hey, Mom." It's like I'm nineteen again and calling her from university.

"Gavin! It's been a while."

"I'm sorry."

"No you're not." She laughs. "You've been busy."

"I have."

"And you're seeing that young woman…"

"I am. Ellie," I add, which is unnecessary because the entire country knows her name. I'm sure my mother has a complete dossier on her.

"When are we going to meet Ellie?"

As soon as possible and maybe never. The thought of introducing her to my family fills me with a ridiculous pride. They'll love her. But I also want to keep her all to myself. "Thanksgiving, perhaps. Christmas for sure."

"So it's serious."

"Very."

"Interesting."

"She's incredible, Mom. Smart and kind. You'll love her."

"I'm sure I will." She waits a beat, then sighs. "It could have been a big scandal, Gavin."

"I know."

"You're lucky it wasn't."

"Did you have anything to do with that?" There are certain arenas where my mother—and my sister—hold more power than I do. Women's groups, some pockets of the media. It's one reason I didn't call either of them as news of the relationship broke. I didn't want that on my call sheet. **PM Strong Runs To Mommy For Approval.**

She laughs. "Oh, Gavin. You're such a cynic. You think people don't look at her and understand that you're head over heels in love?"

I am a cynic. I honestly didn't think that the strength of my feelings was enough of a justification for our relationship. The fact that my mother thinks it is slides over me like a balm I hadn't known I'd needed. "Thank you."

"Thanksgiving, Gavin. Don't make us wait until Christmas. We can come to Ottawa."

"I'll see what we can do."

"I can coordinate with Beth."

I frown. It's not Beth's job to organize a family dinner, beyond getting me a catering menu. "I can handle it."

"She won't mind."

"But I do. And I'd like to discuss it with Ellie first. She may want to invite her parents and have preferences of her own, remember."

"Ah, yes. Of course. And if she wants to get in touch with me…"

"One thing at a time?"

"Right." She turns on a tap in the background. "I'll let you get back to your day, darling. This was a good chat."

"I love you, Mom."

"I love you, too. Tell Ellie I can't wait to meet her. And that I don't bite."

I hang up, and thirty seconds later Beth knocks at the door with my lunch, and two memos to read on human rights violations in refugee camps. Back to work.

45

ELLIE

A WEEK after Gavin tells me about his mother's phone call, I'm sitting outside his office with takeout sushi and two extra-large iced green teas.

Beth smiles at me from behind her desk. "He won't be long."

I don't mind waiting. I don't have any other plans between now and when he finishes work for the day. I had an unexpected day off because my building at the university had a boiler mishap. I didn't even know buildings still used boilers for heating, and even though it's mid-September, it's still warm and there's a gorgeous end-of-summery feeling outside, so nobody is complaining about being kicked out of our offices for the day.

Gavin's flying home to Vancouver for a few days before heading to Asia for a five day trade mission. If the schedule stays as planned, he'll get back five hours after I fly to Colorado for a conference. It'll be nearly two weeks until we see each other again, and since our relationship has become public fodder, there's no such thing as sexting, not even in code. We have tonight and part of tomorrow together and that's it. We might get some brief phone calls if the time zone gods cooperate.

So when he asked me to stop by with lunch, I leapt at the opportunity to have a little more quality time, even if it means getting dangerously close to the Ottawa press corps.

I'm still waiting for the other shoe to drop with drama about us dating. Maybe it won't, but that feels too good to be true.

His door swings open, and there he is. Dark suit, light blue shirt, grey tie today. His hair is looking uncharacteristically rumpled, and my fingers itch to smooth it out. Or maybe mess it up further. Alternating back and forth sounds like a swell plan.

I'll do that while he eats.

"Ellie," he says, his voice rich and warm and just for me in the middle of an otherwise busy day.

I stand and give him a private smile as I lift the lunch bag in the air. "Delivery."

"What did you bring?"

"Sushi." I hand him the tray with our iced green teas and glide past him, close enough to breathe in his subtle cologne on my way by.

"Delicious."

Yes, yes he is.

This is my second time in his office since we fucked on his couch, but I still suddenly feel overheated, like the walls are saying *we know what you did in here.*

But I also feel a little giddy, like *yeah, I know what I did in here.*

This is why I needed to quit. Because he makes me reckless and crazy.

He closes the door behind me as I set the sushi on his desk. I twist around just in time to see him flick the lock.

Oh. Hello, Prime Minister.

He grins at me, lazy and confident, like he knows he can get me to do anything he wants, even though his assistant is on the other side of the door.

You'll have to be quiet, Ms. Montague.

I'll do my best, Sir.

There will be consequences if you're not...

"What are you thinking about?" He stops in front of me and undoes his suit jacket.

I drop my gaze to the growing erection pressing against the front of his suit trousers. "Exactly what you might imagine I'm thinking of."

"In the middle of the day?" His voice is full of censure, and I turn around, cheeks flaming.

"Of course not. That would be—"

He crowds against me. "Completely inappropriate."

"Yes." I rock back against him, shameless in my want for him. "We've been here before. It didn't end well."

"You've already quit, Ms. Montague."

I lick my lips. "Maybe I want my job back. Maybe I'd do anything you want to make that happen."

He groans and squeezes my hips, my waist, pressing me flat against his desk before giving me a slow, teasing swat on my bottom.

Then he walks around the desk and settles in his chair. "Lunch?"

I pout. "That was mean."

"I'm hungry." But his eyes are bright and his eyelids heavy. I can read him like a book. He doesn't want to cross the line.

And he wants to cross it so much it hurts.

I peel myself off his desk and sit myself slowly in the chair across from him. Every inch the prim secretary.

"Salmon roll?"

"Please." His lips quirk as he watches me plate up a few pieces of sushi for him, then help myself.

"So the boiler went, eh?"

I nod. "Afternoon off. Wheee!"

"What else are you going to do today?"

"Sasha wants to go shopping."

"Fun."

I make a noncommittal noise. "Maybe fun. Maybe exhausting. Could go either way. This is definitely the high-light of my day."

"Mine, too."

We finish eating as we talk about our upcoming trips, then he gestures for me to come around the desk. "Come here, Sprite."

I walk around to him, my heart hammering in my chest, the nervous thump reverberating into my throat and down my arms.

He stands up and pulls me into his arms. "I'm going to miss you."

"Same," I whisper, pressing up onto my toes as he kisses me softly, then harder as he moves me back, pushing me against the decorative wooden shutters that cover the windows behind his desk.

"What am I going to do with you?" he asks when we break apart. He rubs his knuckles against my cheek, along my jaw, and I tip my head back, giving him free access to my neck and the v-neck of my blouse below.

"Anything you want."

"The last two times we've done things in here, you've left in a huff."

"The first time you huffed. The second time…I was scared."

"And now?"

"Now I don't feel scared, that's for sure."

"What do you want to do?" His eyes are so bright up close, they take my breath away.

That's a very good question. I reach between us and find the hard length of his cock straining against his dress pants. I palm the rigid thickness and close my fingers around him. The solid weight of him in my hand makes me wet. "I want this," I whisper.

"It's yours."

"In my mouth?"

His eyes flash. "You first."

"Do we have time for that?"

"Ellie."

"What?"

"We always have time for you to come."

Oh. Good answer. I squirm as he hikes up my skirt and yanks my panties aside.

He teases my slit with one hand as he strokes my neck with the other. "So wet for me already, Sprite. Dirty girl."

"I was thinking about blowing you."

"Good. I want your mouth on me. Take me deep as you can and swallow all my come."

I whimper, already worked up.

"Look at you. Hard little clit, begging to be spanked. Wet little pussy, desperate for a finger."

"Or two…"

"Or three?" He runs his mouth along my jaw, his lips finding my earlobe. "Are you going to come on my hand so I can lick it off while you get on your knees for me, Sprite?"

"Yes, Sir." I twist my hips, welcoming his fingers deep inside me.

"Good…" He sinks his teeth into my earlobe as he rolls his thumb over my clit. I buck against his hand. He does it again and my thighs start shaking. He exhales against my neck, grazes his teeth against the skin there, then licks me.

Long. Slow. Totally dirty.

I come hard, my thighs locking his fingers inside my pussy as I grind my clit against his thumb. I fuck his hand like it's my own personal sex toy, and when I sag back against the shutters, he does exactly what he promised he would do.

He slides his fingers out of me and starts licking them.

My legs aren't doing a great job of holding me up anyway, so I sink to my knees and wrestle with his belt and his zipper, until his cock is in my hands, in my mouth and the quiet sound of his groans fills the space around me.

His scent floods my senses and I greedily taste him all over, tugging him deeper into my mouth. He finishes the half-done job of getting his belt out of the way, then leans over me, flexing his hips as I open wide for him.

"Ellie. Look at you. Yes, swallow me. Oh, babe, you're so good at that."

I look up at him and try to see myself through his eyes. Lips stretched wide, cheeks flushed, skirt still rucked up around my hips. I'm his dirty, dirty girl—and I like it.

He grunts and smacks his hand above my head. His hips jack forward and I breathe through my nose as my lips make it almost all the way down to where my fingers circle the base of his cock.

His eyes are closed now, but he reaches down with his free hand and strokes my cheek. "Take me deeper."

I bob again, slicking him up, then take a deep breath and slide him in as deep as he can go. The head nudges the back of my throat and my stomach clenches, but then I swallow and it's fine.

I can't breathe really, but it's fine, because he's thick and hot in my mouth and I can't get enough of his taste on my tongue, his hand in my hair, that press against the back of my head.

He pulls back and I inhale, then he fucks forward again, using my mouth now at will, and I swallow with each pump. Yes, give it to me, yes, yes…

"Fuck," he bites out, hitting his hand against the wall with a crack as the first spurt of come shoots across my tongue. I slide forward, burying my nose against his taut abs as I swallow the rest, neat as can be.

Can't make a mess with *that*, because I'm pretty sure we just damaged something else in pursuit of our depraved chemistry.

Once I've got him tucked away, I glance up. One of those wood shutters has a pair of cracks in it, approximately the same width apart as the prime minister's hand. "Oh, no…"

Gavin just grins down at me. Of course he doesn't care. He just got the world's dirtiest blow job. "Don't worry about it."

"We really can't do this again. Next time it's going to be something irreplaceable."

"Oh, Jesus." He exhales roughly, his sigh turning into a laugh as he pokes at the most damaged slat. "Well, at least this can be repaired."

"What are you going to put on the work order?"

"Definitely not, 'damage caused by significant reaction to PM's girlfriend deep throating him'."

"No. Definitely not." I wink as I hold out my hand, and he helps me up.

"You kind of want me to put that down, don't you?"

"Well, significant reaction…that's something for me to be proud of."

"I'm not sharing your talents in that regard with anyone. But you should be proud. You have a talented mouth and a wicked tongue, and dirty mind that keeps me on my toes."

"On your toes and banging your fist against the shutters." I give him a wide-eyed look as a thought occurs to me. "Think that's the first time they've been a sex casualty?"

"I'm not thinking about the sex lives of my predecessors in this office."

"I am."

"That's my dirty girl. Come here, Sprite." He sits back in his chair and pats his thighs.

I crawl into his lap and he kisses me softly, deeply, tasting himself on my lips and tongue.

He groans and buries his face in my hair when we finally break apart. "I need to get back to work."

"Thank you for lunch," I whisper.

"You brought me—ah." He clears his throat. "You're welcome."

"A little memory to keep us both warm while we're travelling."

"And when you're back, we can start the countdown to Thanksgiving and our parents meeting." His arms tighten around me. "Or we could run away to Bora Bora."

"That's a plan." I slide off his lap and touch my fingertips to his lips. "I'll leave you to your work."

"Love you." He grins at me as he pulls himself closer to his desk again. "I'll be home by seven."

46

____

GAVIN

THE ENTIRE TIME I was in Japan, I had this quiet hope that somehow I'd be able to touch down in Toronto and surprise Ellie for her layover there on her way to Denver. We're two ships passing in the night, or in this case, two airplanes not quite passing in the late afternoon, because I'm stuck in Vancouver.

We landed here to pick up my Defence Minister, but when the pilots went through the pre-flight checklist, a warning light wouldn't go off.

So now we're in the first class lounge at the Vancouver airport, waiting for my plane to get fixed, and Ellie's taking off from Ottawa to Toronto, where she'll be for two hours before flying to Denver for her conference.

I send her a text that she'll get when she lands.

BJ
Love you. Knock 'em dead at the conference. You're the smartest social behaviour expert in the entire world.

It's schmaltzy, but whatever, it's the truth as I see it.

347

Four days later, I'm more excited than a kid in a candy shop because Ellie's coming home. She had an amazing conference and when I talked to her this morning as she was boarding her flight in Colorado to come home, she was pinging off the walls with all her plans and new contacts.

Yesterday, I went and picked out a diamond solitaire ring. Common sense tells me I should wait a while before I ask her to marry me. Common sense can get fucked.

I love her, more and more each day. She brings me joy, and I want to make her my wife. Provided she doesn't think I'm totally insane for moving quickly, we can tell our families at Thanksgiving.

I stick my head out the door of my office. I've been bouncing in and out all morning as things occur to me, so Beth doesn't even look up this time.

"Did I tell you that I'm expecting a courier package?"

She rolls her eyes at me. "You mean the not-so-subtle secret order from a jewellery store?"

"Yes."

"Yes, you told me yesterday when you went on your secret mission that you'd be getting something couriered 'sooner than later', quote-unquote. And mentioned it this morning on your way in."

"Good."

"Stew's pacing in the hallway, FYI."

"In his usual way or a weird way?"

"Kind of a weird way."

I stalk off in that direction and find my Chief of Staff furiously stabbing at his phone, his face tomato red.

"Everything okay?" I ask him.

He doesn't respond.

"Stew?"

He swears under his breath and jerks his head up. "Gavin. Yes. I need a minute in private with you."

I point him toward my office. As soon as the door shuts, Stew looks at me and says, "There's a video of you."

"Did someone catch me littering? I'm sure it was an accident."

"Gavin." He snaps my name harshly and I pull up short. "There's a sex tape."

Blood roars through my ears. I stare at him, rage firing all the nerve endings in my arms. My hands curl into fists as I process what he's just said. "How the hell…"

We've been so careful. There aren't any cameras in my residence or my office.

I raise my hand and point my index finger at Stew. "Who has it? I want them arrested." He doesn't blink, and I hear myself getting louder. "This is an invasion of privacy."

"It's not you and Ellie." He holds out his phone. "I don't know who leaked it, but this is going to hit the news channels in ten minutes."

"What?"

"The video. It's you. But it's not Ellie."

47

ELLIE

I GET off the plane in Toronto and make my way to the concourse level to transfer to my flight to Ottawa. My flight was packed, and so is the hallway. I can't even get over to the wall and pull out my phone, not that I really have time for that anyway. My connection time got shortened to just under an hour this morning, so I need to hustle.

I convinced Gavin I didn't need a bodyguard for this trip, so I'm all by myself, which is kind of nice. Outside of Ottawa, I still feel mostly anonymous, and at the conference in Colorado, I was just Ellie. Academics don't give two figs about who I'm dating.

The Starbucks line is insanely long, so I keep motoring and stop at the main concourse intersection to figure out what gate I'm boarding at. The screen keeps flipping too fast, and I do a slow three-sixty, looking for another departures screen, when an almost as large screen changes from a commercial to a breaking news alert from the station.

It's a video of Gavin, and at first I'm not sure what I'm looking at, because it's obviously him, but he's young. And...naked.

Well, not naked. He's wearing jeans, but they're unbuttoned, and the camera is shaky, so it looks like he's naked.

White, cold, clammy panic slides up my chest and slithers around my neck. Strokes my face.

My boyfriend is having sex on TV. My boyfriend—Prime Minister—is...

That's a sex tape.

And Gavin's holding what looks like a crop. My throat is suddenly dry and I start coughing, but I can't stop staring at the screen.

Gavin smirking down at his sex partner holding the camera, that smirk that's *mine*, and mouthing the words, "you like that, bad girl?"

I know those words. Not exactly the same, not in that order, but the sentiment. I know the shape of his mouth, how it changes when he's turned on.

Of course, my brain is now stuttering on that loop—smirk, bad girl, smirk, bad girl—even as I turn away from staring at the oversized screen.

Does anyone nearby recognize me? Oh, God, I need to hide. I yank on my sunglasses and duck my head, spinning in a circle again. Where the hell can I hide?

I need to get on an airplane in an hour.

How much room do I have on my credit card? I do some mental calculations and speed walk down the main departures hall. Soon I see another list of gates, and mine is up ahead. I'm moving on pure freak-out adrenaline right now, and I'm not sure what I'm about to say makes any sense, but I march right up to the airline staff person at the desk and thump my purse on the counter.

"Is there any room in business class?" I say, my voice only shaking a little bit. "First class?"

Embarrassed girlfriend class? Is that a thing? I'll hand over all the pennies in my bank account if that's a thing.

"I'm sorry, this flight is—" She pauses when I push up my sunglasses. Then she glances at the passport I'm shoving under her nose. "Ms. Montague. I'll see what I can do."

God. The sympathy in her voice makes me want to vomit. Was I the last person in the country to see my boyfriend's X-rated film debut?

"Thank you," I bite out, because I'm still thinking about appearances.

Fuck appearances.

I stand there, refusing to turn around and make eye contact with anyone in the lounge, and she clicks away on her keyboard.

Click.

Click click. "Hmm." Click. "You don't have any checked luggage?"

"No."

Click.

The whole time I'm dying inside. The white clammy feeling has morphed to red hot rage. It's good that I'm about to get on a plane and into a bottle of whatever alcohol they have aboard, because if I were alone right now, I'd be on the phone to Gavin, saying things I know I'll regret once the shock wears off.

It turns out I don't wear jealousy well.

I'm not particularly proud of this discovery.

My phone vibrates in my purse. Maybe it was doing that before and I didn't notice. But now it's not stopping. I don't know if it's a call or text messages, but there's not a chance in hell I'm checking it right now.

The only thing keeping me from being a sobbing mess on the floor is cold dissociation. Any mention of Gavin or the tape or whatever the hell is going on and that's going to crumble hard.

"Yes, we have a new seat for you, Ms. Montague. I'll

take your old boarding pass…" She slides it out from where I'd stuck it in my passport. "And here is your new boarding information. You can wait in the first class lounge over there." She pauses. "There's a private room in there if you need to make any phone calls."

Fan. Fucking. Tastic.

I do my best ice queen impression as I glide across to the lounge, and I swear that chick messaged her friend, because a woman steps out and holds the door for me, and inside it's quiet and I am, for all intents and purposes, alone.

The tears are already falling.

It's old, I tell myself. He was much younger in it. I don't know how much, but…that's not my Gavin.

He must be beside himself angry right now. Where is he? Is he surrounded by press? I need to call him.

I tell myself to pull the phone out of my purse, but it stays where it is because I'm frozen like a statue.

Press.

I can't get on a plane to Ottawa, because I can't get *off* a plane in Ottawa. Not today.

I turn around and move as fast as humanly possible down the concourse again. I push through the security doors and out into the front of the airport. Keep moving, I tell myself. Go, go, go.

I hail a taxi.

"Where are you going today, ma'am?" the cabbie asks as I shove my suitcase ahead of me into the backseat.

That's a really good question. "There's a mall nearby, right?"

"Yes, ma'am. Yorkdale."

"Yeah. Take me there."

I pull out my phone as he slides away from the curb. Missed calls from Sasha, my mother—God, no—, Gavin,

Stew, the Parliament switchboard number—I assume that's Beth—, and Lachlan.

I try to text Sasha, but I keep deleting what I write out. She's sent me three in the last hour, all short.

> **Sasha**
> Call me when you land in Toronto
>
> You okay?
>
> Let me know what you need

I stare at them and try yet another attempt at a response. When I stop, bubbles start up on her side of the screen.

> **Sasha**
> I can see you typing
>
> Where are you?

The cab stops in front of the mall and I pull out a twenty. "Keep the change," I say as I leap out of the cab, my carryon suitcase landing heavily as I wrench it along.

I head in through the main doors and turn into the first high-end clothing store I see.

"I need a black blazer," I tell the clerk, and she grabs two and shows me to a dressing room. I wait for her to walk away before I sink to the floor and hit the call button on the screen.

Sasha picks up on the first ring. "What do you need me to do?"

4 8

GAVIN

"WHAT DO YOU MEAN, she didn't get on the plane?"

Lachlan stands firm in front of me. Dangerous decision, the way I'm feeling right now. "She upgraded her ticket at the gate, and then disappeared from the first class lounge."

"So she's somewhere in Toronto."

"Yes."

"Find her."

"On what grounds exactly are you suggesting that we devote police resources to finding your girlfriend?"

"You don't need fucking grounds." I glance toward the closed door behind him and lower my voice. "As a friend, Lachlan. Do this for me. Fuck, do it for Ellie. Go find her roommate. Sasha has resources. If Ellie has gone dark, it's with her help."

"Maybe you should let her have some space."

My skin crawls and my stomach turns over at the thought of Ellie needing space from me, even though I know it's a reasonable suggestion. I am not a reasonable man when it comes to her. "Find her. Find out if she's okay."

My throat thickens. "Then we'll worry about what to do next."

He nods. "I've immediately increased your security team. Stew has a detailed report on limits for your activity for the next few days—"

"I don't need a reminder that I'm not to go anywhere."

"You sure you don't?"

I know the rules. I'm seriously considering breaking them. "Find her and make sure she's safe. Do that and I won't go anywhere for now."

"This is just an embarrassing news story. It will blow over."

"For me, it will blow over. For Ellie…" Fuck, I want to throw up. We're alone in my office, but as we've learned, Beth hears a lot through that door. I lower my voice again. "The video was taken when I was in university. It was a period in my life when I was discovering a lot about BDSM and trying different things out."

"Ah. The crop? That's what you're worried about?"

I shake my head. "Not just that, but yeah—I've never used any impact toys with Ellie. But that's not me anymore. Doesn't mean I'm not a dirty bastard, but…people are going to think I hit her."

"You do."

I clench my fists. "Not like that."

"That's not judgement, is it?"

"Fuck you."

"Sorry."

"No, it's not judgement. And if Ellie wanted that kind of release, I'd give it to her. I'd enjoy it, probably. But now people will forever wonder if I've used a crop on her, and it's not even true."

He nods slowly. "I'll find her. We're going to move you

to the residence soon. We'll try to do it in a way that protects your privacy, but people are going to know you're there. But it's more secure than here."

"Fine." I spit it out. It's not fine. None of this is fine and as soon as Caroline and Stew come in, we're going to start planning a systematic takedown of whoever did this to me.

This isn't going to end well for them.

I'm going to be fine.

And Ellie?

Fuck.

That's the million dollar question. Because there's no strong-arm tactic, no charming appeal, no persuasive debate technique effective enough to overcome a broken heart.

If this has hurt her, I will do anything and everything in my power to fix that. I just don't know if it'll be enough.

And what if she can't deal with this?

What if it's too much for her?

CAROLINE AND STEW have been working on a statement for more than an hour while I sign letters to Canadians turning one hundred this year, because I'm not fucking stopping work because of this stupid leak.

The news director at CAN News is refusing to say where they got the video. I know who the woman is, of course, a girlfriend from when I was in law school. But I don't think she was the one who shared it, and I don't feel right having the RCMP descend on her today. Last I heard she was married and had a couple kids.

I don't need to take her down with me.

Not that I'm going down.

Assholes. This is prurient and pathetic. That entire news station should have their license revoked.

Caroline assures me that immediate response on Twitter is one of distaste for the airing of it, but Twitter skews toward the margins. We won't know what the average Canadian is thinking until we get some polling done.

I've always known that I could tumble off the pedestal. I never wanted to be on it in the first place, although I know I used that to my advantage in the election.

Maybe this is karma. Payback for pretending to be someone I'm not.

"We have a draft statement for you," Stew says, dragging my attention to the nervous group slowly pacing into my library.

I hold out my hand.

He doesn't pass it over. "We have another option…"

I snap my fingers. We don't have time for this shit.

The statement is short. But it's unacceptable. "This reads like an apology."

"Well…"

"I'm not fucking apologizing!" I crumple the paper into a tight ball and drop it on the floor. "Show me the other one."

It's even worse.

"This isn't working. I'll write my own."

"Time is of the essence," Caroline says.

Stew adds, "You need to take control of the story before it gets out of control."

I slam my hand on my desk. "But you want me to goddamn comment on my own behaviour instead of the fact a so-called news organization has stooped to fucking tabloid tricks?"

"That's one approach to take. Do you want to go with that angle?"

I have no fucking clue. "I'm not saying anything until I know where Ellie is, is that fucking clear?"

"I'm right here."

49

ELLIE

Sasha's driver brought me to 24 Sussex in the end. She wanted to hide me away at her cottage, but I couldn't go another minute without seeing Gavin.

There was a mob of press outside the gates and I resisted every urge in my body to slink lower in my seat.

I'm embarrassed and jealous and even a little angry, but nobody needs to know that. And despite all of those feelings, I know intellectually that he's done nothing wrong, and certainly doesn't deserve to have his private life put under a magnifying glass.

Nobody is running a story tomorrow that I cowered and covered my face as I arrived. I won't give them my embarrassment and let them misread it as judgement.

I wait for the driver to open the door, then I get out and casually walk around to the trunk of the sedan with him, talking and laughing.

The whole time, the press is hollering my name from the gate. They can't really see me, but I can hear them clear as day.

"Ms. Montague! A few questions!"

"Did you know about the tape?"

"Do you know the woman involved?"

Has the Prime Minister ever called you bad girl? I can feel the flush crawling up my chest even though nobody's actually voiced that question. They're just yelling around it.

I don't turn in that direction. Instead, I shake the driver's hand and take my own suitcase in the front door of the official residence of the Prime Minster of Canada like I belong here.

I'm not sure I do.

Gavin's small library is full of PMO staffers. I watch him from the shadows before stepping fully into the room and speaking. "I'm here."

At the first muscle tick in Gavin's cheek, they all get up as one and silently flee. One of them closes the door behind me, and we're alone.

He looks haunted. He's just in a shirt and tie, his sleeves rolled up and his tie pulled loose at the neck, the top button undone behind it.

"Ellie..." His voice cracks and I lose it.

I throw myself across the room and into his arms. Quiet tears slide down my face as he wraps me in a steely embrace, so hard it would hurt if I didn't need to feel that right now.

"I'm sorry. I'm sorry..." he whispers into my hair, over and over again until the words run together.

I shake my head. I don't want to talk about the video right now. I just want to hold him.

"Are you okay?" He pulls back and touches my face, cupping my cheek with one hand as he moves my hair off my face with the other. His fingers are gentle but his stare burns into my skin. "Did the press find you?"

"Only at the gates."

"God." He pulls me back into his chest. "Ellie."

We stand there like that for a long time that isn't nearly long enough. "You haven't made a statement yet."

"We keep going around in circles on what it should be. I don't want to say anything at all."

"Then don't." I kiss his neck, his jaw, little butterfly kisses as I pull him down to my level and press my forehead against his. "It is what it is, and it'll go away in time."

"It was a long time ago. You have to know that."

I know. I nod. "You don't need to—"

"I do." There's a knock at the door and he swears under his breath. "Two more minutes!"

"Do you want me to go?"

His grip on me tightens. "Never. Listen. I swear to you, I'd forgotten all about that video. There were a few of them, none of them dirtier than that…it was a thing with my girlfriend at the time. She usually deleted them afterwards."

Unease curls inside me, twisting against my guts and my heart. "I don't want to know."

Another knock, and this time his muttered *fucking hell* is louder and followed by a sigh. "Come in."

It's a smaller group of PMO staff that comes in, led by Stew and Caroline. To their credit, both of them look me in the eye and give me a smile.

"Another option is to disrupt the news cycle," Stew says, leading off. "Find a bigger scandal about the other guys."

"I'm not stooping to that level."

"Don't trip on your principles," Stew mutters as Caroline steps in between them.

"We can't just blithely move on as if nothing has changed," she says.

What exactly has changed? I hold my tongue because I'm not here as a staffer. I'm the girlfriend, the emotionally invested significant other. I'm the woman who needs to stand beside him as he does a press conference and show that someone still loves him.

Of course I still love him. And I love him because of his principles, not despite them.

"Right," Stew says.

"Does he, though?" I ask. Apparently I can't hold my tongue. I'm surprised I sound more confident than I feel, but my voice is sure and solid, so I keep going. "Maybe Gavin *shouldn't* address it. It's not something to apologize for. It's an appalling violation of two people's privacy, it has zero bearing on his ability to lead the government, and it's not news."

"That sounds great in theory," Stew said, his characteristic bluntness hammering down on my very delicate grasp on a super-thin hope that that plan would work. "But it *is* news, so…he needs to address it."

"And what should he say? Yes, I have sex? I'm a grown man? Everyone else in this room has sex, too, and it's not news."

Stew shrugs. "Nobody else in this room makes the decisions he makes."

Gavin lets go of me and shoves his desk backwards. A sharp crack fills the silence, and I realize he's crushed his chair between the desk and wall. His now broken chair. He's furious, which isn't new. "That's it. We're done with this conversation for now."

"That's not it." I turn and stand in front of him, and the rest of the room fades away. It's just the two of us and it sucks we're doing this in front of his staff, but this is what it is to love the PM. Zero privacy and fights vetted by three levels of communication specialists. "Nothing wrong with saying that you're human, Gavin. But hiding isn't the answer."

"I'm not hiding. I was waiting for you."

"And now I'm here."

"We need to talk."

"We will. But let's get this out of the way so they can start softening the media for our response."

"Our response?" The surprise and relief all over his face hits me in the chest.

I hold out my hand, squeezing my fingers around his when he takes it. "Yep."

"I'm sorry about this."

"You need to tell your country that."

"It's none of their business."

"Tell them that you're sorry your girlfriend had to see a fifteen-year-old video. Tell them you're embarrassed. Tell them it's not something you've thought about since you were in law school, and even if you did remember it, you'd still have run for office. Because having one embarrassing skeleton in your closet is nothing. We're all human. We all make mistakes. But if you don't say, 'yeah, this has repercussions', then you're being deliberately obtuse. You can be honest that this has made you more cynical about privacy. More concerned about the digital sharing of personal content."

He clenches his teeth, his jaw flexing as he searches my face. "Okay."

"Okay?"

He nods. "I'll say that." He jerks his attention to Stew. "That work for you?"

My former boss nods. "Every word."

"Then get out and leave us alone."

50

ELLIE

THEY DON'T JUST LEAVE the library. I hear Stew gather everyone up and they vacate the house. At some point Stew will be back, to tell us the details of the press conference plan, but for now, we're alone.

Except for the RCMP officer standing at the front door.

Gavin stops me when we get to the centre hallway, about to go upstairs, and he points to the constable standing just inside the foyer. "You can wait outside."

"Yes, sir."

He takes his time walking back to me as I wait for him on the stairs. His face is twisted with worry, and it suddenly occurs to me—why I didn't think of it sooner, I don't know —that this might not be the end of this.

"What is it?" I ask, my voice wavering in the quiet stillness of this too-big, too-intense house.

He collides with me, his hands sliding into my hair as his lips part my own. His kiss is a searing brand. *Mine.*

I cling to him and he hoists me up, holding me tight against his front. I wrap my legs around his waist as he climbs to the second floor, not putting me down until we're in his room. He stands me down in front of a chair, not the bed, and I sink into it.

He kicks an ottoman across from the other chair and sits right in front of me, his legs spread wide, bracketing my knees. "I need to tell you something. I should have told you months ago."

"What?" I'm not sure how much more I can take. No, that's not true. I'm strong enough to weather any storm. But I don't want to. Not alone. Not when the storm is swirling out of the man I've come to rely on as my haven.

"The week after you started here…after that day in Stew's office, I flew to Vancouver. Max arranged for a woman for me." He stares right at me, unflinching in the face of what I'm sure is not a good reaction. Icy-cold fear is slithering through me again.

Seriously? What the fuck were you thinking? But I don't say that, I don't say anything, because he's clearly not done. It takes every last bit of my will power to stay silent.

"She was at his place. He was not. And in the end, neither was I. I drove there, and kept going. I took Tim on quite the drive that night. And then I flew back here. I flew back to you, even though I couldn't have you. But it's possible that at some point, that's going to come out. I wanted you to hear it from me. If I'd thought for a second any of this would have happened, I'd have told you first. About the video…about it all."

"What else?" My voice is clipped and chill. "Let's get it all out on the table. We've never talked about our past because I thought that's what it was—the past. But I don't think that's how it works for me. I don't think I get the luxury of truly just moving on with my life, because every inch of your life is going to be picked over. Past, present, future. Right? So what else am I going to learn?"

He doesn't even blink. "I was in a casual relationship

with a woman for two years that ended in January. I believe we ended on amicable terms. During that time I was faithful to her, but our dates were…sporadic. It's possible that she might raise questions about that now, given how intense my relationship is with you, and what was in that video."

I search for the right words and stumble. "Sporadic? Like it was casual?"

"Yes, casual, and strictly vanilla." He blanches. "I dated her because it felt safe. Appropriate for someone with political aspirations. I used her, in a way, and that doesn't feel great."

"No, I imagine she's feeling quite awful right now, knowing that there's a completely different side to her ex that she never saw." I know he meant it doesn't feel great for him, but he's not the only one affected by all of this and I haven't allowed myself to snap yet today. Something's gotta give and apparently it's my patience. "How many submissives have you had?"

"It wasn't like that. That woman in the video wasn't a sub, exactly."

"Who is she?"

"Her name is Valentine DeMasco—or it was. She's married now and I don't know if she's changed her last name. I saw her briefly at a ten-year reunion event for our law class five years ago. She's a practicing attorney in Vancouver and a mother of two. We dated for six months in law school." He hesitates for a second before adding, "She had an exhibitionist streak in her. We recorded ourselves sometimes. We always deleted them after. That video maybe she kept because it didn't show any sex? I don't know."

"Have you talked to her today?"

He shakes his head. "No. There's nothing identifying in it, and I'm assuming she's not the one who leaked it.

Maybe it ended up online somehow and a reporter stumbled on it. Maybe someone's been sitting on it for a while." He shrugs his shoulders. "But I'm not going to give anyone her identity if I can spare her the humiliation."

"You just told me."

"Because you're…" His brow tightens. "Of course I told you."

"Is it of course?"

He reaches for my hands, his fingers warm and strong as they wrap around mine. "Yes."

"You didn't answer my question before." All of a sudden it matters a great deal that I know what his history is.

"Submissives? Nothing like this. Not relationships."

I tug my hands out of his grasp. "Now it feels like you're avoiding the question."

"I'm not. It's not a question that has a direct and easy answer."

"How many subs, Gavin? How many women have you spanked and called bad girl? How many women know your kinky side and can say the prime minister gave them a few marks?" I'm getting wound tight, burrowing back in the chair, but I shouldn't have to spell that last point out for Christ's sake.

He has the good grace to at least look a little embarrassed. "They were mostly women at clubs."

"Sex clubs."

"They're private."

"Like sex tape private or threesome with your intern and your security chief private?"

His jaw clenches. "Are you turning this into a fight?"

"No." Yes. Maybe. I don't know. "You're so damn confident that nothing's wrong, but then I have to see you holding a crop, larger than life in the middle of Pearson

Airport. Can you see where I'm struggling with the whole private thing?"

"And this is damn embarrassing for me, too."

"I know."

"What's this really about, Sprite?" He falls to his knees in front of me, pushing the ottoman back and out of his way. He's big and warm against my legs, and I just want to fold over him and never let go.

I settle for running my hands through his hair, then I trace the contours of his face with my fingertips. "There's still so much I don't know about, isn't there?"

"No." He shakes his head. "I'm thirty-nine. I've had a reasonable amount of safe sex with consenting partners. Some of them wanted some pain with their pleasure. Sometimes I wanted to deliver that for them. That's it. I don't even own leather pants, Sprite. I'm not any different from the man you were with two weeks ago."

When I was the one on my knees, sucking him off in his office in Centre Block. My voice cracks as I voice what's really gripping my heart. "Am I enough?"

He groans and tightens his arms around my waist. "You're everything."

"I'm not, though. You've done things that we never will together, and I knew that before, but now I've seen it with my own eyes, and I can't un-see that."

"No, Ellie…no. It's not like that for me."

"You had me make a list of everything I wanted to do, Gavin." My voice hitches and I realize I'm crying. When did the tears start falling? I can't even feel them, I'm so numb. "But I don't know your list."

"I don't have one."

"Do you want to whip me?"

"I'm here, on my knees, telling you that you're my everything."

"I know you love me. That doesn't answer the question."

"I've…experimented with specific acts, tried them on like a yoga class versus Pilates, hiking versus downhill skiing. It's not the sport that matters. It's not about satisfying a specific kink, Ellie, it's about finding the woman that makes me want to satisfy *her* kinks."

"I don't have any kinks."

"Of course you do. Role-play and bondage. Spanking." He sits up again and wraps my hands in his, tightening his hold on me so I can't pull away as he tugs me closer, moving me to the edge of the chair. His voice is low, rough, and intimate, but still raw. "You're a natural submissive, dying to have something in all of your holes."

I flinch at the crass words, but it's true. My body reacts to the memory of each of those acts in a primal way.

"My kink is simply being in control. Doing all of that to you. Pushing you to the edge of your limits so you can feel that bite. But I'm not a sadist. I don't want to hurt you, and no, I don't ever need to whip you. My arm is more than a little out of practise."

"You've done that before?"

"Yes. Remember I told you about the couple that mentored me early on in my kink exploration?"

I do remember now. Impact toys, he'd said. "Toys."

His grip tightens. "That's the term."

"For whips?" Like, real ones?

"And floggers, dragontails, paddles, canes, crops…" I don't know why I'm speechless, but I am, and he trails off. "Too much?"

"Long day." That's a serious understatement.

He sighs and pulls me close. "Can we lie down for a bit?"

"Yes." I sag against him. "Definitely, yes."

51

GAVIN

LYING down turns into Ellie falling asleep for the night, burrowed deep into my chest.

This means she's out like a light when Stew returns, which is for the best. I go downstairs long enough to confirm that we'll do a press conference together the next afternoon, then I return to our bed and wrap myself around her again.

We always sleep naked.

Tonight we don't, and that's a little thing that feels so fucking huge it hurts my chest.

I drift off after the light outside fades to darkness, and I'm disoriented when I wake with a start, the remnants of an angry nightmare ringing in my ears.

The bedside clock tells me it's three in the morning. I feel like I've hardly slept a wink. Ellie's curled tight into a ball, still facing me, but her knees have pulled up and her hands are clenched into fists. I stroke my palm over her arm, her side, her hip. I want to pull her tight against me again, so tight she imprints on my body, but I don't want to wake her up, either.

It's going to take a hell of a lot to make this right.

To fix this.

And it's probably not the last time we'll face a challenge like this—although I'm confident she knows all the skeletons in my closet, and when I'm not filled with rage, I can objectively rationalize that there aren't that many.

I haven't done anything wrong.

I haven't even done anything wrong when it comes to Ellie, although this is a big fucking lesson in being open and transparent with her.

But still, we're being rocked by waves caused by others, and that's scary.

I lay there, touching her gently, watching her, until dawn breaks.

When she sighs and uncurls her body, finally relaxing after hours of what I fear must have been tortured sleep, I finally drop off again, Ellie draped over the left side of my body.

52

ELLIE

I WAKE up in the morning and Gavin's beside me.

"Breakfast?" he asks softly as he brushes a lock of hair off my cheek.

I must look like a total mess. "Shower first?"

"Sure."

"You want to join me?"

"Always."

He keeps his hands on me in one way or another until we're in the bathroom, then he slowly, reverently strips me out of the travel clothes I fell asleep in the night before. I fumble with his clothes, but he does most of the work there, too, and when the shower is hot, he guides me under the spray and turns me every which way until I'm scrubbed clean.

As he rinses the last of the soap away, he starts talking again, like we're still having the conversation from the day before. "I never wanted this, you know. Growing up, I always thought it would be Pia who'd follow in my parents' footsteps. Even when I ran for office the first time...I didn't think I'd win. I never thought I'd become the de facto leader of a broken party, and end up here two years later."

I blink through the steam at him. I mean, I knew some of that, but not all, and it breaks my heart. "Gavin…you do want it now, right?"

Because if he doesn't, life is too short for this shit.

He gives me a tortured look that says it all. "With all my heart." And at almost any price. He starts to talk again and I don't need to hear anymore. I press against him, silencing him with a soft, wet open-mouthed kiss.

"Okay," I whisper as I kiss his jaw. His neck. I press my face into his wet skin and nod. "Then I want this for you, too. And we'll survive it."

His arms tighten around me and we stand under the water until it starts to run cold.

When we get out, he wraps me in his robe before looping a towel around his waist and tucking the nubby cotton over itself. My eyes tangle on the dip of the fabric there, where he's tucked it in. At the ridge of muscle and the dark edge of pubic hair.

"What do you want to eat?"

You is probably an inappropriate answer right now. But I suddenly crave him. "I'm not hungry."

"Are you sure?" He clears his throat. "Look at me."

I jerk my eyes up.

"Hungry for something else, Sprite?"

I reach for a jar of moisturizer I've left here and smooth it over my face instead of answering. I don't want to lie to him, but sex right now could take us sideways into ugliness.

"It might be good to reconnect," he says quietly, coming closer. He catches his lower lip between his teeth as he tugs on the bathrobe belt. "If you want."

It's the most vanilla sex invitation he's ever given me.

I tilt my head to the side, trying to puzzle out how I feel about that. "Is that what you want?"

He tugs me closer. A little harder. A little less vanilla. "I want you to know that I'm yours in every way. I want you to know that you are my everything. I'm going to keep telling you that until you believe it in your heart. That I would do anything for you."

"And if I freak out? Start crying because I can't get that picture of you with someone else out of my head?"

"Then we'll do whatever we need to do to replace those images with ones that don't make you cry."

"I don't know—"

"I do." His hands are fisted in the terrycloth now, and his expression is fierce. "Let me love you, Ellie."

I nod once, a slow, stuttering jerk of my head.

He exhales and tugs the bathrobe open, dropping it in a puddle around my feet. "Turn around, Sprite."

I face the mirror and he reaches past me to grab my comb. I watch, wide-eyed, as he carefully detangles my hair, starting at the bottom, then combing more and more of it until he's starting at my scalp and slowly sliding the teeth through my tresses to the very tips in the middle of my back.

It's a simple act. One of careful kindness, and not overtly sexual. But with each stroke, my breasts grow heavy and my nipples tighten. Goosebumps break out on my skin, pebbling my entire torso. Gavin grazes me here and there with his fingertips.

Each caress a promise. Here, I will kiss you. Here, I will lick you. Here, I will love you.

He's watching me in the mirror as he gathers my hair, first all in one fist, then he starts dividing it between his hands. Our gazes stay locked together as he braids the strands. Tug, over, exchange hands. Next piece of hair, back to the other side. Each tug shoots down my spine and makes me stand a little taller.

There's a hair clip sitting next to my moisturizer and he picks it up, but he doesn't use it to fasten the end of the braid.

Instead he runs it up my arm and curves over my shoulder. "I've never had a woman's stuff in my bathroom like this." He opens the clip and slides his hand down my chest, until the clip is parallel to my nipples, between my breasts. "One day I should see what sort of fun we can get up to with this."

He snaps it shut and I jump at the sharp little sound.

The burst of adrenaline shifting me from hungry but wary to one hundred percent ready for anything. "Yes, Sir."

His hands fall to my hips and he pulls me back against him. Warm skin and hard muscle. The soft rub of his towel-covered erection against the curve of my bottom. He lowers his mouth to my ear.

"Anything in your head that you don't want there right now, Sprite?"

I shake my head. Only him. Only us. "No, Sir."

He fixes my braid and finishes it with the clip. That won't hold, but it doesn't matter.

Nothing matters beyond him spinning me around and hoisting me onto the counter. The hard shove of his hips between my thighs. His mouth on mine, his lips and tongue. A hard scrape of his teeth against my lower lip, my neck.

The cold mirror against my back.

His hands on mine, pressing me harder against the glass, and then releasing me with a groan when our kisses grow desperate and needy. He brings my hands to his towel and I yank it away, then circle his cock with my fingers.

He throbs in my fist, hot and hard.

"Not here," he growls as I rub the thick crown of his erection against my sex. "Our bed."

Those two words slice heat straight into my belly. Ours.

We tumble together across the blankets, limbs entwined before we're even fully horizontal. Our breathing slows, synchronizes, as Gavin strokes between my legs, spreading my slickness. I wrap my arms around his shoulders, wanting as much contact between us as possible as he notches his cock against my entrance and slowly presses into me.

We have this. Nobody can take this from us. How he watches me so carefully as I stretch around his cock. How I roll my hips to take him even deeper.

My arms fall back against the bed as he surges into me again, and he follows me down, his hands finding mine and holding on tight as he makes love to me.

He's warm and strong above me, his muscles flexing and rolling as he finds all the places that make my breath hitch and my belly pull tight. I wrap my legs higher around his torso, wanting more of *that*, yes, *there*, and he reads my body and mind.

This is perfect, I think. It's not. Outside, the world still rages on, and tomorrow I'll be mad again. But not at him. For him. With him.

But we'll stand together because we have this truth between us. This is love, and it's forever.

53

GAVIN

THE PRESS CONFERENCE doesn't go that well. I get my back up at the hostility in some of the reporters' faces, and Ellie's nervous, but we survive it, and Caroline is thrilled with the viral response to our awkwardness.

"People really identify with how painful that was for you both," she says, and I try not to grind my teeth.

"The other thing that people are responding well to is the rumour that your parents are coming to Ottawa to meet her over Thanksgiving."

"Yeah."

"We'd like pictures."

"No."

"Why not?"

Because I think her father hates me and it's going to be fucking awkward. "It's a private family event."

"How about an interview with the two of you, preparing for your first co-hosted dinner? That's something a lot of millennials can identify with."

I start to make a smart-ass remark about being a little old for that, but I stop because Ellie's not, and frankly, as embarrassing as it is, this is my first time having a family dinner with a serious girlfriend. Pointing out my age won't help the situation. "I'll ask her."

"She already said it would be fine."

"You asked her?"

"Actually the reporter did and Ellie forwarded it to me."

I'm out of my chair and yelling before I can rein it in. "Reporters cannot contact her!"

Caroline just rolls her eyes. "She's a grown woman, Gavin, and a professional to boot. She knows how to handle contacts like that. It's a side effect of her having a public position with a public email address. It's not a big deal."

It's a big fucking deal. "I'm talking about it in the scrum this afternoon."

"That's a good use of your national platform."

"Thanks," I say, ignoring her sarcasm. "Anything else?"

"Not right now. Have a good Question Period."

I intend to. The House is back in session and my government, green and young as it is, is kicking ass and taking names. We're going to make some missteps along the way, but since their leader spent the summer fucking up repeatedly like a goddamn teenager, and still managed to come out of it focused on policy and governance, they can and will survive their own speed bumps, too.

THREE DAYS LATER, I'm raking leaves in the backyard at 24 Sussex for a photo op. Off camera, Max is losing his shit laughing at me and beside me, Ellie is barely managing to school her amused look into something more endearing.

"I'm wearing exactly the wrong outfit for this," I growl.

She picks a leaf off my cashmere sweater and nods. "Yeah. You totally are." She glances sideways at the photographer and gives him a smile so perfect I know whatever she's about to ask for will be granted. "Can we take five minutes for a quick wardrobe change?"

"Definitely." He grins back. "You know what's best, Ms. Montague."

I wait until we're inside to point out that it's rude of him to flirt with Ellie in front of me.

"He wasn't flirting," she says with a laugh as she rifles through my dresser. "Here, wear this Henley. And an undershirt…this black one."

"Can I put on jeans?"

She gives me a careful look. "Sure. But then I probably should as well, right?"

Our carefully coordinated outfits hit the floor and we pull on regular clothes. Jeans—mine darker, hers lighter—and cotton shirts.

"This might be too casual," she says, checking her makeup in the mirror. "But it's us and it's real, and that's all that matters."

Truer words have never been spoken. I grab my now-discarded tie and roll it up, using that as an excuse to go into my dressing room again.

When I step back into our room, she's holding out her hand for me. "Ready?"

"Definitely," I say, taking her fingers in mine. But instead of following her down the stairs, I hold on tight and sink to one knee. My heart is racing, equal parts nerves and excitement. I take a deep breath and squeeze her hand. "I've been waiting for the right moment to do this, Ellie Montague. Thought about a dozen different ideas, all fancy and elaborate. But you're right. This is us. This is real. And I'm not always able to be this guy for you. Jeans and a t-shirt. Raking leaves and being silly. But I want to be, as often as I can, for the rest of my life."

She's staring at me, wide-eyed, and a surprised smile is bursting across her face. "Gavin…"

"Before you I wasn't a whole man. I was all these different pieces, and I couldn't imagine how they'd ever align. I put as many together as I could and pretended that was how it was supposed to be." I turn her hand over and cover her palm with my other hand, pressing the ring between our fingers. "Turns out I needed your pieces, too. You complete the edges of my puzzle and fill in the gaps in the middle, too."

Her eyes are bright with unshed tears. She's never been more beautiful, but I might get shit for making her cry in the middle of a photo shoot. It's worth it if she says yes.

"And like a puzzle, I know that it doesn't take much to tap at us and crack us back into those individual pieces. Work and history and press and family…there are things that will challenge us. I want to glue our pieces together. Forever." I slide my hand out of the way, leaving the solitaire on her palm. "Ellie, will you marry me?"

"Yes," she whispers as a few of the tears slide free from her eyes and roll down her cheeks. "I will marry you in a heartbeat."

Her hands are still shaking as I rise to stand with her, so I help her slide on the ring before I pick her up and kiss her senseless.

We're more than a few minutes late for the photo shoot, but when we get out there, her cheeks are pink and her eyes are sparking just as bright as the diamond she now wears on her ring finger.

54

MAX

GAVIN INVITES me to 24 Sussex for Thanksgiving. Not out of pity, since I'm alone in a new city. No. My best friend—the prime minister of the entire country—needs back up in case his future father-in-law causes a scene.

Apparently Ellie's father didn't take kindly to his daughter being dragged through the media, although she seems to have insulated herself well from the noise.

I'm a good friend. I go, of course.

It helps that their cozy holiday feast is catered by one of the best restaurants in the city and I really like turkey.

Plus Gavin and his nephew are usually good for a game of football, and I'm feeling restless, a fact that Ellie picks up on right away.

"How's the new job going, Max?" she asks as she hands me a beer.

"Great."

"And the house?"

It's big and empty and so far I've had zero sex in it. "It's great."

"In my experience, when things are really great, people tend to elaborate on answers about new jobs and new houses."

I wink at her. "Maybe in my experience, short answers tend to make beautiful women curious."

She rolls her eyes, immune to my charm. "Everything's really okay? We haven't seen you much since you moved here."

Everything is fine. I'm just obsessed with a woman I can't find. "I've really thrown myself into work. I'm still doing some consulting on cases back in Vancouver in addition to building a patient base at the hospital here."

"A workaholic, just like Gavin." She squeezes my arm. "But you're getting a winter hockey team going?"

I nod. No Tate until next summer, because he's captaining a real NHL team, but Lachlan found us a few more people to fill out a beer league team.

"I'll have to bring Sasha to watch a few games." The sly look on her face means she's trying to play matchmaker.

With Sasha? I laugh out loud. "Your roommate is gorgeous and smart and funny, but she's not my type."

"What's your type?"

Glossy black hair, tits that bounce like crazy, hips I can still feel imprinted on my palms three months later. Creamy skin that marks like a dream. "I prefer my women a tad more compliant than Sasha."

Ellie makes an understanding murmur. "Yeah. She's not that."

"Not at all. She'd make an excellent Domme."

She jerks her head toward me, her eyes widening. "You think? No. Really?"

No, not really. I don't know if Sasha's kinky, but if she is, she's probably not a pure top.

But even the sport of trying to figure out which way someone bends no longer appeals to me. As soon as Ellie moves away, keeping her first dinner party moving like the natural hostess she's proving to be—provided someone else does the cooking, I can hear her tease in my head—I let my thoughts slide back to Violet and that night in July.

Violet.

Maybe that's not even her name. After all, I thought she was an escort I'd hired and that had turned out to be…not exactly true.

After dinner, I wander off to the sunroom and stand at the windows, staring into the dark, alone with my thoughts. I don't get much time with them before Gavin sidles up and hands me a beer. "You've been awfully quiet. What's going on?"

"Still dealing with the aftermath of the move. Not a lot of energy left for idle chit-chat."

Gavin gives me that steely-eyed stare of his. "That answer might wash with Ellie, but I've known you too long to buy such a bullshit excuse. It's a woman, isn't it?"

"There is no woman." Not anymore. Where the fuck is she?

"You and those damned rigid boundaries of yours. You may think they're protecting your heart, but they aren't. They're starving it."

"You're deliriously in love, and I'm thrilled for you. Truly. But don't go fucking preaching your happy ever after at me." Because I can never have what he has with Ellie, no matter how much I want it.

"Fair enough. I'm done pushing. I'm still not out of the woods with Ellie's dad and I need you on my side. He wants to play poker."

That's clearly a trap. "Don't worry, I've got your back."

THE NEXT DAY I wrap up my clinic at the hospital an hour earlier than usual because I need to get downtown and meet with my new lawyers.

Nobody told me how much fucking admin work was associated with moving provinces. Now I'm practicing medicine under a different College of Physicians and Surgeons, so from time to time I need to consult an attorney for questions related to my medical practice, plus I'm old-fashioned — I like to actually sit face-to-face with the people I task to manage my money and corporations.

I left Hollywood at sixteen a relatively wealthy teenager, and over the last twenty years I've turned those savings into a significant set of diversified holdings.

So yeah, I need to meet my new lawyers.

Plural, because while there's a partner who will take all the credit for the work, there will also be associates who do the real hands-on stuff, and those are the people I want to look in the eye. I want them to know that I'm not to be messed with.

The offices of Katz & Novak are just off Spark Street, and I make a mental note to arrange time to go and flirt with Gavin's assistant Beth the next time I'm down here. Like Ellie, she's safely off-limits, and therefore the perfect woman for me.

It's hard to be an incorrigible rake and a hardcore sadist at the same time. I learned long ago that the two desires had to be satisfied in very different ways.

Shameless flirting is for women like Beth. Beautiful, clever, and entirely uninterested in anything beyond a double entendre every now and again.

Safe words and carefully negotiated hard limits are for

women I hire. Equally beautiful, equally clever, and carefully vetted by the only high-price madam in the country I trust with my credit card details.

And then came Violet.

Over and over again she came for me. Even when tears streamed down her face, she took another orgasm for me. Let me fuck with her mind in the most beautiful way.

And when it was over, and I cradled her in my arms, she stretched and purred like a satisfied kitten.

Violet.

I'm a week away from hiring a private investigator to find her, but "we hooked up at the Chateau Laurier bar in July and she paid cash for her drink" isn't much to go on.

Plus, the thought of involving anyone else in the hunt for my mystery woman puts a sour taste in my mouth.

Violet is my secret, and I feel oddly protective of her.

I try to shake off the darkness that descends when I think about her and jab the elevator button for the fourth floor. It's a smooth ride up, and the doors open to a high-end boutique law firm that specializes in physician corporations with significant holdings. A one-stop doc shop, a colleague at the hospital called it.

They also come highly recommended by the firm I used in Vancouver.

I give my name to the receptionist, and less than a minute later, William Novak is introducing himself to me. He gives me the expected spiel about how he'll oversee all my legal work, but to keep my billings down—blah blah blah—he'll pull in an associate from time to time.

Like I don't know the drill.

"I'll go grab her now." He flashes a too-white smile and gestures for the boardroom. "Donna will bring you a drink in there. Scotch? Coffee?"

"Water is fine." I adjust my tie, then unbutton my

jacket, pushing it back as I shove my hands into the pockets of my dress pants. The boardroom is in the centre of the office suite, surrounded on all sides by hallways. An interesting set up. No privacy at any time, so anyone deposed in here would feel like they're on display. In a fishbowl.

I make a mental note of that. If I ever have need to be deposed for a case, I'll have it done at the hospital or the courthouse.

"Here's our client," William says from behind me.

I turn around as he introduces his associate.

"Violet Roberts, this is—"

"Max Donovan," she breathes. Her sapphire eyes are wide.

"Have you two met?" the older lawyer asks, frowning at me.

Yes, I think, but she's faster.

"No." Her jaw sets into a hard line as her eyes narrow. "I haven't had the pleasure."

Oh, but my kitten has had the pleasure.

Even as she slams the files in her hand down on the boardroom table between us, I'm already thinking about how I might punish her for that lie.

Thank you so much for reading Prime Minister! We hope you love Gavin and Ellie as much as we do.

Max's book is now available! Visit our website at www. friskybeavers.com for all links. *Dr. Bad Boy* is available at all major ebook retailers.

Also sign up for our exclusive VIP mailing list there. Don't miss a single release alert!

And keep reading to find out more about our other books. Sadie writes kinky musicians, and Ainsley writes forbidden bodyguards.

~ Ainsley & Sadie

ALSO BY SADIE HALLER

If you like kinky classical musicians…

Dominant Cord

One Gold Heart
One Gold Knot
One Gold Triquetra

If you like kinky rock stars…

Tainted Pearl

Tainted Shadow

To connect with Sadie:
www.sadiehaller.com

ALSO BY AINSLEY BOOTH

The Playing Game
a hockey romance standalone

Forbidden Bodyguards
scandal, suspense, and off-limits bodyguards

Hate F*@k
Booty Call
Dirty Love
Wicked Sin
Filthy Liar

Billionaire Secrets
rom com fun

Undercover Billionaire
Her Billionaire Best Friend
A Billionaire for Christmas

Secrets and Lies
angsty erotic romance

Tempt
Shame

To connect with Ainsley:
www.ainsleybooth.com

ACKNOWLEDGEMENTS

[*Ainsley says*... It needs to be pointed out that we wrote these independent of one another. That's just how #same-brain our minds are.]

Sadie says...

It all starts and ends with Ainsley, because she was kind enough to let me tag along on this epic journey. I had doubts about my ability to write, let alone co-write, but when she said, 'it'll be fine,' I had to trust she was right. Because sometimes, you have to take that big leap of faith if you want good things to happen.

Then we started writing, and we couldn't stop. The story just poured out and we were so in tune, there were times where it was like we were two halves of a single brain. Occasionally, that meant one of us taking over where the other was stuck, but usually it meant we could see most of the story and characters unfolding the same way. It was magical.

Of course, the Chatzy crew get our thanks for their unwavering support and urging us on.

Finally, my love and gratitude to my husband for so many reasons, but mainly for not giving me the side-eye over my decision to push back a release to focus on this project.

Ainsley says...

Sadie has been my "first reader" for all things Horus

Group, so when the idea for Prime Minister came up, and she said, "you should write that," I knew the only response was, "only if you write it with me."

Writing this book was a complete joy. From the setting to the plot to the characters—especially the characters—Sadie and I were on the same page at every step. It's kind of freaky to send someone a message and have them immediately bounce back a reply with the photo you imagined in your head…because they were already looking at it. At times it felt like we were finishing each other's sentences.

And sometimes, when we struggled with how to wrap up a scene, we actually did.

As always, the crew in Chatzy get a lot of credit for cheering us on. Melissa Blue and Brenna Aubrey for *needing* this book. Elle Rush (pick-up hockey team) and Tessa Layne (shavasana line) for agreeably letting us steal their responses and work them into the book.

Madelynne Ellis and Vivian Arend gave us valuable beta feedback. Thank you from the bottom of our hearts.

One of our readers, Maria Rose, is responsible for Max in a round about way. Her April Fool's tweets inspired a tweet-response that turned into book 2 in this series. Max's book. As you can tell from the last chapter, we're already well into that one, so we hope you're hooked on these Canadian Doms. She also helped at the proofreading stage, and we're grateful (and kind of embarrassed) for the errors that she caught.

Another reader, Jessica Alcazar, was an early beta reader, and is responsible for the fuckerette definition. Thank you for loving Gavin and Ellie even in their roughest stage!

Marlene Brown and Teri Lyn caught some errors in the earliest ARC, and we're grateful for that.

Rhonda Helms, our foxy editor extraordinaire, gave

PM the very thorough review it deserved, and helped us polish those rough edges until the entire book looked just like we imagined it might if we were super lucky. And then Dana Waganer got out her magnifying glass and did the final proofread.

We are blessed with friends and family that support us. I get a little teary when I think about how awesome my community is. "I'm writing a dirty romance about a hot prime minister!" I say, and they just smile and bring me tea, like that's not super weird.

Until the next book!
~ Ainsley & Sadie